For Monica Hart Koler
and
Naia Elizabeth Hart Poyer

THE
RAVEN'S
BRIDE

LENORE HART

ST. MARTIN'S GRIFFIN ✖ NEW YORK

This is a work of fiction. All of the characters, organizations, and events portrayed in this novel are either products of the author's imagination or are used fictitiously.

THE RAVEN'S BRIDE. Copyright © 2011 by Lenore Hart. All rights reserved. Printed in the United States of America. For information, address St. Martin's Press, 175 Fifth Avenue, New York, N.Y. 10010.

www.stmartins.com

Designed by Kelly S. Too

Library of Congress Cataloging-in-Publication Data

Hart, Lenore.
  The raven's bride / Lenore Hart.—1st ed.
    p. cm.
  ISBN 978-0-312-56723-1
  1. Poe, Virginia, 1822–1847—Fiction. 2. Poe, Edgar Allan, 1809–1849—Marriage—Fiction. 3. Authors' spouses—United States—Fiction. 4. Authors, American—19th century—Fiction. I. Title.
  PS3608.A786R38 2011
  813'.6—dc22
                                          2010038938

ISBN 978-0-312-56723-1 (trade paperback)
ISBN 978-0-312-60433-2 (hardcover)

First Edition: February 2011

10 9 8 7 6 5 4 3 2 1

I have been here before,
But when or how I cannot tell;
I know the grass beyond the door,
The sweet keen smell,
The sighing sound, the lights around the shore.

—Dante Gabriel Rossetti, "Sudden Light"

In door-way where the lilac blows,
  Humming a little wandering air,
I make my shroud and no one knows,
  So shimmering fine it is and fair.

—Adelaide Crapsey, "Song"

· 1 ·

The city's streets lie dark as catacombs beneath a black ceiling of moonless sky. A low fog unrolls across the harbor like a carpet of frost, pushed by a salt-laden breeze. My thin cotton gown is little protection against the chill, but no matter. The cold can no longer make me cough or shiver. This is the harbor of Baltimore, place of my birth, a city I haven't seen in many years.

I walk east, the blowing fall leaves crisp beneath my bare feet, like crumpled pages torn from an old book. Yet they make no sound as I tread on even the thickest drifts. Pulled on as if by an invisible net, I pass a fish market, a haberdasher's and a newspaper office, the Farmer's Bank, then a tobacco warehouse. But none of these are my destination.

At the corner of Broadway and Fairmount I stop before a five-story brick building with vaulted Gothic windows, and hesitate with one foot on the first step. When I lived in this city, as a child, older playmates sometimes whispered of ghastly doings here, in Washington University Hospital. They said body snatchers opened tombs in the nearby cemetery to disinter the unfortunate corpses within. Then they would smuggle these grisly burdens to the hospital's doctors to be cut apart like sides of mutton, before they'd been in their graves a full day. Silly rumors, no doubt. Still, back then most Baltimore residents preferred to die of their diseases at home, rather than suffer the shining knives and toothed saws of the physicians, who so often killed their patients before illness or injury could.

Suddenly I don't want to go inside. If I turn away now, perhaps I can become one of those earthbound ghosts that children whisper of, after the lamps are turned down and they lie shivering in bed, starting at every creak and groan of the settling house. Shrinking beneath the quilts at each flicker of light and shadow. Perhaps I should instead go to Richmond, back to Capitol Square, to haunt our old boardinghouse, and welcome Mrs. Yarrington's new guests.

The thought makes me smile, and so at last I feel heartened enough to go on up the stairs to the open door.

Inside, the high ceilings and vaulted windows mimic some great church, but with no altar, no pews, no crucifix. Beyond the mullioned glass, above the low-lying harbor fog, the great dark sky curves. Still without a moon, but now sprinkled with stars like grains of salt tipped onto black velvet. Across the street a few buildings glow with orange points, a dim earthbound constellation of gaslights.

The hospital is cool and smells of carbolic. Sparsely furnished with white-painted cabinets and straight-backed wooden chairs, populated with distracted people who do not pause but merely pass through in a great hurry. They all ignore me.

I turn in a slow circle to track the progress of a woman clad in the white shirtwaist of a nursing sister. "Excuse me," I whisper, keeping my voice low out of respect for the sick, the injured, the dying. "I'm seeking Mr. Edgar Poe. Could you please—"

She rushes past without turning her head.

From nearby, terrible noises erupt: screaming, curses, shrieks, pleading. The guttural threats of a maniac which rise to fever pitch, warped with madness and pain.

After so long a time spent in solitude, this hellish clamor pierces my head like steel shards. I flee up a wide staircase to the second floor. On the landing I nearly collide with a gray-bearded gentleman. He wears the white coat of a doctor, its material spotted with rusty red and crusted yellow, mementos of former patients. He's accompanied by several young men whose eyes are red rimmed, who are clearly struggling to feign interest in his muttered lecture. One tall, gangly fellow turns away to stifle a yawn in his sleeve.

I suddenly realize I'm blocking their passage down. "Pardon me." Twitching my skirts aside, I wait for them to let me pass. Yet not one man looks up, or smiles, or even nods to acknowledge me.

I fall back in astonishment at this blatant rudeness. Glancing around in consternation I see, in the window on the landing, that the chair and cabinet beside me are reflected in its glass panes. Yet I, alas, am not.

Ah. I had forgotten for a moment this one sure truth: Not everyone can see the dead as we move among you.

Two harried-looking nurses at the head of the stairs exchange brief, knowing nods as they sidle past the lecture group. They brush by as if I'm less substantial than a moonbeam. The red-haired, Irish-looking one does rub her arms, though, and glances back as if struck with a sudden chill. Yet to them I am little more than a draft of cool air through a cracked pane, a faint shadow cast by a flickering lamp.

Actually, this is a freeing thought, and I step off more confidently, no longer bothering to move aside or apologize when a nurse or orderly passes by or even through me.

Washington University is a teaching hospital. The sort of place I might've been well acquainted with, had I not done all my dying at home. I drift onward through its cacophony of ceaseless sound, the sweet scent of opiates, the sour stench of ailing bodies and soiled bandages, the steamy starch of boiling potatoes, because the time is right for one last journey.

As I reach the second-floor landing more screams erupt, shouted curses and pleas, the broken cries louder, even more desperate now. A man is calling my name; he has been calling it all along. The voice is deeper, though, and hoarser than I remember. Coarsened by shouting, illness, and age. And drink, no doubt—far too much drink.

I feel again the old sinking, the vague dread and pity I once knew so well. And love, of course. That too. "Coming!" I say. "I'm coming to you, my dear."

And if no one can see or hear me—well then, why worry? I move out boldly and call again, louder, "I'm coming to you, dear! Peace, Eddy, peace."

At the end of the corridor, in a small private room, the pale dark-haired man I seek is lying on a hospital cot. His limbs tremble and jerk. "Where's my trunk?" he shouts. And then, "I must board the train to Richmond!"

I stop beside the bed, but he does not look up at me.

"For the love of God," he mutters, throwing his lank wet hair from side to side on a sweat-sodden pillow.

They've tied him onto the cot with lengths of stained canvas, but he does not smell of spirits. So the madness comes from within now, not from a bottle.

He shrieks, "Someone find a pistol and blow my brains out!"

I hold out one hand. "Eddy, my dear."

He squeezes his eyes shut. "You aren't there," he whispers fiercely. "It's the fever working on my brain. I told them I have a wife in Richmond, but they said—"

I lean to stroke his pale damp brow. He shudders under my touch like a poor mistreated horse. "I *am* here, Eddy. You can see me. They can't, that's all."

He opens his eyes again. The wild hope in them is heartbreaking. "Virginia? My own dear Sissy. It *is* you!"

"Yes, it's me." I clasp the poor twitching hand to stop its pointless agitations, and we both flinch. His clutching fingers are very hot, while mine—well, to him they must feel quite icy.

The hope slowly fades. His face contorts into an expression of abject fear, of pale staring horror. "My God, my God," he whispers. *"We have put her living in the tomb!"*

I almost laugh at that, but it would be cruel, or seem even more horrible to him, perhaps. For the tomb, I know now, is far from the final resting place I once believed it to be. "That was only a story, my dear. One of your stories. I'm not . . . not *living*, merely—"

But who can explain a mystery, the nature of which they too are not altogether certain? So to soothe him, I suggest the one helpful thing that comes to mind. "I have a tale," I say, smiling down into his wide staring gaze.

He laughs bitterly, as if I've told a mean joke at his expense. Clenches his hands into hard, trembling fists, straining against the canvas bonds as if he'd strike me down, if only the brass buckles were weaker. "You're not her, but some fiend come to torment me! Who sent you—Longfellow? *The Knickerbocker*? My esteemed cousin Neilson? Bastards, thieving bastards all!"

"None of them, Eddy. Please—let me tell the story this time, won't you? If it's worthy, perhaps you'll commend me to your editor."

He rolls his eyes up at the ceiling. His dry, cracked lips twitch into a grimace that's almost a smile. "My *editor.*"

"Yes, I made a joke. Why not? So much in our lives together was not pleasant or amusing, so when the opportunity arises—"

"All right," he whispers, subsiding onto the thin, damp pillow. "All right." He closes his eyes again, and gestures weakly with those long, pale, trembling fingers: *Go on, then. Go on.*

So that is what I do. I sit at the foot of his narrow sickbed, still holding his hand, and prepare to tell a story—of life, of death, and of life-in-death. So that when my dying husband is calm, and finally believes in the message I bring, we may leave here. Depart the flawed, cold, uncaring world of living men once and for all, together.

Still, I hesitate. Only because—for one dizzy, sickening moment—I want to flee back to that calm and solitary peace I was so suddenly called from. Would I stay here, in this loud, bright, hurried world, if I could? To do it all, our lives, over again?

I am not certain.

In any case I can't leave without him, for Eddy needs me still. Even more than he did back then, if that's possible, through all the joys and tragedies and even the most ordinary of our days. So I'll try to recall to him how we came to be here together, and what lies ahead when we leave this place. Together, I hope—but in the end, he is the one who must choose.

I must content myself with simply recounting those twelve years we knew together. That brief span in our lives when I was first simply young Virginia Eliza Clemm—and then, quite suddenly, Mrs. Edgar Allan Poe.

· 2 ·

I met the man of my dreams when I was eight years old.

Oh dear. I can already hear how that must sound. Like the opening line in a sordid tale of depraved men and helpless children. The kind of cheap pamphlet they used to print on rough yellow paper, and no doubt still do, to sell down certain alleyways in New York City and Philadelphia and Baltimore. When *my* story is not really that sort at all.

Shall we begin again?

When I was eight, my family had a small house on Wilks Street, on Mechanic's Row in Baltimore. My mother, Maria Clemm, my older brother Henry Clemm, and I lived there. So did my older first cousin, Henry Poe. That repetition, the fact of two Henrys in one house, used to confuse me when I was very small: one name, with two faces? Also living with us was our grandmother. Granny Poe had long been a widow, and was so old by then that our mother, who was her daughter, had to care for the old lady as yet another child.

On this particular cool April afternoon I was out playing with my little neighbor friends Juliette and Claudine, sisters who lived on the street behind ours. We were skipping rope and acting out all the game songs we knew. We sang first in English and then in

French, for the pretty young mother of my two friends had been born in Paris. And *her* grandfather had been a soldier in our Revolution. But we were small and cared nothing about all that. It was merely history.

I was getting hungry, so I brushed the dirt and powdery coal dust from the knees of my black stockings, said good-bye to the other girls, and headed back to my house. Still singing, still making the sweeping hand motions that went along with our last shared song:

When I was a young girl, a young girl, a young girl
When I was a young girl, how happy was I
And this way and that way, and this way and that way
And this way and that way, and this way went I.

I began the second verse as I came through the front door and skipped down the hall:

When I had a sweetheart, a sweetheart, a sweetheart
When I had a sweetheart, how happy was I . . .

In the parlor Granny Poe was propped up on her settee by the fire, a sight which I'd expected. But a dark-haired young man, in a black sack coat and tie, was there as well. The stranger sat very straight in the chair across from hers. He was frowning, perhaps annoyed by my loud, silly song. Seeing him raise his head to look at me, I felt embarrassed and turned away, to run back outside.

But then he said, in the most pleasant voice I'd ever yet heard come from a man, "My mother used to sing that song to me." He had a soft, drawling Virginia accent—different from the harder, quicker speech I heard every day in town.

Granny put out a hand to beckon me closer. "Come in, Virginia. Your cousin Edgar Poe is here to see us. He's Henry's little brother. And he's just come back from the army."

When she said that, Cousin Edgar made a funny, sour face that made me giggle. But when Granny Poe glanced over, his expression went bland and agreeable again.

"Were you a soldier?" I asked, curious, thinking of my friend Juliette's grandfather. Until that moment I had assumed all soldiers were very old men.

"Was and still should be," Granny muttered. "Imagine what your grandfather, General Poe, would say if he knew of this! It would surely kill him, were he not already dead and gone."

Edgar Poe closed his eyes and pressed his fingertips to either side of his forehead—the palest, highest, broadest one I'd ever seen—as if a terrible pain pulsed there. "Oh, I can imagine the words very well," he murmured. "But no, Virginia," he said, opening his eyes to look at me again. "I am not a soldier. Not at all. And that's why I'm out of the army."

I bit my lip and nodded. Clearly I'd walked in on an argument. And when Granny shook her head and sighed as deeply as if my grandfather Poe had indeed just died all over again, I felt swift sympathy for my older cousin. How well I knew that guilt-making sound! I heard it when I tore my dress at play, or failed to braid my hair properly, or was too slow to set the table for dinner.

But why was she being so mean to my big cousin, who was a man? Many years from now, when I was a grown woman, would Granny still be nagging me about shirked duties and sagging stockings and proper comportment?

"Well, girl, don't just stand there," she said, turning her sharp, narrow gaze on me again. "Go give your dear cousin a kiss!"

But I felt shy, for he was no little-boy cousin, but all grown up.

His brother Henry Poe, who already lived with us, must be even older. But neither of the Henrys—Eddy's brother or mine—ever paid much attention to me. They certainly never asked for kisses. So I lowered my head and hung back.

"You don't have to," he told me in a low voice. "We hardly know each other. But please, do call me 'Eddy.'" Then he rose and bowed as one grown-up would to another.

No one had ever saved me from one of Granny Poe's relentless calls to duty before. I began to look on him more kindly. "All right then," I mumbled, and bobbed a quick, wobbly curtsy to his low, elegant bow.

"Your black hair is very nice," he said as he sat again. "I've always liked long dark curls, and beautiful, dancing black eyes."

I snorted at that remark, but inched a little closer. He looked like an adult, but he didn't talk like one. "Eyes are not black," I protested. "Even on cows. Even on dogs. And they don't *dance*."

"Virginia Eliza Clemm!" scolded Granny. "For shame. Never talk back to your elders, girl."

"I think you're horrible," I whispered, at a pitch calculated not to be heard by her.

But Cousin Eddy must've heard, for he suddenly grinned. "No, no, Virginia's quite right. It is not possible for eyes to dance. And hers are actually flecked with violet. Like the little wildflower that grows in the wood." He leaned over, reached out, and tilted my chin up to look right into my face.

When his warm fingertips touched the soft skin under my chin, a chill or a spark ran from the back of my neck and shoulders all the way down my spine. Eddy started, as if he'd felt it too. Like the tingling jolt you get on cold winter days after scuffing your shoes over a wool carpet, then touching a brass doorknob.

"My! Are you a girl, or an electrical automaton?" he joked. "I am shocked!"

That funny remark was what reminded me. When we girls played at Housekeeping in the backyard, under the maple tree, my imaginary husband always made silly jokes and puns too. He never muttered about needing money for rent and coal and grocer's bills, as my mother and Granny did day in and day out. My imaginary beau looked nothing like the fathers of our neighborhood, men who came home smelling of sweat and dirt or coal dust—or worse, of whiskey or gin or stale beer. Most of them scowled and spoke sharply to any child who got in their way. Not my own father, of course. He had died when I was five. I barely remembered him at all.

But my imaginary husband was tall and slender, dark haired, and well dressed. He always spoke gently and told funny stories when he came home from *his* work—I hadn't quite decided what that was yet. And as he sat and rested from his long day away, I served him tea in an acorn cup. His hands were pale and clean, and as soft as Edgar Poe's felt as he gently turned my head this way and that. My cousin's eyes were large and kind and gray, though his gaze was serious and mournful as a hunting hound's.

Just then Muddy called for us all to come have bread and butter. So we trooped into the tiny, low-ceilinged dining room and sat down. We passed around the bread board and a sweating pitcher of freshly squeezed lemonade, and I learned Edgar would be staying with us for quite some time.

"How long, Cousin?" I asked, remembering to swallow my mouthful of bread and butter first.

"I don't know," he said, setting his lemonade down suddenly without drinking any. "It's the fault of my . . . my foster father. John Allan. If only he had not—" But then he snatched up the glass again and didn't finish whatever he'd meant to say. Muddy and Granny only went on silently buttering bread and sipping lemonade. And I knew no one by the name of Allan.

I ate my warm slice and swung my feet under the table, feeling pleased. Another guest meant I might have to sleep somewhere other than in my own bed, so I was not certain why that would be a thing to feel pleased about. I swung my legs harder, puzzling over this, until my mother finally grabbed my knee and squeezed.

"Ouch, Muddy," I complained, though it didn't really hurt.

She looked embarrassed. "Be still, Sissy, for heaven's sake."

So then I tried. But I did it for his sake, really. Not for heaven's.

He stayed with us a few weeks, though he was out and about town a great deal, on his own errands—which had to do, I think, with poems and publishers and magazines. But in the evenings after supper Eddy sat in the parlor and talked to me. He liked to declaim poems and to read stories aloud, in a clear, dramatic voice. Some of them he'd written himself. Others were Henry Poe's, which Eddy had convinced his shy older brother to finally share with us.

Eddy told me one night that their mother had been a great actress on the New York stage. In fact, on stages in every city: Baltimore, Richmond, even far-off Boston, where he'd been born. "She was beautiful and kind and sweet natured. With a voice lovely as an angel's. And she was also very amusing," he said. "She excelled especially at comedies. Her name was Eliza Arnold Poe."

"What happened to her?" I asked.

His eyes grew even sadder. "She died, Sissy, still very young and beautiful. And then we, her three orphaned children, were given out like parcels. The MacKenzies took Rosalie, for they wanted a baby. Our Grandfather and Granny Poe took in Henry to raise, but said they were too poor to feed and clothe me as well. So I—I was given like a stray pup to the Allans, to be the son they'd never had." He smiled bitterly, as if at some cruel joke. "So you see, because Eliza Poe left this earth while I was still so young, she seems more like the vision of a beautiful angel to me now."

"My middle name's Eliza," I whispered. "I want to be an actress too. If I could only sing someday on a stage—"

I stopped, feeling too shy to go on about such girlish hopes and dreams. Yet also happy that I shared a name with the person most loved and admired by my cousin. His life was a romantic fairy tale with a very sad beginning. If only I were a character in it too! I was certain I could've saved that poor, younger Eddy somehow, and made him happy again.

Then another thought came to me. "But—what about your father?"

He scowled, and his voice grew harder, colder. "An actor as well, though a poor one. David Poe. He deserted our little family before Rosalie was born."

David and Eliza. So his lovely mother must be the same woman Granny sometimes darkly referred to as "David Poe's Great Folly." Of course I didn't tell Eddy that. Anyway, knowing Granny, she'd already told him so herself, more than once.

Then he explained how Henry had been raised by Granny and General Poe here in Baltimore. But Eddy and Rosie grew up in Richmond, and had seen each other often. "She used to follow me everywhere!" He paused, smiling, as if imagining that boy and girl running and laughing and playing again. "I rarely see her now, of course." He sighed. "We were so young, and that was long ago."

I slipped my hand into his and squeezed gently. "I will be your little sister too. That is—if you like," I offered, stammering and blushing. "Or—or whatever you wish."

He gazed silently into my eyes for such a long time I began to feel first enthralled, and then uneasy, but I couldn't look away, not for anything. "You are very good," he said at last. "You are much like an angel too. I should love to come home and see your lovely, smiling face every day of my life."

So then I knew what it was that my pretend, playtime husband did for a living. He was a writer, of course. A maker of stories. It came clear as spring water in that moment when Edgar Poe looked deep into my eyes, and through them to my soul. The shadow man I'd childishly made up, the one who came home each afternoon to my blackberry-bramble kitchen, to sit on a purloined paving stone and sip tea in acorn cups and tell me of his day—it had been my own cousin Eddy all along.

As the months passed, knowing Edgar Poe would be there each evening when I came inside from play made me happier than I could ever recall being in my whole life, up till then. But one day I arrived home for dinner after playing with Claudine and Juliette down the street, and Eddy wasn't there to greet me.

I ran from room to room, up and down stairs, calling and looking for him. "Where's Cousin Eddy," I gasped to my mother, who was at the table peeling potatoes for dinner.

"Gone, Sissy. Off to study at West Point," she said, without looking up, in her terse, no-nonsense voice. "Now go wash those grubby paws and set the table."

That Eddy had gone off to study war seemed to make Granny Poe happy. But he had not even said good-bye to me.

Being a child, I was miserable for a time and then got used to it. In our crowded little house, relatives often came and went. And certain things it did no earthly good to cry about. I'd learned that years earlier, when my father had died, and no quantity of tears, even mine and Muddy's combined, had brought him back to us— not even for a minute.

But my cousin Eddy did come back the following year, shortly before my ninth birthday.

The day he arrived I was playing out in an alley near the home of Juliette and Claudine. We'd brought our dolls outside and were holding them, pretending to be grown ladies, the mothers of infants. In truth, not a very interesting game, because if you're holding a baby on your lap, all you can do is talk. My doll was an old one Muddy had made of leftover dressmaking scraps, with a round, lumpy cloth head. She'd sewed the eyes and mouth on with odds and ends of embroidery thread, so the doll had one green eye and one blue eye. I called her Eliza.

Claudine's doll-baby was similar to mine, except the black eyes and mouth had been drawn on with India ink. Juliette, older by one year and a half, had a real store-bought doll which she'd inherited from their older sister. Its papier-mâché skull was dented in on one side, though, which gave it a demented look.

Mary Etta Wilkins skipped up the alley to join our circle. "May I play too?" The week before she'd received a doll with a painted china face and real horse-mane hair for her birthday, and ever since had made sure no one forgot it.

I started to say no, being sick of her posing and bragging. But she'd already plopped down on the ground next to me. So we grudgingly shifted to make room, then went on talking about our pretend husbands and pretend houses and pretend sets of flowered china. But I felt aggrieved. Next to Mary Etta's shiny, store-bought baby, my homemade Eliza looked even shabbier than she was.

"I shall have a beautiful little shingled cottage with a tall slate roof and a whitewashed fence. And a big, big garden full of a thousand flowers," I said, bouncing Eliza on one knee. "And I shall marry Mr. Edgar Poe and be a singer and an actress. We'll have six children. All girls."

My two friends nodded, but Mary Etta snorted. "A cottage? No lady wants some tiny old cottage, like the Old Woman Who Lived in a Shoe."

She laughed meanly, and after an uncertain moment Juliette and Claudine joined in.

"I didn't say I wanted to live in an old shoe," I protested.

Mary Etta rocked her fancy doll and cooed nonsense into its hard, painted face. "*She* can't sing," she told the stiff, staring doll, then crooned a cracked, high-pitched lullaby that hurt my ears.

"Can so! And much better than that," I insisted. "*You* sound like a shrieking teakettle."

I expected her to strike back, of course. Those were the rules. To call me a know-nothing paddy or a gypsy thief or even a painted Jezebel. Instead she said, "Well, your auntie was a hooer."

Juliette and Claudine stared at her, goggle-eyed.

"What?" I asked, not sure I'd heard right.

"That *actress*." Mary Etta twisted up her mouth like a drawstring pouch. "My grandmama said Eliza Poe was an actress and a hooer too."

She must be talking about Eddy's mother. The first part was true, of course, though acting was no shame as far as I was concerned. But the second word I'd never heard before. So I didn't know how to repel the insult.

Claudine, the older sister, giggled behind one hand and leaned over to my ear. "*Une putain*," she whispered, using her French voice to me. "*C'est une prostituée.*"

I had my own French voice too, from so many hours of playing with the sisters. *"Quoi?* But how . . . what . . . *Qu'est-ce que c'est, une prostituée?"* I could speak simple French fairly well, but knew neither of those words.

Claudine looked around, I suppose to make sure no adult would overhear, then leaned closer. *"Une femme qui . . ."* She paused, and her cheeks turned pink. *"Qui baise les hommes pour l'argent."*

Juliette shrieked and covered her face with both grubby paws. Though I did not take the whole of Claudine's meaning, clearly Mary Etta had just unspeakably insulted Eddy's mother—and thus him. I clenched poor Eliza in both fists, burning with fury. At Mary Etta. At her expensive doll with the stupid, smug china face. At my two best friends for giggling, and for not instantly leaping to defend me and my family.

I rounded on Mary Etta. "Who would listen to your stupid old granny anyhow? Everyone knows she keeps a dirty pig in the kitchen. And that you kiss its bottom every night." The Wilkinses did in fact keep a pig, a big fat smelly one—but in a lean-to off the back of their house.

The sisters hooted at that. Mary Etta leaped up and began to beat me about the head and shoulders with her precious new doll.

I leaped up too, to get away. By then more children had surrounded us; crept in from nowhere, a crowd appearing as it always does just before some schoolyard brawl or just after a bloody accident. This audience lurked at both ends of the alley, so they could quickly run away, if necessary, and pretend to have had nothing to do with whatever trouble was about to unfold.

Mary Etta lunged at me again, shrieking. I, being smaller and faster, dove behind an old, broken chicken crate. When I scrambled out the other side, Mary Etta's madly swinging doll-truncheon slammed the side of my head. I saw spots and tiny stars. I looked all around for a weapon to defend myself. A broken paving stone! I scooped it up, and as she rushed at me for the third time I bounced it off the crown of her head.

She sat abruptly, looking amazed. Her doll tumbled onto her lap, its own china head miraculously unharmed. A thin trail of blood, the same shade as my mother's most expensive embroidery thread, trickled down my foe's forehead. She lifted a hand to touch it, blinked at her sticky red fingertips, then screamed like a banshee.

In a moment the alley was empty, save for the two of us. Without a word I bolted back home to Wilks Street, running all the way. Somewhere I must've let go of Eliza, for she was gone when I arrived. I hid under our back steps, sniffling over my lost dollbaby, until Muddy called me in for supper.

"What in the world ails you?" she said when she saw my sooty, crumpled pinafore, the torn knees of my black wool stockings, the dirty scrapes beneath them. She marched me to the kitchen to strip out of these soiled things, then ordered me to bed with no supper. "No more gallivanting around in the dirt, my girl," she instructed. "You'll stay indoors or on the porch the rest of this week."

That meant I could not go back and look for Eliza the next day. In any case someone had probably already picked her up, rejoicing at a found treasure. I felt despair, but also a glimmer of relief: At least no one had come yet from Mary Etta's to tell on me. I trailed slowly, slowly up the narrow stairs to my second-floor room.

Cousin Eddy was already arrived, and he would be sharing the attic room with his brother Henry. I sat on my bed, afraid to even go up and greet him, expecting momentarily to be exposed as a would-be murderer. But no one from the Wilkins family came banging on our door, crying for bloody vengeance. So perhaps Mary Etta had entirely made up the insult and now was afraid she'd be whipped for even pronouncing such a dirty, mysterious word. Or perhaps the code of honor that binds children in a silent pact against all adults was stronger than her desire to see me suffer.

In the end Mary Etta did me a great favor. Confined to the premises, without my sole plaything, I could only sit on the front porch and amuse myself by singing every ditty I knew. Even Eddy was not permitted to free me; my mother was determined I would learn to be a young lady, and keep my clothing clean, even if I died of boredom in the process. Of course I had no idea, back then, how much trouble it was simply to wash clothing when you had no running water in the house.

On my third endless afternoon of game songs, which were slowing to dirge time by then, a stout lady came puffing up the front steps. "Your mudder, she *ist* home, girl?"

"Yes, ma'am," I said, intimidated by her vast bulk and loud German voice. She carried a parcel of lace, so she must've come to see Muddy about dressmaking. But then, instead of going in, she stopped before me. "It *vas* you zingink?"

I nodded slowly, unsure I understood her. "Yes, ma'am. It was."

"Ah. Zo, you take lessons, *ja*?"

"You mean writing and numbers and—"

"*Nein!* In the voice."

"Oh." I shook my head. "No, ma'am." We could never afford a luxury like voice training, or lessons on the piano. But one never told strangers of family shortcomings.

She looked me up and down, then pushed on through our front door like a bull dressed up in bombazine. She slammed it shut behind her so hard the whole house seemed to shudder with fear.

I slipped around to the back steps, and began drawing pictures in the dirt with a willow stick. I decided to keep quiet and sing no more, until the formidable lady with the German accent was gone.

But that was not the last I heard of it. It seemed that Madame Frieda Fanning was not Irish—even I could see that—but a German who had once sung opera for European royalty. On a concert tour she'd met and married a high-living Irish baron named Fanning. They settled in Baltimore. But he'd played cards too often over the years, and one night was shot in the heart across a faro table, for cheating. The widow Fanning then changed her name to Madame Frieda and hung out a shingle advertising voice and piano lessons. She taught young ladies with musical aspirations, and the ignorant children of merchants and doctors and bankers. Lessons of the type *we* could never justify, because of our poverty—except that Madame Frieda needed some needlework done. And my mother, who'd been poor long enough to be good at it, drove a hard bargain. She'd sew a certain number of items for Madame Frieda, and I would receive singing lessons and a bit of piano instruction from her once a week.

"How wonderful, Sissy!" cried Eddy. "You'll be a famous opera singer someday, and I shall carry bouquets of roses up to you on the stage."

I beamed with pleasure, until something else occurred to me. "But what is opera?" I asked.

By the summer Henry Poe was very ill. His harsh, wrenching coughs shook the house, especially at night, unless he took a good deal of medicine. But laudanum cost money, and Henry and Eddy seemed to have even less of that than Muddy did.

I used to find Henry's discarded handkerchiefs, crumpled and stained with blood, and often heard him roaming in the night like a gasping, coughing specter, unable to rest or sleep. Poor Henry Poe. He'd once looked so much like his handsome younger brother, but now was only a faint, ragged, shadow Eddy. Thin and gaunt and gray—a perfect ruin who might be a hundred years older than his true age, like Rip Van Winkle.

My older cousin rarely appeared downstairs anymore. But a few nights after Eddy arrived he seemed to be feeling better and came down to have dinner with us.

Our long, rickety table, its top stained and scarred, had come from off the street, left by a departing neighbor for the junk man. But this night Granny Poe instructed me to set it with a yellowing crocheted lace cloth, rarely used—not because it was mended and had port wine stains, but because it was the only one we had. So this was a celebration. Perhaps Granny had finally forgiven Eddy for leaving his army service, because now he would pursue military studies at West Point.

Eddy had brought as a gift a small bottle of sherry, not yet opened. Even Muddy had some in a little chipped crystal goblet— all she had left of a set inherited from Granny's mother. Everyone took half a glass, except me. I didn't care. The musty-sweet smell made my head ache.

The liquor made the adults very jolly. Granny Poe smiled at everyone. Henry Poe roused himself to speak of his time at sea, when he'd been to ports like Montevideo and the West Indies and even Russia. "Once, when I was on board *Macedonian*," he said, after our plates were empty and pushed aside, "we were attacked by pirates."

"So the story's true?" I breathed.

Henry had published a romantic tale called "The Pirate" in some magazine when I was five or six, and Granny still showed it to any visitor who happened to be trapped in the parlor with her. I'd read the yellowing pages several times over.

He flapped a hand. "That one? No, no. Young Eddy here's the main character in that." He slapped his younger brother on the back. "*He's* the ladies' man."

Eddy blushed. "Elmira Royster's father read that, Henry. It surely didn't help my cause."

His *cause*? Which had involved a woman named Elmira—a more romantic, exotic name than Virginia, or Sissy, which everyone called me. So the lovers in Henry's tale had been real. Our Eddy, and this . . . Elmira person. I recalled the things hinted at in the story—passionate embraces, long kisses—and imagined Eddy holding some strange young lady in his arms. My stomach clenched around the boiled potatoes and stringy pork we were having for supper.

Eddy announced he and Henry Poe were going into town in an hour or so. "To celebrate our reunion as a family." My own brother Henry, who was thirteen, looked up hopefully from his plate. But Eddy didn't invite anyone else along.

"What about Rosalie?" I said quickly, feeling slighted, wondering if Henry Poe could even walk so far. "Without her your family isn't all here, is it?"

I knew it was a mean thing to say, even as the words left my lips. Some of our neighbors claimed Rosalie MacKenzie Poe was not right in the head, even though she was a young lady now and taught at a fancy girls' school.

She and Mrs. MacKenzie, who'd adopted her, had once come to visit when I was about six years old. I had thought her a very beautiful young lady then.

"Eddy and I always played together when we were small," she'd told me, her plain face glowing. "I follow him everywhere." As if they were still three and five, and she not almost twenty years. As if Eddy stood beside us in short pants, with skinned knees and a sunburned face. "My brother Eddy," she'd whispered, and sighed. "I call him 'Buddy.'"

Rose had insisted on jumping rope with us girls. After she left Claudine had laughed and teased me unmercifully. "Your cousin is *un grand crétin*, Ginny Clemm!" Claudine was older and taller, so I hadn't dared to push her down. How good it would've felt to leave her lying flat-out and sniveling in the dirt. I'd swung the rest of that afternoon between unreasonable anger at Rosalie, and shame I hadn't defended a blood cousin. She was a strange one, no question, like a slow-minded child trapped in a woman's body. But family, nonetheless.

After I mentioned Rose at the table, Eddy lowered his sherry glass and looked at me strangely, lips thinning into a line that might've been slashed by Muddy's paring knife. I shrank under his cold stare.

"Why, Sissy," my mother said, eyebrows raised, broad face slack with shock and embarrassment. "You must apologize."

I shoved back my chair. "I have a headache, Muddy, may I be excused?"

Without waiting for her answer, I ran up the stairs to my room.

I woke some time later to off-key singing and drunken laughter, loud voices and faltering steps on the stair. I closed my eyes and fell asleep again, thinking, *No, Muddy would never allow it. Not in her house.*

I was surprised to see the sherry bottle still sitting on the table the next morning, and even more surprised to discover it empty. My mother was no teetotaler, but she was leery of drink. My grandmother was even more vocal on the Temperance question than on other subjects, pronouncing in grim, front-pew tones, "Alcohol has long been an enemy to the Poe family." She always said this as if speaking of some malevolent person, rather than a beverage, and

would then cast a significant look at any male who happened to
be in the room—usually one of the Henrys. "It's the Old Failing,"
she'd conclude.

As usual Muddy was up before me, already working in the
kitchen. I went in and hugged her soft, thick waist, to make up for
my bad behavior the night before. She smelled of soap and bacon
grease. She pressed her cheek to the top of my head, then gently
pushed me away so she could get on with fixing breakfast—toasted
day-old bread, fried bacon rind, and freshly ground coffee boiling
in a saucepan. A little better than the usual corn porridge.

"Set the table, please, Sissy," she directed, forking crisp hunks
of bacon out of the pan and onto a plate.

I did, then took the old lacquer tray up the stairs to Granny
Poe. I came back down and we waited a few minutes for the men,
as our food cooled and my mouth watered in anticipation of the
taste of salty crisp bacon. But no one came down. At last Muddy
and I ate our share and left the remains under a napkin for them.

"They went into town after dinner, as promised," was all she
had to say on the subject as we cleared. There was no stirring
from their room until well past noon, when I heard the thump of
footsteps overhead. Then, a different sound came, just as Muddy
and I began to peel the potatoes meant for dinner. A single sharp
cry—of pain, or of grief. Impossible to tell which.

We rushed up the narrow stairwell to Henry's room, where Eddy
also slept. I was smaller and faster, and reached the doorway first.

Eddy sat there on the bed, bending over his brother, cradling
Henry's thin, bony shoulders. He was weeping in great gasps that
shook both of their bodies. Henry Poe lay far too still: half out of
the bed, still clad in a nightshirt, his thin legs limp and bare. In the
dim light I gradually made out that the sheets were soaked with
something dark. A brownish red stain.

"Oh," I whispered, and shrank back, staring openmouthed at Eddy. Had they quarreled? Surely he wouldn't have hurt Henry!

Blood and clots also matted Henry's straggly beard. A dark patch had dried like a horrible red dinner napkin on the breast of his nightshirt. Then I vaguely understood. My older cousin had succumbed at last to the consumption, which he'd contracted on one of his sea voyages. The disease had gradually turned him from a healthy young sailor into a coughing, wretched shadow.

Eddy clung to his brother's body fiercely, whispering into his ear, as if he could somehow pull him back.

My mother squeezed past me to touch his shoulder, to draw him away from the ruin of his poor lost brother. "Come now," she said.

My cousin gave one last sob, then threw an arm around Muddy's knees, clutching at her skirts, weeping into the heavy black wool like a grief-stricken child. In the face of such anguish, I could do nothing but stand and bear witness. Finally, sobs rose in my own throat and I roused myself to back slowly, slowly down the stairs.

After a while, Muddy came down to the kitchen again. "We must prepare the poor boy for burial," she told me. Then she called up the stairs to Eddy, "Stay a moment. Help me move him." Again she turned back to me. "Sissy, stay in the kitchen. It's not a fitting thing for a girl to see."

I crept back up anyhow and lingered at the threshold like a sparrow teetering on a wind-tossed twig, but when Muddy saw me she shut the door firmly in my face. So I sat on the top step, and only heard the bed frame creak, and a low, pained moan from Eddy. I couldn't blame him for showing his feelings, his grief at losing his older—his only—brother. I didn't always like my own big brother so well; he teased and pinched, and sometimes jerked hard on my hair. But I loved Henry Clemm fiercely, as one must always love family. I'd feel hurt and lost if he should leave us as suddenly as Henry Poe had.

We buried him the following day in Westminster Burying Ground, near the church my mother and I attended most Sundays. Henry had never gone there, though, and Eddy did not profess to any religion at all.

"He was twenty-four," Muddy prompted our elderly minister, who fumbled with his worn, well-thumbed prayer book and seemed to recollect nothing she told him about Henry. "He was a seagoing man. He wrote poems."

Eddy stared stonily ahead, jaw clenched, speaking to no one.

Only a small band of mourners gathered to send off the eldest son of Eliza Arnold and David Poe. Granny Poe could not come; she was by then confined to bed by paralysis, and we had no proper conveyance. The rest of us stood around the grave in black bombazine and wool, sweating fiercely under the blazing sun and stifling humidity the first of August always brought to Baltimore.

Poor Henry, you had a short, hard life, I thought, as a trickle of sweat slithered wormlike down my side beneath the too-short bodice of my old blue dress, a high-waisted frock Muddy had let out twice already. Henry was being buried in an old suit of my father's, and had looked very respectable, though white and stiff as a waxwork figure in his narrow pine coffin. He'd spent half his life at sea. He had no wife or children. Had he ever been loved by a woman other than his mother or mine? I did not know.

He'd left only a small wooden chest shoved into a dusty corner under his bed. A morbid impulse to know more about my dead cousin, who'd always seemed so grimly mysterious, even a little frightening, had propelled me slowly up the stairs the day before. In his room I had knelt beside the rope bed and tugged at one end of the cobwebbed chest until it slid out into the light. It was unlocked, and when I lifted the lid a whirlwind of dust motes swirled upward like tiny lost souls rejoicing to be set free at last.

Inside, the pitiful leavings included a sheaf of papers, three water-stained stories he'd written aboard ship, one tattered book of Percy Shelley's poems that was missing its back cover, a few creased letters, a pair of black stockings badly out at heel and toe, a broken pocket watch, and a straight razor. Overcome with shame and pity, I had shoved it all beneath the bed again, and run back downstairs.

So this was the sad finish to a man's whole life: a cheap pine box, a handful of sweating, dutiful relatives, and a borrowed minister who mumbled his way quickly through the service, as if worried his dinner was getting cold. At least Henry's brother was there to mourn him. And his sister, though Rosalie kept her adoring gaze fixed fiercely on Eddy, until Mrs. MacKenzie squeezed her elbow and redirected her to attend to the minister, who was still intoning the everlasting rite for the dead.

When my turn came I lifted a clod and tossed it into the open grave, on top of the coffin. "I'm sorry," I whispered as dirt rained down on the pine lid. I tried to envision Henry's face, but could only conjure up one feature at a time—square jaw, gaunt cheeks, a faraway sailor's gaze. "I should've been nicer to you, Henry." I hadn't been mean to him, but he had never seemed very interested in his young girl cousin. He was a grown man who, unlike Eddy, had seemed to have nothing in common with me at all.

We turned away. I looked back to see the undertaker's servants, who'd been standing off at a respectful distance and holding shovels at port arms, step forward to fill in the gap in the earth. As the family walked away, I lengthened my strides to catch up to

Eddy. I slid my hand into his, and squeezed. His fingers tightened almost imperceptibly, and we walked in step all the way.

There would be no stone in the churchyard for Henry Poe; we hadn't the means to have a slab of marble cut and carved. But as we made our way home Eddy vowed he'd erect one someday. "When I have made some money," he said.

Then he left again, the following week. And I felt for a time as if two people I knew had died, not just one.

· 3 ·

The next time I saw my cousin Edgar I was twelve. We'd moved farther out of town by then, to Amity Street, to escape an outbreak of cholera. The brick house was tall and narrow, two floors and an attic, five tiny rooms. I was taller too, but made much more shy by a complexion which Granny Poe bemoaned loudly every time I left a room. "Such a pretty girl till now. But oh, that skin! It spoils her looks. Yes, the Poe men are handsome, but the women have any number of crosses to bear. Just look at poor Rosalie!"

True, Eddy's sister could not be called pretty. Not like their beautiful, funny mother, Eliza. Rose, raised all her life by the MacKenzies, was at least ten years older than me. She taught in the Richmond girls' school run by her mother, and we still didn't know each other well.

Since this time I knew Eddy was on the way, I hovered near the front window, one hand shielding my left cheek where the despised red bumps were the worst. Would he even recognize me? I was no longer a child, not small and plump and charming anymore. My mother had raised one eyebrow that morning as I came yawning into the kitchen. "Soon we'll need to have you corseted, my dear. You're growing so fast I can't keep up."

I was taller, yes, but still short for my age. I had a small waist but the rest of me felt a good deal plumper than it had at eight or even at ten. My new bosom was less of an annoyance since I'd learned to sleep on my side instead of on my stomach. But I feared these changes would make me even more of a stranger to Cousin Eddy than three years' separation must. However, I was looking forward to telling him that while he'd been away, I had been busy—studying music with a real opera singer.

Every other Tuesday I went to Madame Frieda's house, which always smelled of sauerkraut and boiled beef and dusty dried flowers. We could not afford regular lessons, but whenever Madame needed needlework done, or plain mending, or a new gown cut, pieced, and stitched, my mother brokered a deal. So my education in music had been sporadic, but at least it was still progressing.

At Madame's I always sat outside the parlor and listened to the procession of girls, most older than me, who went in to sing scales. Sopranos, mezzo-sopranos, contraltos. They were cash-paying customers, so I had to wait until they were finished for Madame Frieda to devote an hour to me. One after another they'd sweep past, barely deigning to notice me perched on the sprung ottoman covered by an old Turkey carpet scratchy as my grandmother's whitewhiskered chin. For my part, I pretended not to see I was being snubbed by girls older, taller, prettier, or richer than me.

There was one for whom I waited with no resentment though. Angelica Edwards. She possessed the voice of a Greek goddess traversing the night sky in a star-harnessed chariot. A sound so pure and clear I longed for the tall grimy ceiling to lift away, the smokedarkened paneling between parlor and music room to tumble like the walls of Jericho, so I could not only hear but see her singing. I imagined her as Aphrodite enthroned on a crescent moon of gold, her auburn hair ablaze with star dust, her pierced ears hung with tiny blazing comets.

The mantel clock ticked like a metronome as her sweet pure soprano warbled on. I sighed and dreamed, actually thankful that in opera it takes the diva forever to die. It never occurred to me then to wonder how anyone could still sing if the breath was forever leaving her body—as she lay fainting away from loss of blood, loss of love, or both. I'd heard some older students discussing the merits of the various operas. It seemed that, in these, it was the women who most often died. But this realization merely seemed an immutable part of a world set in motion long before I existed. Who questions the moon and stars, the solid earth, the grass growing beneath your feet?

At last the lesson would end and Miss Edwards finally emerge. A tall, slender, pigeon-breasted young lady, her face pale with rice powder, her thick auburn curls pinned with great discipline into a tight chignon. She favored green-sprigged white gowns and dainty green morocco slippers. I gazed in adoration each time she rustled past. She never spoke or even glanced my way. But that too seemed the law of the universe, far beyond my puny reckoning. Why shouldn't a diva, a shining star with a voice of spun gold, treat the rest of the world with graceful, elegant contempt?

Only when she'd shut the heavy oak door behind her did I dare rise and go in for my biweekly bout with the formidable Madame Frieda Fanning.

Madame Frieda always sat on a carved mahogany chair like a round pagan idol, jowly face set off by a gray-streaked bun. She occupied the space between the piano and a huge areca palm, and gripped a heavy walking stick carved from a long, twisted ebony root. Though she seemed very old to me then—much older than my mother, though not quite so ancient as Granny Poe—Madame did not need that cane for walking. So at first I'd wondered why she held it.

I soon found out. On our first afternoon together I'd run through the scales a dozen times. When I paused once for a breath, somewhere between *la* and *so,* Madame scowled and banged the cane on the oak floor. It made an impressive crash, and I jumped. My hands trembled.

"Are you frightened, girl?" she said, smiling grimly. "*Gut!* Again. Go on!"

"Again, Madame?" I inquired. "But—but we've done those so many times already! If you don't mind, I'd like to sing a whole song."

Her eyes bulged. She bared her teeth at me like a bulldog. "*Himmel!* Be glad I am not a man. Manuel Garcia beat his *lieber* daughter Maria for any little error in her singing. He started when she was six, and thrashed the poor little fräulein right out of her natural alto range all the way into a high soprano. All for to sing the opera with him. Do you zink she complained?"

I'd heard of the great Maria Garcia Malibran, of course; the famous, beautiful opera singer who'd died so tragically young. But I did not know a thing about her terrible father. I lowered my gaze to the pattern in the red Turkey carpet beneath my feet, and whispered, "No. I mean—no, Madame."

She banged the stick again, though less violently, and this time I made sure not to flinch. "No *ist* quite correct." She added in a milder tone, "You must to sing the scales to me slow, fast—*ja,* any way at all. For the putting in tune of the voice, as one does *ein* violin, *ja*?" Then, with a fierce glare: "Zo then, begin again!"

And I did, up and down, up and down, until my throbbing

head and staggering footsteps echoed all the way home to *do re mi fa so la tee do.*

I'd longed to be Miss Edwards when I began my lessons. Madame Frieda must've sensed this; perhaps all her silly little students harbored the same predictable, mundane fantasy. For she said to me, at our third lesson, *"Ein Kind* who makes her voice heard among zee rest may hope for a part in zee church choir."

But . . . was that all? I nodded, unsure how to respond, or if I should even attempt to do so.

"But not *ein Kind* who does not practice or take advice. Only one in a hundred will zing a concert outside her own drawing room. And an opera on zee stage? *Mein Gott,* no!"

I felt daunted then. But Muddy was paying with her needle and thimble for those lessons. I would not let her down. And gradually I came to understand and accept that I was not gifted with the same supernatural range as Miss Edwards. My notes left my throat with precision and grace, but did not soar like birds winging toward heaven. I was a natural at the piano though. We had none at home to practice on, but my brother salvaged an oak board from an old building and painted the keys on it so I could practice my fingering.

And then, on the very day of Eddy's arrival, Madame had just grudgingly told me I had a pretty voice. But when I smiled, she'd banged her cane on the floor. "A pretty voice, *mein* girl. Not a great one."

I couldn't help it. A tear trickled down my cheek.

"Ach! Haf you come here for learnink to veep?" she asked, quite gently for her.

I shook my head. Then added quickly, "N-no, Madame."

She nodded as if satisfied. "Zo, you must begin again."

Very well, then. If I could never become Miss Edwards, I would merely be myself, and sing and play as best I was able, and for all I was worth. Not the queen of the opera, but at least a lady-in-waiting, happy to sit on the edge of the glittering royal court.

I hoped Eddy would be proud of me.

Back home I had rushed to the mirror and smoothed stray strands into place. Stared for one despairing moment at my spotted face, so unlike the pale powdered visage of the goddess of music. Then dragged myself to the tiny front room's single window, where I still stood, watching and waiting.

When Eddy finally came up our cracked brick walk he was limping. Perhaps he'd been injured during some practice maneuvers at West Point. Or in a real battle? But I didn't recall any recent wars. I drew back in case he looked up and saw me clutching the yellowed lace, staring out.

"Dear Aunt Maria!" he exclaimed when my mother opened the door. He embraced her and she patted his cheek. "It's like coming home to my family," he said, looking pleased.

"Of course we're your family," Muddy said a bit roughly, as she took his hat. But he had sounded as if he meant something a little different, something . . . *stronger* than she did.

"What happened to your leg?" I blurted out, after promising myself I wouldn't speak first.

He glanced at me, then down at that limb. "This? Nothing much. Merely a sprained knee."

"Were you hurt in a—a battle?"

"No, and I've left the academy. Or rather they—asked me to go. Really a matter of honor. For me, that is."

Granny Poe scowled from her seat by the fire. "Lord God, boy. You're unlucky as a three-legged bird dog. At least your grandfather, the general, didn't live to hear of this."

I scowled in her direction. Eddy bit his lip, or bit back some retort, I suppose. Then he took another, longer look, surveying me head to toe. I jerked a hand up and fingered my cheek, to cover it again.

"Wait a moment." He tilted his head. "Is this—surely this isn't our little Virginia?"

"Ha! Not so little anymore," said my mother, her laugh like a dog's sharp bark. I wished it were permissible to smack one's elders.

Eddy stepped closer and took my bare hands in his gloved ones. "Now let me see. Oh my, Sissy! You're a young lady now, nevermore a little girl. Well. I really didn't expect . . ."

He trailed off, sounding disappointed, as if in partaking of the natural process of growing I had somehow betrayed him. I pulled my hands free and folded my arms across my bosom. "Well, I'm not a lady. Not yet."

A foolish remark, a child's retort. But I felt just then silly and young and unformed and ungainly, whatever he and my mother might think. When he took hold of my hands again, to apologize, the fine hairs on my forearms rose slowly. As if the warm, close room had turned cold as winter.

Suddenly I wished he'd not come back at all.

Eddy this time would share my brother's tiny, sloping room in the attic. At least it was not the same one his brother had died in; we'd left that room behind, back in the house on Wilks Street. And Muddy had arranged a lovely surprise: his sister Rosalie was coming to visit, along with her foster mother, Jane MacKenzie.

Like any child, I had a talent for eavesdropping. So I knew Eddy had lost both foster parents years earlier. Or rather, that he was estranged from his foster father, though he'd loved and been loved by his gentle, sickly foster mother, Frances Allan. But she'd died while he was seventeen and still at the University in Charlottesville.

John Allan had never let Eddy forget he was an orphan, the son of players, wholly beholden to him. After Eddy had grown from a precocious boy into a young man who wrote lines of poetry rather than rows of numbers in ledgers, Mr. Allan had sent him off to the University without enough means even for tuition, then berated him for running up debts. He'd scorned, ridiculed, and finally disowned Eddy. But the kindly MacKenzies had doted on Rose like a true daughter all her life.

The MacKenzies arrived in a shining black rented calash, which they left down the street with the driver, to be admired by a gathering crowd of scruffy, wide-eyed neighborhood boys.

I supposed the MacKenzies were almost as rich as John and Frances Allan had been. Or maybe not, since Jane MacKenzie ran a girls' school in Richmond, and in my experience, well-off ladies did not work. On the other hand it was, according to my mother, the most fashionable female seminary in that city. She didn't need to add that we could never in our lives afford to send me there.

Rosalie touched her cheek to mine. She was no great beauty, as Granny Poe so often lamented. The features that made Edgar distinguished-looking—the broad expanse of pale forehead, the vaguely Roman nose, the heavy, straight brows and large sad eyes—made his sister appear coarse and masculine. Dozens of perfect, dark brown sausage curls carefully arranged above her brow and around her face softened this impression, though, and I decided Granny had been too harsh. Rosalie was not pretty, but she was handsome. She also seemed tall, though most people did, to me. Her lavender silk afternoon gown made my old gray frock look as faded and patched as it really was. I envied her dressmaker-finished clothes, pale doeskin gloves, white kid shoes, the lacquered gray straw hat with its tiny, filmy veil.

At the door Rosalie rushed rudely past me straight to Eddy. She said in a high childish voice, "Buddy! Aren't you going to kiss me hello?"

He bent stiffly and let his lips brush her upturned cheek. Vague distaste flickered across his face, but was gone so soon I decided I'd imagined it.

We gathered in the parlor after I helped Muddy bring glasses of weak tea and mismatched plates with thin slices of pound cake for everyone to balance on one knee, or stand and hold as best he could. We had only one settee and a sprung armchair with broken back that had to be propped against the wall. Muddy's antimacassars weren't numerous enough to disguise the holes in its stained brocade.

Rosalie stuck by Eddy like a burr, even after he'd urged all the ladies to please sit.

Jane MacKenzie was perched on the settee next to Muddy. "Edgar tells me you are musically talented, Virginia," she said, turning gracefully from the waist to look at me. "You must come visit us soon in Richmond, my dear."

"Yes, yes," Rosalie exclaimed, tearing her gaze from Eddy for a moment. "You must come visit us in Richmond."

I smiled but glanced at her curiously. Her words were a near-perfect copy of her mother's, her tones just as well modulated and cultured, yet this mimicry felt unsettling to the ear. As if a parrot had imitated human speech too well. When she'd spoken to Eddy a few moments before, her voice had been quite different—higher-pitched, younger, simple—a petulant little girl's.

"Oh Moses, I see the flowers here are past their prime too," said Jane to Muddy, with a sad little smile. "August is always such a trial, isn't it?"

Before Muddy could reply, Rosalie blurted out loudly, "He brought me a buttercup once."

I started and we all glanced at her. Except for Eddy, who was staring into his glass, fingers gripping so hard his knuckles were a bloodless white.

"Who was that, dear," said Mrs. MacKenzie calmly.

Rosalie tossed her head and gave a little impatient laugh. "Buddy, of course. *Buddy!*"

Eddy winced at this childhood nickname. He and everyone else but Rose had probably discarded it before I was born.

"Oh, I see. You mean, when you were both small," Mrs. Mac-Kenzie said encouragingly, as if acting as a translator for the rulers of two small, unfamiliar countries.

"I used to go everywhere with him." Rosalie's face darkened and her brows drew together. "But he never plays with me now."

Eddy turned abruptly away and drained his glass in one toss, as if it held a shot of medicinal spirits instead of plain China black tea. His expression was tortured, and this tortured me as well. She might be a little slow, but Rosalie was still his sister, all that was left of close kin. Yet he seemed to barely abide her presence, though I'd heard they were inseparable as children. He'd told me how she had always trailed him through Richmond's Shockoe Bottom, imitating everything he did and said, worshiping him. His tone had been amused then, indulgent—even affectionate. I didn't want to think he'd be unkind to her now, even if she was acting strangely.

Finally he turned back, and though his expression was still distant, he gave his younger sister a smile. "Well, Rosie, that was long ago, when we were small. But now I'm a man. And thanks to the whims of fortune I must work for my living." He sighed. "And you—well, there is no more time to play, is there."

As if he'd never spoken, Mrs. MacKenzie said, "And when Virginia comes to see us, you must come too, Mrs. Clemm." She glanced at Eddy. "Indeed, all of you must." I saw in her sweet gaze something steely—a challenge, a rebuke—that she would never voice. And understood, by her tone and the set of her mouth and the line between her eyes, that she would never allow anyone to hurt or insult or slight her daughter. Not even Rosalie's own brother.

Rose clapped her hands. "Yes, oh yes!"

"Won't that be pleasant, Edgar," Jane went on. "I know you're happy to have Mrs. Clemm and pretty little Virginia here with you. But Rose misses her dear brother."

"A visit would be lovely," Eddy choked out, cheeks flushed. "I'll have to see about it, very soon. Right now since I've . . . just left the military academy—well, I must find some sort of position."

When we finished the tea and cake, Mrs. MacKenzie said they must get to the dock and board the steamer for Richmond. "Rosalie has her penmanship classes in the morning," she said, more pointedly than necessary. I was just trying to visualize the tall figure of Rosalie crammed into a school desk, studying handwriting and sums, when Mrs. MacKenzie added, "She is one of my *best* teachers."

Seeing Rose, watching her fawn over Eddy, I'd actually forgotten she was an adult, and a teacher herself.

They left, Rosalie dragging her feet, scuffing her dainty, embroidered kid slippers beyond repair. Eddy seemed morose after that, but why should he not? He'd lost father, mother, foster mother, and older brother. Now his only remaining close family was a sister who—

But I turned my mind away from unkind thoughts then, as

one would rein in a straying horse. For all of Rose's advantages, I was in some ways more fortunate. She was already a spinster, and would probably never marry or have children. No, never, for *she* was still the child, even if a beloved one. While I was young and had a whole long life ahead, just waiting for me.

Something else I hugged to me, which felt warmer than doe-skin gloves or kid slippers or even a fancy fur muff. I owned the brotherly love of Edgar Poe, instead of that reluctant sense of duty Rose seemed to stir in him. And I loved him in return. If Rosalie ever understood the difference, she would probably give up all the fine clothes and musical instruments and certainly all the penmanship classes in the world for one smile of welcome. One willing, affectionate kiss on the cheek from her older brother.

I heard him pacing downstairs late into the night, after Muddy and I went up to bed. Stopping to raise a shrieking window sash, or to drop into the old armchair whose broke-back springs squealed like a snared rabbit. Until I fell asleep, and never found out if he ever went up to bed at all.

· 4 ·

The next morning I sat in our dim little parlor, huddled under the single shaft of sunlight that slanted in through the dusty window glass. I had no music lesson that afternoon, so I was reading fairy tales, an old book we'd had for years. When I was small I'd loved it for the hand-colored engravings of people and flowers. I'd paged through so often the covers were disintegrating at the spine and edges. Now I appreciated the words of the stories more, though they were quaint and old-fashioned, and sometimes puzzling: *There was a queen who was with child, and she dreamed of a daughter with skin as white as snow, hair as black as ebony, and lips as red as blood.*

An odd idea; even odder if you pictured it. A girl so strange, features perfect yet freakish. And the even stranger Little Mermaid, who gave away her voice so she could have legs and walk on land, all for the love of a prince who barely noticed her, who in the end married someone else. Imagine not being able to speak, or to raise your voice in song. Unable to sing popular ballads, love songs, church hymns—at least, the ones not too slow and lugubrious. To have no voice—that part of the tale always made me shudder. For I sang every chance I got, even when not keeping time with Madame Frieda's stick.

Midway through "Sleeping Beauty" I heard a step, the rustle of cloth, and peered over the top of the book. Eddy had come in, his face pale and drawn, nearly as white as fairy-tale snow—a study in suppressed grief. He must've been thinking of Henry Poe.

He paused by my chair. "Ah, what's this?" He picked up my book and gazed at the faded cover. "Oh, for— No, no, Virginia! This is pap for children. You're much too old to read such drivel."

I sat straighter, back stiff, a flush seeping hotly up my neck and cheeks. It was nothing of the kind; they were lively, interesting stories. But I could think of no scathing comeback.

He smiled sadly. "Oh, my dear. I'm sorry if I offended you. It's just that—you're so clever. I hate to see your mind wasted on trivial subjects."

The book dropped back into my lap and he was suddenly gone. I heard him pounding up the stairs, then after a minute or two galloping back down. He thrust a short stack of books into my hands.

I looked at the one on top with dismay and felt my cheeks burn even hotter. I could not read it at all, not even the title. It was in some foreign language.

He frowned at me, then at the book. "You don't care for Homer?" Just as I opened my mouth to confess I had no idea who or what that was, he shook his head. "Oh—of course. You don't read *Greek*! Sorry."

I stared back in dismay. If he read Greek and perhaps even spoke it, how intelligent and well educated my cousin must be. Though I did wonder to whom he would be able to speak such an ancient tongue, here in Baltimore. Perhaps back in Richmond folks spoke it on the street every day, in passing. "Well, no. I can't. That is, I never . . ." I trailed off, mortified.

"Don't look so stricken! I can't read it myself so well. Having been forced to leave after only the one year at Mr. Jefferson's great University, because my parsimonious foster father would not— well, never mind all that."

He took the volume back, then gazed at me expectantly again.

Now on the top of the stack sat some tattered copies of *The New-England Magazine*, a battered novel called *A Lion of the West*, and beneath them, as if hiding out of modesty, two more items. The topmost was a slim bound volume entitled *Tamerlane and Other Poems by a Bostonian*.

I gasped and carefully, reverently cradled it. He'd crossed out "a Bostonian" and inscribed his name. Below that he'd penned: *This copy belongs to Virginia "Sissy" Clemm, the smartest young lady in Baltimore.*

I clutched them to my chest as if someone had dropped a pile of twenty-dollar gold pieces into my lap. We had few books around the house. Most we'd once owned Muddy had taken to a bookseller for the few coins they would bring.

Eddy beamed. "Many of those poems I wrote before the age of fifteen." When I merely gaped at this revelation, he added, "Well, I'll leave you to the pleasure of discovery, then." And went back up the stairs, more sedately this time.

The chapbook opened as if of its own accord, to a very long poem called "Al Araaf."

> *O! nothing earthly save the ray*
> *(Thrown back from flowers) of Beauty's eye,*
> *As in those gardens where the day*
> *Springs from the gems of Circassy—*
> *O! nothing earthly save the thrill*
> *Of melody in woodland rill—*
> *Or (music of the passion-hearted)*

Joy's voice so peacefully departed
That like the murmur in the shell,
Its echo dwelleth and will dwell—
With nothing of the dross of ours—
Yet all the beauty—all the flowers . . .

After some pages of this I paused, perplexed. I liked gardens, and loved flowers, and the rhyme was very well done indeed. But I was only on page 3 and already in over my head. The occasional heaving white breast or burning cheek renewed my interest, but most of the time I was lost in a maze walled with words. It seemed to be about a sort of un-Christian, mythological heaven. One which only two people occupied. Stifling a yawn, I set that one aside for later.

I examined the next item, a handwritten manuscript. Some pages were curled at the edges, as if they'd once been rolled into scrolls. The top sheet was titled *Tales of the Grotesque and Arabesque, by Edgar A. Poe.* I began to read, casually at first, but was soon unable to stop, turning the crackling pages filled with line after line of careful, elegant handwriting. *His* handwriting.

The first story, titled "Metzengerstein," concerned an evil German baron whose true nature was revealed by an heirloom tapestry depicting an ancient murder. A savage, spectral horse figured in the plot too. It was so frightening I paused to look over my shoulder as I read, and my sunny spot seemed less warm. As I turned more pages I encountered a passage about a beautiful, highborn lady called Mary. I read on, enjoying the scene, until I understood she was dying of the consumption. At one point the narrator said, "It is a path I have prayed to follow. I would wish all I love to perish of that gentle disease."

I dropped the page into my lap again, amazed. Eddy's own

brother had perished of the consumption—well, that and drink. An ugly, bloody, drawn-out, painful, ungentle death. A number of women he'd loved—his mother, Eliza, his foster mother, Frances, a Mrs. Jane Stannard, mother of his best boyhood friend—had all perished of that same wasting disease. Why would he make it sound soft and kind?

Perhaps he'd been too young, or not there for the worst of it; perhaps he had not actually *seen* their suffering. Even Henry's, at least until he'd come back to us. And Eddy, who was kindhearted to a fault, would not want to think of anyone he loved in terrible, prolonged pain, racked with coughing, bedridden in endless agony, before death finally thought to come and claim the poor soul. No doubt he preferred to believe they'd faded like summer roses in September; a slipping away, a gentle leave-taking of this unkind world for a better one.

I set the stack aside and went into the front room, where Eddy sat at Muddy's tiny desk. "Shall I sing a song for you now?"

He set quill and paper aside. "Why, yes. That would be lovely, Sissy."

I had no piano. But thanks to Madame Frieda I could get along quite well a capella. I'd mastered several songs of mourning and death, battles and loss, but would not sing those now. Instead, with my small but adequate talent, I would endeavor to woo Eddy from this strange, dark preoccupation. To draw him again into the world of life and of light.

He looked at me expectantly, both hands resting on his knees. "I'm at your disposal. What will you sing?"

Something light and fair, I thought. Something with a castle, and a maiden, and—yes, a handsome young man. If only I had a harp! But no—that might evoke death and angels too. I pondered, turning over titles in my head, then smiled and hummed a note or two. And stood taller yet, with shoulders relaxed as Madame had taught me, for the opening stanza of "The Minstrel Knight."

> *A Maid within this Castle dwelt*
> *More fair than any that grac'd the hall*
> *Tho' many a knight to her had knelt*
> *She loved the Minstrel best of all.*

I sang, taking pleasure in filling my lungs to propel the well-shaped notes, and in the way their crisp sounds vibrated deep in my throat and lungs. I became the lovely Maid—and wasn't Eddy the Minstrel, after all?

He smiled, and nodded, and soon began to keep time with one hand on his knee. And I thought, See, it's not so very hard to cajole a sad soul away from the darkness, and turn his face once more toward the light.

When our grandfather the war-hero general was still alive, our branch of the Poes was well fixed. David Poe the elder had been wealthy enough to loan the government of Maryland and its revolutionary army forty thousand dollars to outfit the troops of the French hero Lafayette. The state had never repaid this considerable debt, though, so since before my birth we'd lived in genteel poverty. Muddy and Granny and I had made many meals of potatoes and vegetables. We cut our worn-out bedsheets down the middle, then turned and sewed them together again to make them last. Often my mother had to ask distant relations for a few dollars to pay a doctor's bill, or to buy cheap smoky lumps of coal during a bad winter.

Yet Muddy still had pretensions to culture. That, I felt certain, was why my practical mother had bartered for my piano and singing lessons. She'd tried to teach me how to paint pastel-hued land-scapes with watercolors, her thick, callused fingers gripping the cheap brush not much more daintily than a feather duster. How I'd hated leaning over the damp paper for hours while the weak, watery colors ran, going every place but where I wanted them.

Well, writing poetry was cultured, wasn't it? Yet no one had ever told me my cousin Eddy was an author.

My mother wrote too. Not poems or tales, but a particular kind of letter addressed to family, friends, and acquaintances. Our precarious financial circumstances gave her so much practice she'd become quite skilled at this homely art.

A week after receiving Eddy's wonderful gift, I came across a letter Muddy was still working on, a scribbled foolscap left out on the dining table while she went to see to Granny's chamber pot. Of course I'd been raised well, for good manners cost nothing, and I didn't make a habit of reading other people's correspondence. However, I couldn't help but notice that this note was addressed to a prominent local judge.

I sucked in a worried breath. Were we in some trouble? With surprise and dread, I leaned closer.

> I am not myself personally known to you, but you were well acquainted with my late husband, Mr. Wm. Clemm, and I also believe with many of my connexions. For a while now my mothers very ill health has kept me from providing for my family, and we shall soon be enduring every privation you might imagine.

I stared at the thin black loops and whorls of the laboriously penned words, feeling mortified. Of course we were poor. But this was out-and-out begging from strangers. Akin to standing in the street with bowl in grubby hand thrust out at anyone hurrying by. Were our circumstances truly so dire? I read on.

> *... I do not ask for any material assistance from you, sir, but only the merest trifle to relieve our most immediate distress ...*

Muddy's step sounded on the stairs. I snatched up the letter, then flung it down and rushed into the kitchen, breathing like a hard-run horse. If we were so impoverished, poorer even than I'd imagined, how could we keep and feed all the people we had now living under our roof? For all I knew, this had always been the way my mother got the money for our food and rent. But what of Granny Poe's widow's pension? I was wringing my hands thinking of it, of all my mother must have dealt with yet kept secret.

We had well-off relations, both Clemms and Poes. But most had opposed her marriage, and time had not softened their stony hearts. When I was younger, we'd had an elderly servant named Edwin— the last visible remnant of my grandfather's lost prosperity. Muddy had sold the poor man for forty dollars. How desperate she must've been! I only knew of it because Granny Poe still complained from time to time of how Muddy had been swindled. Granny somehow blamed Eddy for this failure as well; perhaps he'd helped my mother complete that sad transaction. Those desperate requests and rejections had all been in the family though. While *this*—

I went outside and sat on the back steps, weeping, muffling the choked cries that burst from me from time to time in my bunched skirt, so my mother wouldn't know what a sneaking little spy I was. Or that I'd shamefully read her shameful letter.

That was where Eddy found me—on his way, I suppose, to the privy. By then I'd managed to stop my tears, but still huddled, swollen-eyed and snuffling, ashamed to go inside.

He paused, then sank onto the step below mine. "Has someone hurt your feelings, Sissy?" He twirled a lock of my hair around one finger, his tone light and teasing. As if I were still the grubby seven-year-old he'd met years ago, with no concerns in my head but what game to play next, what silly rhyme to sing—when in fact I was nearly thirteen.

I pulled away. "Oh, Muddy is out of pocket and we have no money. I'm frightened. What will happen to us—to all of us?"

He lifted my chin again, as gently as he had the first time we'd met. "Well, I have great plans," he murmured in that woman-soft tone, looking right into my eyes. "It's in the works still, but soon I'll be the editor of a magazine in Richmond. I'll make a fine salary. I would never let this little family lack for a home, Sissy. I know what it is to be poor and ask for help, yet have none come."

I raised my head and saw with surprise he had tears in his eyes too.

"Do you believe in me?" he said.

I gulped and nodded, then lunged at him, sobbing, smearing his clean white shirt with tears and worse.

Eddy always preferred perfection: in people, in literature, in dress. No matter how worn, his suits were always immaculate: pressed and brushed, not a button missing or undone, his single collar impeccably starched, his black cravat never looped crookedly. So I understood it as a measure of his sincerity, and a firm promise, when he did not flinch or pull away as I wept and crumpled his clean dry shirtfront into a sodden, starchy mess.

A few days later Eddy came up while I was dusting the parlor. "Would you deliver something for me, Sissy dear?"

I nodded. I would've agreed to deliver a block of ice to the devil for him by then. He handed over a note and gave me an address on Essex Street. I glanced at the folded paper and frowned. It bore no name. "But—who is it for?"

He blinked. "A certain young lady. I beg you, don't give it to her mother, whatever you do. The woman detests me."

"Well, all right," I said slowly, as I understood him. Wishing now I hadn't been so quick to agree. A hard metallic taste, which seemed to seep upward from my heart, was actually puckering my mouth: the mingled flavor of fireplace ashes and iron.

I dragged my boots out into the street and scuffed along. Successful delivery of this thin, folded wafer might mean ruin for me, my brother, Muddy, even Granny Poe. For if Eddy liked this young lady, then—

I halted on the street. How wicked I was, to have such faithless thoughts! This note might be a response to a request to read some of Eddy's poems. Or a polite declining of an invitation to a party. I started walking again. Yes, surely that was all.

I turned up Essex Street, only to stop again on the next corner. What if it wasn't any of those, though, but something else? Such as a love letter. Then . . . then Eddy would court this new Elmira. Get engaged, marry her, and forget about Muddy's troubles. And about me. But that was impossible, wasn't it? We were fated to be wed. Eddy was the man of *my* dreams; the kind, adoring husband of my childhood tea parties. The mystery man whose identity I myself had solved. Could it be possible he did not yet know this?

My heart tripped like a tinsmith's hammer, my breath came in shallow gasps. I was swimming in air too thick to breathe, and might soon faint, though I'd never done so before in my life.

Then, as if they had a secret will of their own, my hands began unfolding the note. And as they worked, all the while I looked away, as if those plump, slightly grimy fingers pinching apart the red wax seal and uncreasing the folds in the paper had nothing to do with me.

I stared down at the neat writing in Eddy's familiar, elegant hand. It hit me like a blow to the chest.

Mary whose fair and lovely visage appeals so to me
Shall I wait for a proper invitation to me, poor beggar
One I fear shall not soon come from your house, to tea . . .

"Damn it to hell," I whispered, not caring that the curse was vulgar and worth not just a hard rebuke but a slap; the language of the fishwives at Lexington Market. I held a poem, and even I could tell it was a bad one. As if the mere thought of this young woman had disordered my cousin's brain. Oh dear, yes—a very bad, lovesick verse, addressed to a Miss Mary Starr. A bold, tavern-girl name. I read the rest, hands shaking so the words blurred, feeling more and more ill.

Her blonde hair . . . her blue eyes . . .

I frowned at the last line. *Her Naiad airs . . .* what in the world were those? I could only imagine, and the ethereal, graceful images the words conjured didn't bode well for a short, plump girl not yet thirteen, with a spotted complexion.

I felt glued fast to the cobblestones, yet even as I failed to force my knees to bend, my feet to move along, those devious fingers went to work again. They slowly tore the infernal note from one side to the other. Then again and again, as I watched in fascination and, I admit, some glee. Soon it was nothing but a handful of white flakes with here and there a dash of India black. The guilty particles trickled from my palm to mound at the curb like an out-of-season snow. A reminder of the ice-crusty drifts, sullied with coal dust, that collected there each winter.

No one—certainly no one named Mary Starr—would purloin my handsome, intelligent, gentle cousin. He loved me, and I loved him deeply in return. No silly fool who inspired terrible doggerel would steal my future away.

I kicked the fragments into a blizzard of white and black confetti.

When I returned home out of breath, Eddy was seated at Muddy's little hutch desk in the front parlor, writing. Oh Lord, not more poems! When I hung my bonnet on a hook he looked over his shoulder with a hopeful smile. "Secret mission complete?"

I nodded, returning the smile as best I could, but my lips jerked and twitched.

"You look unwell, cousin," he said, laying the quill aside.

"I'm only . . . I ran most of the way . . . is all," I gasped, breathless, though for different reasons than he must think.

"Oh dear. Did someone accost you? Forgive me for sending you out. I should've taken it myself. Next time—"

Next time. Dear little Lord Jesus, no.

"*No*," I cut in firmly. "I'm well. Just walked a bit fast. The cold got in my lungs." I hacked out a harsh, pretend cough. "I think I should deliver all your messages, Eddy."

He smiled, then bit his lip. "But there was no reply?"

I looked away. "Well, no . . . none. I didn't really, that is, the note is taken care of, but—there was no answer. As yet."

"Ah." He lowered himself back into the chair. "I see." He turned back to the papers on the desk, but did not dip the pen again.

I felt terrible to see him so downcast. Well, too bad. I must harden my heart, and—a line occurred to me from the play Eddy had made us read after dinner the night before—screw my courage to the sticking place. Wherever that was.

I lifted my chin and tried to look older. "Yes, what a shame you must wait. But she said, um, nothing to me. I only took care of that note, and that's all I have to report, Eddy."

He nodded. As I was about to turn away, he sighed and shoved back from the desk. "I shall simply call on her myself, then." He straightened his cravat and grabbed up his coat from where he'd laid it across the settee. He jammed his arms so savagely into the sleeves I heard a seam rip. I stared, openmouthed, unable to think of a way to stop him without confessing my betrayal.

At the front door he halted. "But of course her *mother* will not let me in. Or will have me tossed out." His tone turned bitter. "I am not of sufficient *means*, you see." Still, he squared his shoulders and reached for the doorknob.

"Then I shall go with you!" I cried.

His turn to look astonished, blinking over his shoulder at me. "What?"

"Because," I said, stalling for time. "Because a *lady* would never be rude to you, or . . . or make a scene. Especially not in front of a . . . a *child*." It galled me to say this, but it was all I could manage on short notice.

He tilted his head. "But would it be proper to take along my little cousin?"

Little. That stung, but I tried to keep my expression bland. "Oh, better than proper. It would be above reproach. A social call."

He looked at me as if at a tabby cat who'd suddenly risen from a patch of sun to recite a long, difficult piece of prose. "Yes . . . yes, I believe you're right. That's . . . genius, Sissy."

I had no time to bask or beam, for he grabbed my arm and

dragged me down the steps. The door slammed behind us as I ran to keep up with his long, eager strides.

The Starr house was no gin crib, nor was it a celestial mansion—simply a middling respectable three-story brick foursquare with white trim. We climbed the six steps up and Eddy rapped with the heavy bronze knocker. A female Negro servant opened the door, while a young lady in a pink silk day gown hovered behind, peering around at us. Her pale blue eyes seemed lashless, though they were large—too large, I decided. The goggling gaze of a blond-wigged frog.

"I'll show them in, Melva," she told the servant. Then she clasped her hands before her and beamed. "My dear Mr. Poe! I certainly wasn't expecting *you*."

He bowed. "I'm sorry to intrude. But at the library you expressed an interest in talking further about literature . . . at your home."

She giggled and pursed her lips, then fluffed and fiddled with her curled hair in a way that made me despise her. "Well, yes," she drawled. "I suppose I *did*."

Oh Moses. How would I explain if the subject of the note came up?

Eddy said, "If this is a good time, then—shall we?"

A frown marred her smooth but rather low forehead, which she'd attempted to disguise with carefully placed blond curls. She hesitated, as if this question were on a level with some complicated mathematical formula.

Eddy was still holding his hat, since she hadn't offered to take it. The brim trembled as he said, in a lower voice, "I suggested such a discussion in my note."

Her arched brows rose. "Your note?"

"Yes. The one Virginia delivered earlier."

"I really don't know what to say, Mr. Poe." She turned her palms up in a graceful little gesture of confusion. And I saw with despair she not only had that pale, curled hair and those bright blue eyes, but a dimple in one cheek, as well. On the outside, at least, as perfect as any man might wish. "I have no recollection of receiving such a note." She pursed her rosy lips into a pout.

Just then a stout older woman stomped into the foyer. "Mary Helena Starr! Come away from that door at *once*."

Eddy bowed quickly again at the appearance of this stocky harridan. "Oh, Mrs. Starr. Good afternoon. May I—"

"My daughter's uncle shall cowhide you, *sir*, if you appear on our doorstep again." The woman was red in the face, panting as if she'd run miles. "We do not allow gamblers, drunkards, or poets in this house!"

Eddy's cheeks flared. "Mrs. Starr, I have honorable intentions. I sent a note to your daughter only to request a social—"

"Don't you dare speak of her. We'll have no correspondence or any other dealings with you, Mr. Poe. Mary is engaged to be married to Mr. Nelson, a banker from a *good* family."

Eddy drew himself up. "Are you implying my family is not of good character, Mrs. Starr?"

She sniffed. "Oh, I'm implying nothing. I know all about the Poes. I won't have my only daughter led astray, *sir*. Though that is hardly the proper term of address for a verse-spouting, drink-swilling . . . *artist* who, who"—her squinted, piggy eyes fell on me for the first time and narrowed even more—"who travels in the company of a little girl. I bid you farewell."

She gripped the edge of the door with both hands and began to close it ostentatiously and ponderously, as if it were the gate to a moated castle.

Eddy's mouth tightened. "I will not trouble you again, then."

We descended the steps slowly, our marching music the slamming of the heavy door, the muffled shouting and wails that began behind those pink brick walls.

"Eddy?"

He turned toward me, cheeks drawn, gaze as distant as if he'd been transported to some other place, some other time. I opened my mouth, meaning to say I was sorry. Instead, I gritted between clenched teeth, "That foolish ninny! She's a simpering idiot without a brain in her sausage-curled head."

He took a deep breath, then sighed. "Perhaps you're right. But she approached and spoke to me at the library. Mentioned she'd read my poem 'Israfel,' and I—well, it was flattering. Yet now it seems she's engaged! I wish I'd never written that note. I feel like a fool."

I slid my arm though his, and he patted my hand. Now was probably a good time to tell him about ripping up the cursed note. Perhaps I could phrase it so he'd see I'd done so in his best interests; that he need not feel embarrassed about that part, at least. But what if he didn't see, and was angry? Or thought me a child or a fool too? He might look at me as he did Rosalie.

"Don't worry about that little piece of paper," I said. "I bet Mrs. Starr took it and ripped it into a million pieces, and—and put it in a stew and fed it to the uncle with the cowhide."

Eddy's lips twitched into a smile. "Let's hope he enjoyed every artistic bite."

I nodded eagerly. He'd always liked puns and funny names, so I made one up on the spot, and deepened my voice in imitation of old Mrs. Starr. "Uncle Moo-Cow Starr will love this fine chewy dish indeed."

His low chuckle was so welcome I squeezed his arm and said

fiercely, "Those people don't deserve to have you set foot in their parlor, Eddy. They're vulgar dollar-chasers."

He pulled my arm more securely into the crook of his. "Ah, Virginia. You are my sweet guardian angel."

I smiled up at him and tried not to think of the scraps of his poem, which must even at that moment be blowing about, trampled by boots and hooves and carriage wheels. And then we walked on home together.

After that incident, he received a note, this one sent from Richmond by a man named White. Eddy said he was to help with a magazine called the *Southern Literary Messenger*. He asked what I thought of the name.

"It sounds impressive, and—well . . . maybe a bit long?"

"Just think of it as the *Messenger*, then." He pulled his coat on. "It shall be just that, I think, to the literary world."

He left for Richmond and his new position, while I went on with my music lessons. But I missed him terribly. He became an ache in my breast that hindered my breathing as I sang. I found it harder to concentrate while Madame Frieda thumped her stick in time to my playing.

When he returned a few weeks later, Eddy treated me as an equal, or a friend, and less as an adorable little cousin. Now he didn't just read his new work aloud while I listened in silence; he asked for my opinion. After he pulled out Muddy's chair at the dinner table, he pulled mine out as well, then winked and deftly flicked my napkin across my lap.

One evening after dinner he decided to teach me how to dance. "A young lady must be able to follow in step, in order not to break her partner's toes." He'd had to learn to lead a lady around a ballroom while growing up in the Allan household in Richmond. No doubt there had been many parties and balls there. But he seldom spoke of John Allan, and then only with great bitterness.

"What a good idea, Eddy," my mother said. She agreed to clap to keep time, as we had no harp or piano, or even a fiddle.

"We'll have to pretend there are others dancing with us, for the quadrille," he said, standing me in the middle of the room, clasping my right hand. The fingertips of his left lightly rested on my waist. He showed me the quadrille first, then swung us into something called a contra dance, and finally, the fashionable German.

Eddy might look like a pale scholar, but he'd been involved in athletic pursuits at the University in Charlottesville, and in the army, and at West Point. He'd even set some sort of record while swimming a long distance in the James River. I was no athlete though, and soon grew short of breath.

"Let's stop a bit," I finally gasped, embarrassed that my hand in his was so damp, fearing the slithery trickle of sweat making its way down my sides might soon be noticeable even through layers of chemise and slip and cotton day gown.

Muddy went to prepare a cooling pitcher of lemonade. We stopped spinning and dipping around the room, and I stumbled to a chair. My hair was coming out of its ribbons, straggling down over my right shoulder. I was hopeless at tying bows, especially without the aid of a mirror.

"Drat," I said at last, the ribbon tangled in my fingers, knotted and snarled on one end. "Eddy, could you? You tie such a nice bow." It was true, his black cravat always looked perfect against the white breast of his linen shirt.

He smiled and came over, and I stood again so he could do it without stooping. But I was so short, and he was tall. Finally we had to sit again, he beside me, squeezed into the one seat, so he could reach and unknot the tangles.

At last he laughed and gave up. "Why not let it all down so you match, at least," he suggested, his warm breath stirring the fine hairs at my temple. "Let me undo the other side. I think I can manage that much."

Deftly he untied the blue ribbon that still held up my long dark hair on the left. It fell heavily down my back. He smoothed the curls, arranging them over my shoulders. "It is very like my mother's hair," he said, looking wistful. "Or rather, as I imagine it must've looked and—and felt."

"Do you miss her very much still?" I couldn't imagine being without my own mother, much less to have her die before my eyes. The week before, he'd shown me an oval miniature done in oils, during Eliza Poe's days on the stage. She looked dainty and girlish, lively and mischievous. Her hair was dark and curled like mine, her nose similar too. But in the portrait her eyes had been painted unnaturally large, like a china doll's. All in all, she was much prettier.

"Yes, of course I do." He sighed. "I shall never get over losing her." Then he glanced at me. "When we first met, you reminded me of her. Remember, I told you how much I liked black hair? But you set me straight on the whole mistaken idea of black eyes, or dancing ones."

Oh, I remembered it very well.

"You've set me straight on many things," he murmured, as if talking to himself. "And at such a young age."

I did not know what to reply to that, so we sat silently for a few moments, side by side, not moving. His left hand still rested on my shoulder, though we were not dancing. He was breathing slowly, deeply, though he hadn't seemed winded from the dance.

"We are much alike," he said, so suddenly and unexpectedly I had to suppress a flinch.

"Do you really think so?" That wasn't how I had seen it. I'd meant to be the sunlight to his moonless night. To light his dark path, so that—

"When I am away from here, and from you, I am altogether a different person."

What did he mean by that? I was just turning my head, wondering what expression might be on his face, when he gripped my hand and said, "Sissy. I wish we were closer in age."

I squeezed his hand in return, trying to encourage him to—to do what? Some momentous change seemed imminent, but I was unsure of its nature. "Well, I'm thirteen now. I'll be fourteen in a year."

His shoulders moved as if he were laughing, but soundlessly. "Yes, and then I'll be twenty-six. Suddenly ancient." He sighed. "But if we were to be something else, something different to each other . . . someday . . . would you like that?"

I turned to look him full in the face. "I'd like it now," I said, perhaps too boldly, for he looked surprised, even a little shocked. Women were supposed to let men take the lead, always. I must not forget that. "But . . . perhaps if you could tell me what it is you are thinking of?"

He slid from the settee to the floor, onto his knees. I almost laughed. Was he joking? Was it a game? But his serious expression stopped me from giggling. Then the pose he took, one I'd only heard described in books, made me think, *Dear Lord, is he going to propose?* It seemed impossible, but even more impossible that, once down there on his knees on the warped old floorboards, he would not.

He cradled both my hands between his. His grip tightened as if to stop me from fleeing. It was the last thing on my mind.

"I have good prospects in Richmond," he said quickly, as if fearing his time to speak would be cut short. "Mr. White will make me editor of the *Messenger* soon, I'm sure. And why not? I'm already that in all but name." He frowned as if distracted from his original intentions by this perceived injustice, then shook his head. "Yes, that's true. So . . . so could you have faith I will make a success of myself? Then, when all is arranged, I would send for you."

I stared. So it *was* a proposal. But on the back steps, he had dried my tears and promised to make a home for all of us.

"For me," I said. "To come to Richmond—alone?" My brother had recently apprenticed himself to a Baltimore stonecutter, so I supposed he would not want to leave. But what of Muddy and Granny Poe?

"Well, yes." He ran a hand through his hair, looking thoughtful. "That is, you, yes, and—and Aunt Maria. And . . . and Granny. Yes, of course. All of you."

I smiled then, and nodded. "All of us with you, and in a nice home. As you promised once."

His grip tightened. "So I did. And I will. Your welfare, the comfort of all of you, is always uppermost in my mind." He was biting his lip, but smiling still, gaze distant, as if writing one of his stories in his head. "You all make up my little family. And so, when my position is secure, perhaps you'd even become my dear little wife someday, and they too shall—"

Muddy bustled in carrying a bamboo tray with the old cut-glass pitcher full of lemonade. Eddy released me and sprang up. "Here, let me take that, Aunt Maria."

I felt too breathless and stunned to rise. I'd just received a proposal, a promise of marriage. Me! From the man of my dreams. The fate I had expected, had been living for. Somehow I'd assumed it was still far away, that it would come later in my life. And yet, how many Mary Starrs must there be out there, biding their time, with dreams and plans of their own? No—life was uncertain. This could not, would not wait.

Muddy surrendered the tray willingly, and dropped into the chair by the rickety little desk. I wondered how the scene had looked to her—me there on the settee, Eddy on his knees before me. I could not read anything different in her gaze. I wondered how she'd take the news, if she would be happy or upset. Well, it would have to be Eddy who actually told her, of course. I was old enough to understand that much. The words and wishes of one still deemed a child never hold any weight in the world, unless someone older stands behind them.

A few days later, Eddy did get the chance to speak with her. I was in the parlor bent over an old skirt, mending a tear in the hem, when I heard the murmur of their voices in the kitchen. I was supposed to be there beside him but at the last minute my nerve had failed. If Muddy opposed us, I was afraid I'd hate her as much as I had Granny Poe, for the times she'd been unkind to Eddy. Still, I could not stand to be so near, yet not know how this petition for our future was faring.

I laid the skirt aside and tiptoed across to the connecting doorway, where I hung back, out of sight, and listened.

". . . but she is young, as yet, to consider marriage, Eddy," my mother was saying.

Eddy cleared his throat. Though I could not see it, I could envision him drawing himself up, turning the full force of his dark, serious gaze on my mother. "Yes, indeed, she is young, Aunt Maria," he said—rather too meekly, I feared. "And yet have you never noticed how wise she often seems, beyond the years she's spent on this earth?"

A pause, during which I could almost see my mother gape at that. Then she asked, "What do you mean?"

"Simply this," said Eddy. "That when the subject of a union came up, her first concern was not for a fine ceremony or any of the frippery that might accompany it—as one might well expect in a girl of so few years. Instead, she worried over the fate of her *family*. And extracted a solemn vow that our home would ever be your home too—and Henry's and Granny Poe's as well."

"She did?" My mother sounded a good deal more astonished than I thought complimentary. "Well. Well, then, I suppose . . ."

"Just say yes, Aunt Maria," Eddy urged. "You four are all the family I have left. Save Rose," he added hastily. "Do not deprive me of your company, or the joy of seeing to your comforts in life, please."

"I suppose I would not object to a marriage—in a few years, that is. When Sissy is of an age—"

I think I must've gasped out loud, for a sudden, suspicious hush fell in the kitchen. But it was so unexpected to have my mother bend for once to *my* will, I could not suppress it. I rushed back to my seat, and was calmly sitting and sewing again when they came out. I believe I even looked serene. Even though I had, like the fairy-tale princess in the tower, just clumsily pricked my thumb. I waited, concealing the bleeding digit in my skirts, but neither one said a word to me of what had just transpired. Gradually I grew furious at this oversight, and left the room. Perhaps proving I was still a child after all.

Eddy found me a few minutes later on the back steps, feeding our two remaining chickens. When the door creaked open behind me I rose and turned to look at him.

He sat on the top step and pulled me down beside him. "Aunt Maria thinks you are a bit young as yet to consider marriage," he said in a low voice. "But I believe I've convinced her our intentions are serious. And of course I assured her that she and Granny would always have a place in my—in our home. Is that what you wanted me to say, my dear?"

My dear. I laughed and then, my fit of pique forgotten, threw myself at him and hugged his neck—before remembering that young, betrothed women do not behave in such a fashion, out in public in Baltimore. So I took his arm and drew him back inside, where it would be more proper for him to embrace me as well.

· 5 ·

Eddy left for Richmond again soon after that, pursuing his editorial work. Two months after he departed, as I was just rousing myself on a hot July morning, pulling my damp, sticky nightgown over my head, I heard muffled shrieks and weeping. I jerked my gown back on and rushed to look down the stairwell. My brother Henry, looking groggy in a rumpled nightshirt, came stumbling down the attic steps to do the same.

Muddy was huddled at the foot of the staircase, wringing her hands. "Oh Lord, oh Lord. Oh, now what will we do," she moaned.

I rushed down barefoot and knelt beside her. "Muddy, what's wrong—are you ill?"

Henry came down behind me, with trousers on now, his thick hair standing on end. "What's happened?" he mumbled, rubbing one eye.

Muddy's tear-streaked face, her low groaning frightened me. I flung my arms around her. "Please! Tell us what's wrong."

"Children," she said at last, freeing herself from my embrace, pushing tears out of her eyes with both palms. "Your dear Granny Poe has passed. She's left us alone. And now—"

But she didn't need to finish that sentence. We all rushed to the little room off the parlor where Granny had been sleeping since she could no longer climb the stairs.

My grandmother had been bed-bound for months, paralyzed, but I'd never imagined her sick enough to die. Her care had been a great burden, but Muddy took it up with good spirits. She'd dearly loved her mother, who now lay as she always had in life, hands neatly folded at her waist as if she might soon lift them and say a prayer, or admonish our shocking manners in staring this way. But her stern face had that blue-gray hue of creeping death. I'd seen it before, on my father. Though I was very young then, I'd never forgotten that cold color, so unlike living skin, that had crept slowly from his ankles up, until it tinted the slack, blue, lifeless mouth.

Muddy burst into tears again, sobbing into her apron like a child. I suppose neighbors and even relatives must've always assumed, to look at my mother—who was as large as a man, blocky and square, lacking in fancies or graces—that she was dull as a workhorse and not at all sensitive. Perhaps they even saw her as a grasping sort, with her frequent pleas for help. If so, they did not know how loyal and tenderhearted she really was.

We quickly sent a telegram to Richmond, and Eddy took a train back that evening. She was his grandmother as much as mine and Henry's. He naturally would attend her funeral.

He arrived looking desperately unhappy. At first I took his distraction for grief, though Granny had given him an earful more than once for his choices in life. She'd rarely lost a chance to remark on it whenever he'd failed or disappointed her. Which had been often.

"I'm sorry you're so grieved, cousin," I said. "It's too bad you couldn't see her one last time, before she passed on."

He sighed and took my hand, and turned it over to stare bleakly at my palm. "Oh well. It's not just that. Without my dear, kind-hearted women about me, I feel so lost now," he murmured. "Quite at sea, all on my own."

I caught a faint whiff of brandy, though he appeared quite sober.

At nine o'clock the next morning we followed Granny's coffin from the house at Amity Street to the Westminster Bury-ing Ground. My brother Henry wore a cut-down, rusty black suit that had once been our father's. Accompanied by a few friends and neighbors, we trudged along silently, the family in various hues of black: some dark and crisp, some greenish and faded.

I should've had my mind firmly on my poor dead grandmother, on her recently-released soul and its heavenward ascent. Instead, I could not stop wondering about our own earthly fates. About Eddy. Whether he was not only grieved, but also as worried as Muddy and I about the most crass and shameful and yet important thing, which was money. Our grandmother's pension from General Da-vid Poe's military service—the twenty dollars per month which had been our main household income—had died with her. How would we live now?

Finally we turned into the graveyard at Greene and West Fay-ette. The heavy, ornately-carved stone tablets laid out there made me shudder. For I knew they'd really been set down to keep the dead in place.

Once, many years ago, after a heavy rain, Muddy and I had walked past this same graveyard. As we'd neared the gates, I saw a young man in the outmoded uniform of a Continental soldier come lurching out. At first I'd thought he must've stolen the out-fit for a prank, or borrowed it from an old soldier—his grand-father, say—for he was too young to have fought against the British. But then I saw the coat was muddy and torn, and his bare, abraded skin shone through ripped breeches. And that he had a great horrible gash in one thigh. Though bloodless, it was deep, exposing white bone.

I tugged on my mother's hand. "Muddy, shall we help him?"

The poor man dragged a hand down his face, looking around as if confused. Then his gaze fell on me. He seemed first puzzled, then alarmed, and turned to limp quickly out of view behind one of the great, wide water oaks. I continued to watch, but he did not reemerge on the other side of the tree.

"Help who, Sissy?" Muddy had asked, giving my arm a shake. But I was silent, staring at where the soldier should've been, but was not. And then we were at the gates of the old cemetery. Muddy dropped my arm and exclaimed, "Lord God, the poor souls!"

The underground stream that ran beneath the graveyard had risen. So had a dozen bodies. Men were hurrying to rebury them, digging rapidly through the heavy wet clay with mattocks and shovels. But it was slow going, and the sodden earth kept caving in again. The pale withered limbs and yellowed bones still clad in shreds of leathery flesh and dark, clinging rags made me feel faint and sick. Muddy covered my eyes with one hand and hurried us on.

Sometimes I still dreamed of that scene. And of how, once the closed door of his grave was wrenched aside, the soldier's spirit had been roused to wander out of its proper time and place. The thick stone slabs on the plots were of course laid there to discourage grave robbers. But forever after in my mind, their main duty would be to keep the dead where they belonged.

I also understood this: I was one of those to whom spirits might from time to time make their presence known. I'd heard a few tales from Granny Poe of ancestors in the Auld Country who'd been similarly sensitive—or afflicted, I suppose, depending on your point of view. Muddy had always tut-tutted these reminiscences, and resorted to cajoling different stories out of her, since merely trying to hush Granny was rarely effective. I had looked up at my mother back then, as we hurried along hand in hand, to see if her demeanor suggested she might've noticed anything more strange than damaged graves. But her determined, forward gaze plainly announced that, even if she had, she would never discuss it nor welcome any questions from me. And so we did not speak of it, then or later. But of course I still *knew*.

Now, following my grandmother's cheap coffin, I clasped my mother's hand every bit as tightly as I had that day, and she pressed mine, as well. I felt, through the thin cloth of my glove, small ridges on hers: the worn spots and holes she'd tucked, turned, and mended, as she was forced to do to things every day, in every aspect of our lives.

Then suddenly we were at the tall wrought-iron fence and the Poe family plot. A tall narrow stone marked my grandfather's final resting place. A grave marker for him stood there. There should have been another next to it, carved with these words:

Elizabeth Cairnes Poe,
Beloved Wife of Gen. David Poe
Born 1756 Lancaster County, Penn
Died July 7 1835 Baltimore

But we had no money to buy a new slab. So Granny Poe was laid to rest beside her husband, and had to share his. She was in her coffin, soon to be pressed down under this sodden ground. Never and never again to come out.

I began to gnaw at my knuckles, an old vice.

As the minister read out the service, a low sob escaped Muddy. I could think of nothing comforting to say, so I squeezed her hand and leaned my head against her arm. Granny had been short with us and often intolerant, but Muddy had loved her dearly. We all knew that.

As I stood at my grandparents' grave other things slowly occurred to me: that my mother was a good woman who never lost her temper. That she'd cared for many years for her own mother because she wanted to. Not for the pension, for she'd never complained or shown the slightest reluctance to answer one of her mother's frequent bell-ringing summonses. Her requests for a glass of water, for another candle, for a fresh-baked biscuit even though it was midday, were always granted.

Then it occurred to me that there was something I could do for both my grandmother and my mother. As the minister finished his committal, and the mourners stepped forward to throw a handful of earth, I hung back and stood alone to sing an a capella hymn.

> . . . May a choir of angels receive you
> And with Lazarus, who once
> Was poor, may you have eternal rest.

Eddy had to return to Richmond immediately because he and Mr. White were in the midst of putting out a new issue. Before he left, he pressed a few crumpled notes into Muddy's hand. I turned away, pretending not to have noticed.

Over the next few weeks, the dire nature of our situation became clearer. I'd disliked my grandmother as much as I had loved her, because of her rebukes and reproaches. But now I understood her better: Granny Poe was not really mean, spiteful, and demanding, but a practical, respectable woman who'd worried about and wanted the best for us, and had set the standards we lived by. She'd been the glue that held our shrinking family together—not just with her income, but her insistence on decorum and responsibility.

Eddy wrote us daily, and sent all he could spare. Which was not much, to be honest, and I began to worry that, despite his enthusiasm for the work, magazine editors might not make a living wage. Other relatives wrote to express sympathy for our bereavement. Muddy wrote back asking for assistance until we could set ourselves up in an endeavor both suitable for respectable women to engage in, and adequate for our keep.

In one day she received three replies, all polite but negative. "Since they opposed my marriage to your poor father," she said to me, folding the most recent note into a neat rectangle, "they still believe that absolves them of any responsibility to me and my children." She tied a string around the small, mean stack of condolences and put them away with all the other rejections and refusals in the desk. It was the closest I'd ever heard her come to sounding bitter.

In August another letter arrived. From Neilson Poe, Eddy's uncle and my second cousin, who lived in Frederick. He'd always been distantly kind to us. We didn't see him often, but he wrote several times a year. Neilson was both a lawyer and newspaper editor—a prosperous Poe, if there could still be such a thing.

Muddy came to me clutching his missive in trembling fingers. "Look at this! Cousin Neilson says he would like to take you in, Sissy, to educate you. To see to your upbringing until such time as you are ready to properly marry."

I looked at her, puzzled. At first the meaning of that offer did not sink in. "Well, but I'm to marry Eddy, Muddy. You know that."

She went on as if I hadn't spoken. "Cousin Neilson feels you should take this time in your young life to acquire some social accomplishments. And of course to further train your lovely singing

voice . . . to learn to play a harpsichord. Oh, and—" She looked up
with ecstasy shining in her eyes. "Oh, my dear '. . . and to enter
into society!'"

I'd been setting dishes to dry on a clean old cloth. Her words
made sense, and yet also did not. I was not accustomed to fine
things and for the most part did not miss them. Was a cotillion,
or finer manners, or a nice carriage a substitute for the person I'd
come to love and planned to spend my life with? Was my mother
so very grasping now that she would trade me away for material
goods? I felt a sense of rage so profound it shocked me, even as it
demanded some violent action in order to be dispelled.

I slammed the last cup down and rounded on her. "Enter into
society—what does that *mean*? I don't want to attend stiff soirees
in Frederick. I want to marry Eddy and have a nice little cottage.
A place where you can live too."

She folded the letter and glanced away. When she faced me
again I saw a new look in her eyes, harder and cooler than her cus-
tomary expression. Very much like the one I'd seen in them before
she sat down to compose begging letters.

"Virginia," she said in a steely voice, and I tensed, for it sounded
as if my mother had been suddenly possessed by the angry ghost of
Granny Poe. "I know very well how you feel about your cousin Edgar. And how he feels about you. He's been as good to us as his lim-
ited means allow. But when will he have the money to buy this sweet
little cottage he's been promising? When will he be possessed of the
funds to take us from Baltimore to Richmond and settle us there?"

I wanted to clap my hands over my ears and sing loudly to drown
her out, but that would only have confirmed my lack of maturity.
Or did she guess I'd had these same disloyal, unfaithful thoughts
once or twice myself? "If Eddy has promised," I muttered, "he's
good as his word."

She took my hand and drew me to her. "We can't eat his word, my dear, or take shelter under it, no matter how fine his prose and promises."

I held myself stiffly and did not unbend, even when she smoothed my hair and kissed my cheek. "I told Eddy I would marry him one day, and I will." I had to have him, and only him. I had known this from the first time I set eyes on him as a child—though I could not have put it into those words, back then. "I love him! He loves me. We are . . . sympathetic. We are *suited* to one another. Surely that's important?"

"I insisted on marrying your father too. Have I ever told you that on my wedding day a hundred carrion crows lit in a tree outside our door?" She smiled, as if seeing this weird vision all over again, a grim upturning of the lips. "My mother warned me, but I wouldn't listen. Their black shadows hung over us all our married lives." She paused for a breath after this astonishing speech, then said, "You don't understand what marriage means! Whatever you choose now—"

But crows? What did the shadows of those common birds have to do with me and Eddy? "I'm not a fool or a little child. I know what it means."

Actually, when we were still little my brother Henry had told me a disgusting story about what husbands and wives got up to in the dark, under the covers. A friend from the rougher end of Wilks Street had given him the shocking details. Henry had rushed home, sweating and pale, looking sick, and dragged me into the pantry. He'd held me still and hissed this information into my ear. Then he'd grown furious and twisted my arm when I giggled and told him I didn't believe a word of it.

However, whenever Eddy kissed my cheek, or even brushed my hand, I always felt a sharp and lingering tingle, an electric sort of jolt that was both startling and pleasurable. If he was in the room I longed to sit near him—to lean against his arm, or touch his hair, and he clearly felt the same. This, I believed, was the hallmark of true love. If my mother truly understood what it was to desire your chosen fate so deeply, as she claimed, why could she not see this at work too?

Eddy would someday be a great man; or rather, one day everyone would see and recognize his tremendous intellect and talent. That was clear to me already. But if he had never lifted a quill and set it to paper, I would still feel this *pull* toward him. Would still want him every bit as much. But what daughter can adequately explain such a feeling to her own mother? Nonetheless, it seemed I must try.

"I know what must happen when a man and a woman wed," I repeated. "It doesn't worry me. In fact, I am quite looking—"

Muddy stared at me as I spoke. Her sudden bark of laughter cut my momentous revelation short. "As if that's all there is to be frightened about!" She shook her head. "I can refuse to let you marry at all, of course. You're not nearly of age. We haven't spoken to the Reverend McAdams at church. No banns have been published."

I grabbed her arm. "Oh, Muddy, please!"

Her expression softened. "I won't though. I know good and well how it feels to want a thing everyone else says you shouldn't have."

I moved to hug her neck but she held out a hand to fend me off.

"So here's what I propose," she said as briskly as if we were settling accounts with the butcher. "I'll write to Eddy and see what he thinks of Neilson Poe's plan. If he loves you he'll want the best for you, won't he?"

"Well, yes. I suppose. But what if he *doesn't* believe—"

She frowned at my interruption. "And then if he agrees Neilson's plan is for the best—to wait and educate you, to delay until you are more mature and of age to marry—then will you go to Frederick and take advantage of this offer?"

I hesitated, feeling too pressured to make the right answer. "But what about you, Muddy? Is Neilson offering to take you and Henry in as well?"

She shook her head. "I'm sure he will be kind to us. In any case, I can get along, my dear. Your brother will be earning a bit of money soon." Henry was still apprenticed to the stonecutter, which would at least ensure he had some income in the future. "And Eddy will still send me a bit, perhaps," she went on. "Two can live more cheaply than three."

Oh Lord, how I hated our genteel poverty! To be merely poor was not even a definite hell, but a low-placed purgatory that offered few choices, all of them flawed. Now a different life was dangling before me—yet one not necessarily, God help me, with Edgar Poe.

Imagine *not* having to give up even small, ordinary things in order to simply survive. To live in a well-heated house with a few servants and hot meals three times a day. Meat and fish, maybe even cakes. A grand piano to play. To become an educated, accomplished young lady. How proud Eddy would be of me! And yet—yet it seemed I had to give him up in order to *become* that person.

Oh yes, Muddy had said, "until you're of age." But how many Mary Starrs also lurked in Richmond like hungry doorway spiders— how many not already engaged to bankers? Perfect young ladies with blond ringlets and cheek dimples. And shining dresses not stitched crookedly beneath the light of a single candle, by their tired, eye-sore mothers, out of the cheapest cotton remnants.

So there it was: the possibility I might be giving up everything else I desired, for a man who in the end might just as easily change *his* mind. Though I could not believe Eddy would do so. Yet perhaps about this much my mother was right: Why not wait just a bit, and then know?

"All right, Muddy," I said meekly, forcing down like a pressed flower my urge to shout it out, to demand we send for him at once, hoping she'd take my calm, reasonable tone as a sign of good sense and maturity. "Write to Eddy for me, and we'll see what he thinks."

His reply came swiftly. Muddy dropped the opened envelope on the table in front of me without comment and stalked off. I heard her banging pans in the kitchen, though suppertime was hours away. I closed my eyes but couldn't decide what I ought to pray for, much less formulate a coherent plea.

I smoothed the crumpled pages, then picked up the first page.

> *Aug: 29th*
> *My Dearest Aunty,*
> *I am blinded with tears while writing this letter—I have no wish to live another hour. My bitterest enemy would pity me could he now read my heart—My last my only hold on life is cruelly torn away—I have no desire to live and <u>will not</u>.*

Oh, Eddy, my dear! Why couldn't I close my eyes and transport myself to his side? I bit my lip and read on.

> *. . . All my thoughts are occupied with the supposition that both you & she will prefer to go with N. Poe; I do sincerely believe that your <u>comforts</u> will for the present be secured—I cannot speak as regards your peace—your happiness. You both have tender hearts—and you will always have the ref-*

*lection that my agony is more than I can bear—that you have
driven me to the grave—for love like mine can never be gotten
over.*

I was startled by my own sob. My cheeks were wet, and drops
were falling upon the letter, spotting the pale, cheap ink. I could
not keep reading.

I had to keep reading.

*It is useless to expect advice from me—what can I say? Can I,
in honour & in truth say—Virginia! Do not go!—do not go
where you can be comfortable & perhaps happy—and on the
other hand can I calmly resign my life—life itself.*

It was unbearable. But I had to bear it, and read on. This was
my life too. Muddy had warned that what I decided now would
set it forever in stone. I had already begun to picture a huge boulder hanging over my head, casting a dark shadow as I sat and talked
and ate.

Eddy went on to explain he'd found a perfectly sweet little cottage for us in Richmond. Even so, Mr. White had given the *real*
editor job to another. I bristled. How could that be? No one could
do a finer job of making a literary magazine than Edgar Poe!

However, White had at least raised his salary to sixty dollars a
month. I smiled through my tears then, for that was three times
more than we'd lived on with Granny's pension. So, surely—but
there was more.

*The tone of your letter wounds me to the soul—Oh Aunty,
Aunty you loved me once—how can you be so cruel now?*

You speak of Virginia acquiring accomplishments, and en-
tering into society—you speak in so <u>worldly</u> a tone ... do
you think anyone could love her more dearly than I?
*   ... Adieu my dear Aunty. <u>I cannot advise you.</u> Ask Vir-*
ginia. Leave it to her. Let me have under her own hand, a
letter, a letter bidding me <u>good-bye</u>—forever—and I may
die—my heart will break—but I will say no more.

Kiss her for me—a million times
E. A. P.

I lowered my head into my hands and groaned. *No.*

I could never write such a letter. And his tone frightened me. Not just the hints of suicide, but his feelings, which swept off the page like a black, howling cyclone. Words that hinted at something beyond what I had ever imagined Love to be. Something more binding, but also much darker. Yet how could I fear, at least for myself, when these words were penned by my dearest cousin, my husband-to-be, my very own Eddy?

There was more, including a note to the effect he had enclosed five dollars for Muddy, which she had apparently already removed. But what drew my eye again was his postscript.

For Virginia,
My love, my own sweetest Sissy, my darling little wifey, think
well before you break the heart of your cousin Eddy.

By then I could've more easily plunged a dull paring knife into my own bosom. So we would lack for money? Better to starve and live in the street, then.

No, I thought, rising and pushing away from the table to go and face my mother. I paused to smooth my disheveled hair, to blot wet, swollen eyes on one sleeve, for I had no handkerchief in my pocket. Actually, I owned no decent handkerchief at all. But I must look like a grown woman, appear self-possessed, when I finally went into the kitchen to make the most important choice of my life. At least no crows were darkening the tree outside our front window. Not even a red-winged blackbird.

In the opera, there was always only one great love for the characters. In Eddy's tales there was always only one love as well—yes, even after death. Everything I had read or sung or felt said this was always the case. If you ignored this great truth, if you gave up on it for being too hard to hold on to, or let it slip away to have mere *things,* no real meaning could be left in life. My one great love was surely Eddy, so how could I write such a cruel rejection to him?

I couldn't. Not even if the massed shadow of a thousand black birds even now waited to gather overhead, to jeer and dog me for all eternity. I could not do it for all the wealthy second cousins and grand pianos and silk dresses and society parties that had ever existed in this world.

No, not ever.

· 6 ·

My brother Henry disappeared the following month. He'd been complaining for weeks of the powdery dust at the stonecutter's, which drifted and billowed through the shop, got deep into his lungs and made him cough. It coated his hair and clothing so thickly that when he came home he looked like an exhausted ghost. His hands were curled into claws from gripping the chisel and hammer; I had to massage them back to life before we could sit down to eat dinner. Still, he had revived enough to go out in the evenings and come in late. He'd been spending more and more time away, though he'd never say where he went or who his friends were, growing surly if we asked.

"Well, the boy is near seventeen, a man almost," Muddy lamented as he slammed out the door yet again. "I can't tell him to stay in, or forbid whatever it is that he does away from here."

I frowned. She seemed to have no trouble telling *me* what to do. Henry was still childish, I would've said, had anyone asked my opinion. He and I argued now more than when we were little.

On a hot July morning I'd gone upstairs to rouse him for breakfast and found, instead of a snoring older brother, a large square note pinned to his pillow. It had been written on the back of a torn handbill advertising a tonic medicine to boost "male powers." Whatever those were.

> *Muddy and Sis—*
> *Im a man now and will make my own way. I have gon and signed on a steemer bound for Panama. When I return Deer Muddy Ill bring plenty of money for you and a pet monkey back for my Sissy.*
>
> *—Yr son, Henry*

I crumpled the note, thinking with a sick chill of poor Henry Poe, who'd gone to sea and seen exotic lands, but returned a broken, coughing, rum-tortured wreck. Our older cousin had found no happiness in foreign ports, as far as I could tell. Nor had he made plenty of money. He most certainly had not come back with a pet monkey, or even a talking parrot, a more fitting companion for a sailor. Henry Poe's only happy hours had seemed to be the times Eddy had returned to live with us. They'd talked and read and drank together, at least when Henry felt well enough. He'd liked his liquor to the last, when he could still get it, and had also urged the stuff on Eddy—who could not refuse his brother and always took the drink, then would be dreadfully sick next morning. It didn't seem to matter whether Eddy imbibed one glass or ten—the result was the same.

Then poor Henry had died in blood and pain and tangled sheets. I hoped Eddy would not be persuaded so easily by low companions in Richmond.

But how would my own brother fare at sea? Would we ever even hear from him? I carried the note slowly down to Muddy.

She read it through, then again, lips moving as she scanned each word. She set her mouth in a tight line, and turned silently away.

I hoped he would write us soon and tell us of his wanderings. But our Henry had never been one for reading or writing, or for lessons in general. As he got older, he'd kept more to himself, going out at night with those mysterious companions who never came in but waited for him down in the street. Perhaps long days with nothing but wild green sea and stormy sky to look at would make him miss us. Perhaps those far-off ports would hold not just exotic animals for sale, but a post office as well.

"We'll hear from him soon," Muddy said every morning. But we did not.

What she didn't know was that his leaving was really my fault. I'd spoken to him sharply when I'd come into the kitchen the day before he disappeared. He'd been sitting at the table eating bread— all that was left of the loaf I'd baked earlier in the week—and we were out of flour.

"I work too," he'd grumbled, scowling at me.

"I suppose you do," I snapped back. "But we so rarely see you. You're out at all hours with those ruffian friends of yours. Who can tell?"

He'd thrown the gnawed heel end at me and stalked out. And I'd wondered, as I stooped to salvage it from the floor, *Why did I just do that? It's only stale bread.* But later he'd glowered at me so fiercely at the dinner table, I hadn't been moved to apologize. I'd made him angry, ashamed, or both—his little sister rebuking him over such a petty thing. So he'd left us and gone away.

So our household gradually shrunk from five people to two women, yet there was still not enough left to feed and house even us. Muddy took in a bit of fine sewing. I tried to help, but was not nearly as agile with a needle. My fingers itched instead to press the keys of Madame Frieda's piano again; I'd had to give up my lessons entirely, for there was no way at all to pay for them. I dreamed hopelessly of a chance to pluck the strings of a harp. But we no longer could afford to trade piecework for artistic luxuries. So I told my fingers to be still and mind more closely the flashing needle— only to impale myself yet again with bloody results.

Another month passed. We had little but flour and dripping left in the pantry. Now, one can live on this humble fare for a long while. But we began to avoid going out, lest we encounter our landlady, Mrs. Upshur, to whom we owed two whole months' rent. She had not yet knocked, but even that saintly woman would resort to more forward means of collecting eventually. Eddy still sent Muddy funds from Richmond from time to time: three dollars here, five there. It helped, but was not enough to cover food, rent, and coal for the stove and parlor grate.

One morning Muddy looked at me over our breakfast of plain yellow grits and said, "Perhaps your cousin Neilson would still take you into his home, Sissy. Then I might go into service, or find a job as a seamstress."

I stared down at the dry mealy dollop in my bowl. "No, Muddy. Eddy will have an increase of salary, and then send for us. If our family's to stay together, you and I must stick close."

She looked at me with something oddly like pity.

Well, so be it. The fact was, I pitied her more. It was clear to me by then my mother had no idea of what real love actually was, or meant. Perhaps she had forgotten after my father died. In any case, it seemed the chance for that sort of joy had already passed her by. So I pretended I hadn't seen, and spooned up another mouthful of crumbly, unsalted grits.

Instead, the next week Eddy wrote to say he'd quit his job with Mr. White at the *Messenger*. The same day we received this shocking letter, before we had time to absorb the full impact of the blow, Eddy appeared on the front stoop, clutching his hat.

He looked up wild-eyed when I answered his knock. "Sissy, thank God," he said, and rushed in. The edges of his shirt collar were outlined in gray, his coat and trousers unbrushed, his black stock tie pulled askew. He was wrinkled and soiled, so unlike himself I stepped back a pace as if from an unsavory, too-forward stranger. Edgar Poe's clothing, no matter how old or worn, had always looked as neat and well-tended as those of any gentleman. It was all I could do not to wrinkle my nose, for he smelled strongly of whiskey and old sweat.

Who are you? I wanted to say. "Eddy, are you well?"

He laughed and grabbed my hands. "Well? I was suffering under a depression of spirits such as I've never felt before. Driven even to drink. But now I know the cure! I must have you with me, always, at all times."

It felt odd he should put it that way—not that I was the love of his life, but rather a sure means of imposing temperance on himself. Though great men were often prey to drink, it seemed. Even more so than ordinary ones. I supposed I did not mind being the instrument of reason, in that case, because I already knew how much Eddy cared for me. "But I *will* be with you, when we wed," I pointed out. "It won't be so very long now."

He wrung his hands as he paced back and forth before me. "No, no. You don't understand. It's the Imp again."

I frowned, wondering if I heard him correctly. "The what?"

He stopped and turned to face me, looking abashed. "Oh well— it's just a pet theory of mine. I came to it recently by realizing that when I see . . . a danger . . . even knowing that I should shrink away, should no doubt *run*—sometimes I go ahead and do the very thing

I know I should not. The Imp of the Perverse seizes my heart, and so instead I reach for my own ruin with both hands."

"You mean, the bottle."

He nodded, sighed. "Yes. In this case."

I too sighed. "I see. But since you understand all this so wonderfully well now, could we merely delay a little while longer, as Muddy requires? And then be married."

He shook his head. "I can't wait till you are sixteen, Sissy. Two years and more! I cannot, not another month. If you can't be my wife yet, for the love of God at least come to Richmond or—or wherever I shall soon be working, to live with me. Otherwise, God knows what I shall—"

Just then Muddy cried, "Eddy! For heaven's sake." She stood between parlor and dining room, holding a wet plate and a dripping dishcloth. "A respectable girl can't live with a man, without . . . without . . . oh, what am I saying, you know all that quite well."

He dropped my hand and began to pace again, frowning. "No, no, indeed that's true," he muttered. Then he brightened and whirled to face her again, smiling. "Oh, but Aunty, *you* will be there. And so Sissy will not be alone, and what better arrangement than that her adult companion and chaperone be her own dear mother? The woman we both love most in all the world."

The unflappable Muddy's mouth opened, yet no words came out. She appeared dumbfounded, amazed. But Eddy had discussed this part of our great life plan with her! The bargain we'd made that day on the back stoop: that he'd never ask me to leave my family. That we would all be together, always.

Before I could apologize or further enlighten her, my mother burst into tears, turned from us, and stumbled back into the kitchen. I thought she was simply upset we'd taken matters out of her hands, aggrieved at our terrible presumption. For no one, I realized, my cheeks heating with shame, had ever asked what *she* wanted to do.

No. But then had they ever? I ran after her, Eddy trailing in my wake.

She was sitting at the scarred table, sobbing, blotting her eyes on her crumpled apron.

"Oh, Muddy, I'm so sorry. We should have consulted you about it, but I thought—"

She looked up, smiling tremulously, eyes glittering with new tears. She did not look upset, but rather *transported.*

"It's just, I thought you two would wish to be alone if you married," she said. "To have your own home. Most women do. And—and people have often needed me, but—no one ever wanted me before to, to . . . just to be *with* them."

I was struck silent at this. "But you married Pa for love, Muddy! You told me so. How you chose to marry him even though your family didn't want you to, and the black crows came, and all because—"

Her shoulders shook, and I feared I'd set her off again. Then she raised her face and I saw she was laughing. Yet the sound was bitter. "When I first saw your father, and he paid such kind attention to me, I could've loved him for that alone. No man had ever looked twice at me before. Such a face as this does not inspire much poetry," she said wryly, glancing at Eddy.

"Aunt Maria," he protested, but she held up a hand to silence him.

"William Clemm was a harried widower with a house full of small children. Oh, he *needed* me desperately, of course." She shook her head. "And he was never unkind. But as for true, fated love— the sort I would naturally hope for you to have, my dear—well . . ."

She trailed off with a deep sigh, perhaps thinking back to all my much older stepbrothers and stepsisters, whom Muddy had raised. We never saw them anymore, now.

Eddy looked stricken. He rushed up and took her hands in his. "But we both love and want you with us, always. You shall be my mother too! This is my little family, and will be forever. I'll take care of you, Aunt Maria, and Virginia too. My dear Muddy and Sissy." He lifted his arms as if to an angel hovering benevolently above the kitchen table. He too looked transported. Then again I caught that faint whiff of brandy, and wondered if Muddy had noticed.

"And so," Eddy said, letting his arms fall back to his sides with a dull slap, "I am returning to Richmond tomorrow on the train. A man fulfilled and renewed."

We both looked at him, gaping. "What?" I gasped.

He grasped my hand and squeezed it. "I shall simply get my job back from Mr. White."

"Oh, well, but Eddy," said Muddy slowly, "perhaps you should write him first."

He nodded. "An excellent idea. I shall compose a letter, asking for my position back, assuring him I will be everything he admired in me previously, and more."

He did so, and posted it that afternoon.

White's letter in reply came two days later, and I discovered what the problem in Richmond had truly been, when Eddy gleefully showed it to me.

My Dear Edgar,
I was attached to you—and am still.

My, that did sound promising. I glanced up at Eddy with a smile, then took a deep breath and read on.

But Edgar, when you once again tread these streets, I have
my fears that your resolve will fall through—and that you
would again sip the juice, even till it stole away your senses.
No man is safe who drinks before breakfast! No man can do
so, and attend to business properly.

Oh Moses. Before breakfast? I lowered the letter and stared
over it at Eddy.

He smiled back as if its contents were nothing. At least until he
seemed to truly take in my expression, and then his face fell. "I
know what you're thinking, Sissy, but don't you see? White wanted
me to live with him, in his house, to keep watch over me like some
prisoner, or a small child. But there will be no need, with you and
Aunt Maria there! It's only when I'm alone, and become so low in
my mind that the blue devils come over me, and then—"

So it *was* that. What Granny Poe had always referred to as the
Old Failing. Like Henry, like David, like so many Poe men before
him, Edgar was in danger of falling into a bottle and drowning
there. And yet, sitting across from me he looked so earnest and so
miserable, at last I nodded and continued reading.

If you should return and become drunk, our relation would
end immediately. But if you can separate yourself from your
bottle companions, I will gladly take you back. Tell me if you
can and will do so—and let me hear that it is your fixed
purpose never to yield to temptation.

"Can you do that, Eddy?" I asked, fingers tightening on the
pages until they crackled. "Give up your . . . your evil demon, and
never yield to it again?"

He slid the letter gently from my hands, then leaned down and kissed the crown of my head. "With you, darling girl, I would gladly drink only weak tea and well water the rest of my days."

Perhaps it was faithless of me, but I needed a more binding oath. "Yes, but will you *swear* it?"

"On what?" he asked, glancing around. "Perhaps you should choose."

What would be the most effective yet loving bond to impose? Finally I had it. "Swear that you will never yield again, and do so on—on that which you love best in the world."

He blanched a bit at that, but his hand did not tremble when he raised it and said in a steady and even voice, "I swear I will never touch a drop of spirits ever again—I swear it on the life of my darling and wife-to-be."

I nodded then, mostly satisfied. He would do his best, I was certain, and Mr. White would grow even more fond of him when he saw how earnest, how brilliant, how *sober* Eddy truly could be. And if my beloved ever should begin to waver, then both of us would be there to redirect him firmly to that Path—the only true one which I knew, in his heart, he devoutly wished to tread.

· 7 ·

We went to take out a marriage bond at the courthouse on the twenty-second of September. Eddy escorted me up the steps, then down a musty high-ceilinged hall where the humid air simmered with dust and smelled of boiled coffee and mildew. He was to hand the clerk in the records office a paper signed by Muddy and witnessed by a neighbor, a letter giving her consent for us to marry.

The man behind the big oak desk was thin and balding, eyes narrowed behind rimless spectacles. His snow-white sleeves were caught up in black garters to spare them from the ink he must constantly dip into to sign decrees, licenses, deeds, and contracts: the ordinary papers he transformed and made official, to render people happy or unhappy, richer or poorer. We got in line behind an elderly lady with a property claim, and two gentlemen who wished a business contract witnessed.

When finally it came our turn, the clerk glanced up briefly. "How may I help you?"

"We're here to obtain a license. Miss Clemm and I are to be married." Eddy's voice was pitched deeper than usual, but I detected a slight tremor. "We wish to do so soon."

The clerk took the paper from Eddy's hand, adjusted his spectacles, and peered down. His lips moved faintly, like those of a schoolboy not fully at ease with books. He looked up suddenly at me, then back down to the paper, which stated Eddy and I were both twenty-one years of age. Then up at me again, as the lines in his forehead deepened.

I first thought to smile to reassure him, but instead decided to make my expression serious, befitting a young woman of twenty-one, who was perhaps a schoolteacher. I gazed back at him somberly and laced my fingers together in my old, too-tight gloves so they would not tremble and give me away.

The truth was, I wanted to laugh. Dressed up in an old gown cut down from a castoff of Rosalie's, and a borrowed pair of gloves, with my mother's last whole handkerchief tucked into my sleeve—it all felt like a game. Better than any childhood hide-and-seek or dressing up. I knew I looked older than my true age, having bloomed early, as Muddy put it. Though short of stature, I had a womanly figure. Would this man, an expert with spectacles and stamps and papers and pens, believe what my mother had written? For really I was just thirteen, and my betrothed twenty-six.

Eddy's face never changed but I felt his hand under my elbow growing warmer and damper, even through the cloth.

At last, with a grunt, the clerk dipped his quill. The moving point scritched and scratched like insect legs skittering inside a drawer. I shivered. Eddy's hand tightened, but I didn't dare look up, for my jaw was quivering again.

I could not suppress the shaking of my hand as I took up the quill the clerk handed me so I could carefully inscribe my name at the foot of the license. Until then, I'd never signed anything more important than a personal letter. Now the great day was coming to pass: my entry to adulthood, just as it happened in novels. Shortly I would no longer be Virginia Eliza Clemm, an inexperienced girl, but Mrs. Edgar A. Poe: a married woman who made her own choices, commanded her own fate. One whose life had been firmly set in stone. And the first thing I would do—

"May I have my pen back, young lady?"

I blushed and handed it over. The factotum sprinkled sand over the paper to set the still-shining swoops and flourishes of India black. He shook the whispering grains off over a little wooden box, then handed the license to Eddy.

What adulthood would entail I was unsure, except that it would be nothing like my life up till then. No more miserable cold rooms and empty kitchen shelves. No more begging letters from Muddy to relations. A neat white cottage, fenced and twined with ivy. No—with a cedar vine, a great old venerable one. And Eddy seated by a sunlit window scribbling at stories. While I bustled about my whitewashed kitchen in a fashionable dark dress with a ruffled apron. The room was lined with cupboards of beautiful dishes, the pantry with jars of preserves and sacks of sugar and flour and cornmeal and shelves of bread and smoked ham and cakes. But I was not merely a housewife, of course. A harp and a piano both waited in the parlor to be played; stacks of sheet music lay in a cabinet, songs I'd practice and perfect to later perform at . . . well, I knew not where. Not yet.

And Muddy? Why, she'd be rocking away in a fine oak chair, snug by a cheerful fire—

"Come along, Virginia," said Eddy, more formal than he sounded at home. He was turning from the counter, away from the narrow, cynical gaze of the balding clerk.

"Coming," I whispered, catching and schooling myself not to wave good-bye.

We strolled out of the courthouse, arm in arm. Eddy led me to a stone bench out front shaded by a pair of elms. We sat there, but he said nothing until a dray wagon had clattered on by. Then he squeezed my fingers gently. "Don't worry, my dear. Of course we won't use the license yet."

Startled, I glanced up into his eyes, which seemed full of both relief and trouble, as if he knew the answer to a difficult philosophical question but had not yet resolved how to write it out.

"What do you mean?"

"Virginia—Sissy, my dearest. I fully understand you're too young to be a wife yet. But this way we are officially promised, and can marry when you're older. No one can stop us now, thanks to that simple scrap of paper. And then you *will* be my little wife in full—my dearest friend and helpmate."

I blinked in dismay. No vows? No wedding? No "Mrs. Poe" to sign my letters with? The cottage, the piano, the harp slowly took wing and lifted out of sight. "But Eddy—"

"Do you not see? Now no one can prevent our being together forever, my dear." He leaned forward and kissed my hand. Then, quickly and more discreetly, my cheek, even though people were passing by. This made me smile a little and blush. But I was angry at him, and at her.

I assumed he meant not just the vague "no one" but rather our cousin Neilson. When he'd written to Muddy to offer to take me in as his ward, he'd certainly suggested between the lines that I was far too young to marry anyone just now, though he hadn't mentioned Eddy by name. While I was convinced girls my age, or very close to it, married all the time in Baltimore and everywhere else. If the groom was a bit older, well, there was nothing so startling about that. Our ages had nothing to do with our feelings for each other. But it was easy to imagine Poe relations far and wide gathered like a flock of undertaker crows, discussing our fortunes, and me and Eddy, and Muddy's official agreement to allow us to wed. Who were they to judge?

I took a deep breath and forced myself not to pull away from Eddy's hand. For one weak moment, the heavy cream pages of Neilson Poe's letter, and those colorful dresses and sheets of fine music and a gilded harp—and yes, even crystal flutes brimming with fizzy champagne—flitted through my mind. And then, like birds migrating to some more congenial southern shore, they swooped higher and soared away. I bit my lip and told myself, *What is champagne but mere alcohol, the devilish liquid that has fueled so many of our family's sorrows, past and present?*

Besides, Eddy had promised me and Muddy he would ensure I became well educated in all the usual academic subjects. The artistic ones too, especially music and voice. He'd sworn to protect me, assured me that I would lack for nothing. I did wonder how he could ever afford all of that, but had no doubt he'd find a way. After all, he was a wonderful poet and an editor too, with books already in print. His future both with the *Messenger,* and in the halls of publishing, could not be more promising. The world would soon take note.

Still, it seemed hard he held such a grudge against Neilson Poe, who'd no doubt only meant to be kind. "To be honest, I thought our cousin generous to offer me a place in his home," I said.

Eddy looked down at me, mouth open. Then squeezed my hand again. "Bless her little heart," he said, as if I were not even sitting there. "She always sees the good in people."

Now that was not true. But before I could protest Eddy jumped up and began to pace. "Still, my dear, you surely must see that my esteemed cousin Neilson—"

"My cousin, sir. Your uncle," I reminded him.

"Yes, yes, of course," he said, waving away the convoluted pedigrees and lineages of the extended and intermarried Poe family tree like so many tattered, sticky cobwebs. "Don't you understand? The little dog is bent on destroying my happiness! I consider him my bitterest enemy now. And I always will."

He looked so angry just then, his pale face even whiter when drained by rage, that I thought better of contradicting. No doubt he'd get over this fanciful hurt soon enough. Probably sooner if I didn't fan the flame by arguing for the opposing side like a graceless, misguided lawyer. In any case, I now had *most* of what I'd longed for. The rest would soon follow.

"Do you see him yet?" I asked Muddy, for the second or third time.

She sighed and shook her head.

It was the morning of October third, and she and I stood together on the Light Street wharf at Baltimore Harbor. Three battered old trunks were stacked next to us in a small, untidy pile, ready to be carried aboard the Norfolk-bound steamer. The smallest box contained all I owned in the world: one shirtwaist too tight in the bosom; one day dress of dark cotton and one of gray wool; a moth-nibbled shawl; a spare lisle chemise; one flannel petticoat, too short; a mourning brooch made of the braided, infant-soft brown hair of the dead sister I'd been named for; and a straw summer hat, its brim bent. And of course the books Eddy had given me, wrapped carefully in the old petticoat.

My mother walked around the trunks, looking anxious, then gazed along the wharf toward the post office again. "Oh dear. I do wish Eddy had received another letter from Mr. White," she murmured.

I was fiddling with my bonnet strings, which kept coming untied. "Saying what?"

"Some final confirmation of his, his—oh, I don't know," she said, wringing her hands like an actress in a melodramatic play.

She seemed afraid, but of what? All her life—all of mine, at least—she'd faced down illness and death and poverty and bitterly hard work without complaint. Why should leaving the place we'd been so miserably poor and cold, and often hungry, to begin anew in happier circumstances, worry her so?

"Well, he'll be here soon," I said, drawing my good shawl around me, standing straighter and trying to look grown and tall, though that last of course was impossible. I meant to show her it was my burden to shoulder too, this rushing off to a new life. "And no matter how we wish to see the future, Muddy, we cannot. So we must go on to Richmond, letter or not." I paused, surprised at the peremptory tone of my own words, wondering if I had been too sharp.

She was staring at me with mild surprise, as if a spirit from the past had risen and addressed her, as they sometimes did in novels. "Why, yes—yes, of course we must. That's how it is in life for females, Virginia. We must follow Eddy wherever he goes, no matter the circumstances. Good or bad, rich or poor, we won't complain. In any case, you can't complain of things to a man, for you see, it only irritates and makes them angry. At least when it's not something they can quickly remedy."

I stared at her, feeling dismayed. I had no response to this depressing revelation of the true meaning of womanhood; I'd never really considered the practicalities of the state before. And yet if I looked back over my mother's life her words seemed fairly accurate.

I shivered as a breeze kicked up off the water, blowing strands of hair into my face. Very well, then. Even before I stepped onto this pier I'd chosen the path my life would take—whether in cheerful sunshine, or deep in the shadow of that invisible overhanging boulder I'd set in place myself. So I lifted my chin, smiled at my mother, and took a deep breath of the crisp harbor air. Which was so weighted with salt and fish and smoke it made me cough.

What if he didn't come?

For a moment I wanted to cling to my mother, gripping her skirts to force her to think only of me; for her to stroke my head and murmur reassurances. But people were thronging all around us. Such behavior would look so childish that even the dark sober traveling dress Muddy had cut down and restitched for me would no longer be sufficient costume to mark me out as a grown woman.

I turned away to look out across the basin toward Federal Hill. Clipper ships were moored there, tied up like sleek, exhausted horses resting between dashes to Brazil and New York and Cuba. Their tall naked masts and spiky yards were bare of sails, their snarl of lines a thick forest without leaves. Smaller craft scooted in and out. Timber rafts wallowed along, while skipjacks and bugeyes coasted in, carrying in their shallow wooden bellies piles of black duck and terrapins and muskrat. Or crates and barrels of Chesapeake Bay oysters and clams and blue crabs. These would be flung, battered but still living after a hard voyage, into display crates and copper cooking vats and steel tubs, or onto blocks of ice from New England, in the various fish markets along the wharf. Where soon they'd meet their fate.

Suddenly I couldn't breathe.

Stop this foolishness, I told myself in the calm, firm tones of my mother's voice. Her broad bombazine-clad back was to me again as she continued to scan the harborside. What if Eddy had stopped somewhere to say good-bye and a bad acquaintance had insisted on buying him a farewell drink? And then . . . black spots

rose like a swarm of gnats before my eyes. I waved a hand to shoo
them off.

Breathe.

I inhaled as deeply as my corset allowed, past the hard knot in
my throat. The waterfront's smells were strong—raw fish and seaweed and mildewed hemp and hot pitch and, more pleasantly,
green coffee beans slowly roasting to rich brown. The wet-steel stink
of steam. And underneath that, a fainter odor of shipped goods
leaked from containers: tobacco and molasses and the sharp meaty
tang of salted beef as stevedores, black or white arms and faces
gleaming with sweat despite the dry cool weather, trundled hogsheads and crates and barrels of freight past. Amid all this rumbling,
banging chaos sat my one shabby little trunk.

I really was leaving Baltimore, the only place I had ever lived.

A sob rose like a bunched fist, its knuckles digging at the inside of my throat.

Just then Muddy pointed. "There he is!" She did not add, *Thank
the Lord,* but I heard it all the same.

So I swallowed the hard thing back, and only then realized I'd
been gripping my collar, pulling the cloth away from my neck. I
let that hand fall to my side and composed my face. Then turned
with a smile to greet my intended.

Stevedores came to check the marking on our trunks, then hoisted
them aboard.

"There's the purser," said Eddy, pointing at a uniformed man
at the top of the gangplank, hands clasped behind him, surveying
us rabble below as if God himself had come to check our tickets.

At last the bell sounded and we assembled to board. The passengers around us seemed not much more finely dressed than we, though certainly more colorfully. Well, we were in mourning still, and I thought Eddy's black sack coat, black trousers and black stock, his broad pale forehead, dark brown hair, and muttonchop sideburns set him apart to advantage. He looked serious, poetic, somber. Yes, as I looked around again, all the embroidered, colored waistcoats, pastel-hued trousers, the fall dresses in primary colors, seemed garish and cheap. I straightened my shoulders, lifted my chin, and walked up the gangway behind him and Muddy. When she murmured tremulously, "It's so high, I fear I might fall," he gallantly took her arm.

We stood near the stern on the port side, as people crowded to wave madly to friends and family on the pier. There was no one to say good-bye and see us off, though; we'd already written or called on the few family and friends left in Baltimore. But it was my first voyage. So, even though I was sure it would not be my last, I waved from my spot at the rail. Muddy gave me a strange look, but Eddy smiled and slid one arm around my waist. "She's waving good-bye to Baltimore," he said, with satisfaction. Then he lifted a hand too.

I expected to feel ill once we were out on the water, perhaps even to be sick all the way to Richmond. The Chesapeake is rough as any ocean when the wind turns and the sky bunches overhead like a knotted gray handkerchief. But after the engine gave a steamy sigh and the big paddlewheels began to slowly slap the ash-streaked water of the harbor, to propel us with more and more force into the Patapsco River, it was Muddy who had to excuse herself and retire to the ladies' waiting room. We could not afford a cabin.

I could've retired as well, but chose to stand at the stern rail with Eddy. The wind tugged like a naughty child at my shawl, making a snarled mess of my hairdo which Muddy had so carefully pinned up. Eddy, the seasoned traveler, held my arm and pointed out the sights—mostly trees, and more trees, and the occasional private landing or small farm or lonely cabin. Then finally only gray water.

"Mr. White has given me an increase in salary," Eddy said as we gazed out over the Bay.

I let go the rail and clapped in delight. "How wonderful!"

He snorted. "But he's still waffling on the question of my title."

"He'll see the light soon, and put you completely in charge," I assured him.

The boat we boarded in Norfolk to continue on to Richmond was smaller and a good deal slower than the Baltimore Line steamer. Our trip up the James was more leisurely too. So smooth and calm Muddy came on deck again to admire the flocks of black duck and mallards, and the honking, straggling dark arrows of geese flowing south. She and I were curious about the great plantation houses, at whose wharves the boat stopped to unload chests and parcels and hogsheads into the uplifted arms of dark-skinned servants. We gazed at the twin brick chimneys of Berkeley's great house, perched on its own hill; at the steep roof and ancient boxwood hedges of Westover; and peered with puzzlement at the strange white knob atop the roof of Shirley Plantation.

"Oh, that? It's a pineapple," Eddy explained.

I frowned, thinking he was making fun of me.

"No, truly. You see, the carved fruit is a signpost. An assurance to travelers they are welcome. Unlike at some places one could name."

He always turned away at these stops, becoming greatly occupied with relighting his segar or brushing lint I could not see from the cloth of his coat or trousers. He must be thinking of his foster father, or of the death of Frances Allan, or perhaps the inheritance dangled, then jerked away. His childhood would've made a good story for Mr. Dickens; a start in life which had promised so much, then left him an impoverished orphan again. The son of forgotten actors, scorned by his cold, wealthy foster father. But I knew better than to lay a hand on his arm or give him any pitying looks. Eddy hated pity above all else.

Beyond the confluence of the Appomattox, the James grew narrower and wound in great loops around Bermuda Hundred. The current ran more swiftly there, shoving its relentless force against gray rocks and lush low peninsulas which twisted the channel into a shallow, treacherous serpent whose narrow back we must ride. At this point I did begin to feel sick, not so much from the motion of the boat, but from thinking of what it must be like to steer it, to hold the lives of so many in your hands. To know a moment of inattention, one forgotten snag or rock outcrop, or an accident with the boiler could take everything away from us all.

About three hours down the river I caught sight of a white-columned structure rising high above the rooftops of many other brick and stone buildings on the north bank. "Look, there it is!" I cried. "There is Richmond, I think."

Eddy smiled and nodded. "The capitol. If you could climb to its dome you might see the misty peaks of the Blue Ridge, off to the west. The city sits on seven large hills, like Rome."

By the time we docked the sun hung low, its bottom curve already obscured by city skyline. Eddy arranged with a porter for our baggage. "We shall stay at Mrs. Poore's," he said. "In two nice rooms."

"Ah, good. You've made arrangements?" my mother asked.

He shrugged. "It's a large house. There's always space."

I slid onto one seat of the wagonette. Eddy helped Muddy up beside me, then took the place opposite.

"But I just heard the driver say this vehicle is bound for the Spottswood Hotel," she persisted, brows lowering.

"Mrs. Poore's is quite close to the hotel," Eddy assured her.

Our wagonette was nearly empty, but the docks were very busy. We would lurch forward, only to stop for a dray loaded with sacks of flour and cornmeal, or an empty collier's wagon rumbling and rattling over cobblestones toward the coal yards upstream. Or coming more slowly from the yards, the horses sweating and pulling hard to move mounds of shining black ore.

We finally rolled up the hill, swaying and jolting over the cobbles. The horses turned left at a tobacco warehouse of their own accord, picking up the pace to a clattering trot, as if relieved to have completed the hard pull to the top. The driver reined to a stop at Eighth and Main. The other passengers began gathering parcels and carpetbags, gentlemen jumping down and holding up their hands to steady their ladies' descent.

Muddy and I both looked at Eddy for guidance. "It is only a bit farther, but we must go the rest of the way on foot," he said.

He steered us through the throngs on the sidewalk: men in well-cut dark suits, ladies in low-necked, jewel-toned gowns, all apparently on the way to some grand function, many ascending the sweeping steps of the Spottswood. We turned away from its gaslit elegance and went on down Main, past cafés and taverns and saloons. I kept my eyes ahead, not wanting to see if Eddy gazed at any of these longingly—or worse, with familiarity. Or perhaps worst of all, resentment. What if the Imp of the Perverse stirred to life in his breast now? Then he might wish himself once more free to be drawn in by the invisible webs of fiddle, clarinet, guitar, and twanging banjo notes which echoed in more or less pleasing combinations from each doorway.

We walked through clouds of tobacco smoke flavored with the eye-watering fumes of beer and rum and gin, past the rough male music of laughter and shouts. No wonder Eddy, when he'd lived alone, walking these very streets each night, had been tempted into bad habits and worse company.

He turned us at last off Main and down a side alley. We came out facing an open park set about with small trees and a few marble monuments. Above it rose the towering white Capitol, Mr. Jefferson's architectural marvel.

"Capitol Square," he said. "Mrs. Poore's is the next house on Bank Street."

We turned into the yard of a two-story brick structure with a whitewashed Greek portico facing the neatly-planted square. Within lay a wide, well-lighted hall. Eddy opened the door without even ringing a bell or knocking.

Muddy glanced at me doubtfully. "Well, he used to live here," I whispered, though I was taken aback too. In the foyer he picked up a brass handbell from a candlestand by a hall tree heaped with coats, and shook it till it rang out clear and loud.

A tall, broad-shouldered man appeared at the rear of the hall. He wore no coat, just uncollared shirt and suspenders, and was wiping his mouth on a large white napkin.

"Hello, Thomas," said Eddy eagerly. "We've interrupted your dinner, forgive me."

"Not at all," the man said, as his tongue pushed at the side of his cheek, dislodging some trapped particle of meat or vegetable in his lower teeth.

Eddy introduced us, then said to Muddy, "Mr. Cleland is Mrs. Poore's son-in-law. Also a pressman on the *Messenger,* so we know each other well."

Thomas Cleland bowed to us. "We've been missing you a great deal at the shop, Eddy. And now you'll need a room again, I see. Or rather, rooms?" He smiled at me and Muddy, then went to the foot of the stairs. "Oh, Mother Poore! Mr. Poe is back. Do you have a place for him and his little family?"

A door creaked shrilly on protesting hinges upstairs, and an equally high voice called down, "What was that, Tom?"

Mr. Cleland took a deep breath and bellowed, "I *said* Edgar *Poe* is back, and he—"

"That's what I thought you said," the woman shouted. "Well, you can tell him for me, I do not have lodgings for him, and am not likely to have any now or later!"

The hinges squealed derisively as the door slammed again. I flinched, feeling as if I'd been slapped. What could've made a lady behave so rudely?

Cleland turned back, avoiding our eyes. "Ah, well. It seems my mother-in-law has no vacancy here just now."

Eddy stared at him helplessly. "But I—then what are we to do?"

"Excuse us a moment," I said to Muddy and Mr. Cleland, as I drew Eddy off to the side. "Is there something the matter?" I whispered. "Is that lady for some reason angry with you?"

He shrugged. "Can't imagine why. I suspect she simply does not like artists."

This seemed an odd, somewhat evasive reply. But we were not alone; the woman's son-in-law stood a few feet away. In any case, I dared not even glance at Muddy now. "Surely there must be other places," I said, raising my voice. "Perhaps Mr. Cleland knows of one nearby?"

"Of course!" Thomas replied, looking relieved. "There's Mrs. James Yarrington's—down the street at the corner of Bank and Twelfth. A fine house, also facing the square. John Ferguson lives there. And Will McFarland." Cleland said to my mother, "They work at the *Messenger* as well, ma'am."

"Is it a decent house?" she asked sternly, and then I longed to melt into the floor.

"Is it—why, of course," said Cleland, clearly flabbergasted. "I shall take you there myself." And without bothering to get hat or coat, or to discard the napkin still clutched in one hand, he led us down the street.

Mrs. Yarrington's looked so much like Mrs. Poore's, I glanced over my shoulder to reassure myself we had not somehow walked in a circle back to our starting place. The same neat square of clipped yard and long painted portico, the same half-glazed doors, and Thomas swept in without knocking as if he lived here as well.

He called down the landlady and introduced us. "Mr. Poe is, ah, assistant editor at the *Southern Literary Messenger,* and—well, my mother-in-law hasn't room for, uh, the three of them. So we thought you might."

This was very clever, for that *we* made it sound as if Mrs. Poore herself had sent and thus approved of us.

"Why yes, I believe so," said Mrs. Yarrington, who nevertheless looked us over discreetly. "There's a nice large front room for the ladies. And an adjoining one for Mr. Poe."

She turned to Eddy, who quickly said, "My aunt, Mrs. Clemm, will decide. Would you show the rooms to her, please?"

Muddy smiled then, and so did Mrs. Yarrington.

I started after them as my mother followed the landlady, but paused at the foot of the stairs, gripping the bannister. I was Eddy's fiancée, not yet his wife. What if the women sent me back down the stairs again? So I returned to the men in the foyer and stood trying to smile and look self-assured. Eddy sighed now and then, one hand playing with a loose button on his coat. He fiddled with it so long, tapping the round disk of horn with a nail, I began to grit my teeth. I resolved that I—not my mother—would mend it as soon as we had unpacked.

When they came slowly back down, I heard Mrs Yarrington saying, "I don't usually let to females. But as you are a respectable widow . . . and with Mr. Poe, a male relative, here to protect the two of you . . . I have other lodgers who work at Mr. White's establishment. Quiet, hardworking men. No trouble at all."

Eddy lifted his head and grinned at Thomas, who winked back and then, with a triumphant flourish of dinner napkin, departed.

Our sitting room was large and high ceilinged, warm looking in the light of several fat white candles, which Mrs. Yarrington must've just lighted to show the rooms. They burned luxuriously in spotless hurricane globes on the mantel and a brass candlestick on a round oak stand. The room was all she'd claimed, with a fine view of the capitol beyond the glowing gaslights which illuminated the street. The mahogany four-poster was made up with a spotless white tester and valance. Next to it sat a marble-topped washstand and dresser, tall wardrobes with carved pediments, a heavy claw-footed desk, a sewing chair, a new rush-seated rocker, and two ladder-backed chairs. Except for the desk, where I could already envision Eddy working, it was clearly a lady's room.

"The gentleman's room adjoins," said the landlady, pointing at the far wall. "Divided of course with a *very* solid connecting door."

My face burned. Our circumstances were so far from what I had envisioned in my daydreams of love and marriage.

"These are my best rooms. They belonged to the former owner, a maiden lady. It will be nice to have one family living in them," she conceded. "With board it will be nine dollars a week in total."

Across the room Eddy looked as relieved as I felt; with the recent increase in salary he could afford that. Mrs. Yarrington gave a little bow and excused herself, leaving us to await our trunks. Eddy said Thomas would divert them from his mother-in-law's house.

He took both my hands in his. "I will never be lonely now, with two beautiful ladies by my side. We can be comfortable here, don't you think, Sissy?"

I squeezed his long, gloved fingers. "Yes, indeed. It will be lovely, until we can move into that little white cottage on Church Hill you described in your letter."

He frowned. "Oh. The cottage? Well, I—"

His grip fell away. Muddy shot me a frown, and I understood I'd just said something amiss. But he'd promised a cottage. Had written he'd settled on the one on that very street, and said he longed to see us in it soon.

Muddy said quickly, "Why, that was over a month ago. I'm sure the place has been let by now. Eddy has enough to worry about without chasing after fairy-tale cottages. We can live quite comfortably right here. It's a clean, respectable home."

I stared at my mother, tears pressing at the corners of my eyes. Yes, it was respectable, with its chipped marble mantels, painted china lamps, polished oak floors, and flowered wool carpets. But why speak as if I were an eight-year-old with grubby hands and hopeless fantasies? I'd only mentioned what Eddy himself had written. If he'd misrepresented things in his letters, the least he could do was spring to my defense. I lowered my head, waiting for his certain reply.

"Don't worry, Sissy," he said at last. "I'll see if the cottage is still available. But we can surely be just as happy and comfortable here. As Muddy says."

Her face went soft, as if she were gazing on the Baby Jesus

himself. And Eddy sent my mother such a look of gratitude and love that for a moment I was stabbed with a bolt of pure jealousy. Though it would've been hard to decide why, or to explain over which of them I felt it.

· 8 ·

Without Edgar Poe in the office, Mr. White had gotten so far behind he'd been forced to cancel the October issue. He told Eddy he was thinking of scrapping November as well. He wanted to concentrate on a special Christmas number.

"He welcomed me back as one would the Baby Savior," my cousin gloated the next evening, and Muddy did not rebuke him. He was in good spirits and consequently so were we.

The very next day he took us down to the building at Fifteenth and Main which housed the *Messenger,* to formally introduce Muddy and me to Mr. Thomas Willis White. When we stepped into the second-floor offices they were quiet except for the muffled metal-on-metal clatter of a printing press in the back. The rooms were light and cheerful, if dusty, though smaller than I had imagined. They smelled of stale segars and damp paper and a pungent inky aroma that prickled the nose.

A man with a round Irish countenance, arched brows, and the generous rosy mouth of a girl, rushed in from the back clutching a sheaf of papers. His collar was askew, his black stock untied. He glared about as if ready to strike someone, or perhaps jump out a window. Then his gaze fell on my husband. "Edgar! There you are. The November issue is missing copy."

Eddy smiled. "Took care of that problem yesterday. The new pages are already with Sam."

White's tense shoulders drooped. He raked at thick auburn curls hard enough to tear them out, then glanced at me. "Ah! This must be the good angel herself?"

"Mr. White, this dear lady is my aunt, the widow Mrs. Maria Clemm. And here also is my fiancée, Miss Virginia Clemm. They arrived from Baltimore only last week, as I mentioned."

The editor bowed and so did we. And then—seemingly overcome with some great, gripping emotion—he stepped forward to seize and kiss my hand. "My dear young lady! You've wrought a miraculous change in our Eddy. Done what her chaste majesty Temperance could not."

I heard Muddy's sharp intake of breath. What in the world was the man suggesting?

Mr. White's ruddy Irish cheeks turned a deeper carmine. "Oh, I—I hope I can make myself plain, my—my *dear* Mrs. Clemm," he stammered, gaze skittering from me to Muddy and back. "I merely meant, of course, Miss Clemm, that it is your *presence*—indeed, your combined presences—which will keep Edgar in good spirits and good habits. And so I congratulate you! Both of you, ladies," he said, bowing again, gazing around to include everyone.

Muddy, who still looked taken aback, spoke up. "It's only right for us to bring my nephew a steady home life, sir. And why not—we know we'll always have someone to love and care for us, in Eddy."

Who, meanwhile, was standing by, face a pale mask of composure. As if he were not being discussed in his presence like a two-headed calf. I ached for what this conversation must do to his always-prickly pride. Eddy would never let it show, of course.

"Well, I believe it is acting as your editor which will *keep* him in good spirits," I said quickly, throwing him a smile.

White's eyebrows rose a fraction. "As my—"

Eddy cleared his throat. "Mr. White is of course the *editor* of the *Messenger.*" I heard, if no one else did, the bitterness beneath his polite, self-deprecating tone. "And I am the—now, what did you call it, again, Thomas?"

White frowned, looking sheepish. "Manager of the editorial department."

I felt a sinking within, for I'd heard in White's voice and seen in his hardening expression that he held his magazine close as a doting, vigilant father would an ailing only child. Like Eddy's foster father, White's pride of ownership would make him jealous of titles, stingy with control. No matter how much he might need Eddy. At least, unlike Allan, he was generous with money and praise.

"It sounds very grand, very . . . responsible," said Muddy, nodding.

We left soon after, once Eddy had shown us his desk, a scarred and ink-stained but good-sized mahogany secretary with many tiny drawers and assorted cubbyholes in its tall cabinet. But the chair was very odd; most of its back had been sawn off.

Eddy caught my puzzled stare. "Oh, that," he said, rolling his eyes. "White cut it down. He doesn't like me leaning back. Says it looks unprofessional."

"Oh," I murmured. "I see. I suppose."

The desk's hinged surface was heaped with manuscripts: submissions to the magazine which he would read and ponder, then accept or reject. I recognized a few of his own distinctively-rolled scrolls in the jumbled pile as well. He always carefully glued his beautifully-penned fair copies of stories or poems end to end, then rolled them like a royal proclamation, and tied each with a length of black ribbon. Once he'd used my favorite and only black velvet hair ribbon. It was lost forever, but he'd been so abashed and apologetic I forgave him. It had not occurred to me that as editor—or rather, *manager*—he could also still publish his own stories and poems. But why not? No one wrote half so well, no one was his equal, not even Mr. Longfellow. But while managing everything for Mr. White, would he still have time to keep writing poems and stories too?

Then and there I resolved that, in between my own lessons in music and voice, I would strive to make things at home pleasant and easy for him. So that we might both practice and excel at the different arts we loved.

The next week we dutifully paid our first visit to the MacKenzies. I was eager to finally see the large sunny music room Jane Mac-Kenzie had described on her visit to us in Baltimore. It had sounded like heaven. No doubt that's why I climbed into the calash she'd sent with much more alacrity than Eddy. Muddy had decided to stay behind to sort out our rooms, unpack clothing and brush it; to set up or put away what few belongings were still in our trunks.

Duncan Lodge, the MacKenzies' rural home, looked grim and forbidding as we rolled through the wrought-iron front gate down a poplar-lined drive. A brick Georgian foursquare with a col-umned portico, it squatted on the grounds as thick shouldered and solemn as a judge. A colored manservant greeted us, and a uniformed girl took my coat and bonnet off to some place deeper in the house. Then the butler, if that was the proper title, escorted me. Eddy remained in the parlor.

"Oh!" I whispered when we entered the music room. And then whispered, "Oh," to myself again. For it was all I'd imagined. No— even more. The walls were wainscoted with oak, and above that papered with a lively design of painted musical notes. A plaster Mozart brooded from a pedestal between tall windows which over-looked a formal garden. The shrubs and box bushes out there were clipped into stiff geometric shapes in a Frenchified style. The scent of tea roses drifted in through the open windows. A Chickering grand piano draped with a tapestry held a silver candelabra, and a tall mahogany cabinet displayed a large collection of music books. On the wall hung a framed oil painting of a performing trio: vio-linist, cellist, and pianist.

But this chamber was no wealthy dilettante's showcase. On a practice table flanked by music stands waited a small harp, two violins with bows, a flute, a conductor's baton, a metronome, and a stack of sheet music. A tall case clock ticked steadily beside the table. Two floor-length mirrors in opposite corners would allow musicians and singers to view their posture and technique. The only other furnishings were a dozen straight-backed chairs with upholstered seats, which players and audience could arrange as they wished.

I stood on the thick Turkey carpet gazing around with awe and delight. Surely Cousin Neilson Poe could not have provided a more elegant setting!

"Good afternoon, Virginia," said a well-modulated voice.

I was so startled my stomach jumped. I turned, expecting to see Jane MacKenzie, but it was Rosalie. The uncanny similarity of their voices brought gooseflesh to my arms. "Oh! Cousin Rose," I said, moving to clasp her gloved hands. "Thank you for inviting me. The room is so lovely."

In her blue serge skirt and white shirtwaist she appeared very much the schoolmistress, looking down with an intent expres-sion I could not read. "Where is Eddy?"

"In the parlor, waiting for Mrs.—for your mother." I could barely meet her gaze; I was sure he'd stayed there mainly to avoid his sister.

"All right. Then let's begin." But she hesitated. "What shall I teach her?" she murmured, as if alone and talking to herself. "I write a beautiful hand. I teach the little girls at Mother's school manners and proper comportment and etiquette too."

"Well, I know how to write." I added, in a joking tone, "And I certainly hope my manners are up to snuff!"

"The taking of snuff is a disgusting habit," she said, frowning, her tone so eerily like Mrs. MacKenzie's that again I felt the fine hairs on my arms rising.

"Yes, yes, I know," I stammered. "I only meant—I don't *take* it of course, it's just an expression that my older brother used to—"

But she'd let go of my hands and was moving away, toward the piano. "We shall start with a music lesson," she tossed over her shoulder, as if I were to follow like a spaniel. I hesitated, struggling with the resentment rising in my breast. That would not do; I was after all not the mistress here, but the poor relation and fortunate recipient of MacKenzie largess. So I took a deep breath, and walked obediently over to the great, polished bulk of the Chickering.

Rosalie slid onto the bench, tugged off her white kid gloves, then smoothed her billowing skirts. "Sit here beside me."

I did so. "What shall we play?"

"*I'll* choose," she said, as if we were ten and competing to go first at a game of marbles.

We played "Kindermarsch," an easy four-handed Schubert duet, without too many mistakes. Then Rose said, "This one is my favorite." She pulled out a sheet with Haydn's "Gypsy Rondo," which appeared approachable, though I'd never attempted it myself.

She began to play it alone.

Rosalie was not an incompetent pianist, but she seemed even less skilled than I. Still, she played with great enthusiasm and many unneeded flourishes, hitting wrong chords without blushing or faltering as I would've done. She merely plowed ahead like a small, determined skiff caught at sea in a storm. Still, I began to wonder what she could teach me about music. Perhaps Mrs. MacKenzie planned to instruct us both in some more difficult pieces, later.

As we were finishing another four-handed duet, her mother came in. She stood by silently until we'd played the last notes, then applauded softly. "Lovely, girls. Now, come to the parlor, and we'll have tea."

Rosalie sprang up like an unruly boy. "I'm starving, Mama," she exclaimed. "Is Eddy still here?"

"Yes, my dear," her mother said, lifting a hand to smooth the curls on Rosalie's forehead, turning on her adopted daughter such a devoted look I had to glance away.

As we entered the parlor Eddy was perched on the horsehair sofa, at the very edge, as if thinking of rising to take his leave.

Rosalie squealed, "Buddy!"

He flinched, but rose graciously as she rushed over.

"I shall sit here beside you, brother," she declared, and sank onto the sofa gripping his hands, dragging him down next to her. He glanced my way, but all I saw was resignation, mixed with a dose of pained endurance.

A slight young servant girl wheeled in a silent tea cart. Thin-skinned china cups and saucers, steaming gilded teapots, and plates of small yellow cakes topped with fancy sugar icing were all fitted carefully together on the top tray like a breakable jigsaw puzzle. She began to unload and set up this feast before us on a low table.

"That looks very nice, Tessy," said Mrs MacKenzie, nodding. I wondered what it felt like to be the mistress of such a house, to call for whatever food you liked, and generally order people about. Though Mrs. MacKenzie spoke just as softly to her servants as she did to us.

"Yes'm," said the girl. "I fix 'em just like you said." Then she bowed and left, wheeling the well-oiled cart before her. Beneath her apron, her gray wool skirt and white blouse looked better pressed and newer than my own.

Mrs. MacKenzie poured, and we sat for a while in silence stirring, sipping, and eating. The cakes were fresh and soft, flecked with brown specks of vanilla bean. But after a few bites the confection grew so painfully sweet my mouth ached. I had to set my plate down and sip more tea.

Rosalie had already eaten two or three little cakes by then, yet somehow had not actually gobbled them. When she was not overcome by the sight of her big brother, her manners were indeed impeccable. She drained her teacup and set it on the saucer, then rose and went over to a hammered-brass chest by the fireplace.

She took out a set of draughts, set up a lovely inlaid checker board at a gaming table beneath the window, and beckoned to Eddy. "Look, we can play a round."

He stood, set cup and saucer down with great care, and walked to the table with the enthusiasm of a man who'd just seen through the clouds of Time all the way to his own execution.

Mrs. MacKenzie rose too. "Come, Virginia. Let's stroll in the garden and leave them to get reacquainted."

I did as I was bid, wishing I could rescue Eddy without hurting Rosalie's feelings, or incurring her foster mother's displeasure. For I was beginning to—well, not love her, precisely, but to care greatly what Jane MacKenzie thought of me. To respect her. To want, even, to be like her. Rather than like my own poor, well-meaning parent.

We strolled arm in arm between well-pruned rosebushes and

chrysanthemums with tightfisted buds that trembled impatiently for the cool summoning hand of late fall. Jane MacKenzie was so calm and immaculate, so graceful and assured, I had to remind myself not to stare at her.

"Did Rosalie make a good instructress, Virginia?"

"She has such lovely manners." I was careful not to look her in the eye. "She told me—oh, a great deal about etiquette and manners and—and, well, so many other things."

"She also paints," said Mrs. MacKenzie. "Would you like lessons in watercolor and china-painting?"

I bit my lip, but that small self-punishment did not stop me from blurting, "I love music. I like to sing. I want to learn to play the harp, the flute. To improve myself on the piano. I want—"

She laughed softly and patted my hand, then tucked it into the crook of her arm, as if gently restraining a kitten for its own good. "The enthusiasm of youth is charming, my dear. I'll be happy to tutor you in all those things. Along with Rosalie, of course."

Then she paused on the path and tilted her head, as if reflecting on some suddenly-realized truth. "Now that I think about it, Rose has had plenty of music lessons from me already. She can visit with Edgar while we play. Shall we say, every Thursday at this time?"

I thought of the great room with its gleaming well-tuned piano; the ebony clarinet and arched violins and the gold-leaf harp all lying there waiting for the eager touch of my untutored fingers. Of my breath warming their wooden or metal skins. Of the viola, a beautiful amber-hued instrument I wished to pull into my lap and cradle like a child. The long practice table glowing with beeswax, the curved, graceful chairs waiting to be arranged for an audience. No satisfactory words to express my longing for all these riches, or my joy at their proximity, came to me.

I took a deep breath and pushed Eddy's pained face from my

mind. Then nodded at Jane MacKenzie, understanding we'd just struck a bargain terribly complex and binding. An invisible contract the frowning clerk back at the Baltimore courthouse might not recognize or deign to seal, but one that nonetheless had just committed me—and the absent Eddy—to an arrangement based on mutual gain, and mutual guilt. A more compelling security than notarized paper could ever offer or uphold. And Eddy could not possibly disagree, for how else would he fulfill his promise to my mother—to educate me in all the subjects and skills and graces Neilson Poe had dangled before us a few months ago?

"Wonderful," said Mrs. MacKenzie, with a faint smile. We took another leisurely turn about the garden, then went back inside.

Eddy and I decided to take our time and walk home. As we strolled, he said, without looking at me, "What do you think of Mrs. Jane MacKenzie now?"

"She is so good and generous. And—well, a bit daunting too."

When he laughed, the tones rang back from the surrounding buildings more bitter and cynical than they had leaving his lips. "Yes. A difficult woman to say no to. And what about my sister?"

I swallowed. "Oh . . . Rosalie?"

"The only one I know of. How was your lesson with her, Sissy?"

"Well, we talked a while." I decided it best to embroider a bit. "She says I speak very well."

"Of course you do! Being naturally and in all ways a lady."

"And then . . . we played." I added quickly, "I'm going to learn your favorite song next week, Eddy. I've found the music for it, and—"

He stopped in the street and turned to face me. "Yes, I heard the playing. All those wrong notes were yours?"

"No." I looked away. "Not all of them."

"My God, how can *she* teach you anything?"

I hurried on, hoping to soothe him. "Mrs. MacKenzie will instruct me in instrumental music, and singing as well. While she does, you and Rosalie . . . well . . ."

His forehead creased like crumpled foolscap. He peered down into my face. "Yes?"

I told him of the arrangement concluded in the MacKenzie garden.

His eyes narrowed, his mouth slackened. Suddenly he resumed walking, his arm once more through mine, now dragging me along. "And this will be . . . *every* Thursday?"

I nodded miserably, wanting to plead, *Don't take it so badly.* "I think I'll love your sister, Eddy. How could I help it, she is so much like you!"

I meant she had the same large, deep eyes, the same soft, dark brown hair.

He stopped and released my arm abruptly. Teeth gritted, he said in a low, rough growl that scoured my ears, "*We are nothing alike.*"

For a terrified moment I thought he meant he and I were nothing alike; that we were opposites, or strangers. I reached for his arm again, but he shook me off as one might discourage a misbehaving pet. Passers-by glanced over and then hurried on their way, preoccupied with their own problems.

"I didn't mean *that*," I said, unwilling to give voice to words that would underline what all the whispers and taunts I'd grown up hearing had implied with smug cruelty. *Poor Rosalie. Poor unfortunate Rose. Ginny Clemm, your cousin is a dummy!* "I only meant—"

"We are *nothing* alike," he repeated, voice shaking. He shrank back when I held out a hand. Then turned his back to me and walked quickly away, ducking down Bank Street and disappearing before I could call out or run after him.

I stood on the sidewalk, tears crawling like snails down my hot face, not caring anymore who might be watching or judging. If Jane MacKenzie could see me now!

"Eddy, wait!" I cried. "You'll miss dinner. Mrs. Yarrington will be put out!"

He was already gone. I looked around, then wiped my nose quickly on one sleeve, too full of despair to bother fishing for a hanky. Why did he feel such disgust at his own sister? Why did he always look as if he wanted to shrink from her as he just had from me? She had her flaws, yes, but lack of devotion to him was not among them. He was very fastidious, but then so was Rose, in both dress and manners—or at least in her uncanny simulation of her mother's gracious demeanor. Was that it? Perhaps he saw her imitative skills as somehow unnatural, like a dog in ruffled collar dancing on its hind legs. Or perhaps he felt bitter that, despite all her shortcomings, his little sister had still gained the love of her adoptive parents, while his own foster father had coldly abandoned him. But that was not Rosalie's fault.

He had been so upset, I only hoped that if—no, *when* he returned, it would not be from one of the gin cribs or taverns lining Main Street, with smoke in his hair and on his person—and the harsh, sickly stink of liquor on his breath.

And that, by then, he would have forgiven me for bartering his Thursdays away, for my own gain.

A half hour later, at the long oak dining table, I lied through my teeth to Muddy and Mrs. Yarrington. "Eddy's had to return to the office." I fixed my gaze on the slice of bread I was buttering with great care. "A lost review, which Mr. White needs desperately."

"What a shame," they said in unison.

I shrugged and nodded as the other boarders chewed and sipped. As a child I'd been hopeless at making up stories, even to save myself from a whipping. Yet now lying seemed quite easy, a skill I'd been born to wield.

Still I could not eat much, though the table was set with a huge roast of beef steaming in its bloody juices, and baskets of hot, floury dinner rolls, and an oval china tureen of runner beans from the garden plot behind the boardinghouse, boiled with bacon. Later, when Mrs. Yarrington carried out a four-layer chocolate cake, the memory of those tiny iced vanilla confections in the MacKenzies' parlor backed up in my mouth like sweet sickly bile. I excused myself and rushed upstairs, barely making it to the washstand. I wiped my mouth, loosened my stays, and lay on the bed, wishing only to sleep.

When I opened my eyes again the room was dark, and Muddy lay snoring beside me. The sounds of someone moving about next door had roused me. My heart leaped and bucked, a rabbit escaping the hawk. So he *was* here, he'd come home, of course he wouldn't simply *leave* us.

A tap sounded at the connecting door. Muddy murmured, "Come in." She sounded so wide awake perhaps she hadn't been asleep after all.

"I wanted to say good night," Eddy muttered from the foot of the bed. Still in his jacket, though his tie was undone. He came around and kissed my mother's cheek, then moved to my side and pressed his mouth to mine—no warm, lingering kiss, but not a cold one either. His lips felt dry, slightly chapped, and he smelled faintly of segar smoke and Mrs. Yarrington's lavender soap. He did not explain, and I did not ask where he'd been. The faint illumination from the gaslight outside our window cast deep shadows on his face; he looked gaunt and hollow and tired.

"It's good to come home to such love and beauty," he whispered.

Then he withdrew. I heard the click of the latch of Mrs. Yarrington's much-vaunted connecting door. Then I lay back, fingers on my lips, which were still moist from the kiss. There'd been no taint of liquor on his breath. Perhaps that was why he'd kissed me full on the mouth, in front of my mother. So I would know that.

I looked over at the heavy paneled door, at the glass doorknob only ten feet away, and imagined getting up, tiptoeing over. Could see myself there already, turning the knob. And then—

But my mother lay beside me, breathing evenly. Too evenly. She was still awake, and in any case, what was I thinking? What would *he* think of a young woman who could even conceive such a bold act? My face flushed in the dark, cheeks burning as with fever. I lay back on the pillow, sick again—now with shame. He'd kissed me in that beguiling way only to prove he'd kept his word and hadn't imbibed a drop of spirits. That was all.

I lay as still and straight in the dark as a maiden under fairy-tale enchantment, my fingertips resting on that same spot on my lips. At last I stopped pondering and turned over to go back to sleep, thinking, *No, it was a real kiss.* Given freely, for all the reasons a man presses his lips to those of a woman he still loves.

· 9 ·

Eddy was rarely at home with us during the day, so when he returned in the afternoons I tried to be downstairs to greet him. I did so with all my heart, flinging my arms around his neck, whispering, "We both missed you today. But *I* missed you especially, my dear." He must understand he was loved and appreciated, if we expected him to stay away from the things that would mislead and hurt him.

Was I perhaps too enthusiastic though? One morning, as my mother and I were coming down a little later than usual to breakfast, I neared the door to the dining room and heard one of the other boarders saying, "Yes, but have you seen how she receives that young man in the evenings, Mrs. Y? With such unseemly forwardness!"

I could not make out the specifics of our landlady's reply and doubted Muddy, who was behind me, had heard either. I could've stepped off the thick wool runner onto the oak floor then, so the gossipmongers might hear our footsteps approaching. Instead I deliberately kept to the soft Turkey carpet and entered, hoping my face was still composed.

"... and that young Mr. Poe," the old man seated at the table was saying, as he speared a thick slice of salted ham. "Have you seen how he—"

"Good morning, Mr. Powell!" I said, loud and cheerful, nodding at the gray-haired fellow, and then at our landlady. "And to you too, Mrs. Yarrington."

He stammered a surprised greeting, and after a moment so did our landlady. Then she sat back and compressed her mouth into a lipless line. Muddy and I took our seats. I would not transform myself to mollify two gossipy old busybodies. Eddy and I were engaged. There was nothing improper in being young and in love. I would not be shamed like a child.

But one aspect of communal life I could not complain about was the table, loaded at every meal to the point of capsizing. Always three kinds of hot bread for breakfast, and salted fish, and covered dishes of baked or poached eggs, and those thick slices of salty Virginia ham which old Mr. Powell across was still greedily stuffing into his toothless mouth.

After breakfast Muddy and I would tidy our rooms, take care of the laundry, and hang our things up to dry near the open windows. I had no music or singing lessons this day. Perhaps my mother would wash my hair. She was old-fashioned, always insisting it was unhealthy to do so more than once a month, urging me instead to just brush it a hundred strokes morning and night. But I could not abide the itchy, greasy feel of dirty scalp. I loved the smell and feel of clean hair dried in the sun, in fresh air near the window, as if I too were a piece of fragrant hand-washed linen. As my long, heavy wet hair slowly dried, I felt my head becoming lighter, until it all but lifted to float above my shoulders. As if more than simple city dust and oil had been washed away into the basin with good lavender soap and water and vinegar.

I would never have said so aloud, but on those mornings I felt like a princess framed in the window of a castle tower. I was too afraid back then of sounding like a little girl. But it was true. I could sit in the sun and watch the carriages down in Capitol Square, or read one of Eddy's books, or a story or poem he'd just written. He alone seemed to value my advice. No one else ever really had. Not even Muddy.

Yes, I thought, helping myself to a thick mealy slice of bread, a generous scoop of fig preserves, and two large slices of ham. Today we'll wash my hair. It must be shining and sweet and clean, because tomorrow I will put on my new blue dress, and the new white hat with a real ladies' veil. Then, once I look my best, we'll all go downstairs to the same parlor Muddy and I had just walked past a few moments ago. Because today was the fifteenth of May. And Eddy had promised that on May sixteenth he would leave the *Messenger* office early. We would go to the Hustings Court for the City, taking his friend Tom Cleland along for a witness, and file a new marriage bond.

It was Muddy who'd decided the time was right to take our actual vows. The week before, after dinner, she'd sat us both down and said, "While it's all well and good to stay in a respectable house, and keep separate rooms, I fear this arrangement may provoke unseemly gossip if it goes on too long."

Eddy had frowned, looking thoughtful. "I suppose you're right. I get so busy with the work at the magazine I tend to forget such things."

I was on the very edge of my seat—which was the chair at Eddy's writing desk—and could stand it no longer. Again, my fate was being discussed and decided as if I were not even in the room. "So we are to be married at last?" I blurted out.

For a moment they both looked astonished, as if the landlady's cat had spoken. "I think it would be best," Muddy conceded at last, "to take *that* particular step."

She gave Eddy a long look I did not understand. Nor did I

care. The day I'd longed for was coming to pass. What else could matter?

And so on a mild May afternoon, after the bridegroom returned home to Mrs. Yarrington's establishment, we would finally, finally be married.

I lay awake the whole night before, barely able to restrain myself from sneaking over to the connecting door. To softly turn the glass knob, which seemed to wink at me tauntingly in the moonlight. To rush in, muffling my laughter. To leap on Eddy's bed and jump up and down on the feather mattress.

Beside me my mother slept on, breathing evenly, a soft snore escaping her lips from time to time. As if everything were as usual. As if tomorrow weren't to be the most momentous day in all our lives. But no, what was the matter with me? Imagine jumping around like a silly little girl playing in a Baltimore alley. Like a child skipping rope, on the eve of my wedding.

I sighed and turned over. No, no. Wouldn't do. I could no longer behave so in front of Eddy. I knew better than to do such things, from experience.

Just the week before, Rosalie and I had been strolling in the MacKenzies' garden. She'd picked up a skipping rope from a bench and, to my astonishment, began to turn and jump it, laughing and chanting a rhyme. I'd stood by at first, staring wide-eyed at the sight of a twenty-five-year-old woman hopping around a formal garden like a mischievous girl, her carefully curled hair bouncing about her ears. I watched first with amazement, then sourly as a disapproving schoolteacher. Though I was supposedly the pupil, while Rosalie—

But she was having so much fun! And so, when she tossed the rope to me, gasping and out of breath, I only hesitated a moment. Then I began to skip, singing my old favorite:

When I was a young girl, a young girl, a young girl,
When I was a young girl, how happy was I!

Of course it would be at that moment—as I was beginning to perspire though my shift, and Rosalie whooping and clapping, looking on like a delighted big sister—that Eddy arrived to fetch me home.

I hadn't noticed him at first. He stood at the curve of the smoothly raked pea-gravel path, his old top hat in hand. Stood very still, staring, with revulsion or disgust or perhaps even fear flickering across his face. At least he'd seemed to be staring at both of us. Perhaps he was only looking at Rosalie. As soon as I saw him I had dropped my hands, and let the rope slither limp as a dead snake to coil at my feet.

"I came to take you home." He'd turned away as if to go back alone.

Rosalie would never let him get away so smoothly. "Buddy!" she shrieked, though I had tried often to tactfully explain he did not care for that old nickname. She bounded up like a runaway lamb, skirts flying, and flung herself at him.

I set the coiled rope on the bench and waited, while Eddy muttered strained pleasantries and tried to gently disentangle himself.

After we left, he'd said very little to me all the way home. I thought I understood his distress. Eddy valued art, literature, learning—the finer things life had to offer. Yet he had no inheritance, no impressive First Family name, no automatic claim to being a gentleman at all. He owned only his talent, his carefully-presented demeanor, and of course that fine intellect. How disturbing to him, then, it must be to see that Rosalie—a product of the union between the same two parents—was so clearly not his intellectual equal. To know people might draw conclusions from this, make remarks and spread gossip that would take away the veneer of dignity that, for one in Eddy's straitened circumstances, at times grew so thin.

And yet I also did not understand. Did being an adult mean it was necessary to never have any innocent fun? To nevermore act or know the world as simply as a child does, merely because of Rosalie? Were we to grow dry and grim and dull together, the whole while acting as if we were eighty?

Now, waking on the morning of the sixteenth of May, I glanced out my bedroom window and saw only a perfect blue sky, a warm fair day. But of course! I was at last a bride. I wouldn't have cared if I looked outside and saw we'd been struck with a tornado, and half of Richmond was whirling away.

I sat up and glanced at the turned-back quilt, surprised to see Muddy was already gone. Perhaps she was down in the kitchen, baking. I hoped she and Mrs. Yarrington weren't bickering again. They hadn't been on good terms. Whatever she told Eddy, Muddy clearly disliked not being mistress of her own home, no matter how humble a place it might have to be. And Mrs. Yarrington did not care to hear suggestions of either economies or improvements. At least not, it seemed, when they sprang from someone else's imagination. Oh please, let them not be arguing—or rather, not speaking except to murmur a few cold, meaningless, unavoidable phrases: *Kindly pass the saltcellar. Thank you. Pardon me, please.*

Oh Lord, not today.

I stripped to my shift, poured water from the pitcher, and splashed my face, neck, and under my arms. I rubbed my skin with a towel until it shone pink. Then yanked on my dress, buttoned it crookedly, and had to begin again, fuming at the delay.

I raced out of our room but slowed halfway down the stairs, realizing how silly it would look for a bride to gallop. It was almost nine, so I'd missed breakfast. Someday I would have a little watch to pin to the bosom of my dress, like the small gold timepieces Rosalie and Mrs. MacKenzie always wore. How grown-up that would make me look! As grown as I knew I already was, and would be from now on, as Eddy's wife.

I stuck my head into the dining room. The table and sideboard had been cleared—except for one setting, with silver and coffee cup and saucer . . . and a single rosebud in a cut-glass vase. I walked over and saw a calling card propped there: Jane MacKenzie's. *For the beautiful young bride,* someone had written in a perfect copperplate hand, below her embossed name.

I smiled and sniffed the sweet, tea-and-honey scent of the yellow bud from her garden. Then slid into my chair and took a big slice from the napkin-wrapped basket. I slathered it with dense yellow butter and peach preserves, more thickly than I would've had anyone else been sitting there. I bolted the bread in seconds, washing every other bite down with strong black coffee from the pot on the sideboard. It was still, magically, warm. I felt I could eat the whole loaf and drink the whole pot, then call for more like a famished giant.

The door between kitchen and dining room was propped open. A murmur of voices drifted out. I pushed away from the table, suppressed an unladylike belch, and went to see who was inside.

Imagine my surprise to find my mother and Mrs. Yarrington

with heads close together, leaning over the scarred worktable like old friends. They were frosting an enormous, three-layered Lady Baltimore cake.

"Oh my," I said in a tiny voice, afraid to speak too loudly lest I break an enchantment. "Look at that."

"Here she is!" Mrs. Yarrington cried, and gave me a delighted smile, as if she and not Muddy had given birth to me.

"Good morning, Sissy." Muddy had a smear of icing on the end of her nose. "We've been cracking eggs and beating butter all morning. Our arms are about ready to fall off."

I could easily believe it. The hollow wreckage from many a hen's nest lay all about. So did two depleted sacks, one of flour and one of sugar.

"Oh, but it is very elegant! And so are you," I said, laughing. I picked up a dishcloth and carefully dabbed the icing off her face. Then found an old wooden spatula, and joined the party.

At a quarter to five I was up in our room again, finishing my preparations. I'd left the door ajar; now I heard someone walk in behind me. Certainly not Eddy; he was confined to the first floor. Mrs. Yarrington had caught him at the foot of the stairs, about to ascend, and ordered him back down. "It is mighty unlucky, sir, for a bridegroom to see his intended before the ceremony," she'd warned, hands on ample hips. Muddy had not contradicted her.

And though Eddy did not hold with superstition or even much with ordinary religion, he'd backed down and retreated into the parlor with his friend Tom Cleland.

So I assumed this must be Muddy, come to assist with buttons or hairpins. I picked up the stiff-brimmed white hat we'd purchased the week before at Hooper and Graff's Fashionable Virginia Clothing Store, opposite the Bell Tavern on Cary Street. It had a useless, sweet little veil and I'd loved it on sight. "Yes, a perfect bride's hat," Muddy had agreed then.

Still gazing at it in the mirror, I asked, "Could you help me pin this on straight?"

"I'll try," said an unfamiliar voice, higher pitched and much younger than my mother's. I whirled openmouthed to see a girl my own age, very small and thin, even shorter of stature than I. She stood just inside the doorway, staring.

"I didn't—who are you? If you please."

"I'm Jane Foster. My mother is a good friend of Mrs. Yarrington's. They went to school together, at least a donkey's age ago," she said, looking curiously around at our furnishings, at the bed strewn with the day dress and stockings I'd thrown there. "Mrs. Y told me to come up here and see how the bride was coming along in her toilette." She looked around again, as if searching for someone else in the room.

"Oh. Well, I'm Virginia Eliza Clemm." I felt a drop in my belly when I realized this was the last time I'd ever introduce myself so.

"We've just arrived to spend the day in Richmond." Jane came closer to stand on tiptoe and peer at my hat. "Are you getting dressed to go out and make a visit?"

I was speechless, then vexed she could not see immediately that I was a bride. "Of course not! I'm to be married this evening."

"Married?" Her eyes met mine in the mirror, and she frowned. "You mean, *you* are the bride? But—how old are you?"

"Fourteen." It was almost true. I *would* be, in three months.

Her eyes widened. "But I'm nearly fifteen, and my mother would never—" She pressed her lips together and stopped. "Well then, who's the lucky gentleman?"

I looked down and fiddled with a pile of hairpins, no longer wanting to see her expression in the mirror. "Mr. Edgar Poe," I muttered.

"Oh!" she said. "Why, I just met him in the parlor a moment ago. I thought he said—" She paused again.

"What?" I demanded, looking up to stare at her in the mirror again.

"Only that . . . do you know, Mr. Poe is my idea of absolute romantic male perfection," she murmured. "That soft dark hair. Those sad eyes. Well, I did notice the parlor was decked out with a pile of spring blossoms. But didn't realize you and he were . . . *you know.*"

"But what did he say?" I persisted. Though I'd grown used to being gainsaid by adults, I felt a growing unease that someone so near my own age also seemed shocked at the idea of my marrying Eddy. I decided she must be jealous.

Jane became suddenly interested in some sight or sound outside the door. "Oh, just that you were his cousin. But dear me, you're so young! And he seems a good bit older. So I, well, I naturally didn't think—oh, you know. Oh, I am so stupid! Really, it's nothing."

I decided not to respond to this nonsensical speech. "I need help with my hat," I repeated firmly, handing over a wicked mother-of-pearl-tipped pin borrowed from our landlady.

"A bride should wear a long trailing veil," Jane said, wrinkling her nose. "Not a little pouf of one stuck on a hat." She didn't move to take the pin.

How annoying the girl was! "I don't see why not," I huffed. "It's a lovely hat."

"Because," she said, as patiently as I might've replied to one of Rosalie's questions, "it's *traditional.*"

I gritted my teeth. "Well, we are not so old-fashioned here. And you may call me Mrs. Poe," I said stiffly. "At least, you may in a few minutes." I'd meant it as a rebuke, but it sounded so funny put that way. Our gazes met in the mirror again and we both burst out laughing.

"I'm sorry," she gasped, wiping her eyes. Just then my mother rushed in, saying breathlessly that the Reverend Mr. Converse had arrived, and for heaven's sake, hadn't I finished primping yet?

She led the way and Jane followed us down. My hands shook so I had to grip the railing. If I tried galloping now my knees would give way. People were standing in clusters below in the foyer. The two parlors were indeed a vision of spring flowers, as Jane Foster had reported. Someone had even rigged up a sweet little bower before the mantel in the larger one.

There the Reverend Amasa Converse waited, prayer book in hand. He too was a friend of Eddy's, and the editor of the *Southern Religious Telegraph*. The murmurs and greetings grew in volume as more guests came in, among them Mr. White, his lovely blond daughter Eliza on his arm. I wondered how she felt about attending Eddy's wedding. We'd been invited to their home for dinner, and the whole evening she'd giggled and tossed her curls and flirted with Eddy quite as shamelessly as Mary Starr had back in Baltimore. But she appeared jolly enough now, laughing and talking to Tom Cleland. They were followed by the foreman and apprentice from White's, and of course the other boarders, who by now comported themselves as if we were family. And perhaps in a way they were—even gossipy, ham-swilling Mr. Jabez Powell, who might stand in for a grizzled, dotty old grandfather.

The whole house seemed filled with Eddy's friends and coworkers and acquaintances. I had no friends of my own in Richmond yet, only people he'd introduced me to. But once married I was sure I'd find it easier to meet other ladies. To talk to them about the things married ladies discussed. I wasn't sure what those would be,

but I could learn. Hadn't Jane MacKenzie called me the brightest
pupil she'd had in many years?

Eddy was already standing before the fireplace, next to the
Reverend. My dark, handsome bridegroom. A "vision of romantic
male perfection," just as Jane Foster had sighed in my room. I forgave her as I looked at him. Indeed, how she must envy me! What
woman in all of Richmond would not? He was so tall and graceful,
his thick hair brushed back from his broad handsome brow.
The brow that concealed so much knowledge and talent it almost
frightened me. His black suit coat and trousers were immaculately
brushed and pressed, without a speck of lint or dust. His stock was
tied perfectly. Only a hint of snowy white collar punctuated all
that dark perfection.

Then I caught my own reflection in one of the tall mirrors that
flanked the fireplace. It took me a moment to realize that the young
girl who seemed to be playing dress-up in a fancy day gown was
indeed me. I felt deep dismay. Was this how Eddy saw me too? Im-
mature, callow, a mere playacting child? While he, in contrast—

No, I told myself firmly, looking away from the unsatisfactory
reflection. *I will allow no one to spoil this day. Not even me.*

I took a deep breath and let the love in his eyes draw me forward.

The ceremony was short and simple.

"Do you, Virginia Eliza Clemm, take Edgar Allan Poe to be
your lawful wedded husband? To honor and obey him in sickness
and in health, to cleave—"

Just then I glimpsed Jane Foster in one of the tall mirrors that
flanked the fireplace. She was up on tiptoe, straining to see over
other folks' shoulders, watching us. She might still be thinking a
real bride ought to wear a long, trailing veil. However, looking up
at the smiling face of my bridegroom, at his obvious joy and satis-

faction, I no longer cared what Jane or anyone else thought. All that mattered was that Eddy and I would now live as one, inseparable all the days of our long and happy lives.

Suddenly I noticed he and the minister were both peering at me anxiously.

"Yes, yes I do!" I blurted, then felt my cheeks tingle as suppressed laughter rippled through the parlor.

We adjourned to the other parlor to partake of wedding cake and sweet sherry. Mrs. Yarrington served the boarders and guests. I went back up to the room, mine and Muddy's, to change into my blue traveling dress—the same I'd worn on our sea journey from Baltimore to Richmond. I hung my new wedding frock on a hook, and changed into my traveling dress. Then dropped onto the rumpled bed, looked around me, and burst into tears.

Good Lord, what ailed me? I was the happy bride! But I stroked the quilt as one would a sympathetic cat, and thought, *I will never sleep in this bed again.* Or rather, I will never sleep in this bed again with my mother, as a girl. When Eddy and I return from Petersburg, I will be a lady, a wife, and sleep forevermore beside my husband. Muddy would move to Eddy's bachelor room. And then soon—very soon, I hoped—we'd take a house of our own, and Muddy would receive boarders to supplement our income. She'd already written to her brother, George Poe, for a hundred dollars to finance this venture, and miraculously he'd sent a draft for that sum. Muddy had not yet cashed it, but when we returned . . .

I dried my eyes on a corner of the quilt and smoothed my hair. What a sentimental fool! Had I expected to remain a child and yet still be a wife, to have it both ways? I snorted, then pushed up off the sagging mattress to go down again.

Jane Foster stood at the bottom of the stairs. She was holding an old carpet slipper—just one. When I stared at this worn, scuffed object, she laughed. "I borrowed it from Mrs. Y, to throw after you and the handsome Mr. Poe. When you depart in the carriage on your wedding trip."

"Oh," I said, wondering what this strange custom meant.

She leaned in close to my ear, so close her breath, fruity with wedding punch, stirred the fine escaping hairs which tickled my cheek. "Your traveling dress is very sweet," she whispered. Then pulled back, smiling.

I waited for her to add some barb, to tell me she'd had one just like it when she was ten. Instead she appeared awed as she eyed me up and down. As if now that I could sign "missus" in front of my name I'd taken an enormous leap past and she'd never catch up, no matter that she was a year older and always would be. As if I already knew some uncanny mystery, like the secret that lies beyond the grave.

What incredible fancies I have. How foolish my mind gets! Well, perhaps she *is* jealous, I thought. Perhaps she's fallen in love with Eddy. What a queer thing, to feel envied. I did not know how to behave or respond.

"Thank you," I said finally, nodding. Feeling like an actress in a play, a little girl in rouge and stays impersonating a woman. Then I went on across the foyer. My new husband was waiting at the door, and the carriage outside would drive us to the railroad depot, where we'd board for Petersburg. I stared at the darkly varnished cabriolet. Somehow it looked ominous, an evil conveyance sent by a demon lover in a fairy tale to carry me off to perdition, rather than what it was: a plain rented hack seen every day on the streets of Richmond. How I wished I could make myself the same age as Eddy now. Or that we were both really twenty-one, as was written on our marriage bond, sworn to by Thomas Cleland. Then such silly notions wouldn't even enter my head.

I looked again at Eddy, who stood by the wheel of the carriage, and felt even younger than almost fourteen. And a little frightened. I glanced over my shoulder for Muddy. But no one takes her mother on a honeymoon.

He put a hand under my elbow, helped me onto the seat, and climbed in after. Then, amid a lucky hail of old boots and worn-out ladies' slippers, and the ear-pinching snap of the driver's flicked whip, we lurched forward and clattered away as if pursued.

As we jolted through the streets of Richmond, heads turned. Little girls pointed and jumped and squealed, I suppose imagining themselves sitting in their own honeymoon carriage one day. Little boys shouted and chased us. Dogs howled. Eddy said ruefully, "Someone's tied a bunch of old shoes to the hack. And then there's the sign."

I frowned. "What sign?"

"On the back. It says JUST HITCHED."

"Oh my." I hadn't realized that part of being wed meant you were suddenly fare for public entertainment, a street fair to amuse strangers. I felt I'd been shoved out into the road clad only in chemise and petticoat. Eddy must've felt it too, for he sat stiffly upright at the opposite end of the bench. The driver, who'd shot off in a great hurry, took the time to drive us twice around Capitol Square with the most pertinacious of the young mob still in hot pursuit, before turning down Ninth toward the depot.

So that was how we journeyed, after our blessed joining together as one—with strained smiles and averted eyes, in stiff, self-conscious poses—rattling through Richmond's streets toward the train to Petersburg. Where I would finally shed this outgrown girl's life like an old, too-small skin, to make room to grow into another.

· 10 ·

Our locomotive was waiting at the station, puffing like a tea-kettle. Only three cars were attached, the first piled high with cotton bales to protect the second, the Ladies' Car, from flying sparks and hot cinders. The conductor paced the platform in a high hat and blue uniform, cupping a huge silver watch in his glove.

Unlike Jane Foster, he knew me as a bride at once. He looked us up and down and bowed slightly. "Going to flout company rules, folks, and seat you all in the second coach." He grinned at Eddy. "Already cleared it with the ladies aboard."

When we climbed up no one looked askance or asked how old I was. Of course, if a female is veiled and reasonably well filled out, it's hard to tell her exact age anyhow.

The conductor left after admonishing the groom, "Smoking is restricted to the gentlemen's car at the rear, sir." And Eddy, who had just been withdrawing one from the fistful of huge Cuban segars Tom Cleland had presented him with after the ceremony, sheepishly slid it back into his coat pocket. "Thank you for the information," he said. "In any case, I seldom smoke."

Two of the younger ladies giggled behind gloves. I pressed my lips tight and tried not to do so as well. It was difficult; he looked so abashed.

Despite the shielding bales, my first train ride was noisy and dirty. The rumbling and hissing of the Yankee engine, the loud, rhythmic clacking of the steel wheels over the rails, all made conversation nearly impossible. At first I felt afraid to move or speak, for I'd read of so many horrible accidents involving trains colliding, or rails coming up through the floors, or trains derailing after striking carriages or even cows on the tracks.

So we lurched and jolted along silently, swaying like roosting hens on our seats. Eddy gazed down at me at last, and I looked up, and we both smiled at the same time. I felt for that moment as I'd always read a bride *should* feel—radiant. But as we gazed on each other, the ladies too were gazing expectantly. They cooed and murmured and clucked, ruffling their feathery shawls so much like the three Orpington whites Muddy had once kept out back in Baltimore that we quickly turned from each other again in embarrassment, and stared at the passing scenery instead.

As we chugged away from the confines of Richmond, Eddy leaned over and shouted the names of landmarks into my ear: "Gamble's Hill. The State Armory, there. Oh—and the Tredegar Iron Works." By the time we stopped briefly at Manchester, on the opposite side of the James River, he'd fallen silent again, either out of names or out of breath. By then I was content to sit in drowsy peace, lulled by the regular clacking of the wheels, only needing to smile politely now and then at one of the ladies seated across. I felt exhausted by the events of the day, though the view was lovely: vast meadows of blue chicory set off by the twining green fingers and bright orange blossoms of trumpet vine, all perfumed by sweet, starry white jasmine. Two white-faced cows that lifted muzzles from their lush, grassy dinners to mildly regard us. A flock of blackbirds rising from a sunbaked cornfield. Every now and then, wisteria vines draped the gate posts of a cottage. Such sweet little peak-roofed, whitewashed places they pained my heart, and I had to glance away.

Sometimes smoke swirled around inside the car like an evil genie, stinging our eyes and making us cough. Whenever that happened Eddy bent to me with concern, until I smiled and shook my head to let him know I was fine. Then the ladies would cluck and twitter until I felt like stamping a foot to shoo them as I'd done with our chickens. During the rare moments the ladies weren't looking our way, I'd slide a hand along the seat behind the swell of my skirts, capture Eddy's fingers, and give a quick squeeze.

Petersburg lay twenty miles distant. "The trip should take a little over an hour," he informed me. "Unless there is some delay. Or"—he paused and I caught my breath—"a careless carriage or wandering cow."

"So we'll arrive in time for a late supper." I doubted I could eat a thing, after so many odd bites of ham, and the cake with sweet boiled icing, and a whole glass of sherry. Each time our swaying coach gave a sickening roll, I wished I'd eaten nothing at all.

We crossed the Appomattox after sunset and rolled into the Petersburg depot before full dark. As we descended from the car Eddy spotted our host, Hiram Haines, the cheerful, balding publisher of the *American Constellation*. What Mr. Haines's pate lacked in hair he made up for with enormous muttonchop whiskers. His smile pushed his cheeks up into twin red apples.

"Welcome to Petersburg, Mrs. Poe," he boomed. I looked at him blankly, then quickly bowed to hide my flaming face. He was the first to informally address me so. His wife, who sat smiling in their surrey, waved to us. Then her husband helped me up into the back with her, and we took off for our honeymoon abode, the Haineses' country house.

Hiram Haines asked whether the trip had tired me out.

"No, not a bit," I assured him. Then, fearing that sounded rude, added, "Well, perhaps a little."

Mrs. Haines laughed. "Pshaw. She can't possibly be tired, Mr. Haines. Remember back when we wed? There were no trains then so we rode all day long on a stagecoach to our honeymoon cottage. And yet I was not fatigued, not one little bit!"

I could think of nothing to say to that, or the images it evoked. So I merely nodded and murmured occasionally, and let Mrs. Haines do the talking. She seemed to prefer it that way.

Petersburg was a quiet town. A few lamps glowed in windows along the way, though from much bigger places than the sweet cottages I'd glimpsed earlier. In the dusk, the Haines house appeared even larger, and very well kept. A sweet musky perfume of jasmine drifted from the walled side garden. Inside, the rooms were lit with the warm golden glow of both candles and whale-oil lamps.

"Now, we only planned a quiet little supper," warned Mrs. Haines. "So you needn't dress up, my dear."

Dress? Oh dear. I was already wearing my best frock, next to the blue wedding gown I'd left in Richmond. I wondered if I could in all good manners simply retire to our room right then. "I'm not very hungry," I began. "Though it was kind of you to go to so much trouble."

"Nonsense," insisted Mrs. Haines. "You need to keep up your strength after a journey."

Suddenly a colored maidservant appeared to show us upstairs, while a tall, broad-shouldered manservant went out to retrieve our luggage: one small trunk I might've managed myself. We seemed to keep falling short of Petersburg standards.

Our room was spacious, with a very high ceiling. Its windows overlooked that dark, fragrant garden. I could just make out light-colored paths paved with crushed stone or marl, winding through neat flower beds and clipped shrubs. Against one wall stood a huge four-poster, with curtains to draw for privacy or against insects. So the mosquitoes must be nearly as bad here as in low, swampy Richmond.

The housemaid was slender, with a graceful neck; her hair smoothed back and pinned, posture as upright as any Richmond matron's. She wore a crisp apron over a gown made of finer wool than my day dress. I fiddled with my hat for a long time; I was unused to being waited on and hoped she might grow tired or bored and soon go away. Yet she lingered silently by the open door as if expecting orders. I could not even look her in the face, which was silly. But I didn't *feel* married yet. At last she did leave, closing the door softly, leaving on the washstand a basin of water and a pile of tiny starched white towels embroidered with our host's initials.

Eddy dropped onto the bed, then started and stood again. "Well, so we're here," he said, without looking at me.

"Yes, and I'm glad. I ought to wash off this soot and grime."

I took off my hat and gloves, then started to undo the top of my dress. My fingers froze on the second button. I hadn't grown up or shared a room with even a sister—only the faded story of little Virginia Maria, who'd died as a toddling baby the year before I was born. I'd never in my whole life undressed before anyone but my mother. I wasn't certain if it was proper, or expected, for a wife to disrobe before her husband. But then how . . . ?

Before I could glance up at Eddy for a sign, some unspoken guidance, I heard a latch softly click. I was alone again.

The quiet meal promised by Mrs. Haines turned out to be a second wedding feast: a steamship round of beef, a whole smoked ham, mounds of tiny roasted red potatoes, turnip greens swim-

ming in pot liquor, boiled snap beans, squares of buttery corn-
bread and browned dinner rolls in separate covered baskets.

The men talked of the publishing business and the people they
knew between them who were in it. Mrs. Haines asked me if we
would live in Richmond when we returned.

"Oh yes," I said. "My husband—" I hesitated at this unfamiliar
phrase, then plunged on. "My husband has a position there with a
magazine."

"Oh, that's nice. And you will keep the house, while he does
work much like my husband's."

"Yes, I suppose so. When I'm not taking lessons in music and
voice."

She frowned. "Lessons? But you are married now. That sort of
thing must fall by the wayside when you have a home and family."

I looked at my plate. "Oh, really? But I had thought—"

She smiled and patted my arm. "You'll see, my dear. You'll be so
busy, there won't be a spare moment to think about music and . . .
whatever it was you mentioned."

What did she mean? But I could not imagine contradicting
such a dignified older lady, who was also our gracious hostess. I fell
silent again, listening to a dull pulsing in my ears that seemed to
accompany a growing pain in both temples. I turned my head and
coughed into my palm.

Mrs. Haines did not remark on my silence. Instead she said, "The
best remedy for that is three bulbs of Indian turnip, cut up and left
to pickle in a quart bottle of good whiskey. I'll write it down for you,
my dear."

She prattled on about home remedies as I cast about for something to say that would not make me sound like an inexperienced
fool. Nothing came to mind.

She passed me the basket of dinner rolls again. "I hope these are fresh enough. They were baked this morning, before it got too warm."

"Oh, they're excellent," I assured her, relieved to have the proper response, or any sensible answer at all. Indeed, they were—light and buttery yet crisply browned at the edges, even better than my mother's and Mrs. Yarrington's, a thing I would not have previously credited.

"I can give you the receipt," she said archly, as if offering treasure.

"Oh, I never bake," I said without thinking. "My mother does that."

She stared a moment, then burst out laughing. "Oh, my dear," she gasped, when she had her breath back, "you'll find a number of things change after one marries."

I looked down at my lap and pretended to laugh too, but she'd already turned away to her husband and Eddy, to repeat our conversation to them word for word.

She didn't understand. Muddy would be with us, still doing the things she loved and insisted on doing. Neither of us would dream of living anywhere without the dearest mother in the world. I did not attempt to explain all this, however. No doubt I would only sound more foolish, and in any case, where would I begin?

After dinner we sat out on the piazza, the men smoking the wedding segars. It was pleasant, even with the fumes from the huge Cubano Robustos—which Eddy had told me had cost a shocking fifteen cents a piece. To me they looked disturbingly like dried animal droppings, and smelled only a little better. After an hour or so, a large clock slowly struck ten deep within the house. Mrs. Haines called for lights out and we all went up the stairs. Eddy, who'd been so jovial and charming, fell quiet. He silently took my arm and we ascended the wide staircase, which we could walk side by side.

He paused at the landing. "I've left something downstairs. You go ahead, Sissy. I'll join you in a moment."

My pulse jumped. I took this to be some cryptic married code. He must mean I was to get ready—for bed with him, the place one shared with a husband—and then he would join me there, in our curtained bower. So this is how it is done, I thought. In fairy tales you never learned what happened *after* the wedding.

I sleepwalked the rest of the way up, and undressed quickly, not knowing how much time remained to prepare. Pulling off everything, even my chemise, hoping Eddy did not return right in the middle of this graceless, frantic disrobing. I hung my clothes on brass hooks in a huge walnut wardrobe, then yanked over my head the new nightgown Muddy had sewn. In the pier glass set back in one dim corner, the bit of lace around neck and cuffs looked very grown-up.

I drew back quilt and coverlet and slid between cool white sheets which felt new and freshly pressed. A strange tingling had replaced the lurch and leap in my stomach, and I pressed both hands there to still it. But the feeling seemed lower, not in my belly at all. "Oh Moses," I whispered, worried I was about to be embarrassingly ill and would need to run to the privy. And where was that? Oh Lord, was there at least a pot under the bed?

But really, this was a pleasant feeling, not the sickening cramp of watery bowels or the monthly flow I'd experienced only a few times as yet. So I sighed and lay back, folding my hands gracefully on top of the covers.

I lay and waited, but Eddy did not come. For a while I watched the single whale-oil lamp I'd left burning low. It was under siege by

foolish winged insects who flung themselves bodily at the flame. I
began to feel sleepy, then would jerk awake; how could anyone sleep
through her wedding night, before the bridegroom arrived? What a
silly story *that* would make to amuse the Haineses tomorrow morning. I resolved not to tell even Eddy.

I must've dozed off for a while, because I jerked awake as the
feather tester sagged and a weight eased onto it. I heard soft breathing and smelled bay rum and stale segar smoke.

"Eddy?" I whispered and touched his arm.

He started. "Oh! Yes, it's me."

I giggled and rolled over, right up against him. He held very
still; perhaps he was nervous too. But no, surely not. He was older
and a male. I rose on one elbow, leaned over, and planted a kiss on
his lips. "We're alone, finally. I was running out of things to think
of to keep me awake," I whispered.

He said, *"Virginia,"* in such a peremptory tone that I froze.

"What?" Shouldn't he take me in his arms now? To show his
love for me, since from this day on it was sanctioned, wedded bliss.

He sighed. "I don't quite know how to say this."

My heart speeded up to the tripping pace of a steam-powered
piston. My mouth went so dry I couldn't speak. He was about to
reveal—what? That we'd made a mistake, or he found me repul-
sive, or—

"I love you very much," he whispered.

I pressed against him again. "Yes?"

"Don't," he said sharply, and I drew back, confused. "I mean,
you can't do that—not yet," he added.

I frowned. "But now we are wed, so—"

"I promised your mother."

I sat up, though it was so dark I could not read his expression.
"Promised her what?"

"She agreed to the wedding on the condition you remain . . . I mean, that I as yet refrain from—"

My mother? What agreement? "That you refrain from *what*?"

"That I—that we—refrain from those . . . normal relations between husband and wife, until such time as—"

"*What?*" I gasped, for in all the waiting and then our frenzied preparations, and my mother's obvious excitement, it had never occurred to me there might still be obstacles, or complications, to my becoming fully a woman and wife. "What, you mean—*never*?"

Stupidly, I began to cry.

"Oh, my dear." He took me in his arms. "Please don't."

But I did, sobbing even louder. What now of my great plan for my life: to become a grown woman, have my own house, become the mistress of my fate, and learn more music, to sing and perform someday? In my mind it had all seemed to hinge on one secret act, a thing of which I was not totally ignorant but not actually clear as to the specific details.

"Shh, hush," he said, as if to an inconsolable child. At his tone and those words I went rigid with anger, for I thought he was only worried the Haineses would hear and assume . . . whatever they'd assume.

"Not forever, no," he whispered, and I took in a deep shuddering breath. My soft bosom, which so often got in my way, was pressed up against his firm, muscular chest. The hard chest of an athlete, for when Eddy was only fifteen he had swum six miles up the James River against the current, a feat never yet equaled by anyone. Well, he was not behaving like some brave adventurer now. He swallowed, and his throat clicked.

"But *she* isn't *here*," I hissed, wishing I could see his face, his eyes, in the dark.

"A gentleman doesn't go back on his word."

"How long, then?" I let a hand rest on his chest. Thus I discovered he was not still wearing all his clothing, as I'd assumed, but only a thin cotton nightshirt. I shifted one leg tentatively and my bare foot encountered a naked shin—his.

A sharp intake of breath; his or mine, or both together.

"Well . . ." he began, then seemed unable to go on.

I tapped his chest. "Are you—unclothed? I mean, beneath this."

"What? Well, yes I am." He began to draw away.

I slipped both arms around his neck and hung on. "No, wait. So we're to sleep in the same bed for some time yet, perhaps years. But to remain as—as we are now?" I meant chaste, or virginal, but it was said men were different and not subject to the same rules. It struck me that I didn't know if he'd ever been with a woman in *that* way. Perhaps if he had, he found me wanting now, and that was what this conversation was really all about.

I felt him shake his head. "No, not after this. It's just that—I couldn't very well ask the Haineses to provide us with separate accommodations on our wedding night! When we return I'll sleep in my room, and you and Muddy will share your same bed. As we have done up till now."

I felt a true, white-hot rage igniting in my breast. How dare my mother pull the strings to make us dance like marionettes, senseless wooden puppets, taking only the steps she preferred? If she hadn't wanted me to be married, why had she agreed to it, or signed that paper attesting to our false ages?

I tried to pull his face down to mine, for I felt some vague instinct stirring too. If I could just press my soft, curved body against his own, which felt so very much the opposite, he must surely change his mind.

But Eddy fended me off with one hand while gently disengaging mine from his neck with the other. Then carefully but firmly he slid me to my side of the bed. As he was accomplishing this maneuver, I felt something odd. A hard protrusion which nudged my hip and thigh—something of *him*, hidden under the nightshirt. I wanted very much to look, to ask about it. But by now I understood that my husband—if he could truly be called that—was not really on my side. He had no more intention of assisting me into womanhood than did my mother. Or at least not enough conviction, enough love and desire, to sway him to do so. I might as well still be that eight-year-old he'd met in a homely Baltimore parlor. The one who'd skipped in singing, then rushed out again to join her little friends, to weave a blossom band from dandelion flowers. A false bride's crown.

I lay on the far edge of the feather tick, fists clenched, rigid with thwarted fury. But what could I *do*? Against two conspiring adults, nothing. Nothing, except . . . endure. Find and keep my resolve. Suffer, if need be. In that, at least, they could not stop me. In that, at least, I could be a woman.

Eddy began to breathe regularly, then to snore. While I stared into the gloom of our honeymoon chamber, and it all—the walls, the pictures, the wardrobe and washstand—gradually seemed to grow fainter, darker, less than real. Until finally I too slipped away. From hard, dry-eyed anger into an equally hard sleep, inhabiting dreams full of shipwrecks and sea monsters, and cruel-beaked birds, and stone castles ringed by forests of bloodred roses with black, wicked thorns.

· 11 ·

We returned to Richmond a week later, welcomed by Muddy's enfolding arms. I stood in the front room and let her embrace me, for by then my anger had cooled.

It simmered up, though, when I saw her talking alone to Eddy. Was she asking about our so-called nuptial night? Perhaps she wanted his assurances I was still the same innocent maiden she'd sent away on that false honeymoon. I gritted my teeth and thought of several clever, mysterious replies to make if she asked anything of me—but of course she did not. Children should be seen and controlled, I thought bitterly. But never truly heard.

Thomas White made a new proposition to Eddy on our return. The editor of the *Messenger* wished to rent out a new house he'd purchased on Seventh Street.

"Mr. White wants to board himself and his family there, with us," Eddy said. This arrangement would ensure the comforts of his family, and assist with the finances of ours.

Eddy was so excited he'd already agreed, and gone out and purchased two four-poster beds, one large and one small, as well as chairs, a settee, and an oak table, all on credit. Only to find, when we examined the premises next day, the house was barely large enough for one family.

"We must move in as agreed," Eddy said.

My mother protested, "But it's all cost now, and no income."

"Yes, the moneymaking scheme is set aside for now. But," he reminded her, "a gentleman's agreement is binding."

How well I knew it by then! So we kept our word, leaving my mother without paying guests, and Eddy with a debt of two hundred dollars for the furniture.

This was not the cottage of my dreams, but still our own house. Every morning my mother and I set out down Main Street to the Old Market. Sometimes as we walked I wondered what passers-by thought of us: Muddy tall and broad, sturdily handsome, dignified in widow's black, with a wicker market basket on one arm and her other arm linked with mine, a round-faced, smiling girl. But surely I no longer appeared merely that? No one really knew what exactly had transpired—or had not—on our wedding night.

Once when I sighed deeply, thinking of this, Muddy asked, "What is it?"

"Nothing. Nothing at all." And I turned away, hoping she'd wonder, even worry.

At least I could no longer be addressed by acquaintances and shopkeepers as "Miss Clemm," or "Little Virginia," but only as "Mrs. Poe." I reveled in this inarguable change, at least, and felt an inch taller. I cast about for other ways to mark out my new station.

The following week I got my own basket and carried it hooked around my elbow as married women did. I no longer clung to Muddy's arm or stared at the sights and chattered to her. Instead I swished my skirts along sedately—in her company, but no longer her little girl. Now and then she looked down and something— doubt, concern—flickered across her broad face, like the quick- winged shadows of black ducks skimming an autumn pond. Did she wonder whether Eddy had truly kept their bargain? A lady would never question his word. Still, perhaps she wondered how *much* of a woman I was now. Well, she'd not bothered to consult me, so now she could not ask.

That shadow crossed her features again, then was gone like wingtips brushing water. I smiled slowly, as if I had a sweet, thrilling secret. Then picked up an apple from a grocer's stall, and turned away, humming.

That fall Eddy's "Berenice" and "Morella" were published in the *Messenger,* so we had a little more to live on. The first story was about a man who falls in love with his cousin—or rather, her beautiful white *teeth.* Instead of cutting a lock of hair to mourn over, he opens her casket after she dies to pry out those beautiful molars and incisors and bicuspids he'd worshiped, for a keepsake. In the other tale, a powerful man marries a beautiful, learned young lady who dies after giving birth to their daughter.

"It is so—very well done," I'd murmured as I handed back the manuscript. "I see no flaws in the execution." But I thought, *Why the cousin, why the mother, why the daughter?* "And yet," I added, "you quite often write of beautiful young women who die."

He smiled and pulled me onto his lap. "My dear little wife," he said, stroking my hair, playing with the curling ends. "The only truly fit subject for poetry is the death of a beautiful woman. Don't you see? Nothing is more sad, more tragic, yet so filled with ethereal grace."

He'd said *tragic* and *sad,* yet kept smiling. What thoughts were turning beneath that fine, pale forehead? "But these are stories, not poems," I pointed out.

"True. But my goal is to make each one as perfect as the best poetry. To evoke the same strong emotions from readers, even as I recount a thrilling or ghastly event."

Perhaps I still looked doubtful, for he went on. "To be widely read, a writer must grab the mob by the nose."

"And its nose is . . . its imagination?" I ventured.

He laughed with delight. "Yes, such as that may be. Longfellow has his little professorship, Fenimore Cooper his European audience. But I intend to be the first writer to make my living in America by pen alone. Do you see?"

I looked down at those long, beautiful, ink-stained fingers, and remembered the cruel, bloody end of Henry Poe. *How can death be full of ethereal grace? Sad, tragic—yes. Certainly grotesque. But how can it be pretty?* It sometimes seemed to me God gave us things only to snatch them away. Eddy's mother, my own father, the baby girl who'd come before me—the sister I'd never gotten to meet. Then Granny Poe, and Eddy's brother, Henry. Sickness and death were horrors we all must endure eventually. But why did Eddy so often smile when he talked about them?

"Yes, I suppose I see. But the women in your stories . . ."

He lifted my chin to gaze at me again. "What about them?"

"Your mother died before your eyes when you were scarcely two."

He sighed. "I was told about the event so many times, I feel I recall it. Yet the scene I see is a beautiful young actress lying pale and still, the star of a tragedy—gracefully bidding her friends and three small children farewell."

Imagine watching Muddy lie coughing herself into death. Fear squeezed my throat like a hard hand. She was *my* mother, mine. What would I do if *she* was taken?

Each time I thought of the young Eddy, my love and tenderness grew so great I wished to fly back in time and prevent him from being orphaned twice, first by the death of Eliza Poe, then the passing of his foster mother, Frances Allan, who had also loved him. And both had succumbed to consumption.

Then John Allan, who'd only wanted some stout, hearty, ledger-minded heir to take over his business, had treated him brutally. Calling him a beggar, the son of players. Sending him off with too little money to pay tuition at the University, then blaming him for running up debts. Dangling adoption like a tidbit before a starving hound, then snatching it away. Eddy had grown up with fine clothing, books, good teachers. He'd been schooled in England for six years; a most beautiful child, my mother had told me. "What *do* you recall clearly?" I asked.

"That when I was five or six, my father—" He stopped himself in correction. "My *foster* father would lift me onto the table at dinner parties, and bid me recite a dramatic poem or a portion of Shakespeare. When I performed like a trained pet he loved me well enough."

We'd always been poor. But Eddy had not. No wonder deprivations small and large stung and humiliated him. And if the women he'd loved had all died young, painfully and tragically, perhaps all he could do now for comfort was to change history on paper. To make a pretty, romantic notion of it.

Of course, he had me, and I was young and plump and healthy. We had our whole lives ahead. Our children would not know cruelty as Eddy had, nor poverty as I had. Someday, we would live in that little rose-covered cottage, and be happy forevermore.

That month Jane MacKenzie began teaching me the violin. She first had me stand and hold the instrument under my chin, to get used to the feel. I'd done so facing the long mirror in one corner, while she stood behind me.

"You have a slight tendency to slump, my dear," she said, pulling my shoulders back.

"Sorry," I had mumbled. It was my bosoms, which were heavy and sometimes in the way.

Today she was showing me simple fingering. "There! Practice that while I go see to something for a moment, please."

I tried, but each finger seemed to have a mind of its own. At last I grew impatient and set the violin down. To occupy myself until her return I looked through the books and sheet music piled on the practice table. There were Irish and Scottish works; songs not simply mourning death and lost loves, but about marrying, or having your sweetheart stolen away, and even comic ballads about playing tricks on people. These surely weren't opera. Madame Frieda would turn up her nose, but I liked their simple, natural rhythms.

When Mrs. MacKenzie came back I picked up the violin again and played a few bars, with less shrieking and scraping than the lesson before. "Might we play some Irish ballads, when I get a bit more skill? I like the way they are composed."

"Why is that, dear?" she asked.

"They seem natural and . . . and cheerful. I wonder if I can ever capture that with the violin. I fear I'm not very good at bowing."

She smiled. "Well, you've only begun."

I lowered the instrument again and perched the bow on the stand. "Yes, but it seems so choppy when I play, not at all like the piano. Couldn't a composer write so the music comes out with a more . . . more graceful sound?"

Her eyebrows rose. "Why? Are you planning to compose music, Virginia?"

I hadn't been thinking of that, but now I wondered if it might be possible. I could already read music, I had a good ear. I sometimes helped Eddy to find a better word or phrase in his stories.

"Because if you are, well." She laughed softly. "A few ladies have written novels, it's true. And poetry. But our sex, I fear, has very little gift for composing."

"Oh. I see," I said.

She handed me the bow, signaling our talk was at an end. I went back to work obediently, sawing away again at the poor wooden box. Perhaps violin would not turn out to be one of my talents. And though the idea of writing music was novel, appealing, perhaps that too was not to be. But if I were ever to attempt it, I knew one thing already: My song would not feature a beautiful woman lying helpless at Death's door.

In the end, we could not keep the house.

It did seem a cruel blow at first, for Eddy told me that in the previous twelve months he had increased the circulation of the *Southern Literary Messenger* from seven hundred subscribers to nearly fifty-five hundred. Yes, sometimes he was prone to exaggeration, but his salary had risen over the same period to almost twenty dollars a week. Surely he'd already made Mr. White rich. Yet despite this great success under Eddy's hand, while he gladly gave my husband more work, White refused to relinquish any authority. He denied him even the simple title of editor. Eddy's honest critical reviews took apart the pretensions of bad writers, and he composed these so wittily many purchased the magazine solely to enjoy the resulting commotion. "Tomahawking" was what Eddy called this unvarnished criticism.

At his cluttered office desk he chose articles, poems, and stories of the first quality, only to be overruled by White when the owner wished to strike a more sentimental tone, or flatter some wealthy amateur poetess. At last, in despair and outrage, Eddy turned in his resignation.

"The drudgery was excessive," he told me when he came home early that November afternoon, shaken but defiant, and sank into our tattered armchair. "It is 1836—almost 1837! I work for a rich man who owns a magazine and much else besides, yet my salary is contemptible. All I could gain from employment there was my reputation, and I've secured that."

Muddy turned away, back to the kitchen, with no words of sympathy, but none of complaint or criticism either. Later I discovered her weeping in the pantry as if someone had died. But I did not cry. For I knew a thing she did not: Eddy was writing letters to various important men in Washington. Recalling to them the sacrifices of our illustrious grandfather, David Poe. He was filing a claim on Muddy's behalf, to regain the fortune General Poe had so trustingly lent to Maryland to finance the new government and pay Lafayette's troops. The recovery of this capital was to be his great Christmas gift to her. When he had gotten back that forty thousand dollars, even shared out among the various cousins it meant we'd never want again. Eddy could write all day if he liked, or start his own, superior magazine.

But the official reply a few weeks later informed us that our grandmother Elizabeth had died before the act allowing such reimbursement to patriotic old benefactors had been put into effect. We had no claim. Eddy was crushed. We did not even tell Muddy about his efforts then; it seemed too cruel.

There was no December issue of the *Messenger*. White pleaded poverty, illness, and a printers' strike. But the January 1837 issue announced, in very small type:

> Mr. Poe's attention being called in another direction, he will
> decline with the present number the Editorial duties of the
> 'Messenger.' His critical notices for this month end with Pro-
> fessor Anthon's Cicero—what follows is from another hand.
> With the best wishes to the Magazine, and its few foes as
> well as its many friends, he is now desirous of bidding all
> parties a peaceable farewell.

Eddy quickly started a novel, a romance called *The Narrative of Arthur Gordon Pym of Nantucket.* The pages I'd read so far contained mutiny, shipwreck, famine, and massacre. This longer work would make his reputation, I was sure. Laboring like a navvy for Mr. White every day, he would never have managed to write it. But the most exciting development was that we were leaving what Eddy called "the backwater village of Richmond," and moving north to New York City.

Poor Muddy looked bewildered by this news. "We left Baltimore, and now Richmond too? But—it is become our home."

I stroked her arm and leaned my head against her shoulder. "Yes, that is just the problem. We've never lived anywhere but the South. Eddy says that's why we must leave. There are so many opportunities in New York. It's the heart of the publishing world. He'll be offered a job there worthy of him at last."

And Manhattan held opera houses and recital halls and music schools and—

Muddy sighed. "I suppose," she murmured. "But how?"

"He has many connections there, important people he's corresponded with through the magazine. They all admire his work." One New York editor had recently written to him, saying, "I wish you to fall in with your broad-axe amidst this miserable literary trash which surrounds us." The literary world also had a second beating heart in Boston, but after all the shots Eddy had fired across the poetic bows of Longfellow and other members of the private club of New England writers, he'd not be welcome there to anything more friendly than tar and feathers.

At the thought of regular employment and improved wages, Muddy brightened. So over the next few weeks we sold our furniture, paid off what debts we could, bade relatives and friends goodbye, and prepared to depart in late February.

· 12 ·

The cold.

That was the first thing I noticed when we arrived that February. A perpetual frigid wind ripped down the broad main way like a crushing wave bent on flattening anyone who dared stand before it. As a consequence, Manhattanites always walked very quickly and at a forward slant, as if battling their way up a mountainside. Nothing was safe from the winds that barreled down the city's narrow building-lined canyons and converged at their points. Every item of apparel not buttoned, clasped, buckled, or tied down soared skyward on the updrafts.

We searched for lodgings in the less expensive Village. This meant much trudging while gazing up at towering three- and four-story architecture until our necks creaked. We finally happened on a shabby but inexpensive place on the corner of Sixth and Waverly. When we went up to view the rooms, we were offered the sharing of one floor with a Scotsman named William Gowans.

Muddy looked about doubtfully. "Hmm . . . Scots-Irish. And what's your trade, sir?"

The bearded, red-haired man smiled. "I've been gardener, stonecutter, stevedore, newsboy, and store clerk."

Muddy's eyebrows rose with each job title, until I thought I would have to tactfully intervene. Eddy had wandered across the room to a tall shelf and stood with his back to us, nose buried in a book.

"But most recently, madam," said Gowans, his faint burr buzzing, "I've moved my book peddling from our city's fair streets to the auction and commission trade at Long Room. That's at 169 Bloomingdale, the broad main way."

Behind me, Eddy snapped the volume shut. "A bookstore?"

"Seems a good omen, doesn't it," I said, taking my mother's arm and steering her toward the hall. "Let's look over the rest of the floor, Muddy."

As we were inspecting the rooms, wondering how much it would cost to coal the little stove in the corner, Eddy burst in, ecstatic.

"Do you like it?" I asked, meaning the cramped little suite.

He laughed. "Like it? Gowans just said he doesn't encourage people to browse in his store and handle the books. But *I'm* to come in when I like, and read whatever I like. And who but important literary men frequent a good bookshop!"

"I'll tell the landlord we'll take it," said Muddy, with only a little resignation.

Despite Gowans' fine phrasing, the streets of our adopted city turned out to be anything but fair. Downtown surged a malodorous crush of hawkers, hucksters, rude white pedestrians, impudent dark ones, and pushcarts heaped with fish. Shining mounds of oysters packed in seaweed emitted the same salty, marshy scent as the harbor of my childhood. Then, for a moment, the city smelled like home.

But New York was not as amiable as Baltimore or even Richmond. The wind was freezing, the food more varied but also much dearer. The walkways were treacherous with dirt, potholes, rain puddles, trash, shining tobacco slicks, and occasional lumpier brown shapes I did not care to identify. Whole fleets of carriages and hacks rumbled past as one walked along, each throwing up a muddy bow wave to foul and drench the stoutest wool skirt in a moment.

The shops and cafés smelled of roasted beef and boiled coffee, and less deliciously of stale segar smoke, pickled eggs, and the sharp oniony sweat exhaled from the pores and dirty clothes of gin-swigging laborers. Above those seething streets, beyond the roofs of the buildings, our communal ceiling of cast-iron winter sky only changed when it yielded to sudden flurries of wet, cold snow which was instantly churned into freezing cakes of mud for us to skate on. Then the sky disappeared altogether, as if we inhabited a snow globe shaken for amusement by a bored, peevish god.

Against this cruel Northern cold Muddy seemed impervious, but my old wool shawl didn't keep out the wind. The afternoon Eddy realized this, he chafed my blue-tipped fingers, then dragged off his old West Point greatcoat and slung it about my shoulders. The boiled wool smelled of him—soap, leather, tobacco—and the warmth was luxurious. But then he had only a thin sack coat himself. And I hated the pitying or scornful glances better-dressed pedestrians threw our way, as if to a street denizen in cast-off rags and tattered horse blankets. A beggar, a Little Match Girl, a real-life Cinderella. So I made him take the coat back.

"But you're still cold," he protested. "And we're many blocks from home."

I shrugged, holding back the next shiver with sheer will. "It's too heavy. It tires me out just to carry all that weight."

So he pulled the coat back on, then threw an arm around my shoulders and hugged me to him, as if that could shield me from

the blasts that raced between the buildings. And under this shel-
tering embrace and loving gaze, I did feel warmer.

When we returned home I coughed for a long while. Even sitting
beside our glowing little stove I still felt the cold, windy fingers that
had slapped and numbed my face, and pushed down my throat,
probing at my lungs and pummeling my ribs, making it suddenly
hard to do such a simple thing—to draw in a decent breath.

Eddy meant to be lucky in New York, even though Granny Poe
had often bemoaned the lack of that quality in the Poe men. Had
she seen the future, or cursed us by predicting it? We'd met Mr.
Gowans and that had seemed fortunate. Especially when he invited Eddy to a dinner at the City Hotel, held in honor of distinguished authors by the city's booksellers.

"Washington Irving will attend," Eddy told me breathlessly.
"And William Cullen Bryant, and Halleck and Inman."

"And you," I added. Finally my husband would move in the
company of his equals.

He smiled wryly. "Oh yes, I'll have my own plate. And a fork
and knife and napkin. But I'm not accepted as one of their company. Especially by the Bostonians."

"But you will be. No one can know you or read your work, and
not see the genius there."

He pulled me onto his lap and called me his dear little wifey.
Normally I enjoyed such embraces. But he was humoring me,
though all I'd said was true. And I didn't want to be kissed and
petted and laughed at; I wanted to help. To be of use in some way.
Of course I could not work at a man's job to help support us. I did
have talent, but the decorative sort. The kind meant for singing
and playing, entertaining dinner guests in parlors. I was no opera

singer, as Madame Frieda had judged, and could not perform in a tavern or saloon. Music schools and tutors and concert halls abounded in New York, but we were too poor as yet to afford lessons. For now I spent my days helping Muddy keep house, marketing, cooking, and tending a few pots of flowers I'd set on the sill of our room. When the weather warmed I planned to plant them outside near the narrow alley beside our building. I had sweet William and petunias and even a tiny rosebush I'd found half buried in a pile of leaves down the street. It amazed me, the good things people threw away.

But my plan was already laid. When Eddy made some money, I would have the means to build on the foundation given me by Madame Frieda and Jane MacKenzie, and avail myself of more instruction. Soon; but not while we were still so poor even food was almost too dear. In the meantime, I practiced my scales as I worked—when the soot and smoke that filtered even inside was not thick enough to set me coughing.

Eddy went to the authors' dinner the following week. He spoke to other writers, and a number of editors and publishers. Many were familiar with his critical writings. A few even took him aside and directed him, saying he might find work at this magazine or that newspaper. But 1837 was a bad year, especially for banks. And thanks to uncertain finances and what Eddy explained was bad management, many magazines stopped publishing. The worst blow was the death of *The New York Review,* edited by his friend and supporter Dr. Charles Anthon. Eddy had pinned his brightest hopes on that publication.

In the end, it turned out to be not a good omen that New York literary men knew his work from the *Messenger.* He'd tomahawked some authors they all held dear. His most grievous fault had been to criticize a novel called *Norman Leslie,* by Theodore Fay, the editor of *The New-York Mirror*. Now Fay's fellow newspapermen stood by him, and the name Edgar Poe opened no doors in Gotham.

When he was not pounding the pavement and being turned away from one office or another, Eddy was home writing stories.

"More tales about beautiful young ladies who die?" I asked, tugging on a corner of one page, trying to pull it out to read.

He slid the manuscript out of reach. "When it's ready, your wise and beautiful eyes will be first to gaze on it." I must've looked disappointed, for he squeezed my hand, his quill dripping ink across the table and onto my cuff. No matter. It had many fellow stains for company.

My mother was still determined to take in paying guests, but we needed more space for that. So in April we moved from Sixth and Waverly to 113½ Carmine Street, near St. John's Church. It was an old street with leafy oaks, beeches, and elms overarching in a canopy, and a grassy churchyard with eroding marble monuments. Mr. Gowans moved with us, and became our first boarder.

As soon as we unpacked, Eddy sat down and began two more stories. For the next eight months he slaved at his desk, and was so domestic in all his habits I felt we'd never have to worry about his old weakness for spirits again. Really, he was nothing like the picture so many seemed to envision after reading his stories.

The night he moved in, Mr. Gowans turned to me at dinner and said, "Your husband, Mrs. Poe, is one of the most courteous, gentlemanly, and intelligent companions I've ever met in all my journeying over the globe." Then he raised his sherry high. Eddy returned the toast with his glass of water.

Sometimes I think I liked my husband best when he retired to an inner world of shipwrecks and mutinies and decaying castles, brooding over dark tarns, muttering and clutching his head one minute, than laughing out loud at some clever turn he put into a plot. Perhaps because, though we could not afford to go to the theater, to see and hear Eddy was as good as a play.

"Is he finishing his story about cannibals?" Muddy might whisper to me as she passed his room on tiptoe.

"Oh no," I'd reply, just as hushed. "He is now in Scotland—or perhaps it's England or Wales—where a young man has just buried his sister alive."

"Lord God," Muddy would whisper, and shake her head, looking astonished and often unnerved. Then we'd part, and turn back to whatever it was we were doing. Thinking from time to time of the wild adventures and ghoulish murders going on in the next room.

Even then my mother still treated us both like children. She began insisting on doing all the shopping, though complaining each time before she ventured out at how strange New York was, how unlike Virginia or Maryland. I no longer demanded to accompany her, to assert my station in life in that way, for I'd developed a persistent cough the outdoor air and smoke made worse.

When the weather finally warmed in late spring, Eddy and I went to stroll among the departed at St. John's Chapel and the Burying Ground. The churchyard was lovely and cool under the shade of its trees. He took us there almost every day, until I told him, "Since I'm certain we'll both lie in such a place for all eternity, I'd rather spend my living days getting out and seeing other sights."

He looked surprised, as if this had not occurred to him. A writer can be quite perceptive about the desires of his characters, I've noticed, and yet much less so about the real people around him. Then and there he turned us about, and we headed down to the Battery.

After that we took many different routes through the Village, and sometimes went on boat trips around the harbor, for such expeditions were either free or very cheap. That is how we passed the warm gentle spring, hot summer, and very cool fall of 1837.

Those seasons still did not prepare us for the winter to come.

Eddy caught a very bad cold in December and couldn't shake it. We couldn't call a doctor because of the fee. He finally dragged himself down to the Northern Dispensary, where he was looked at by a Dr. Mott, and a kind nurse named Mrs. Shew. When he returned he told me, in a voice low with misery and shame, "In the next room, when I suppose they thought I couldn't hear, the nurse remarked to the doctor, 'That poor man looks as if he's existed for months on nothing but hard work and broken promises.'"

"Never mind," I said. "Those promises will soon become opportunities."

His mouth twisted into a line too bitter to be called a smile. "Oh yes, I almost forgot. We live in the City of Opportunities."

The only real one which arose came when William Gowans introduced Eddy to James Peddar, an Englishman who wrote books for children. Mr. Peddar was about to leave for an editing job in Philadelphia. He assured Eddy *that* city was now the publishing center of the country—not New York. "Come there," he urged. "Join me. I'm sure I can put you in touch with something."

Eddy returned home from this meeting quite excited, but it seemed a vague promise to me. "I see, but—what does he mean by 'something'?"

Eddy shrugged. "That I write a longer work, a potboiler. Only novels make money now. Something light and full of action."

That sounded familiar. "But what about your Pym book?" He'd been working night and day to finish *The Narrative of Arthur Gordon Pym,* which employed cannibals and South Sea voyages and other marvels. I'd read most of the manuscript by then: the scenes with the hero's plague-stricken ship, the cannibal feast. At times it was heavy going, when Eddy stopped to expound on the scientific details of South Sea voyaging. One moment I was filled with terror for the characters, then the next felt profoundly bored.

The story had struck me most strongly with this idea: that the men in it had much less to fear from harsh elements and disease and inhospitable uncharted seas, than they did from *other human beings*. Just now, thanks to the recommendations of a few friends, the manuscript sat in the publishing offices of the Harper brothers.

"I don't need to be in New York to write more books," he said. "And no one here seems inclined to employ me, do they?"

That did seem true. And if he could make no money here, where it cost so much merely to live, we could not stay. I hadn't been able to avail myself of even one New York music tutor or voice instructor, and tried hard not to mind. I looked away each time we passed a music school or rehearsal hall, or even one of the many raucous beer gardens from which tinny piano notes emanated. I always felt a bitter pang that stayed with me for many city blocks.

But Philadelphia was a great city too. Surely it would hold similar opportunities, and less animosity toward my husband. Still I dreaded my mother's expression when Eddy informed her we'd once again be pulling up stakes.

He got down to it quickly, at dinner that night. "The gypsies of literature are headed south again," he joked.

Muddy frowned. "What do you mean, Eddy?"

I kept my eyes on my plate after that, but couldn't eat. She must've given him a shocked look after he explained, because he hurried to add, "My very first story was published in Philadelphia, do you remember? That city has always seemed amiable. It's inhabited by so many gentle Quakers. Don't you think so?"

Silence around the table then, even from Mr. Gowans. Eddy

seemed to have forgotten that, aside from him, none of us had ever set foot in Philadelphia. Did he notice Muddy's bewilderment, then the slow onset of resignation before she shrugged and looked down at her plate too? Already thinking of what we could afford to keep, and what we must sell to finance the journey.

"When will the move take place?" I asked.

"Spring would be best, I think. James Peddar's sisters will be opening a boardinghouse there soon."

Mr. Gowans looked downcast. "I shall miss you all," he said, but raised a glass nonetheless to toast our future.

Money was so tight, and tickets so expensive, we could keep only a few sticks of furniture and some pots and pans. Muddy still had to borrow to cover our steamer and train passage. But in the early spring of 1838, a month before we left Carmine Street, we had good news. Harper's had decided to publish *Arthur Gordon Pym*. Amid great rejoicing, we postponed leaving for a bit. The book would be brought out that July. And he'd always said a novel would make more money than a poem here, a story there.

So it seemed to me, as we prepared to move to yet another new city, that despite Granny Poe's dire predictions the Poe luck might be turning after all.

· 13 ·

We arrived in Philadelphia on April 22. It was a Tuesday, though I thought it must be Sunday, on account of the impressive quiet—so unlike the streets of New York. The Peddar sisters' boardinghouse, a large brick Federal, stood on Twelfth Street between Arch and Race. They were recently arrived from London, and still unpacking and hanging pictures, but the place already looked more luxurious than Mrs. Yarrington's in Richmond. A haven of refinement after the small, cold, dirty rooms we could afford in New York. Muddy immediately set to work helping the sisters establish themselves in their new home. Or perhaps it was to *reconcile* themselves, for they seemed used to even finer things, and took them so for granted, I wondered to Eddy, "Why did they leave England at all?"

"Something to do with the British economy. And I believe an inheritance," he said. "They can live much more cheaply here, and make a nice living to boot." The rent for our rooms would help them do so.

The first week it seemed every day was washday in Philadelphia. The neighborhood's housewives or their servants were forever out on the front stoop on hands and knees, scrubbing steps and pavements. The whole city looked clean as a nursing ward compared to the hearty, casual filth of the Village.

But a refined life with the Peddars was still too much for our pocketbook. We had to bid the genteel sisters good-bye and move to more modest rooms at Fourth and Arch. We felt more prosperous by September, and looked to rent an entire house, settling on a tall, narrow redbrick with white stone trim and the requisite gleaming, scrubbed stoop. It stood near Fairmont Park at 2502 Coates Street and had a walled garden. As close to a cottage as might be found in any downtown.

"I like a house and a yard," Muddy said, as we stood looking up at the façade. "A row house may be fine for most. But I'm tired of other folks' noise and messes."

"I was sure you'd like it, Muddy dear," Eddy said, looking proud as he slid an arm around my waist. "But someday we'll take a real cottage in the country, with an acre of grounds at least."

"Maybe we'll have sheep," I added. "Imagine me in a flowered skirt, carrying a crook, spinning yarn from our own wool." Eddy looked so alarmed I laughed. "I'm joking, my dear. This is fine, and paid for out of your earnings. Truly, it's all we need."

His arm tightened on my waist. He pointed to the narrow dormer windows on the third floor. "That will be my eyrie. You and Muddy will have the master bedroom on the second floor. There's a lean-to kitchen on the back, though you can't see it from here. Come on, I'll show you."

Not *our eyrie*, but his. My smile faltered. By then he was already leading us around the yard, showing off lush rhododendron and rosebushes, the two buttonwood trees in back, and some bordered but overgrown flower beds. When Muddy poked the dirt there with a stick it gave agreeably, black and moist and crumbly. "A kitchen garden here," she proclaimed. "Onions and potatoes and greens."

I went to stand next to the shortest bed, near the wall, and looked at her. "But here, we'll have flowers."

She eyed me narrowly, then shrugged as if it had never mattered what we planted. I felt I'd won a small victory and aged a year all in one moment.

"Of course, Sissy. We'll want lots of fresh flowers in our home," Eddy agreed.

My mother gave him a strange look—of sadness, of annoyance? I couldn't tell, but felt ashamed I could not keep from asserting myself; that it seemed so important to have my own way. She'd raised me herself and worked so hard. Had been good to both of us. "Yes, but it's Muddy's home too," I added. "We ought to spoil her for a change."

She laughed. "Oh, I'd like to see you great big children spoiling me the way I've spoiled both of you!" But she touched one eye with the corner of her apron. "I'd like to see that indeed."

The new place was only three rooms stacked atop one another like a child's set of blocks. But they were large, each with its own fireplace drawing into a common chimney on the north wall. The spacious parlor was papered with woodland scenes, only slightly faded. The lean-to frame kitchen, crude and three sided, was stuck like a barnacle to the outside back wall. It even had space for a small table.

The only part I didn't like was the narrow stairwell, so dark and musty. There hung eternal, unwhiskable cobwebs that always brushed my face as I passed. The stairs were enclosed by a cupboardlike door on one side of the slate fireplace downstairs. The only benefit I could see was that when you emerged from it on the second floor, mine and Muddy's room, or at Eddy's third-floor eyrie, both rooms felt even more spacious and filled with light after the dark, gloomy ascent.

All three rooms were beautifully lit with mullioned windows, so Eddy would have plenty of light to write by. We could read or sew and actually see what we were doing until night fell.

"We might entertain friends now," said Eddy. As if he'd been too ashamed to bring anyone home before.

"We have none yet but the Peddars," I noted. But Eddy's natural charm and fine manners would soon add to that short list.

So Muddy and I unpacked boxes, and polished the front stoop like true Philadelphia housewives. We walked to the produce market on High Street, or rode the Chestnut Street stagecoach all the way to the Headhouse Market at Second and Pine, where the real bargains were found. Eddy began spending one evening a week at the Falstaff Hotel, at an informal gathering of writers and reviewers and artists. "The Pennsylvania Intellectuals," they called themselves. Best of all, he never came home smelling of drink, not even after a whole evening in their bohemian company.

The artist Thomas Sully, also a member, came one day to our house to paint an oil portrait of Eddy. "It makes you look Byronish," I said, squinting at the still-wet results after Mr. Sully had departed. I wasn't sure I liked it, but Eddy looked pleased at that association.

We furnished a bit at a time, buying a second bed, painted straight-backed chairs, and a wicker rocker for Muddy. In early May we had to purchase a sturdier desk for Eddy. One night his old one had groaned and then buckled like a spavined horse under the weight of all the books he'd stacked on one end.

The following week he came home and found me downstairs reading. "Go sit in the kitchen with your eyes closed, my dear, until I tell you to come out."

I went, but didn't shut my eyes. Instead I stood staring at the pattern on a set of Chinese dishes, cast-offs bestowed on us with an air of great magnanimity by the Peddar sisters when we'd left them. The kind Muddy called "Blue Willow." An incomplete set, all a bit chipped or cracked. And yet, "My dishes," I whispered. "My kitchen."

While I stood worshiping the god of china, from out in the parlor came a good deal of heaving and grunting, and a muffled curse in a male voice I didn't recognize. "What in the world," I muttered, "is going on out there?" But I'd promised not to look.

Eddy burst in again. "I *said* to close your eyes," he scolded, so I did. Then he grabbed both my hands and dragged me back into the sitting room.

I stumbled after him, laughing. "Wait—what're you doing, we'll both fall!"

"Open them now," he ordered.

Sitting in one corner—in fact, filling that end—was a piano-forte. Not as large as the baby grand in the MacKenzies' music room back in Richmond, but it looked enormous just then. When I slowly drew closer, I saw the lid had a splintered corner and that the varnish was savagely scratched, as if by music-hating tigers. No matter; I gazed hungrily. It was lovely.

"I'm afraid we dinged the varnish a bit getting it through the door," Eddy said, wiping his forehead with an already-soiled hand-kerchief, nodding toward two men in laborer's clothes who lingered near the open doorway.

His face shone with a look I could only describe as joy, which must've been echoed by my own. I couldn't rip my gaze from my piano. *My piano.*

"It—this—you mean, it's really for me? Oh, Eddy, it's—oh, my dear—but surely we can't afford—you'll have to send it back!"

I realized my mistake immediately. This instrument was a sacred object, a true work of art, so much finer than anything I'd ever known—a luxury not even to be dreamed of. How could it possibly be mine? But Eddy, who'd been raised in luxury, then had had it all taken away, was trying to recapture that. To give the same to me freely and with generosity. "It's your birthday present," he said dully.

"And it's—oh, it's the most wonderful thing I've ever, ever seen," I cried, trying with all my heart to recapture that first moment. To look only joyful and enraptured. To not begin automatically to tot up the cost, as we always had done. To reckon what would have to be sold or cheapened or done without to pay for this new thing.

But dear God, had he spent all of his *Pym* advance? And if so, how would we pay the rent for the next months? What would Muddy say when she saw the pianoforte sitting there like a varnished elephant, crowding the drawing room?

"Oh, Sissy, there'll be plenty of money now. Besides the short articles, I've got a new deal in the works with Billy Burton."

"The English comedian?" I asked, confused. "Oh. Will you be writing . . . jokes for him?"

Eddy burst out laughing. "Good Lord, no! He also publishes *Burton's Gentleman's Magazine*. For what gentleman is complete without his own magazine?"

Certainly *he* longed for one, and even had the first issue all planned out.

"Besides," he continued, recapturing my hands. "*Pym* will do well. It's a *novel*. You'll see. We'll be fixed for quite a while."

I nodded, and squeezed his hand back, and finally, finally felt I could allow myself to enjoy the outrageous gift set like a banquet - before me. I approached again slowly, as one would a shy horse that might spook and bolt out the still-open door. Eddy dragged out the bench and I sat, spreading my skirts. I looked up at him, then down at the ivory and ebony. As if of their own accord my fingers began to move, playing "I'll Think of Thee, Love." Mr. Heman wrote with

an elevated mind, and I adored the gentle curve of its Italianate vocal line. So I began to sing on the second chorus, adding in the ca-
denza at the end of each chorus:

> *I'll think of thee, love, when the dark shadows sleep*
> *On the billows that roll o'er the emerald deep:*
> *Like the swift speeding gale, every thought then shall be—*
> *I'll think of thee, dearest—and only of thee!*

What a heavenly feeling to press smooth, cool keys and realize
I hadn't forgotten a thing Madame Frieda and Jane MacKenzie
had taught me. My fingers moved surely and independently, small
intelligent creatures sending out a happy message to the world.
They next played a bit of a Bach sonata, then Rosalie's favorite, the
"Gypsy Rondo"—and with only one error. It was some time before I even recalled that Eddy was still standing there. Then I noticed my mother had come into the room. She was perched on the
edge of our threadbare settee, eyes shining.

Arthur Gordon Pym did not sell so well after all, though some of
the shorter tales Eddy had worked on in New York were published.
I still read his stories first, before he sent each one off like a cherished child into the world.

My husband overestimated my literary abilities, I fear. Still, I
always took the pages eagerly, setting them out in neat piles on
the kitchen table. No doubt I should've warned him more strongly
against those stupefying passages of technical detail that had
marred *Pym*. Reviews had not been very good. *The Knickerbocker*
claimed it was told in "a loose and slip-shod style," and too liberally stuffed with the horrors of bloodshed and battle. *Burton's*

Gentleman's Magazine had piously complained of errors in geography and nautical information. "An impudent attempt at humbugging the public," the reviewer fumed.

Nautical details aside, I'd noted some of those flaws myself, and should've told Eddy in stronger terms. But I hadn't, so did that prove I was not a fit critic of my husband's work? But I'd assumed readers more formally educated than I—picturing men, I suppose—would find such dull, studious prose engrossing. This possible error still worried me. But I was also selfish; I did not want to give up my place as Eddy's first reader. "My muse," he liked to call me. Yet I had nothing to do with the stories, really, until *after* he'd written them.

Late in the summer of 1838 he set a new manuscript before me. "Another one ready for your keen eye, my dear," he said. "A Gothic tale."

With the familiar excitement I always felt when he handed me new work, I picked up "Ligeia," and began to read.

He'd taken a poetic conceit from the long verse he'd written years ago, "Al Araaf," and turned it into prose. I read on, fascinated, as the young wife sickened and died, and then—*then!*—as the husband sat and mourned and slowly faded from grief, Ligeia gathered her will *from beyond the grave* to return once more.

I shuddered and glanced over my shoulder at the dark stairway behind me, yet could not stop reading. Soon I'd bitten my nails down to the cuticle, and was tasting bitter black ink, as if I were chewing at Eddy's fingers rather than my own.

I disliked the rich, supposedly noble husband, even though he doted on Ligeia. For when his first darling died, he not only quickly took another wife, he treated this young, innocent replacement very badly. Then, when she too sickened, he merely watched the pale, fevered Rowena struggle as if battling some unseen assailant.

Gradually I understood: the second wife, Rowena, had met the first one, Ligeia, as her soul too began to enter the Other World. Now they were locked in combat there.

Oh yes, the husband sponged her brow and tended bandages, but his thoughts were all with Ligeia. He sent his first, best-loved wife moral support, perhaps even . . . a sort of *permission*. So when the seemingly-recovered Rowena rose from her bed and loosened the bandages from her face, in place of her childish, fair-haired visage stood Lady Ligeia, alive again before him.

"Oh God," I whispered. Could such a thing truly happen? Perhaps I should've rejoiced for the poor first wife, struck down so cruelly in the midst of her youth, her beauty, her great learning, her everlasting love for her husband. Yet somehow I felt more for the young, naïve, and witless Rowena, sold much as an African slave might be to a man who despised her simply for *not* being Ligeia.

It was a good story. I shivered whenever I thought of it. In fact, it was difficult to stop picturing the scene. This must be what Eddy had meant by seizing the reader's imagination, and not letting go.

With a contented sigh, I turned to the next sheet, which was a new poem still in the rough, early stages; many words had been crossed out and replaced. "The Haunted Palace" seemed to be about the ruin of an ancient stronghold, but I understood, after I read it a third time, that the palace was really a person, or rather a human soul. The "evil things in robes of sorrow" were bad deeds, or wicked thoughts. Did he mean it to be about his foster father, whose estate had prospered as he had betrayed and rejected Eddy? If so, he was brave to write it. For who likes to speak of such things in a family? Much less reveal them to an audience in a venue as public as a magazine.

But as I read, I also wondered, did Eddy love me in that way, to death and beyond? I suspected that variety of love would have to do with much more than just sympathetic intellects, or even physical beauty. It would be a timeless bond forged only by couples who shared absolutely everything—and we certainly did not. At least, not our interests, for he was immersed in literature and writing, while I had music and song. And then too . . . unlike other married couples, we did not share a bed, or even the same room. I still slept in the double four-poster with Muddy, like a child, while Eddy had a narrow cot upstairs, like a bachelor soldier. All thanks to the bargain the two of them had struck without consulting me.

So *was* I in fact a wife, truly?

I discovered the music shop the following week. It had rained for three days straight; by that Friday everything felt damp and mildewed, outdoors and in. Muddy had slipped and fallen on our polished front steps the previous afternoon. One knee was bruised and still swollen, so I'd left her propped up on the settee and set out alone for High Street market.

On a side street two blocks from High—not the one we usually took—I happened to glance into a shop window. It held a display of musical instruments: an old harpsichord, an oboe, and a flute, all set against a Turkey carpet and some artfully stacked leatherbound volumes on music. I paused, looked again, and drew closer. J. G. MACGREGOR'S MUSIC SALON said the gilded sign over the door. Beneath that: SHEET MUSIC OF THE WORLD, ALL VARIETIES.

I could not afford to buy my own music—the sheets were very expensive. So I was forced to play the songs I could recall by heart, over and over. The sight of that dully gilded lettering drew out of me a sharp covetousness as strong as biblical lust. A gripping want the like of which I had not felt since the Christmas long ago when

Claudine and Juliette had both gotten new dolls and green velvet dresses with black silk sashes. I had been pleased with my orange and walnuts and homemade cloth ball, until they'd come over to show off their gifts.

I should not go in. No good would come of it.

After debating a few moments, I stepped closer and tentatively shoved at the door. It swung open. A bright brass bell tinkled overhead.

The first set of shelves held classical compositions. The next, old favorites such as "The Bloom Is on the Rye" or "Rise, Gentle Moon." I pulled out a stack from where someone had boldly inked onto creamy card stock, *The Latest in Fine Songs This Year!*

I set one sheaf on the scarred table that stood in the middle of the quiet shop, and began to leaf through. Beneath my fingers lay new songs, just released, as the sign promised. I flipped through "All Things Love Thee, So Do I" and "Flow Gently, Sweet Afton" and "'Tis Home Where the Heart Is," and "Mary of Argyle" and "A Life on the Ocean Wave."

Oh my Lord. I'd never heard of anyone swooning for joy— from shock, yes, or terrible grief. But there was a humming in my ears, and I saw black spots whisk across the pages, and the blood fizzed in my veins. Yet how could I faint? No, not now!

Bracing an arm on the tabletop, I took a deep breath and picked up the next sheet, titled "Annie Laurie." No writer's name; just *Anon.* But the music had been arranged by a Finlay Dunn.

> *Her brow is like the snowdrift, her throat is like the swan*
> *Her face is the fairest that e're the sun shone on . . .*

It was sentimental but so lovely, especially as I imagined how it would sound being played on my own piano at home. I was humming the first stanza when a deep voice behind me said, "That 'un's written by a lady."

"Oh!" I gasped, and whirled to face him. As I did my hand flew up and knocked the sheets to the floor in a fluttering cascade, like dying white-winged moths.

He was an older man—that is, a bit older than Eddy—but quite handsome in a ruddy Celtic way: green eyes, clear fine skin, thick auburn hair. So he must not drink to excess like so many of his countrymen, I decided, then felt ashamed. Not only had I thought ill of a stranger, I'd just decimated much of his new stock.

Then a chilling realization struck: perhaps he would want payment for the scattered sheets. "Oh Moses," I gasped, and dove to pick them up.

"Dinna trouble yourself," he said, taking my elbow to help me to my feet again. "Accidents happen, 'tis no harm done."

I sprang up too quickly, then wobbled and swayed, feeling warm, while my face was suddenly cold with perspiration. He caught my arms and steered me to a chair.

"I don't faint," I protested. "That is, not normally. But the heat. And the—"

"I'll gather oop the music. Sit still and recover yourself. Would ye perhaps like a glass of something?"

"Just water," I said hastily. "Yes, please."

He smiled. "Happen t' have a drop."

He went to the back and for a moment I thought of leaping up and bolting out. All I had was the few coins Muddy had thrust into my hand to buy carrots and potatoes and an onion for dinner. Not enough to pay for even one new sheet of music.

But by then he was back, carrying a fairly clean glass half full of water.

"Thank you, oh dear, I don't wish to be a bother." I took the glass but then held it in my lap, afraid I'd spill it, my hands were trembling so.

"Ach. 'Tis no bother." He simply stood there, expression mild, jingling coins in his pocket. Then abruptly he turned away and began to scoop up the sheets I'd spilled, humming to himself.

I dreaded to see what condition the pages were in, and what he'd say next. But he merely tapped the stack on the tabletop to neaten it, then set it down. "'Tis no harm done," he repeated, and I nearly wept. "Something in particular ye were looking for?" he added.

"No," I said. Then, afraid that sounded rude, I murmured, "I love music, but cannot purchase any today, so I—I should go now. Sorry to have troubled you." I leaned over and set my glass carefully on the floor.

"'Tis pity, that," he said, and I stiffened. But then he gave me a hand up, and added, "Money ought not to matter, if ye love music. Come in again and look all ye wish. Does no harm and costs me naught. Though I'll be careful not to affright ye next time."

We both laughed at that, though he the more heartily. Then I bade him good day and went out, torn between humiliation and ecstasy. I rushed off in the direction of the market, nearly colliding with a tottering elderly lady who gave me a sharp glare. As I slowed down, I began to understand a return visit was impossible. It would not be proper to come alone and take the man up on his offer. My mother would consider it a shocking proposition. Eddy would never set foot in the place if I told him what had happened.

No, it was not possible. I could never return to J. G. Mac-Gregor's Music Salon.

I went back three days later.

My excuse was that Muddy's knee was still feeling sore, and

we needed some things from the market. "Potatoes," I said pointedly to Eddy, who seemed uninterested as he finished his breakfast of two smoked herring and a leftover biscuit.

"And greens," I added sharply. "And, perhaps . . . yes, a ham hock."

"I'm late," was his sole reply as he kissed my cheek, then hurled himself out the front door.

A young gentleman exiting the Music Salon doffed his hat, bowed, and held the door for me. The little bell tinkled derisively as I stepped inside, closing the door softly. I tiptoed to the rack of classical music this time and began browsing. I soon became engrossed in oratorios, concertos, sinfonias. An opera seria, an opera ballad, and then—oh my, a French opéra comique? I held it between trembling fingers and read greedily, knowing most of the notes at once, stumbling over some, lips moving. Trying to somehow memorize—oh, it was impossible!

Again I felt a presence. I lowered the sheet and looked over my shoulder. "Mr. MacGregor," I said faintly. "Good day. I was just—"

He bowed smartly. "Please don't mind me, maid. Go on about perusing."

I bit my lower lip. "Actually, sir, I'm not a . . . that is . . ." But it would not be proper to discuss my marital status with a male stranger.

He wandered away and began to dust the shelves at the far end. Every now and then I felt someone's gaze upon me, but dared not look up. Instead I fed my greedy brain with all the scores and lyrics I could stuff into it.

Some time later Mr. MacGregor cleared his throat behind me again. How did such a large man move so silently on a pine plank floor?

"Pardon me, maid. But I've a new crate in the storeroom. It's not been opened yet. Would ye care to look over the sheets before I set it oot?"

Would I . . . ? Clutching my reticule, I nodded. Then, glancing over my shoulder, I followed him to the velvet-curtained door of a small back room. There I paused. Inside lay a close, dim space. And while Mr. MacGregor seemed a respectable merchant, one who'd shown me courtesy, it would be unseemly to enter in his company.

He seemed to realize this as well, for he turned back to face me and smiled apologetically. "I'll just light this lamp and then go back aboot my business."

I stood aside. As he passed I could not help but inhale a scent of leather, and paper dust, and bow rosin, and pomade, and lime water. My knees felt oddly weak, my head light. But then, it'd been another unusually warm day. Hot enough out on the sidewalks to fry the gizzards inside a chicken.

Mr. MacGregor had pried the lid off a crate and left an oil lamp on the table next to it. I lifted out the top stack and set it on the tabletop, then began to peruse the latest songs from Paris, from Belgium, from Austria. I did not sit, though—that would seem too familiar.

I don't know how much time passed before he was there again. I smelled his scent first, and felt that same knee-weakening, the tautening as of a bow string in my belly. He stood close behind me, breathing faintly.

I turned slowly and he smiled down. In close quarters he seemed very tall. "Is any of it of interest to ye?"

I had to swallow first to make my throat work. "It's all wonderful. But really, I've taken up too much of your time and good will, and cannot stay longer. Because," I began, then stuttered to a stop. I could not think of why, or at least how to say it.

"Stay all you like," he said mildly, again jingling coins in his pockets. The lure of that kind, handsome face seemed equally as powerful now as the lure of the crate. I wanted to look into his eyes almost as much as I did at the music. I'd tucked my gloves into my reticule to better grasp the slippery sheets. Now, shockingly, I could imagine Mr. MacGregor drawing a hand from his pocket and taking mine. Could hear him murmuring endearments into my ears in that soft burr. Even watching while he kissed each of my fingers, slowly, one at a time, then turned my hand over to kiss—no, to lick the palm. I would not even mind that his own might taste bitter and metallic, like the coins in his pocket.

He took one step forward, put a hand on my waist, and drew me forward until my bosom was pressed against the embroidery on his waistcoat. I felt the faint *lub dub lub dub* of a heart, mine or his, as he lowered his face toward me. His breath, which smelled faintly and pleasantly of coffee, warmed my mouth. I closed my eyes. At that moment, I was certain I had been made for no other act than this.

He pressed his lips to mine and I slipped my arms around his neck. He pulled me to him so tight I could not draw breath, and did not mind. A low noise which came from deep in his throat might have signified either pleasure or despair. He slid two fingers between the buttons at the top of my dress, caressing the soft skin there.

"Oh!" I whispered, for his fingertips felt callused, and hot even through the thin cloth of my chemise.

Just then, the tinny brass bell over the door jingled madly, jealously.

I broke free and rushed out, through the curtains, past a startled old man with some sort of reed instrument cradled in his arms like a sick child. I slammed out the front door, the muffled shrieking of the bell bidding me to never, ever return.

I did not stop until I was at the market. I stood panting, smoothing my hair, relieved to tears that my reticule still hung by its chain, that I did not have to slink back to retrieve it and the little bit of silver it held.

I walked up and down the street until I felt calmer. Then went to buy the vegetables for our dinner at the very first stall, from a woman Muddy had often dickered with. Whose hard little eyes were like black marbles as she looked me up and down, as if she could somehow see—

"Three potatoes," I gasped out, "and—and that bunch of greens!"

She looked surprised, then sly, when I made no attempt to bargain down the price. Next I went to the butcher to procure a ham hock, with no concern for its meatiness or lack thereof. I rushed home, trying to forget the dim little room that had held, for one wicked moment, a taste of what seemed now a distant Paradise.

But I could not forget it. Especially when I lay in bed that night, and the next and the next, beside my peacefully sleeping mother. While my husband—my husband!—lay in a narrow bachelor's cot in another room, on another floor, door firmly shut. I stared at the ceiling and tossed and turned until sometimes my mother, always a sound sleeper, would wake and say, "Lord God, Sissy, what ails you tonight! Have you got a bellyache?"

Ah, if only I could tell her. Then perhaps she could instruct me in a cure.

Slowly, too slowly, it turned to July. On the fifteenth of August I would be sixteen. Old enough by anyone's reckoning to be married, surely. To make my own decisions, grasp adult life with both hands and hang on. To be a wife in every sense of the word, and thus out of reach of the arms of strange, beguiling men. Safe from my own recent dreams. Otherwise, I had a terrible feeling eventually I would find my way back again to MacGregor's Music Salon.

I decided our odd sleeping arrangement had gone on long enough.

The next night I lay feigning sleep long after Muddy had begun snoring, then slid from beneath the covers by inches, making sure not to jostle the bedding. I'd brushed my hair an extra fifty strokes, and before we'd blown out the light had sponged myself all over at the washstand.

I tiptoed across the floor, stepping over the creaking plank just before the threshold, and climbed each step with excruciating slowness. Another loose board lay at the top of the stairwell. I grasped the cool white porcelain doorknob and turned it gently, taking my time so the stiff mechanism didn't grate or squeal. Finally I was able to push the door open soundlessly, slip through, and seal it behind me.

This topmost room was not very dark, even without a light burning, for a street lamp was always lit below Eddy's window. He lay on his back in the narrow bed, illuminated in squares by the panes the lamp shone through.

I stood looking down at him like Psyche secretly gazing on the sleeping Cupid.

How beautiful he was, for a man. Quite different in many ways from Mr. MacGregor—but no, I must banish that name, that person, from my mind. So I gazed on Eddy's thick, dark brown hair, his smooth white skin like a porcelain doll's. Surely Lord Byron could not have been more handsome. One arm lay straight at his side, the other flung out so his right hand hung over the edge. He wore his old white nightshirt, the one I'd sewed up a tear in the day before. It felt strange, swaying there in the dark as if I'd been drinking sherry, or had just gotten up from a long illness too soon.

I took a deep breath, lifted the sheet, and slid onto the plain iron-framed cot, right next to him—no easy thing, since the straw-stuffed ticking was barely wide enough for one.

He muttered something, then flinched and bolted upright. He stared down, eyes wide. "Why—what in—*Virginia*?"

My lips felt numb as I moved them to answer. "Yes, my dear. It's me."

"But—but what are you *doing* here?"

I pulled a corner of his pillow over my mouth to muffle a laugh. "I'm your wife. Husbands and wives sleep together."

"Yes. Well, they do, but—I told you why, I mean about what I promised your mother. And you're not yet—"

"I'm almost sixteen."

He shook his head and sighed. "Not quite."

"But soon. Are you planning to publicly announce a change in general sleeping arrangements at my birthday dinner?"

He drew back. "Of course not!"

"Then this seems by far the better idea. Much less awkward."

I slid closer, so that my hip and bosom pressed against his side, in part because I was in imminent danger of falling off. Eddy was breathing quickly, staring with an expression that seemed to mingle fear with longing. But he made no move. At last I took one of his hands and placed it on the curve of my hip. "There," I said matter-of-factly, as if he were teaching me how to hang a picture, or fix a broken latch. "What comes next, dear?"

For a moment his fingers tightened on my hipbone, then slid up the curve of my waist, pulling the cloth of my gown with it. But then he let go abruptly, as if I were a hot kettle. "Get up," he said hoarsely. "You can't stay here. What if your mother comes in?"

"She's asleep. And anyway, we're married."

He didn't argue. But then I did get up to stand beside the bed again, because something else had just occurred to me. A terrible thought, unbearable. For it was plain that Eddy—my own husband—was not behaving toward me in the way Mr. Mac-Gregor, who was a stranger, had when he'd drawn me to him in that tiny back room.

"Eddy," I said. "Is it that you really don't want me in here at all? Not—ever?"

Once this idea crept in, a new and unsettling suspicion followed close behind. Everyone in the family had always called me "Sissy." The name Henry had bestowed when I was a baby, because he could not pronounce all the complicated syllables of "Virginia." I'd always assumed it meant little that Eddy also called me by that name. I knew he loved me, but now I began to wonder whether it was more in the way a brother loves a sister—rather than as a man, or a husband, loves a wife.

My brief, exhilarating, shameful experience in the music store had complicated my life more terribly than I'd first imagined.

Eddy laughed a quiet bark of dry humor and despair mixed. "Oh, certainly not that."

No? In that case, I thought, perhaps if he were to finally glimpse more than just the heavy flannel of my nightgown . . . Perhaps if, like the smitten, possessed husbands in his stories, he were to see those female parts they always seemed to gaze at and so fulsomely yet vaguely praise . . . to touch my bare skin as Mr. MacGregor had wanted so badly to do . . . Perhaps then Eddy would wish me to stay. Perhaps then he'd want *me.*

I took hold of the seams of my gown and slowly pulled upward. The fabric crept up over my shins. Soon the hem reached my knees, rising, uncovering them.

He sat up. "What're you doing?"

"Just showing you what I look like. Don't you want to see?"

Without waiting for an answer, I pulled the gown higher and higher, all the while watching his face. He stared as I lifted the hem as high as my bent elbows could make it would go. Then I thought, Perhaps I should've unbuttoned the neckline instead, and let the thin cotton fabric fall gracefully away from my shoulders, instead of pulling the gown up, as one did when in the privy. My bosom was attractive enough, I thought, round and smooth and white. I could see most of it in the small round mirror over the washstand, when I stood on tiptoe. But I was much less familiar with the appearance of the rest of my body, especially the shadowy parts below the waist. We had no full-length pier glass.

Just as I was about to give up and let the skirt fall again, and undo my top buttons instead (for I could not imagine simply yanking the whole gown off over my head, to stand suddenly stark naked, pimply with cold shivers, like a plucked chicken), Eddy reached out and grasped my wrist. Then slowly, carefully—as if I were a wood nymph about to turn and flee; as if this hadn't been entirely my own notion in the first place—he drew me toward the cot. And then slowly down onto it, next to him again.

I stretched out and smiled up at him, but when he slid one hand under the rumpled cloth of my gown I flinched. His palm was so hot it scorched my bare skin. I felt no calluses, though, as he ran his hands over my neck, my bosom, and finally over my ribs and waist.

"You are beautiful," he whispered, as he helped me undo the tiny mother-of-pearl buttons, from top to bottom.

And as he finally began to show me what came next, I wondered, Why for so long did I simply take the world as it was presented to me, like a willing, passive child? Why had it never occurred to me before that a grown woman could change things, get what she desired, by stepping boldly forward and taking hold?

I had that much, and more, for which to thank Mr. Mac-Gregor.

Somehow we managed to sleep much of the night in that narrow bed without one or the other of us rolling off and crashing onto the hard planks of the attic floor. Early the next morning, as the moonlight was chased away by pink and yellow sunlight streaming in, the stairwell risers creaked.

It had to be Muddy coming up. I pretended to be asleep and lay there barely breathing. I felt frightened and defiant, sad and exhilarated. Then, simply afraid.

From outside the glowing window came the faint early-morning rumble of carriage wheels, the soprano cries of a newsboy, the dull *clop-clop, clop-clop* of a draft horse plodding up our street. Ordinary sounds, ordinary day. Yet in this small dim room, a revolution had taken place. Even if out there nothing had changed.

It matters in life who has the upper hand. I knew that now; I simply hadn't understood before that the order of command could change. Now would she confront us, rage at me, make a scene? Blame Eddy, or perhaps cry, "I no longer have a daughter!" Then I would only have to act again to somehow prove her wrong. But already, in any case, she no longer had absolute power over me.

The door opened a crack, but didn't swing any wider. Muddy did not come in, nor did she say a word. At last I heard her pull it shut again. The latch clicked into place quietly behind her.

· 14 ·

Eddy finally did get more work. Before we left New York he'd discussed, with a publisher, writing a textbook on seashells for young students, called *The Conchologist's First Book*. He worked on it all through the winter and spring. The book had a very long subtitle, impossible to remember. One which made little sense to me, though I was impressed to learn it would have two hundred and fifteen illustrations.

"Oh, it's just hackwork," he lamented. "But I'll be paid, at least."

Classifying seashells seemed a far cry from staging cannibal feasts and raising the dead. But we did need money, though not quite as desperately as at other times in the past.

I'd put in a flower garden out back, with seeds and offerings from neighbors, or rooted cuttings surreptitiously pinched from the flowering hedges that walled downtown estates. From late summer into the early fall, my shallow beds full of dahlias and forget-me-nots and chrysanthemums and even heliotrope had bloomed well, until the real cold came. The following spring I weeded and dug again, sinking my bare hands into warm rich leaf mold Eddy hauled from a nearby wooded lot. I hummed and sang, anticipating the joy of finding myself with child soon. I had some idea of how one could know this, but not what that condition might feel like. As the months passed, I had armloads of beautiful flowers, yet no other happy news to offer Eddy and Muddy.

So it seemed prescient that in the spring of 1840, Henry Haines, the newspaper editor who'd hosted us on our Petersburg honeymoon, wrote to offer me something else in need of a mother: an orphaned fawn found by their gardener. Mrs. Haines had been feeding it with a bottle capped by the thumb of an old canvas glove. He proposed Eddy send for the young deer so I could keep it as a pet in our walled garden.

"Oh, how wonderful," I exclaimed. A graceful deer would be better even than a flock of sheep on a green hill outside a cottage. "The garden is large enough for it."

Eddy lowered the letter, looking doubtful. But it was Muddy who spoke up. "A wild thing has no business being penned up in a city. It's against God and nature."

"But what will happen to the poor little creature?" I protested. "It's tame now, used to people. They can't just release it back into the woods." I envisioned a long-limbed, spotted fawn, legs limber as willow branches, with mild dark eyes and long graceful neck and silky coat, walking right up to a party of hunters. Like a bewitched unicorn, it would blink long-lashed, liquid eyes, then lay its head in their laps. "Eddy, we must save it! Why not keep it here?"

Muddy stuck her sewing needle into the shirt she was mending, and nipped off the end of the thread with her teeth. "Virginia, you can't have everything on a whim. What if the dogs next door jumped the fence and killed it? What if that dirty-faced rascal from down the street brought his bow and arrows, climbed on top of our wall, and shot the poor trapped thing for sport?"

"But Muddy—"

"Don't be foolish," she said, and rose from her chair, mouth set, face closed. As if we were back in Baltimore and she was dismissing a childish plea for a full-grown elephant to ride, or the moon pulled to earth and sealed in a canning jar. "How would it get here?"

I bowed my head then; I didn't know. And really, she was right. To keep a wild creature here, a few yards from hustling traffic and tall buildings and busy, hurrying people, would be against the very laws of the universe. How unhappy it would be set down in this hard-edged, coal-smoky, soot-coated world. I myself could take lessons in any number of subjects and artistic pursuits, acquire social graces, learn to bow at introductions, and when to smile and make idle small talk. But a truly wild thing would not adapt so wonderfully.

"Then what shall I say?" asked Eddy, gripping the letter with its incendiary offer, glancing from one to the other of us as if afraid to offer any opinion.

Yes, my mother was right. But I wondered, as I contemplated her placid, stolid expression, which thing she took more pleasure in: saving a wild creature from the dangers of a large city, or putting me for those moments back in my place.

"I suppose you must write back to Mr. Haines," I told Eddy, looking away from them both, out the window. He had not taken my part; only sat back and let two women fling words at each other like sharp stones. I heard the warped drawer of his secretary as it was pulled open, the dry rustle as he drew out sheets of paper and a quill. When I looked back again he sat with the sharpened tip poised over the page, as if I were a famous writer and he merely my amanuensis.

Very well, then. I cleared my throat. "Tell him . . . you must say, 'Thank you for the offer of the fawn for Mrs. P.'"

He scratched that line, then looked up again, waiting for me to direct him.

"Say, 'In fact, she desires me to thank you with all her heart, but—'" I drew in a deep breath, to forestall the childish tears that suddenly were pressing behind my eyes. "'But unhappily I cannot think how to . . . how to . . .'"

Eddy looked up, a line between his eyebrows. "How to convey it?"

I took another deep breath. "Yes, 'because . . . we cannot point out a mode of conveyance. And so, unless some friend from Petersburg soon pays us a visit, we must decline. But please accept our best acknowledgments of your kindness, just as if the little fellow were already nibbling the grass before our windows in Philadelphia.'"

So I had no large, gentle pet to enliven my days. Then, a week later, Eddy brought home something smaller but no less in need of a home: a fuzzy calico kitten, colored orange and black.

"She's called 'Catterina,'" he said. "I meant to let you choose the name, but she seemed to be demanding that one all the way home, like an imperious princess of Muscovy."

I laughed, for it was true—the clinging ball of fur had all four clawed feet calmly but firmly embedded in Eddy's sack coat, as if he were a public conveyance she'd called for. The kitten didn't appear frightened, and she did look back over her shoulder at me as imperiously as any Russian princess. I understood she was saying, "All right, here we are. Now, where is that cream you mentioned?"

I loved Catterina, who stayed in the garden with me all day as long as it was warm enough. And when it turned too cold to linger out of doors, she perched like a tortoiseshell parrot on Eddy's shoulder, watching with great interest as he sat at his desk and scratched black wavy marks onto pale blue pages.

Still I clearly imagined a child. Our daughter. A sweet little girl with my eyes and Eddy's dark brown hair, with round pink cheeks and a face lit like the sun. If not in this waning year, then the next. And why not? Most nights Eddy turned to me in our shared bed, and everything between us worked well enough. I was by then sixteen and a half, quite as old as other ladies in our neighborhood who went about gravely and importantly pushing carriages down the sidewalks. It seemed to me that all I lacked was this undeniable outward sign to be fully entered into the world of adults, and privy at last to all its mysteries.

I sang and played music; I gardened and walked to the market. But summer and fall passed, and no child arrived to complete my passage to maturity. By winter Catterina had grown into gangly, furry girlhood, and the following February the daffodils and crocus I'd planted began to bloom. Yet I did not. Spring was uneventful until May, when Eddy finally did bring the popular comedian Billy Evans Burton home for a sherry. Muddy got out our good glasses, those least cracked or chipped. She poured only water in Eddy's.

"We've seen you perform at the Walnut Theater, Mr. Burton," I said, unable to look him in the eye, shy to be speaking to an actual stage personality in our shabby parlor.

Burton was large, but more avuncular and jolly than imposing. His rubbery mobile face seemed to register every emotion available to mankind and perhaps a few new ones.

"Please don't tell me how funny you found me," he begged. "I can never get a beautiful lady to take me seriously. One occupational hazard I've become sick of, my dear Mrs. Poe, I can tell you that!"

Muddy set her glass firmly back on the table, and frowned. I was certain I'd read somewhere that Mr. Burton had a wife and a

number of children back in England. I decided to change the subject. "It must be hard work though. Being a comedian."

Eddy shook his head. "Oh, I don't know—it seems to come to
Mr. Burton naturally."

They both laughed.

That wasn't what I'd meant. "No, truly. I was thinking that—
that comedy seems to me a very serious business. Even a burden.
How difficult if one *must* make people laugh, no matter what! To
have to work so fast and so hard, yet not let any effort show."

Mr. Burton stopped a piece of pound cake halfway to his mouth.
He lowered his laden fork. "It is indeed," he agreed, looking at me
more seriously. "No one's naturally funny, always, no matter what
people say." He turned to Eddy. "I may hire your wife, if she can
play that pianoforte across the room as well as she can philo-
sophize."

Hire me? I felt my face and neck heat up, and looked down to
hide the sudden eagerness I felt at this attractive yet not entirely
proper suggestion.

Eddy chuckled again, as if it were a jest, even though Burton
hadn't smiled when he said it. "She's even better at singing than
playing," Eddy told him, gazing at me with pride. "But on the way
here, Mr. Burton and I were actually discussing my ideas for a
magazine."

"You mean *The Penn*?" That was what he'd been planning to call
his own literary magazine, for both the artistic and geographic as-
sociations. I wanted to find out what this meant, yet also wished just
as much that they would keep on discussing my musical talents.

"No, my dear. You may recall Mr. Burton already has a magazine of his own. He's been putting it out for two years now."

"Though I'm really more actor than literary man," Burton admitted, stifling a belch with his fingertips. "Which is why," he

said, turning back to Eddy, "I've been wanting to ask him to share his expertise, and improve the tone of my modest screed."

It seemed he wanted Eddy to come in two hours a day, to write reviews, and edit and prepare the copy for the printer. For this my husband would receive fifty dollars a month, and three dollars the page for his own contributions—as well as he'd been paid at the *Southern Literary Messenger.*

Muddy appeared overjoyed, I sighed, and Eddy looked triumphant. On top of this great news his stories, collected under the title *Tales of the Grotesque and Arabesque,* had been accepted by the Philadelphia publisher Lea and Blanchard. The very manuscript of tales he'd dropped into my lap so long ago, when I was still a child back in Baltimore, was about to be published as a real book. It would finally assure Eddy his rightful place in the world of letters. Our days of struggle and poverty truly must be over and done.

Perhaps, I thought, as I listened to the men making plans, watching them over the nicked rim of my glass of watered sherry—perhaps a baby will be next. Surely she will come now, when we're so happy and fortunate and well.

The next day Eddy hired a little rig and a bay pony from the livery down the street to drive us out to one of his favorite spots, a gorge cut by Wissahickon Creek. I packed a basket with cold chicken and sliced cake and a bottle of lemonade, fending off Muddy in the kitchen, determined to do it all myself.

We'd invited her along, but she refused. "Have a day of it, just you two," she insisted. "Catterina and I will be fine on our own." I looked for martyrdom in her face, but saw none.

More reason to do everything myself. But I hesitated, looking over the basket's contents, which seemed meager compared to picnic meals my mother had concocted. I rooted once more in the pantry, and tossed in a triangular hunk of yellow rat cheese. Then covered everything with a clean napkin, and went out front to meet Eddy.

He handed me into the springy little rig, wedging the basket between us. He kept the pony stepping lively down the ridge road at a fast trot. We swayed on the seat for several miles, then turned down a narrow dirt lane lined with tulip poplars and evergreens. This rough track we followed bumpily until it ended on a bluff high above the winding creek.

"Eddy, how lovely!" I'd forgotten how nice the country could be since we'd been living so long in cities. Of course, the only time I'd seen much countryside at all had been from the train, on our honeymoon trip to Petersburg.

He jumped out and helped me down. "We can stay all day if you like."

I slid the basket out while he unhitched the blowing, stamping bay, and then walked it to a shallow pool. He hobbled the pony loosely in some high grass, under a sweet gum.

Then he suddenly turned away from me and slid stiff legged down the riverbank, disappearing from sight. I gasped and rushed to the verge. There he was, ten or fifteen feet below at the water's edge, dragging a flat-bottomed skiff from a clump of myrtles.

I stood looking down, a hand on my hip, mouth open. "Well! Where did you get that?"

"It's only on loan. I don't feel wealthy enough to own a boat. Even one this small."

"You don't mean we're stealing it?"

He looked reproachful. "No, Sissy, of course not. Merely borrowing."

I looked about doubtfully. "What if the owner comes while we're out?"

"He can steal our horse in revenge."

That seemed fair. How young and relaxed he looked today, not gloomy or depressed, not a tired writer with the cares of the world and unpaid bills weighing down his shoulders. He was actually instigating a game. Yet I, the younger party, had apparently forgotten how to play. That was the moment I understood my old wish had been granted: I was indeed an adult, no longer a child who understands make-believe and needn't be cajoled or have it all explained.

It felt more a letdown than a triumph. "He can take the horse and the buggy," I agreed, trying to enter into the spirit of things. "Then we'll have to trade him back, or possibly pay an enormous ransom!"

I had to lie flat on the damp ground to hand down the heavy basket. Then, with a whooping cry, skirts flying and snagging on roots, I too slid down. Eddy caught me in his arms, squeezing so tight I couldn't breathe. He handed me into a seat in the bow and climbed in to face me. A bit of tannin-browned, leaf-strewn water sloshed in the bottom, wetting my best, my only slippers. But by then to care about such a thing would've been dull and petty, the trivial complaint of a boring matron.

Eddy seated himself amidships, fitted unvarnished oars into wooden pegs that served as locks, and cast off. He pointed us upstream and began to pull.

"What beautiful scenery. Why don't you write a poem about this?"

"Perhaps I will, when we return."

"But your poems and stories are always set somewhere else.

Europe, or perhaps England. In fact, I never really recognize the landscape."

"It's true," he admitted. "And every stream in France and England has been celebrated in song and story and poem ten hundred times over. Yet . . . I suppose it's because of my childhood years spent there, in school. You're right. Why shouldn't our own landscape be as famous?"

And why shouldn't a story—just once—have in it a beautiful woman who doesn't die, one who manages to thrive and live a long and happy life? But I bit those words back. I could not tell Eddy what to write. His visions were his own, as my voice and my hands were mine. He enjoyed hearing me play and sing, but so far had never tried to make me do it some other way, one that he'd prefer.

The morning sun was not yet high enough to shine between the mossy rock walls of the gorge. The Wissahickon was a chain of quiet shallow pools haunted by large, wary catfish, and linked by small rapids in the middle channel. Dragonflies flitted and buzzed above the water. Now and then a fish jumped, then slapped down with a faint splash. Even on a warm day in May, the air was cool. I pulled my shawl closer, glad I'd brought it along, matronly or not.

We ate cake and cheese and cold fried chicken on a rock ledge. The one small bottle of lemonade was not nearly enough. So after we finished it Eddy dipped water from the chilly stream for us to drink. After lunch we sat on the rock in the sun, then he shifted to lie with his head in my lap. And I wondered why we had to come so far from our own home, which I felt was truly a happy one, to find such peace. But I knew the answer. All our joys and all our griefs resided back there, side by side.

We were getting into the boat again when I saw something on the cliff overhead. "Look," I called softly to Eddy, holding very still. "Up there. See it—see the deer?"

He followed my gaze. "Oh yes. But—is it? Yes, I believe it's an elk, not a deer."

An elk, how strange and exotic. The huge animal, who stood almost directly overhead, gazed down at us—or rather, seemed to look through us—with mild, unalarmed eyes. As if to say, *You don't belong in my world, so you aren't really here.*

"How beautiful and unspoiled it still is here," I whispered. "What a wild place, to have such a creature in it."

"Perhaps someday we'll live in your dream cottage, just there, overlooking this river," he said, squeezing my hand. "And he will be our neighbor."

Perhaps, but I would change nothing else.

Just then a tall man in a sporty tweed suit and bow tie stepped out of the shrubs behind the elk. I opened my mouth to shout, to startle the creature into flight, so it would leap and run and save itself.

"Oh, *there* you are, Adonis," the well-dressed fellow scolded. Instead of raising a gun, he held out his palm flat, with a white lump of salt or sugar sitting on it. The elk did not flinch or bolt, but turned its head to gaze serenely at him, large brown eyes accepting and unconcerned. Our wonderful, mythical beast nodded and stamped and then, just like a fat tame pony, took the treat from its master's palm. The man grinned and waved to us, then slipped a halter on the creature and led him away into the woods.

"Unspoiled, my britches," muttered Eddy.

"I wonder whatever happened to the little fawn Mr. Haines offered to send to me?" I said. I imagined he—no, *she*—was grown now. She'd be content, but not too docile, and live in a large green enclosure on the Haines property, I decided. Mrs. Haines had fed it herself with a bottle. No woman who'd done that could let an animal go back to the wild, to be tormented or shunned by its own kind for its strange human ways. Or killed for its fatal lack of caution. No, she'd keep it close and never let it go.

As we rowed back, the lovely day turned gray. Though it was May, a cold, prickly rain began to fall. I pulled my shawl tight around me, but soon it was sodden. As we drove back to town, biting gusts flew out of the north. Before Eddy pulled up in front of our house, the liquid downpour had turned to pellets of sleet. He kept one arm tight around me, but I could not talk—my breath was gone. I shivered in fits, sucking short gasps of damp, chilly air. Like shards of cold iron, these seemed to stick halfway down in my chest, to congeal around my heart.

Eddy half dragged, half carried me inside as I was racked with fits of hard, barking coughs.

Muddy put me to bed and brought a saucepan of scalded milk, which I gagged on. Then she offered hot water with lemon squeezed into it, feeding me half a spoonful at a time, and I could not even thank her. "You have a fever," she said, feeling my forehead with gentle callused fingers. I nodded, but didn't believe her. I was so cold, how could I also be burning up?

After Eddy returned from dropping off the rented buggy, he sat at the end of my bed looking miserable. I wanted to say it was worth it, I didn't mind, he should not feel guilty. But this might sound unconvincing. Instead I managed to ask, in a hoarse whisper, "Would you read to me?"

He did so gratefully, all evening. Muddy cast a frown at him every now and then. I saw she *did* blame him for my terrible condition, though she'd never say so to his face.

The next morning I could not rise, even to use the privy. I burned and sweltered and sweated, and kept impatiently throwing off the covers. Yet each time some unseen devil would tuck them in around me again until I was sure I'd melt and flow away across the quilt, off the side of the bed, then over the floorboards like the Wissahickon, down into one shining pool after another. The pain in my chest was a cartload of broken bricks and glass shards. My throat was so parched its walls stuck together. Yet I choked whenever Muddy put a glass of water to my lips.

Eddy's face hovered like the moon—or perhaps the pale oval I saw really was the moon, shining in through the cracked window of our eyrie. Someone came, I think it was Dr. Hentz. He said I was on the verge of pneumonia. I smiled, for earlier I'd seen a deer, or was it an elk, also on the verge of something. So I too was standing at the edge of some great void. I hoped no one would try to make me swallow such a big lump of salt as had been given the poor deer, for my mouth was already dry as an ancient seabed.

Some time later I saw Rosalie sitting at the foot of my bed and told her, "Now, Rose, don't ever call him 'Buddy' anymore." At least I tried to, but perhaps it wasn't Rose, only a picture of her, for she looked peculiarly flat and dim. She said to me, "Has Eddy been partaking of drink?" Then she was gone, and a small, dark-haired woman with round face and large luminous eyes—unlike Rose, very pretty and petite—had taken her place. This one, whose gown was low-cut and old-fashioned, didn't speak, only stood by the bed as poised and graceful as an actress, smiling at me.

Suddenly Muddy loomed in her place, rubbing my cold aching feet. Then Eddy came. He was always beside the bed, reading or standing over me, looking down with anguish while Muddy or the doctor tried to coax tea or broth or medicine into me.

Then one morning he was gone.

"Where is he?" I mumbled.

"What?" asked Muddy. "Who, Sissy?"

"The deer. Adonis," I whispered. "No, Byron."

She stroked my forehead. "Do you mean Eddy?"

I nodded, or tried to.

"He'll be right back," she said, smiling. Such a kind liar; he did not return.

"Where is he, where's Eddy?" I asked the next morning. At least I think it was morning.

"Gone out." Muddy tightened her lips and shook her head.

"He'll be here soon," someone said in a bright strained voice so much like Rosalie's parrot-speak I shivered, because it made me hear Rose when I could not see her. Then Muddy pulled the heavy covers up, and I began to sweat like a draft horse again.

After what seemed many days Eddy did come back looking quite ill himself, perhaps worse than me. So he'd been out drinking. I turned my face away, to the window, where the curious yellow moon peered in at us and seemed to laugh.

The next day he was gone again. Rosalie did not return, if she'd been here at all. Nor did the pretty dark-haired woman in the low-cut gown. Muddy had been sleeping on a pallet by our four-poster. In the early afternoon our former landlady, a nice old Quaker lady, brought a bowl of beef tea. I didn't want to ask about Eddy again, so I didn't talk to either of them.

"You must zee she eats up all de broth," the Quaker lady was saying. "Her face is nice and round still. But *mein Gott,* she is gettink so thin!"

Muddy brought the stewpan in to give me some in a coffee cup, and it tasted like the sweet steaming nectar of the gods.

I wanted to ask for Eddy again, but did not wish to upset Muddy. Or to make her tell me something she didn't want to speak of: that he'd gone off again, under the influence of the Old Failing.

At last she told me on her own. "Eddy's here, asleep in my room, Sissy. He can see you tomorrow."

I turned my head so my cheek brushed the sweat-damp pillow. "Rosalie said he'd been drinking."

My mother looked startled, then quickly smoothed her expression. "Quite right. So he has."

"What happened?"

"While you were ill he sat by the bed day and night, until finally he gave a dreadful cry and rushed out. He said he couldn't stand it anymore. To see you suffer so, and nothing to be done."

"He thought I'd die. Like the others."

"Oh, surely not. No, we never did." But she was gripping her apron in both fists. "A friend found him at the Falstaff and brought him home." She looked so very tired I wanted to make her lie down in my place. "Well, get some rest," she said at last. "When you wake, Eddy will be in to see you."

My husband is a dipsomaniac.

There, I'd said it, at least to myself. Never mind Granny Poe's euphemism, the Old Failing. Was it more noble to drink to excess and blame it on your ancestors? I did not think so now. Yes, Eddy had suffered. But so had my mother, and she did not take to the bottle whenever trouble loomed. Back in Baltimore, the men on our old street had often smelled of drink. They staggered and reeled about sometimes even during the day, and cursed any child who got in the way. The children of the worst of them wore bruised faces. Screams and shouts were the music that issued from their open windows on warm nights. The mornings after, their wives looked drawn and haggard; they would not meet your eyes on the street. So I had invented an imaginary husband, a man nothing like the fathers of our old neighborhood.

But my husband was not imaginary. And Eddy didn't smell of sweat and dirt or coal dust. He didn't beat me or curse my mother. Like my pretend beau of old he was tall and slender, dark haired, well dressed. He spoke gently and told funny stories when he came home from work. Muddy often served him tea, when we had it. We kept little or no liquor in our home.

A terrible thought struck me then. What if—what if those men back in Baltimore had *started out* more like Eddy? Then taken to drink, and slowly but surely changed. Yes, Eddy's hands were soft and pale and clean. But when they lifted a glass of spirits they would not set it down until he'd drained the last drop from the bottle.

Of course I had married him, the man of my dreams. Up till then the only men I had really had to compare Eddy to were the rough, gin-soaked denizens of our old Baltimore neighborhood. And the Henrys—my own brother, and Eddy's—one a boy barely older than me; the other a pale, cough-racked wraith. And of course my poor father, who'd died when I was five. I could barely remember him at all now. William Clemm was a dim patchwork memory: a kindly figure who used to set me on his knee and sing Irish ballads; a pair of gentle but callused hands; a set of whiskers that sometimes scratched my cheeks. Fathers had been a thing that other children had; some of them, anyway. Until Muddy and I had cast our lots with Eddy, my life had been as poor in male companionship as it had been in worldly luxuries. But perhaps we should not always be given everything we dream of, and think we want?

These thoughts exhausted me. I wanted the question to go away. At last I fell asleep and it did.

Eddy came in later, or perhaps it was the next day. "I'm back, my darling."

"Yes, I see. You needed some rest. But did you have to—" I forgot what I was going to say next.

"Yes," he said, looking miserable. "It was the Imp stirring again. I meant to take just the one glass, of course. But after that— well."

It was true. Whenever he went out, if he took one drink, it might as well have been a whole bottle. As his friends could attest, his weakness was this: One glass made him quite as drunk as ten. And yet after the one he would not stop until he'd swallowed the bar, the tavern; drained the whole city, the whole world of alcohol.

He sank to his knees by the bed. "I couldn't bear to see you lying there, it was happening—you were dying again." He laid his forehead on my hand like a child. He *was* my child—the only one, I dimly understood by then, I would ever have. So I lifted my other hand, which felt terribly heavy despite the good Quaker beef tea, and rested it on his hair. Beneath my fingers his scalp felt hot, his hair uncombed, the strands oily. The bed shook with his sobs.

He meant the deaths of his mother and Frances Allan. And then there was the mother of his best friend in school, Jane Stannard, whom he'd loved and admired. She'd died horribly of a consumptive brain fever, and so young—the one for whom he'd written "To Helen." One by one they'd died, and left him. But I, the woman he'd written more poems and stories about than all of them put together—I was yet alive, if damaged. So he must be rehearsing my death already, mourning me in advance, over and over.

How many times would be sufficient to prepare him? Would any number be enough? My fingers tightened in his hair as I thought of this, but he sighed and didn't flinch.

I felt so tired. Filled with envy for every insect and lizard and bird and stray dog, who would never have to know how close they stood, each day, to a dark abyss.

But I am barely seventeen, I thought. Too young to die, and become merely a pretty name etched in black lines on a white page.

· 15 ·

As the young mostly do, I recovered, though slowly. Over those long months, as I lay regaining my strength, Eddy went to work for Billy Burton.

The *Gentleman's Magazine* expanded under his direction, and he added his own contributions. "The Fall of the House of Usher" was the tale of a cursed family to which one bad thing after another happens—for they were all as mad as hatmakers—until the brother ends up accidentally putting his sister in the family tomb before she's quite dead. When she claws her way out and totters into the study to reproach him for this unseemly haste, she falls on him and he dies of fright and remorse. Then the rotten pile of stones that was their ancestral manse topples into the adjacent tarn—which sounds exotic but is merely a common Scottish lake.

Eddy had imbued the most ordinary objects and people with desolation and terror and ruin. The doomed Roderick is a romantic weakling who, realizing his mistake, doesn't have the gumption to get up and undo it. His sister Madeline suffers from a rare blood malady which is only cured by that brief sojourn in the tomb. Perhaps the sole place she could escape him? I shuddered as I read, enjoying the terror, yet feeling an odd unease that I was still able to do so, considering my own condition. Sometimes with ill health, as with ill luck, comes a graveyard bravado as well.

After a few months, though, relations between Eddy and Burton were not going half so well as the magazine's subscription figures.

"You'd think a man would appreciate the success of his own magazine," my husband fumed one evening after dinner, while we were sitting in the front room.

I could eat heartily again by then, and had enjoyed the roasted chicken and fresh peas my mother had made. "Doesn't he?"

Eddy was sitting at his desk, hair tousled, tie askew. I was lying on the settee, rereading his *Tales*. Catterina, who'd grown into a big heavy lady-cat, lay across my bosom. She made an excellent blanket, her substantial weight warm and pliant and pleasant.

Eddy threw up his hands. "Apparently not! He's always looking for reasons to be angry with me. Claims I owe him money! When I produce figures which prove I don't, he only becomes more angry. The man's an ass. I wrote him a letter today saying so."

Oh dear, I thought. Not again, so soon. "Perhaps he's more interested in the theater than in literature. He may not understand how you—"

"He's circulating vile rumors about me, Sissy." Eddy got up from the straight-backed chair and came over to sink onto the settee.

He pulled my stocking feet into his lap and stroked them with one hand, the cat with the other. I noted a hole near the toe of one; perhaps I could darn it tomorrow. "What sort of rumors?"

"That I drink heavily. That I can't be trusted, and tell enough lies to fill the deepest well. That *he* must do all the work himself, poor fellow."

I especially gasped at that first accusation, for of all the assertions, it was the most untrue. Eddy had gotten terribly drunk, yes, but only that once when he'd thought I was dying. My chest swelled

at the injustice. "Oh dear, that's terrible," I croaked. The outrage
swelling in my chest brought on a cough.

"He wants to run the magazine like an amateur-night contest,
and print free material from ignoramuses. The most wretched swill
scrawled ungrammatically on cheap paper—oh, my dear, are you
coming down with pneumonia again?" He seized one of my hands
so quickly he knocked my book to the floor.

"No, no, just a touch of pleurisy."

He smiled, and I smiled back. Reassured, he told me about his
day. On top of his quarrel with William Burton, that afternoon
Eddy had outpointed a young lieutenant at the gymnasium, shoot-
ing with pistols at targets. Then the man tried to insult him. "He
said no wonder I'd been discharged from the army, as everyone
knows poets lack common sense and intelligence, and should never
be trusted with firearms."

I laughed, then stopped when I felt a growing pressure, as if
I were about to be struck with a new bout of coughing. "But if you
outpointed him, then—"

My reasoning seemed not to cheer up Eddy much. "Oh God, I
feel terrible," he groaned, lying back to join me completely on the
settee. Catterina turned to look, her slitted green eyes widening.
She flicked her tail, then leaped off my chest and stalked away.

The next day Eddy took to our bed, and I stayed there too.
Muddy climbed to the third floor with a tray. She laid it across our
laps and Eddy fell to with an energy which suggested more sulk
than sickness. "My two invalids," my mother muttered each time
she came up, but in a mostly good-natured way.

Under her mustard plasters and alcohol rubs, my pleurisy
slowly disappeared. However, she would not let me get up again
until I'd been free of fever for more than two days. So Eddy and I
lay there together and gradually grew bored—of ourselves, of each

other. We took turns reading aloud; first from the books in the room, then from creased back issues of the *Weekly Messenger*. No *Gentleman's Magazine* though.

After he deciphered a supposedly difficult word puzzle in an old *Messenger* in less than three minutes, Eddy had a brainstorm. "I'll write a notice offering a challenge to all Burton's readers. To stump me with any sort of difficult cryptogram they can devise," he said. A moment later he was up rummaging for clean linen. Then in record time bathed, dressed, combed, and on his way out the door, apparently fully recovered.

The next day I was up too. I would not be a fainting maiden from some old oil painting, nor a doomed bride in a Gothic tale. Look, I thought, as Muddy fastened my stays. See how soon I've gotten over this! Clearly Eddy's fears were baseless; unlike the others I would live with him a long, long time.

The day I understood this might not be the case, I wasn't lying in bed with pleurisy or a new fever. I was sitting at the piano in the parlor, playing and singing, entertaining a room full of people.

In January, to welcome in the new year, Eddy and Muddy and I were hosting a supper. I'd invited one of our Baltimore cousins, Dolly Herring—Mrs. James Warner now. We'd lost touch with the Herring side years ago, but Muddy and I had been shopping on Chestnut Street and bumped into Dolly at a milliner's. I was buying plain satin ribbon, Dolly trying on a fluffy concoction like a pink serving platter piled with egret feathers, topped with a stuffed dead dove. The poor bird's glass-bead eyes seemed to reproach Dolly in the mirror for both its fate and her terrible taste.

What no one else knew was that this dinner was a rehearsal as well as my informal debut. I'd been practicing faithfully, both voice and piano, and felt ready to offer myself to entertain in concert at private gatherings. I'd already spoken to Mr. Heddy, a music master who was willing to give me more lessons—lessons which would be partly paid for by showcasing my singing at some patron's home.

When Dolly and James arrived, I was relieved she wasn't wearing the terrible pink hat. "Virginia!" she exclaimed as I met her at the door. "You look well."

"So do you," I said, and Muddy took her cloak. We linked arms and strolled to the parlor. Eddy greeted the Warners there, looking handsome and well dressed, for Muddy had just brushed his coat and mended his best trousers. His hair was clean and shining, swept back off his forehead in a dark wave.

"See Eddy looking at you," whispered Dolly, giggling. "My dear, how he worships you!"

He was just then offering James Warner a glass of spiced apple cider. Yet even as he served Dolly's husband he was glancing my way, and nearly spilled cider on Dolly's skirt. She gave a little shriek and hopped back. Eddy blushed and apologized.

We would not be drinking anything stronger. Eddy hadn't taken a drink for nearly a year, even though he'd been working so hard at the *Gentleman's Magazine*. The amusing Mr. Burton was not invited, but we were expecting the poets Henry Hirst and Thomas Dunn English. We'd stretched the budget tight this evening, but all of life can't be drudgery.

The last to arrive was English, who'd recently graduated from the School of Medicine at the University of Pennsylvania. He was only a couple years older than me, but so upright he looked like a soldier or a young pioneer. He liked to gaze down on you as he spoke, while stroking his mustache, and was so fond of his new title everyone tried to work it into the conversation as much as possible.

"Your husband's going to publish some of my verses," Dr. English said to me. Like every other person on earth, it seemed, he too wished to be a poet.

We all sat down at seven. My mother had outdone herself with an elegant platter of sliced smoked ham and new peas preserved from the previous summer. We sat and talked and laughed as Eddy impersonated other writers from the Falstaff Hotel crowd.

Inevitably the men set off like a pack of baying hounds on the trail of literary injustices—mostly against themselves. We women rolled our eyes at each other, and Muddy and I rose to clear. As I reached for her fork and knife, my cousin Dolly touched my wrist. "You will sing for us tonight, won't you, Virginia?"

"Yes, of course." I whisked her plate away. "As soon as I catch my breath."

Muddy, who was coming around the table toward us, her hands full of plates, said sharply, "What do you mean?"

"Nothing," I said. "Only that I've scarcely been able to . . ."

If I had said *breathe*, that would've been a mistake. My husband was well enough known that the gossips in Philadelphia would soon be whispering, "Poor little Virginia, the child bride of Edgar Poe. Did you hear?" By breakfast they'd have me in the tomb, like Madeline Usher. Even though I was now quite, quite well.

". . . scarcely been able to rest," I finished. "Just run off my feet all day long." Then I turned and walked out to the kitchen, feeling their probing gazes like tentacles of creeping ivy.

I planned to play several light selections and one difficult piece, an aria from Gioacchino Rossini's *La Cenerentola*, inspired by the fairy tale "Cinderella." The opera had just come from a triumphal run in Baltimore to play at the Academy of Music Theater, and Eddy had taken me to a matinee. Later I'd found a water-stained copy of the lyrics in a book stall at the market. I would attempt the final aria, sung by Angelina at the wedding. At the end of the opera she ascends in her white shimmering gown to the top of a huge structure shaped like a giant wedding cake, still singing, as all around her men and women throw glittering confetti into the air.

I felt in some ways like a Cinderella, a young woman risen from the ashes of illness to good health and back to music again. Nothing would make me happier than performing tonight. So after the table was cleared and every guest had finished his coffee, we went into the parlor. As they found seats I stepped up to the bench and arranged the few sheets I owned in the order I wanted to play them. The rest I had by heart. Then I glanced at Eddy, whose smile lit his face. I knew what he was thinking: Perhaps he'd never have a great house, or impressive wealth, or the fine clothes and beautiful things of his lost youth. Yet his whole countenance said, *You, my talented love. You are worth all that and more.*

I smiled, then turned to the keyboard and began with "Come Rest in This Bosom," just for him.

> *Come rest in this bosom my own stricken deer,*
> *Though the herd has fled from thee,*
> *Thy home is still here.*

Everyone applauded after the last notes faded. I bowed and tried not to blush, which was impossible. Then Dolly shouted out, "'Woodman, Spare That Tree'!" Please play that, Sissy."

I did happen to know it. So I played that one and a few more, then tackled, "It Is Said That Absence Conquers Love."

I knew I needed to embark on my final selection, the Cinderella aria, before my breath began to lag. The tempo was quite fast, the notes repetitive, and the song called for much coloratura. But I had practiced a great deal and was now able to get through it all nonstop.

I turned to that page and played the introduction. My voice flowed smoothly through the lyrics, and did not sound tired or strained. And though I could not turn to look into my audience's faces, their admiration and awe flowed over me like a warm, welcome breeze.

But halfway through the aria, a sharp pain stabbed my chest. And suddenly my mouth was flooded with salt and hot iron. I stood from the bench and raised one hand to clutch my throat. I clamped the other over my lips, but still hot liquid trickled, then gushed between my fingers. A stain spread like a red bodice over my pale blue dress. Ruby droplets pattered, then rained onto the yellowed ivory keys.

I turned to Eddy, unable to ask for help, eyes blasted wide with fright. I felt I'd been standing there forever, a bleeding statue. Yet it must've been a second or less, for my audience was still leaning forward raptly, as if to better appreciate the music. As if this sudden bloodletting were some artistic effect, a new and messy brand of opera. In slow motion their looks slackened to puzzlement, concern, then horror. And then everyone sprang forward as if released like tightly-wound clockwork toys, all rushing toward me.

The piercing pain was gone as quickly as it had come. All I felt was embarrassment: what a terrible scene, what a sickening mess.

Eddy reached me first, then Muddy, but both stepped aside for Dr. English. "It's vocal strain. She's probably just burst a blood vessel," he said, but his voice quavered and he was biting his lower lip, as if holding back some pointed comment. "Come, let's carry her to the settee."

I was lifted by several pairs of arms and borne like a sacrificial offering to the sagging green velvet sofa. Being carried so across the parlor felt ridiculous; I opened my mouth to laugh and protest that I was fine. But a new gush filled my throat and I choked on fresh gouts of blood.

After that I could hear nothing but my own harsh breath, the rasp and gurgle heavy and loud in my ears. Even as I grew lighter, floating like Ophelia across the room past a vase of flowers. To where Muddy stood, her face, normally so ruddy, pale as tallow while her shaking hands arranged thin silk pillows to receive me. All else was a blur, save for one more face: Eddy's. Full of pain, of horror or fear, and how must I look to him? His dear, dainty little wife laid out corpselike on a secondhand altar, smeared with blood like a pagan hecatomb. I turned my face into the cushions. But in that pose I could not breathe, so I rolled it back again, to stare at an angular water stain on the ceiling shaped like a dark bird poised overhead.

"Go out, get my saddlebags," Dr. English snapped. Someone—it sounded like the heavy tread of Henry Hirst—ran off to do so.

My mother and Dolly had disappeared. "Where's Muddy?" I tried to ask. I wanted my mother, but speaking meant to risk choking again. Oh God, who'd have thought I had so much—was there no end to all the blood in me? Something had torn inside and I feared it would never be mended now.

Muddy reappeared with Dolly, the two holding each other up, looking like frightened girls. My cousin's face swam closer, tight with fear and I think a certain excitement too. So much was happening, but not to her. Together she and Muddy sponged my cheeks and chin and throat. When Dolly kept scrubbing at my tucked bodice, the sodden rust-stained lace of my dress, I nearly laughed at her intent frown. Couldn't she tell when a thing was utterly, hopelessly ruined?

Muddy set a glass to my lips and I took a cautious sip. "Here, my darling girl," she whispered, and I spat the cool water out in a gush of pale red, into the chipped white bowl under my chin. Then English's serious mask, his doctor-face, hovered again. "Feeling better now, Mrs. Poe?"

I thought of a brave tin soldier. I parted my lips to speak but feared if I did it would start all over again. So I nodded once. Then Eddy dropped to his knees beside the settee with a thump. He grasped my hand and wrung it so hard I had to grit my teeth to keep from crying out.

"Just lie quietly now," said English. "It would be good if you could rest or even sleep."

"Her bed is ready upstairs," said Muddy. "If we can all carry her there."

Eddy kissed my hand, lips trembling, cheeks wet. "You tried to leave me," he whispered.

I turned my head. *No,* I mouthed silently. *Never.*

Someone, I think the young doctor, raised a spoonful of milky fluid. I obediently parted my lips. The thin trickle was white and bitter. Laudanum, to make me sleep. I did not want to waste my life, to slumber it away again like a cursed princess in a briar-wrapped tower. Yet I felt too tired to protest.

More of the bitter juice trickled down my throat. I swallowed it all. And then, someone extinguished the light.

· 16 ·

The next morning, or the next, I woke and could hardly tell day from day. Or even day from night. Someone was always by the bed—usually Eddy, sometimes Muddy or our kind neighbor Mrs. Deidrich. My husband would sit for hours waving a palm leaf fan with such a determined look—as if he could force more air into my lungs and heal me all the sooner. And I *would* feel better for a time, but then I'd begin to cough again, and they'd pour into me more of the bitter brew I now thought of as Sleeping Potion. Then I had no choice but to smile at the hand that held the glass, and sink back into drugged dreams.

In that dream life many people came to me, sometimes walking right through the wall into my bedroom. I didn't want to think I knew them, yet sometimes I did. Granny Poe was first. Yet she was younger, slimmer. So different. Then I realized why: She was walking along on her own, with no help, as if nothing hurt. But what did it mean, seeing her here now?

Another night I heard a racket of hammering in the next room, and thought with detached despair: *So, they are knocking together my coffin.* But then the hammering ceased, and footsteps approached. I looked up in the dim light to see my brother Henry.

He must've been building something with odds and ends of found wood, as he used to do when we all lived in Baltimore.

"When did you get back, Henry?" I whispered. "What does a sea island look like?"

Here he was home, and no one had said a word! I wondered what marvels he'd seen out in the world. "Did you buy a blue or a green parrot?" I asked, though he hadn't answered my first question yet.

He smiled and shook his head, as if to imply I was not to tire myself. Everyone always wanted me to save my strength, though they never said for what. Or perhaps Henry only meant to tell me I didn't need to say it out loud—that he already knew what I was thinking.

When he sat on the edge of my bed the ticking didn't sag. He patted my arm just as he used to when he was little and I even smaller, if I was crying about some silly slight or thwarted desire. I saw his hand clearly—its tanned back, the knuckles with black hairs, the thin white scar where his chisel had once slipped when he worked for the stonecutter. But I could not *feel* it. I stared up at the strange things twined in his too-long black hair—iridescent whorled shells like tiny, pearly ears. Thin green ribbons of seaweed. The lacework bones of a tiny perfect fish.

I wept then, for I understood at last: He was dead, drowned, and I had sent him away with my harsh words. No wonder we'd never heard from him again. How could I have thought gentle, quiet Henry would be so unkind as to not send a letter to his own mother and sister?

We sat like that for a long time, he smiling and silent, I weeping. But I must've fallen asleep, for when I opened my eyes again it was morning and Henry was gone. I wondered how in the world I could tell Muddy of this. No, I could not. Would it not be better for her to still have a healthy son she could merely miss, to be gently chided in absentia from time to time for his youthful thoughtlessness in not writing a single letter? I would weep and mourn secretly for both of us. Little enough else could I do for her.

Over the following months I was not allowed to even feed myself, having become Muddy's baby girl again. When what I wanted was to be a woman: to walk, cook, shop, tend a garden, hold a child, make a dress. Sing a lullaby. Laugh at some silly joke. And finally, to sing and play before a real audience. Especially if I was going to die soon. No one had to tell me to save my strength now, or not to speak. But what good in the end was faith or hope or effort or even love, if one still died and became nothing? I did not wish to say a word, and would not be comforted—no, not even by the promise of angels.

One morning a week later Eddy was sitting in a straight-backed chair he'd brought up from the kitchen, reading a poem he'd just finished, called "A Sonnet—Silence."

There is a twofold Silence—sea and shore—
Body and soul. One dwells in lonely places,
Newly with grass o'ergrown; some solemn graces,
Some human memories and tearful lore—

No beautiful dead girl in it this time. The lines seemed almost a eulogy for poor Henry, as if Eddy somehow knew or sensed my brother's fate too. Oh God, it made me sad. I couldn't listen to another word. "Eddy," I rasped, sitting up from the pillow which he'd propped behind my back.

He lowered the manuscript page. "Yes, my dear?"

"I must get up. I want to."

"Of course you do, and you shall. Just as soon as the doctor says it's wise. You're my only and dearest little wife. I'll take care of you."

I lay back again, despairing. His old army greatcoat was spread over me, on top of the blankets and quilts. Catterina perched atop all those layers, a queen enthroned on her woolly mountain. I was sweltering. It was May or even June, for heaven's sake. I kicked at the whole swaddling pile. But the blasted coat was so heavy—made from a whole flock of sheep, no doubt—it barely moved. Catterina raised her head and purred, gazing from her cliffside perch through green eyes slitted with pleasure. Cats love to find a person sick in bed so they can lie there too, and purr and knead you like overworked biscuit dough all day long.

But there were too many things I had not yet done! I had not sung a concert. I'd never played the piano for money, as Billy Burton had suggested. I hadn't even planted the garden with new flowers, white hollyhocks and blue iris. And I had never had a child, our child. Perhaps heaven was to be my destiny, to sit with gentle Jesus—but no! Not yet, not yet.

I refused to lie still while despair pecked at my heart like a persistent black bird. But I could not say any of this to Eddy. We could talk for hours about nearly anything—except my health. He would not hear or discuss the possibility that I was ill and might die. Perhaps he believed that if we said these things aloud it would make them come to pass. So we could not even contemplate together that what was wrong with me was not bronchitis, or fatigue, or even pleurisy. That it was certainly not, as Dr. English had so kindly and vaguely assured us, a mere burst blood vessel in my throat.

The truth was my secret. I was left alone with it on top of my mountain. This solitary knowledge would eat away at mind and heart, its small sharp teeth gnawing. Until the keeper finally understood that like an irrational, ravenous beast, the secret would swallow everything—houses and people and all the love within them—leaving only dust.

I opened my mouth again, to unlatch the gate and tell. As if he could read my mind, Eddy was out of his chair. The poem slid to the floor. He rushed to the chest of drawers, picked up a scrap of newsprint, carried it back to me.

"Look," he said quickly, the note of excitement in his voice only a little false. "Have I shown you this? The actual prospectus for my *Penn* magazine, from the *Saturday Evening Post*."

I took it from his trembling fingers.

To the Public. —Since resigning the editorship of the Southern Literary Messenger, at the commencement of its third year, I have always had in view the establishment of a Magazine which should retain some of the features of that Journal, abandoning or greatly modifying the rest.

A long description followed, and it did sound fine. To be published in Philadelphia, on the first of each month. Subscription price five dollars a year, the first number to be issued on the first of January 1841. "Six months from now," I murmured. "So soon."

I'd been a writer's wife long enough to know such an endeavor would require a good deal of cash in advance. To start up a publication of the quality described here might take three or four thousand dollars. We were unlikely to ever hope for that much in our whole lives. Eddy must've planned to interest a financial backer, some well-off patron of literature who happened to read this notice.

When I looked up again he appeared so hopeful I hadn't the heart to discourage him.

"Well, it sounds grand," I said at last, and handed the clipping back. "Really, Eddy, I can't wait to see your first issue."

But even after a second notice appeared in the January issue of the *Post,* Eddy enticed no patron. Once again he put his plans on hold.

I gradually felt better, though, and a few months later rose from my sickbed. I went out with Muddy to the High Street market, which in spring was stocked with large, perfect fruits and vegetables grown in rich black dirt by somber Amish and Mennonite farmers, at market stalls tended by their sober, fertile wives and sturdy-limbed daughters. Fat poultry, freshly-caught game, yeasty breads of every kind from crusty white to grain-studded wheat to stonelike rounds of heavy black pumpernickel. The farmers brought in pale tubs of thick white butter, large speckled brown hen eggs, and crisp green and red apples.

I still felt weak, so we strolled slowly through the clean, orderly Philadelphia streets, past redbrick houses and scrubbed white stoops and dry-set stone wells. Everyone walked those miles of square blocks during the day, bowing and tipping hats as we passed. A city resident called for his mail at the post office, twice a day if he liked, reaching across the counter to take a stack of foolscap notes with wafer seals from the postmaster's ink-stained hand. We had no money for postage though. Unlike the vegetables and eggs at market, its cost was sky-high.

Eddy was still trying to finish the curious shell textbook, so we went out often to give him peace and quiet. He finally finished editing *The Conchologist's First Book* in April, and published "The Haunted Palace." But for this poem and "To Ianthe" he received less than six dollars in total. He grew even more angry about Billy Burton.

"The man was pipe-dreaming when he said the assistant editor's daily work could be accomplished in two hours," he fumed. "I'm stuck in the office day and night, trying in vain to make a literary silk purse out of amateur-contest sows."

I'd always wondered at their initial mutual admiration, for just to see them together—the loud, ruddy Englishman and the pale, soft-spoken Eddy—was a study in contrasts. But the quick and clever Burton had clearly known a useful understudy when he saw one. He'd printed Eddy's name with the title "associate editor" way back in the July 1839 issue, without even consulting him. Eddy had only agreed to initial the contract provided he do very little editorial work, that monster which ate away his time and left none for his own writing. Yet a hill of just such material had immediately risen upon his desk. More stacks arrived daily, because the British thespian had so many other irons heating in the fire. Burton would slip off to New York for days at a time to attend the theater, leaving Eddy to slave in the tiny office.

"I agreed to write for this flawed sheet, not to edit it," he complained to me and Muddy each evening.

She only shrugged and nodded. To her, work was work. What difference? She mainly cared that money was coming in to feed and house us, and who could blame her? Eddy had promised that much, and she'd left her lifelong home because she believed him.

Despite his loud complaints he could never stop himself from improving even the slightest, cheapest excuse for a magazine. Over the course of a year he'd turned Burton's lightweight, gossipy, fashion-plate-stuffed organ into something much finer. And himself into a harried, overworked wreck inside the cramped office at Bank Alley and Dock Street. Business with printers, engravers, and binders pulled him out into the streets daily on a furious round of errands. Once he passed by a foot from me and Muddy on Bank Street, and I'd said, "Why hello, my dear!" He only strode on past, so intent, muttering so darkly to himself, he never looked up or recognized us.

We'd glanced at each other, Muddy and I, and just shaken our heads. I wouldn't criticize my husband aloud—least of all to my own mother—but it seemed to me that he sometimes brought problems on himself. Yes, the owners of magazines were a prickly, prideful lot, desiring fame and monetary rewards while someone else did the yeoman's work. Still, Eddy always signed on for these jobs eagerly enough, toiling like an indentured servant at each new venture— only to suddenly throw it all over because of some vague dissatisfaction or a passing slight. I was forced at last to conclude that my husband—such a good, hardworking one—was nevertheless his own worst foe. If he'd only stayed a bit longer with the *Messenger*, we might be in better circumstances now, and he not suffering from overwork but merely in a different location.

Again and again, though, as soon as he became totally enraged at the genial, duplicitous Burton, something would change Eddy's mind. Like the notice clipped from the St. Louis *Bulletin* some admirer forwarded:

> Let it never be forgotten that the first impetus to the favor of literary men which the Southern Literary Messenger received, was given by the glowing pen of Edgar Allan Poe, now assistant editor of Burton's Gentleman's Magazine . . . few writers in this country can compete with Poe . . . his is a high destiny.

I could not agree more. But when would the rest of "this country" ever acknowledge it and reward him?

One warm summer night he came home with an armful of newspapers, calling out, "Sissy! Muddy! Excellent notices for my *Tales* from the *United States Gazette,* the Philadelphia *Pennsylvanian,* and the *Star* and *Evening* Post—of New York! 'There has been no such art before in America,' they say."

I threw my arms around him and Muddy applauded. But then he threw the papers onto the settee and dropped beside them, head in his hands.

I sank down next to him. "What is it? Aren't you happy?"

When he raised his face it looked older, ravaged. "Oh yes, very. But why, with all this favorable commentary, is the best I have to offer so cheaply bought? Why can I get nothing for it but favorable reviews? Can we eat paper?"

He grabbed one section and wadded it up. He did not smell of liquor, so I feared for a moment he'd truly gone mad and would stuff the offending paper in his mouth.

"Eddy, no!" I gently pulled the newsprint from his fist and tried to smooth it on the settee.

He laughed bitterly, but then pulled me onto his lap. "Huzzah! I'm the literary lion of the New World. But at the going rate our little pride will starve."

I met Muddy's eyes over his head. She turned away and went back to the kitchen.

Poverty did make us all enterprising though.

Next door lived the Detwilers, a genial German family. The bluff, stocky mister took a liking to Eddy. As did their son Billy, who loved to go out on the marshes with my husband. He'd paddle a rowboat down to Gray's Ferry while Eddy loaded his gun and took potshots at any ducks, coots, or geese that flapped by. Then, like a faithful bird dog, young Detwiler would leap into the chest-high water, even in winter, and wade out to retrieve the game. They'd bring in a bag of assorted waterfowl and divide it between our two households.

I secretly pitied the poor, limp birds that lay on the kitchen table, feathers still glistening with water droplets as their black eyes dulled. Soon to take the last leg of that final journey, when Muddy would plunge them into a boiling pot, pluck that fine plumage, and plop them naked into a pan.

Eddy was gleeful after these trips. I could see what he must be thinking: *Today, at least, I have provided like a king for everyone. We won't starve this week.*

At last Eddy wrote a scorching parting letter to Billy Burton, severing their connection and giving up his position. Right afterward, growing nervous at the thought of no income, he wrote Burton again. To everyone's surprise, he received a kind, magnanimous reply. So he kept on working for the Englishman, but now a shadow hovered over him. His work suffered under its pall. There were more great notices and high praise for his cherished *Tales,* but no more payment to acknowledge that genius.

The state of our finances meant I could pay nothing at all toward voice and piano lessons from Mr. Heddy. When I went to his studio to tell him so, he said, "That is a shame, Mrs. Poe. But may I suggest a solution?"

I nodded. "Certainly. I very much want to continue my studies."

"Well . . . you may defray the cost by performing, if you feel able."

I felt nervous but intrigued, imagining a performance much like that I'd presented in our parlor, though with a less dramatic ending. I would eschew any piece as difficult as the one that had felled me then.

"There's to be a benefit concert for a gentleman who's been ill for months. To help out his family," Mr. Heddy said. "I agreed to supply a vocalist. The performance would cover more than a month's worth of lessons. If you think your husband would approve?"

A benefit concert sounded quite proper and also would be a good deed. But I did not intend to tell Eddy, who'd see it as some form of charity—for us. So I only said, "Oh yes, of course he would."

The following week the music master sent a note detailing the time and place: at noon, at an address on Potter Street, which lay west of Market. Thus the next afternoon, after Eddy finished his lunch and left for the office, Muddy and I set out. I imagined this would be a drawing-room event, a fancy tea attended by ladies of means who liked to dabble in charity. No more onerous than singing to a parlor full of friends.

Following the directions Heddy had enclosed with his note, we turned off Lancaster into a narrow unpaved street. It gradually constricted even further, and the houses became lower, rickety, much older dwellings, their doors framed with dark unfinished wood and precarious hanging porches of knocked-together wood scraps.

Muddy looked sideways at me. "This Mr. Heddy is a decent gentleman?"

I sighed. "A respected music master, Muddy. Very talented. He studied in Italy."

She sniffed. "A foreigner, then."

"No," I said, trying not to grit my teeth. "An American music master. He only *studied* in Europe."

"What did he tell you of this concert you're to do?" Before I could answer, she added, "Except for fine needlework and a bit of painting, ladies do not work, Sissy. I don't approve of it."

I came to a stop. "What do you mean? You agreed to come along, so—"

"You've always been dreaming of something beyond this life.

The life that's our lot. Always thinking and pining for other, better things, like Eddy. So I'm coming along to see to it you're safe,
and—and to see you get what you want, this time."

After this remarkable speech she set her lips in a firm line and
would say no more. So, after a moment, we silently went on.

This part of Philadelphia lay close to Crow's Hill, where gypsies
often camped. The windows were flung open to the street. Women
leaned from some, talking and laughing, shouting at friends across
the narrow dirt lane. Some threw us frank, curious stares. People
passed carrying canvas bags and baskets, and I had the uneasy
feeling some of these bulging sacks did not contain simple dry
goods or the makings of a meal. The occasional wagon forced us to
draw closer to the buildings. On the inner edge of the broken half-
cobbled walk sat booths or stalls, sometimes the odd wheelbarrow
of meat or fish or vegetables. Everything for sale looked used and
battered.

A vendor caught my eye. "Lovely oysters from Baltimore,
madam!" Another shouted, "Try this good iron pot, miss!", with
a metallic clatter of pans. Muddy scowled, grabbed my elbow,
and dragged me on. Bent umbrellas, grayed shirtwaists, patent
medicines—all were displayed in a jumble. Women sauntered the
length of the street, returning to gaze at a cheaper bundle of rhu-
barb, a wilted head of lettuce, bantering with each other and the
vendors. Most carried infants who looked thin and jaundiced, already world-weary. A sparrow of a girl in faded calico, struggling
to haul a market basket half her size, was arguing with a grocer like
a canny old matron.

The hot air reeked of spoiled fish and vinegar; of decaying
vegetable skins and the musty sweat of secondhand garments. At
one stall fried fish and potatoes hissed in boiling grease over an
open flame, the smell turning my stomach. I'd been unable to eat

for thinking of my upcoming performance. I meant to sing the classical selection of sheet music tucked under my arm.

We passed one doorway where tight crowds of men and women, and even children, were drinking at the bar or waiting their turn to do so. A haze of tobacco smoke wreathed their heads like fog.

"Where *is* this place then?" my mother muttered.

I paused to glance at the number painted on a nearby post. "This is it," I said, looking with a sinking heart at the tavern.

Muddy stared, her face swelling with outrage. Just then a man strolled out in vest and shirtsleeves. "You her? That singer, Miss Poe? We been waitin' for you."

"Yes," I said. "But—"

"Mr. Heddy's ill himself, but said for you to come on in and we're to take care of you." He peered closely at me. "It's a respectable place. We do benefits often here, miss. For the poor, and those who's fallen on hard times, in the neighborhood."

"It's 'missus,'" I said faintly. "And I suppose—"

"You can't," said Muddy.

"It's only a few songs, and I agreed to help out. For charity," I reminded her. Besides, how else would I pay for lessons? "Only half an hour, Muddy."

Before she could drag me away I darted inside, following him. Near the door a placard set on an easel proclaimed:

A Concert on Friday afternoon
Two O'Clock on August 2
To Benefit Mr. Bill Moultrie
the well-known Apothecary of Potter Street
laid up with a Broken Leg and the Pleurisy.
Come forward Give the Support
a Man deserves.

People were seating themselves on a variety of benches and straight-backed chairs. About the room hung grimy paintings of hunting scenes, of oddly-proportioned racehorses, of politicians and pugilists. A piano hunched in one corner.

The master of ceremonies stood fidgeting on a raised platform. His red necktie was crooked; a daisy wilted in his buttonhole. His short, choppy haircut seemed a homemade job. A man sitting by the door held a dented soup pot, into which each customer threw some coins on his way inside. On the rows of benches men, women, and girls clasped pewter mugs or glasses. The air was thick with pipe and segar smoke. Finally the pianist, a young pimply man in a seedy sack coat, struck up a popular melody. The room by degrees grew full.

"Set yourself on that chair to the left of the stage," instructed my escort. "'N wait for him to announce ye." Then he melted into the crowd. Laughter rang out above the hubbub. I declined a proffered cider and shrank into my seat. Yet after a few minutes the singing, and even the uproar, began to give me a certain pleasure. The females who sat with glasses of beer, flirting with nearby young men, appeared to be young factory and workshop girls. If they lacked refinement, was that their fault? They must toil for ten or twelve hours six days of any week, for little pay. Yet they'd willingly thrown their hard-earned pennies into the soup pot. I could have ended up one of them, instead of having a loving husband and mother to care for me. Why shouldn't they enjoy themselves a bit?

Suddenly the master of ceremonies announced my name. The pianist played a prelude with great flourishes. I rose shakily, hesitated, and the announcer leaned down and whispered encouragingly, "Well then, c'mon up and sing something, young lady. Go on. I hear you're good."

I glanced again at the audience, then set my classical music on the seat of my chair. I climbed the pile of crates assembled as makeshift steps and centered myself on the small stage. My trembling knees felt boneless as a cloth doll's. "I'll begin with—do you know 'Woodman, Spare That Tree'?" I asked the pianist. He launched in enthusiastically. I hummed along, then raised my chin. Looking out over the heads of the audience, I closed my eyes and began to sing.

Woodman, spare that tree
Touch not a single bough
In youth it sheltered me
And I'll protect it now!

The rowdy room fell silent. Not a foot stirred, not a throat was cleared. At the second verse I felt more confident, and rose boldly to the upper notes. By the end I was singing my best; better than I'd known I could.

The applause that followed was deafening and not, I decided, merely due to the liquor being consumed.

"Have a drink," said the announcer, thrusting a glass in my face. "Only ginger beer; it can't hurt you."

I drank it off. Then sang again, this time "Flow Gently, Sweet Afton." I followed with every popular ballad I could recall, and the pianist kept up. I meant to leave the crowd satisfied after their rapt appreciation. I no longer felt I was doing wrong. I sang another song and another, and each time the room hushed. Again came the rapturous applause and shouts of "Another! Another!" I could not refuse. Their praise fell like sweet warm rain, sweeter than any I had ever received before.

One more, I decided. Then I would go out to Muddy. I glanced at the door where she waited outside for me. But she was here, inside, her face a study in disapproval—no, horror. Yet I saw that along with these emotions also struggled pride, even joy.

"I *must* go soon," I whispered to the announcer. "What's the time?"

"Only just after four," he said. "Now, will you sing—"

Oh Moses. Eddy would be home soon. "Oh dear, I must go at once!" I cried, and rushed away, then turned back to grab my sheet music. I jumped from the stage without waiting for a hand, and wound through the cheering crowd. Hands reached out to pat my arm. A man in a butcher's smock stood and clapped, as two girls cried, "Bravo, miss!"

I needed fresh air, to get away from the smoke and heat. I took Muddy's arm, pulling her through the doorway with me.

"Don't say anything," I begged, and gazed back imploringly. "Don't tell Eddy."

I started to add, *I'll never come back. Or ever do this again.* But that was not a promise I could swear to keep. My head ached from the noise and smoke. I longed to hurry away. I longed to go back inside and sing just one more song.

"You're hurting my arm," said Muddy very gently.

"I'm sorry," I said, and let go.

"I heard you from outside, and then came in. I hadn't enough for the donation, so I just stood at the door. Oh Sissy—how they clapped for you! A man at the counter said, 'Who in the world's that?' and I told him, 'My daughter.' I see why you dream of things that I—I never—" And then my sober, stoic mother burst into tears.

When she recovered she murmured, "No, that wasn't a fit place for you. And yet—but no, I will never tell Eddy."

By then we were on a different street, a quiet one with no market stalls and plenty of gas lamps. "You can't imagine what I felt in there, Muddy," I said. "Singing before that crowd . . . it made me realize . . ."

She peered at me, frowning. "Realize what?"

Soul, breath, voice—they are all the same for me.

I wanted to shout this out loud. But I'd been so ill before, it might alarm her. She might misunderstand.

"Realize I can't give up hope," I said at last. "Not ever. Not as long as there's a chance I might do that again someday."

She nodded and linked her arm with mine, and then we headed for home.

We did not know that while—aside from my secret concert—all of life proceeded seemingly as usual, Billy Burton had advertised the *Gentleman's Magazine* for sale without saying a word to Eddy. The comedian had been away more than usual, leaving Eddy to shoulder an even greater load. My husband was furious; he'd just gotten a bit of support for *The Penn.* Some days he turned up at home far too early, around noon, and would only answer Muddy's anxious queries with, "I am expected now to do double duty, while Burton takes in a new musical or drama, and stays away. Well, two can play at that game."

Finally Eddy too stayed away, for a whole week, and learned from a man on the staff that Burton had to enlist a friend named Rosenbach to manage. They'd carried the huge bundle of manuscript by carriage to Rosenbach's home, and sat up all night sorting pages. So the March 1840 issue was published without help from Eddy. Burton sent a letter on May 30 dismissing him for negligence. Eddy fired one back the next morning, taking issue with all the allegations therein.

"Now I'm without a job and without prospects, my dear," he

said after he returned from mailing it. "I had better resign myself and get used to it."

He went straight to bed, looking ill-used. Of course that would be the day Frederick Thomas, the lawyer turned novelist who'd only corresponded with Eddy up till then, arrived at our front door without notice.

Muddy greeted him. "Oh—Edgar is not yet ready for visitors," she murmured. "I am—I'm just getting him a late breakfast. Won't you come in?"

I bowed hurriedly, wishing I were wearing something other than my shabby white day dress. Though everything in my cupboard now showed hard wear or failing seams.

"I'll leave Virginia to entertain you," said my mother. "Please go into the parlor." She hurried away, leaving me with the full burden of our surprise and dismay.

Thomas took my hand. "My dear Mrs. Poe, lovely to meet you!" He was tall and slim; his brown hair waved over a forehead nearly as high as Eddy's. "You look pale," he added, peering at my face. "Have I come at a bad time?"

"No, no, certainly not." I begged him to have a seat, then noted his fine black wool trousers. Our settee was coated with Catterina's long orange fur. When Thomas crossed the room I saw the poor fellow had to walk leaning on a stout walnut cane. I was wondering whether to offer to brush the trousers, or if it would even be proper to mention them, when Eddy tottered in.

"I'm glad to finally meet you," he said to Thomas in a meek, subdued tone. He came over and stroked my hair. "Are you feeling well today, my dear?" He looked so anxious and beseeching, I couldn't be annoyed.

We had dry rye toast and black tea. Our guest was courteous, praising the simple fare and our home. He spoke of his great admiration for Eddy's work, while Eddy complimented Thomas's novel, *Clinton Bradshaw*. By then his presence in our parlor felt like a belated gift received during an otherwise disappointing year.

The last week of October, Billy Burton completed the sale of the magazine. But he must not have spoken ill of Eddy to the new owner, for George Graham got in touch in December and coaxed a new story out of Eddy. It was "The Man of the Crowd," about a fellow who walks the streets of a city, endlessly regretting some great crime, unable to stand being alone.

The character's struggle with conscience seemed to mirror Eddy's own battle. He muttered and cursed, threatening to sue Burton. Instead he went back to bed, all his plans to move forward on *The Penn* abandoned again. I suspected he hadn't had as much support, nor as long a list of subscribers, as he'd claimed a month earlier.

We finally had to sell my pianoforte to pay the rent. I assured Eddy I didn't mind. "No, really. I like singing a capella," I insisted. "And—and it's easier to make my voice heard now when I'm not competing with the music."

But inwardly I mourned. I'd mastered the beautiful, battered instrument with patience, and got great joy from playing it twice a day. On the days when my breath had come too hard and shallow to allow me to sing, I could still sit down and play.

By then we had nothing more nourishing in the pantry than molasses and bread. Still, on some afternoons—though I had no idea where in the world he got the money or the credit—Eddy would rise from his sickbed and murmur something unconvincing about a business appointment. He'd set off in the direction of downtown. And come home late, reeking of spirits.

· 17 ·

January 9 was Eddy's thirty-second birthday. The date was also supposed to herald the first issue of *The Penn,* but he'd postponed its publication until March. He was still ill, or at least firmly convinced he was. By then George Graham, who made cabinets by day and studied law by night, had merged *Burton's Gentleman's Magazine* with his own, *The Casket,* under the new name *Graham's Magazine.* I read with interest his announcement promising the new publication would be "embracing every department of literature, embellished with engravings, fashions, and music arranged for the pianoforte, harp and guitar."

I thought wistfully of my pawned piano. Of the sweet harp I'd long desired but not yet owned. The guitar was less elegant, not an instrument I'd ever felt much interest in. And yet, it *was* inexpensive . . .

I was beginning to wonder if I myself might somehow work for such a magazine, which was interested in music and songs— though doing what?—when Eddy received a summons from George Graham.

He got up, dressed, and by the time he was headed out seemed nearly recovered. Muddy and I set to work on the heaped sewing basket, for when you cannot afford to make new clothes you must mend the old ones frequently.

"Perhaps he'll offer Eddy a job," I said, jerking the thread tighter. Sewing made me feel clumsy and impatient; I'd never been a clever seamstress like Muddy. Two of her neat tiny stitches could've fit inside one of my large, sloppy ones.

"Careful, you'll snarl it," she admonished. Then, in a milder tone, "My dear, the cupboard is bare. If only we had a nice fresh fish for dinner. Or one of those fat ducks he used to bring home by the bagful."

"Surely Mr. Graham has the wit to know a good man, a good editor, when he sees one," I said.

"Surely," Muddy echoed, but she bit off the end of her next thread more savagely than needed to sever it.

I dropped the thin chemise I'd been working on, the rip in its seam only half repaired. What use was sewing a seam back together if the worn material would simply part again?

When Eddy returned, he rushed into the parlor. Shoved Catterina from the chair she'd been lying on, cleverly evading her lunge to nip his wrist. He sat, and before we could ask, gasped out, "Mr. Graham has invited me to be his editor at the new magazine!"

Muddy looked ecstatic, and I cried, "That's wonderful!"

"He says if I'll put *The Penn* aside for just six months, or at most a year, he will join me on it then."

"Well. Mr. Graham seems a far more reasonable man than Mr. Burton," said Muddy, though she'd liked Billy Burton and his silly old jokes.

"No question," Eddy agreed. "I'll supply my own work too— stories, poems, articles, critical reviews. Graham knows I shall get names for him—contributions from the great literary men of our time. The work will be octavo, ninety-six pages. The paper of excellent quality, the typeface new, clear, and bold. The circulation will soar!"

He paused to take a breath. Muddy, her eyes still on the sewing in her lap, murmured, "I suppose this agreement is set down on paper."

Eddy waved a hand. "The agreement is a verbal one, between gentlemen." But a shadow did pass over his face. "He offers right now only eight hundred dollars annually, in monthly payments. The best offer I have yet had."

"Quite the best," I agreed, nudging Muddy to remind her to act pleased too. "Where will your office be?"

"The other side of the city, Chestnut and Third. The top floor of the old Ledger Building. Up three flights, so I'll be fit again in no time." He leaned in to capture one of my hands, then winced and jerked away. He'd grabbed the one holding the sewing needle. "I begin at once. My salary starts this very month." He sucked a drop of blood from his finger. "I'll buy you pretty things, Sissy. A new piano. An Irish harp. Decent furniture. Perhaps even jewelry! And Muddy, you'd like a new tea service, wouldn't you?"

My mother's face glowed. We'd had to pawn the old china set. What a pleasure it would be to toss out the few chipped, mismatched cups that now sat on the bare open shelves in the kitchen. I'd help carry them into the alley behind the house, where we could smash them against the back wall.

"With—a new flowered teapot?" she added hesitantly, as if those homely items were normally cast in pure gold.

"Good Lord, yes," Eddy said. "And bone china cups and saucers to match!"

Now every morning an immaculately dressed man came down to the kitchen, to breakfast on a cup of coffee, a hard roll, and a salt herring. He left the gate at eight sharp and walked across the city to his office. There he worked until midmorning.

"At eleven Mr. Graham punctually appears to discuss any important decisions, collect the mail and any bills or banknotes for deposit. His wife is usually along too," Eddy remarked, with a funny little smile. "Then I go back to my heavy labors as that handsome, well-dressed pair descends to their carriage and the set of matched bays waiting below."

He gave me a wry look, but I think, really, that he was happy.

After the noon hour he met with artists and illustrators. "I do the work so Graham can do the prancing," he remarked. By the time he could put on his hat to leave, often Dr. Thomas English was waiting to accompany him so they might talk poetry all the way home.

Even Eddy's reviews were becoming more tolerant. He did less tomahawking, though still made a point of correcting the grammar and rhetoric of aspiring authors. I burst out laughing when I read aloud to Muddy his review of Lambert Wilmer's new poetry anthology: "'Mr. Bryant is not *all* a fool, Mr. Willis is not *quite* an ass, Mr. Longfellow *will* steal, but perhaps he cannot help it . . . and then it must not be denied that he touches nothing that he does not adorn.'"

I resumed my studies with Mr. Heddy, hoping soon to take up the harp. Perhaps we could all be happy and content. Eddy was writing again, at a prodigious pace: "The Gold Bug" and "A Descent into the Maelstrom." And by summer Graham's new subscribers numbered *fifteen thousand*.

Mrs. Graham sometimes stopped by in her carriage to take me and Muddy downtown, to visit the shops or have a cup of tea. Eddy had insisted on buying both of us new articles of dress, even underclothing. Then one afternoon, as we were putting up a batch

of jam from the raspberry canes I'd grown against one wall out in
the garden, men in denim work clothes arrived. They came slowly,
slowly, rolling in a tall gilded harp like a pair of dusty, uncouth
angels. They left and came right back carrying a sweet little ebony
pianoforte.

"Eddy! Oh, it's too much," I protested that evening—though I
loved both instruments.

"Don't even think of it," he said, beaming at my joy. "I'm even
now writing articles to cover the cost."

I caressed the silken ebony finish, smooth as the skin of a baby.
But I didn't want to think about babies. So I stroked the harp's
carved golden whorls instead, and sang to it in a high sweet voice.
My mother hovered, as if she feared I'd strain my throat again.

"Don't worry, Muddy dear," I soothed her. "I decided just now
I'm going to live forever."

"Don't be impious." She swatted me with a dishcloth, then went
back to the kitchen to inventory the pantry. It was well stocked
now, for Eddy set his paycheck in her lap as soon as he brought it
home. And finally, after it had appeared there month after month,
she admitted it might not be wrong to buy a few pretty things.

The next week we took delivery of a red Turkey carpet and had
it laid down before the black slate mantel in the front room, to
surprise the Editor. The motley chipped dishes had already met
their violent end out in the alley, smashed to bits as I'd prophe-
sied. We had a new matching Chinese Blue Willow set, and sturdy
mahogany chairs to replace the three oft-mended pine ladder-
backs. I felt breathless again, but with pleasure.

Yet later that day I came into the kitchen to see my mother
seated at the table, head bowed, weeping. My first thought was,
Dear Lord, it's about Henry. Somehow she's found out.

I rushed to her side. "Muddy, what's wrong? Do you have a

pain? Has a neighbor been unkind? Tell me!" I demanded, as if I could force her grief to be something other than what I feared.

She wiped her eyes on her apron hem. "It's just that—Eddy is making such a magnificent reputation for himself now," she whispered. "And—and everything looks so nice!" Her tears came even harder and more copiously.

So then I understood. Yes, things were going well now. But what if he should begin to fall off in attendance at the office? What if one of his authors or artists insisted on taking him out for a glass of wine? If he touched one dram, it could spell ruin for this new career, the end of our new comfortable living. And it would weigh hard, so very hard now, to go back to the old want and deprivation, the plain bread and molasses at every meal.

"Here, darling, let me help you up," I said, taking her arm.

She scrubbed at her eyes with both palms, muttering about "foolishness," laughing at herself. I could not bring myself to join in. Her fears were not unfounded.

Eddy sometimes attended lavish suppers and dinner parties given by the Grahams, who could afford to entertain as often as they wished. The fancy food and beverages, the mounded arrangements of cut flowers, on the few occasions I'd attended, had been impressive. The liquor had flowed freely. But with the colder weather a low, persistent cough settled into my lungs, and many nights I didn't feel well enough to go out. To keep watch over him.

I urged Muddy to go in my place.

She hesitated. "I feel uncomfortable among them. Those artists and society people and famous writers."

I laughed. "But Muddy, what do you think Eddy is? And you live with him here every day!"

"No." She shook her head. "Not without you there to talk to."

Yet so great was her fear of his possible fall, my mother began waiting until Eddy left the house, then pulled on her faded black shawl and trailed him like a shadow to the hosts' home. Where she would wait in the kitchen like an old nursemaid, in that fine house on Arch Street. Seated alone, stared at by servants, while a gay party went on in the next room. While a long mahogany dining table was set with bottles of wine and sherry and fine Scotch whisky, and spread with steaming biscuits and big rosy hams and juicy bleeding roasts and fancy iced cakes. Which the most distinguished artists, writers, and society people in Philadelphia picked and pecked at like a flock of cawing, preening, gem-studded ravens.

Muddy told me once that, as a serving girl swung the kitchen door open on the crowded, noisy dining room, she'd seen the great orator Henry Clay, in the flesh.

I stared, openmouthed. "Well . . . what was he doing?"

"Making a toast to Mrs. Graham. Calling her the most beautiful woman he had ever yet seen in Philadelphia."

I giggled. "Oh my. *That* must've made him popular with the other ladies."

She laughed too. But still I worried. Thomas Sully, the portrait painter, or John Sartain, the English engraver, or even good old Henry Hirst might take Eddy aside. And then, simply because they liked him and wished him to join in the fun, press a glass of liquor on him. And then . . . when it came to temptation, my husband was in some ways still a child.

"Does Eddy—mind?" I asked my mother. "When he leaves the party and sees you waiting there for him, like . . . like a . . ." But I couldn't think of a word that didn't insult either him or her, or both together.

She laughed. "Lord, no. He says, 'Why, there you are, Mother dear. Thank the Lord. Another fine evening wasted floating on the cream of society!' Then he laughs, takes my arm, and we walk on home."

He never complained to me, and always seemed glad to see her in the evenings. To see us both, waiting here for him. Yet sometimes he did remain away overnight, and then neither of us could sleep for worrying.

We were all happiest when he was home and at his desk, working on a new story or poem. Now it was a new kind of tale he called a "detective story."

"What in the world is that?" I asked. "I've never heard of such a thing."

"That's because I've just invented it. A story to be worked out as a puzzle is solved, by logical reasoning. Like solving a cryptogram."

"Hmm. Sounds more like work than an entertainment," I pointed out. "I wonder . . ."

"Wonder what?" He tilted his head like a curious bird.

"Oh, whether such a thing would catch on . . . very *widely*," I said. Really, though normally I trusted Eddy's judgment in things literary, I doubted many people would wish to read whole stories based on the arcane activities of policemen and criminals.

He turned back to his desk with a smug expression, as if he could already see the glowing future of his latest brainchild. This story was set in an ominous dark street in Paris. When he told me the plot I shuddered, not so much because it contained a grisly double murder, but because there was an ape in the tale.

"Ugh," I said. "Perhaps I won't read this manuscript, my dear. Will you mind terribly?"

"Not at all," he replied. As I rose to go help Muddy finish in the kitchen, he went on, "I'm going to read it aloud to both of you. You can hold Muddy's hand so she isn't frightened."

Men, I thought. And oh, how I hated monkeys, those sly wizened little half-humans. Thank goodness neither of the Henrys had ever brought one home from sea. But then my eyes filled with tears as I thought of my poor lost brother. I should tell Muddy what I feared—what I *knew*. But she might not believe it. Or else grieve herself sick when she learned her son lay at the bottom of the sea, with no burial rites and no shroud, only crabs to pick at his bones. And where, *where*? I had no idea at all.

Night after night that winter Eddy labored on his detective story, hunched at his desk, breathing at times as if he were running a marathon instead of pushing a featherweight quill pen across paper. His face was a study, as if his own word-pictures filled him too with equal measures of horror and fascination. By the third week I wanted to ask how far he'd gotten, but he was so absorbed I didn't dare disturb him.

Muddy rose and said, "I'll put more coal on the fire. It's getting low, I'm sure."

In any case, it was heavenly to have enough coal. To not have to worry or wonder, or stare at a few broken bits lying in the bin and think, It's all gone, almost, and how will we ever get more?

To simply have *enough*.

The next day was less cold, and fair, and Eddy had promised me a walk. But noontime passed, then three o'clock. At last I went to stand in the parlor doorway. "Are you nearly finished, dear? We should go, it's getting late."

He was slumped in the chair, staring at the opposite wall. When he turned to me his face was glowing. "Done at last. Tonight I'll read it aloud. I'm going to call it 'The Murders in the Rue Morgue.' You'll never guess who the killer is!"

"Murders?" Muddy was in the parlor too, and she looked up from her new teapot, as she was straining the leaves to pour a cup. "Eddy, you're such a kind, gentle soul. Why must you write of such terrible things? Phantoms and ghosts and shipwrecks and corpses. The living buried underground." She laid the pewter strainer aside. "Why not some pleasant thing instead?"

"I've got to take as a subject what readers want, Muddy. And what they want is to be frightened—to be taken, shaken out of their humdrum lives. To be *appalled*." He rose to help me on with my shawl, then slipped his arms into his old sack coat. "Though lately I've been thinking of a new poem. One with a bird in it."

Muddy smiled. "Ah! Now that sounds nice. Cheerful and sunny. More like it, dear." And she smiled and sipped her steaming cup.

His lips twitched. His face was a study as he steered me out the front door. So I suspected the bird he had in mind was no everyday robin or homely sparrow, but something much darker. A hawk, a vulture? Really, I feared to ask.

We set out at last on our delayed walk. The close of the year was bringing a brilliant, prosperous season for the magazine—and for us. I still missed Baltimore from time to time, but not often. Philadelphia had brought us at first new worries but, in the end, acclaim for Eddy. A greater measure of comfort for us all. We were finally, truly settled. And whether Mr. Graham understood this or not, the incredible success of his new magazine was due to this industrious genius: the pale, serious fellow who was handing me down the front steps just then as if I were made of glass.

"I'm not eighty yet, my dear," I said, laughing. "I'm sure I can make it down without breaking anything."

How funny he was, to still act as if I were less durable than flesh and blood, and might at any moment shatter like a decorative vase. All I had, after all, was a tiny cough.

· 18 ·

Graham's published Eddy's "Murders in the Rue Morgue" that April, and the magazine's circulation soared to over twenty thousand subscribers. It was the most popular periodical in the country. Eddy couldn't walk down the street without being stopped and praised and congratulated. People stared and whispered in a smiling, envious way.

"You are celebrated," I murmured, squeezing his hand with my gloved fingers.

He frowned. "Perhaps. But they also say I am an opium addict."

It was absurd. Perhaps he feared being taken seriously, or feared it would not last. Yet when he published "The Masque of the Red Death" and "Life in Death," circulation soared again, to over thirty thousand.

In early summer Eddy again heard from Frederick Thomas, who'd just secured a clerkship in the Treasury Department, under President Tyler's new administration. He carried the letter into the kitchen, where Muddy and I were peeling peaches for preserves. He stood near the mounds of pits and skins, grasping the letter, its pages trembling with his suppressed excitement.

"My hands are sticky," I protested, when he tried to hand it to me. Sweet juice ran in golden rivulets down my forearms.

"Freddie says here, 'I leave my desk each day at two o'clock,'" Eddy read. "And that its surface is so clear of work, if he wishes to write a story, then he does." His fingertips grew white clutching the thin paper. "And for this onerous labor he receives a thousand dollars a year!"

Muddy frowned. "But is a political job such as that secure?"

Eddy waved a hand. "Thomas *knows* people. And don't you see? So do I!"

He *had* been slightly acquainted with Tyler in Richmond, and they were both Southerners. But Eddy was a Whig and Tyler was a Democrat. Surely that party had their own hangers-on with hands outstretched. Then, as the implication of his words grew clearer, I felt suddenly cold. "You mean, you wish to leave *Graham's*? To move to Washington, like Frederick?"

Muddy looked horrified. "Mr. Graham has been nothing but civil and kind to you."

He glanced away, as if ashamed. "Yes, yes, he has. But—but—" He clenched his jaw. "The magazine is filling up with fashion plates again. And love tales! What next, society gossip?"

I didn't recall the last issue having a frivolous look. "But your stories! And you have the cryptograms, and—" Oh Lord, he was doing it again. Giving himself reasons so he might leave with a clear conscience. "What is really bothering you, my dear?"

He stared at me, mouth open. "Well, I—what if I can no longer do it?"

"What?" Muddy asked, looking mystified.

I thought I knew. "The stories?"

"Yes." He sagged. "And the damned—pardon me—the poems. On top of the editing, the reviews, the planning, the design—all of it." He sank into one of the kitchen chairs and leaned his elbows on the tabletop, heedless of the peach juice soaking his sleeves. He whispered, "What if I'm all written out?"

Before either of us could speak, he said, "Thomas went to a dinner at the White House and saw my old friend John P. Kennedy—he's now in the House of Representatives! If they can do it, why not me?" He lifted his head and scowled as if we'd scoffed. When we kept silent, finally he got up and left.

Eddy wrote back to Thomas in late June and received a warm reply, but in the end nothing came of it. Except that now we knew: He was no longer happy at *Graham's*. He had reason, it's true. Mr. Graham paid Eddy the agreed-upon eight hundred a year without complaint. He paid his authors liberally—very liberally—and of this too Eddy certainly approved. But how galling for him to work like a dog for Graham, and continue to receive the same steady but low salary, while the Grahams themselves became more and more wealthy through his efforts. For him to see nothing come of George Graham's earlier promises to help launch his dream of *The Penn*.

He was cheered briefly by a visit in March from Charles Dickens. Eddy had been able to guess the ending of *Barnaby Rudge* before its serialization was complete. His letter to Dickens had impressed the British novelist enough that he looked Eddy up on his travels in the States.

"We had a pleasant visit," Eddy told me that evening. "He promised to try to secure the publication of a volume of my stories in London. For payment, that is." The prospect buoyed his spirits for weeks.

Then Thomas wrote back, mentioning the possibility of a job for Eddy, perhaps at the Custom House here in Philadelphia. That was enough to fan the fires of dissatisfaction again. And so Eddy did it: He turned in his formal notice.

"Mr. Graham is a gentleman, yes," he told us. "But exceedingly weak. The salary was steady but didn't begin to repay me for all the labor I bestowed. And the magazine! It's become a catalog of contemptible pictures, fashion plates, popular music, and—and love tales!" He flung his hands up. "To stay on would only tarnish my reputation, which—God knows—is really all I have."

Muddy and I nodded, careful not to look at each other, or him. All he'd said was true, and yet—could he not have waited at least until a new position was certain, rather than an offhand comment in a friendly letter? Still, Muddy might fear for our futures, and worry about money, but she would never, ever accuse him. And I— what rebuke should I offer to a husband who took me with him always, who hovered to protect me from anything, even the lurking presence of a disease he would not admit I suffered from, with the fond anxiety of a mother for a newborn? My slightest cough caused him to shudder, to mount a renewed, devoted vigil.

"Who will replace you at Graham's?" I finally asked. "Do you know?"

Eddy smiled in fond condescension. "Rufus Griswold. An ordained minister, and a rather poor poet. But a nice enough fellow."

I frowned. "The one whose poems you tomahawked a year or two ago?"

I'd met Mr. Griswold at a party at the Grahams' house. What I'd noticed most was the way his eyes followed Eddy around the room, as if—as if he either wished to kill him, or to *be* him. I would not have trusted this Griswold with the care of my oldest, shabbiest pair of gloves, much less the workings of a magazine. I'd thought of him that night at the Grahams', with his somber ecumenical garb, his heavy brows and dark glances, as the Evil Genius.

"And you . . . approve?"

"Oh, he'll do well enough. He has some taste, and certainly

more tact than I. He's a worker. And he has forgiven me the hard review. He said so."

I doubted that. But there was nothing more to say. We'd have to get used to it, as we had done before. "Well, there's only one thing left," I said, and Eddy looked at me quizzically. "You must start up *The Penn* again. For now you can devote all your time to it."

He busied himself instead with more stories, to bring in a little income first. Finally, by the following January, we convinced him to see Henry Hirst at his law office. Hirst and some other men had expressed interest in Eddy's magazine venture, at a dinner months earlier.

But on the morning of the meeting my husband was still lying in bed at nine o'clock, refusing to come down to breakfast. I climbed the stairs and sat on the edge of the mattress. "Should I go in your stead?"

He turned his head on the pillow and gaped. "You?"

"I will, of course, if you are ill," I said, then forced a little cough. I felt terrible tricking him like that, but sometimes a husband needs a push to get him started doing the very thing he already knows he should.

"Oh, for heaven's sake!" he cried. "No, of course you can't go downtown alone and talk to a bunch of men who, who—"

I grinned. "Whom I know?"

"I'm getting up now," he grumbled. "Tell Muddy I'll be down directly."

I thought of walking with him to the end of the street, but it was growing colder outside and my mother fretted I'd take a chill. She accompanied him instead. So I sat by the fire waiting, drowsing in the heat, thinking about where our lives had led us. It seemed to me much like the course of the rocky Wissahickon River—sometimes a narrow, constricted stream, at others a wider, wilder torrent rushing on, carving its way tortuously through deep gorges which offered occasionally a glimpse of something finer, more pleasant—such as a country road, or a tame elk. Already the current had rushed us past so many whom we could no longer, even looking back with longing and great perseverance, still see.

Yes, he must commence *The Penn.* He had to have that much, at least. I would not allow it to fail. Somehow we must ensure its success.

Muddy came back and hung her shawl and bonnet on the rickety hall tree. "He seemed in better spirits by the time I left him."

"I hope Mr. Hirst has good news for him. For us."

"Whatever the news, he'll be the better for getting up and going out."

She made us a good hot supper of vegetable stew. "It'll keep, no matter what time he gets in," she said, practical as usual.

But that night Eddy did not come back. Not for dinner, not even by the time Muddy and I were both yawning and unable to stay awake any longer. I looked at the parlor clock and saw with alarm that it was midnight.

"Nothing to be done tonight," she said stoically. "I'll go down to Mr. Hirst's office first thing and ask after him. I'll take some books along to sell."

Whenever we were in dire straits, she would take a few volumes from Eddy's small library and sell them to book dealers. Usually with his permission, but sometimes not. He'd gotten upset on more than one occasion when she'd sold a book borrowed from an acquaintance. Then he had to try to buy it back, to avoid embarrassment. We'd both spoken to her about this habit, but if it came to a choice between books and food, Muddy always came down on the side of comestibles.

I slept that night in her bed again, for the first time in a long while. Or rather, I tossed and turned, and stared at the attic room's rafters, while she snored beside me. I had terrible nightmares and sudden fearful awakenings. So, when she got up just before dawn, though I did not like early rising, I jumped up too. We ate cold left-over biscuits and coffee, then I helped her dress. After she left me to go downtown I became a domestic whirlwind, washing dishes, sweeping and dusting the parlor, changing bed linens that did not need washing. I did it all, and still had idle time on my hands to sit and brood, to cough up the cursed dust I'd liberated and then in-haled.

I leaped up again at four-thirty and prepared dinner for three. More biscuits. Sweet potatoes buried in the hot ashes of the stove. Finally I heard the front door creak open, and I rushed to the hall.

There was Muddy with Eddy. He looked worn, and was lean-ing heavily on her arm. He also carried something in a wicker cage, and when he saw me there in the hall he lifted it. The cage must've been heavy, for he could only raise it shoulder high.

An agitated black-feathered bird hunched inside. It turned its head and fixed one fierce black orb on me, then opened its beak in a silent scream. Someone had split its long ribbon of pink tongue to make it an unnatural creature—to make it talk like a man. The wind blowing in behind them ruffled its feathers, which stood on end like the black cape of some savage prophet. I shivered in the cold draft, and took a step back.

"Thomas Clarke has agreed . . . to proceed with plans for *The Penn*," Eddy slurred. "Only we are agreed on . . . on changing its name to—to . . . what was it? Oh yes, *The Stylus*. More universal appeal. Less provincial."

I wrinkled my nose at the fumes of alcohol pouring off him, then nodded at the cage. "Yes, but—the bird?"

"Filthy creature," said Muddy, shaking her head. "Rooks are bad luck. Didn't I once tell you—"

"Shut up, you old bitch," Eddy snarled. "It's a gift for my wife."

Muddy blinked, but did not otherwise react, as if she doubted her own hearing.

"Eddy!" I gasped.

He looked sullen. "Graham isn't pleased with Griswold these last three months. Offered my old job back." He lurched a step closer.

"So . . . you took it?" I asked, flinching away when the blackbird or rook or crow let fly a profanity that made Muddy turn red and huff.

"Not—not yet. But I will, damn it. I will. So . . . looked for a gift, to celebrate. All the shops . . . too dear . . . not good enough. Then I see this stall in the market . . . you like pets. So, say hello to Pym." He shook the cage like a bell.

The poor creature. I reluctantly bent to peer in again. The rumpled black bird sidled away to the far end of its bamboo perch and screeched, "Dead! Dead!" At least, that was what I heard.

Eddy laughed. "Clever-tongued devil," he said. "I picked a talker."

"Dear God," I whispered. When he drank, Eddy became another person. One I did not know, or wish to. He simply stood there grinning at me, swaying and bleary, stinking of rum and sweat and stale segar smoke. I began to feel as if I were living in a madhouse, or a circus. But who were the keepers, and who the inmates? I turned away and went up the stairs without waiting for either of them. Muddy could take the poor damned bird back in the morning, or pawn it, or give it away. I didn't care which.

Eddy was still in bed late the next morning. I felt first annoyed and then concerned, for now he did indeed seem ill. He'd been complaining of terrible headaches and taking far too much calomel. When he finally rose again, a week or so later, he apologized for his behavior.

"My old Imp of the Perverse has been stirring," he confessed, head hanging. "I could not keep the devil in his place." But then he went out and sold "The Pit and the Pendulum," and "The Murder of Marie Roget." Still, our finances dipped dangerously low.

The next time it happened I wasn't singing, or exerting myself in any way. Merely sitting in a chair, rereading "The Masque of the Red Death," a story fraught with phantasms and colors, mostly black and red. Looking for entertainment before it was time to cook dinner, I'd plucked it idly from the shelf.

As I finished the tale my chest tightened, and I had to cough. Again the terrible pain, the familiar gush of bright red. I could not even cry out, and feared I'd drown in my own blood. *Is this what Henry felt, before he died?* This terrible pressure, the burning hunger for air but the air does not, cannot, come? Only the liquid fist of that choking, smothering sea of red. I knew too well what Eddy had meant, in the story he'd written. *Blood was its avatar and its seal— the redness and horror of blood.* There was nothing more horrible: the unstoppable tide rising in your throat, the hot salty metallic taste. Then, the drowning darkness.

Yet unlike Henry, I did swim up to the surface again. I came back to myself in our little room upstairs. A pallet was laid out across the room, so Eddy or Muddy had been sleeping there, watching over me. Oh no, I thought. Now *he* will be ill again too.

But at that moment it was Thomas Dunn English who bent over me, my wrist captured in his long, warm fingers. He was taking my pulse.

"How long do I have left, Dr. English?" I murmured, remembering his beloved title.

He flinched, so intent on counting off pulse beats he apparently hadn't noticed I was awake. "Oh—Mrs. Poe. You're back with us."

I wondered if he intended to answer me. No doubt he meant to be kind, to keep me ignorant so I would not feel Death's finger tapping my shoulder. But I had to know. For, while in my girlhood I might've been the mirror for Eddy's moods and opinions, the last few years I'd seen that his emotions had come to depend on my condition. If I was well, he wrote like a beautiful, genial madman, turning out reams of prose and poems. If I fell sick, he did too. Not always in a physical way; sometimes only his mind reflected the strain of deep despair. And of course, the turning to drink. When I recovered he once again became the dutiful provider, the celebrated author. It was a heavy responsibility, keeping myself in good health for the benefit of another.

So I fought back the Sleeping Potion. I gripped Dr. English's wrist as hard as I could and had the pleasure of hearing him gasp. "I know quite well what is wrong with me," I said. "You may call it pleurisy, or catarrh, or triple pneumonia if you like. But it's consumption, is it not?"

The poor man sighed. "Very well, Mrs. Poe. If you insist? The diagnosis would be phthisis, yes." He held up one hand as if to forestall hysteria. "Though you may outlive all of us yet."

I tightened my grip and he winced. "Of a hundred patients

you've seen in my condition," I went on, not certain English had yet at his tender age even treated so many, "what number will live on for five—no, ten more years?"

His smile faltered. "You sound so much like a detective, Mrs. Poe. As if the stories Mr. Poe writes—"

I squeezed the trapped wrist again, harder. "If you tell my husband, it will drive him mad. He'll be dead by nightfall." I no longer felt guilt at making such gross exaggerations. "But if you don't give me an answer I'll call him in now."

Dr. English's face sagged. I was giving him a hard time of it, this kind, earnest young man who did not wish to distress his patients. Who felt helpless, no doubt, when he could not heal them. "All right," he said dully. "At medical college I was taught that ninety out of a hundred will live five to seven years after the first hemorrhage. But the other ten might live twenty, even fifty years." He smiled uncertainly. "You might be one of those ten."

But this was not my first hemorrhage.

"Thank you. Is there any way until—" I took a slow, deep breath to calm myself. "Until that unfortunate day, to avoid the—these terrible, sudden attacks? They are killing my husband even faster than me. And my mother—"

He patted my hand. "Perhaps, if you can cooperate. My colleagues prescribe a number of different treatments. A diet of red meat and eggs is often urged. As is exercise. A regimen of walking, even horseback riding. But in your case I do not think exertion would be efficacious."

"What else then?"

"First, you must go to bed for months—perhaps as long as a year—and stay there, regardless of how ill or well you may feel. No matter what happens to your husband or your mother. Eat well and stay warm. Boiled eggs every morning, and plenty of hot beef tea and milk and roasted mutton."

Ugh, mutton. "I see." So I should be fed like a baby, and entombed alive for a year. Like Ligeia, like Madeline Usher and Morella. "And then I shall be resurrected?"

"Pardon?" Dr. English frowned. "Oh, I see—a little jest." He didn't laugh though. "Your body must be completely at rest. Avoid damp air at all costs. You mustn't move even your little finger unnecessarily. I would keep you sedated for much of that time, to make sure."

Buried and drugged. "So I will be dead for a year."

He looked shocked. "No! You'll sleep, like the fabled young beauty in the fairy tale. And wake as young and lovely and refreshed as she was."

At least he didn't promise me a prince and a castle. "Then I shall rise and live again?"

He nodded. "If we can slow the progress of the disease, you may outlive us all. As I said. In any case, this treatment will give yourself and your husband time to, to . . ." He paused and cleared his throat, looking away. "More time."

So I must be content to exist mostly in dreams until then, like Sleeping Beauty. Even more a prisoner than the poor foulmouthed crow, Pym, in his wicker jail that Muddy kept hanging in the kitchen, where it hypnotized and enraged Catterina. My practical mother hadn't had the heart to return the miserable bird to the dirty market stall where Eddy had found it.

I would live, but only under the stupor of the Sleeping Potion. I decided to start calling it my "Sleeping Poison," that bitter dream-milk as insidious and all-powerful as any magic elixir in a fairy tale. Yet I had to love and cherish it too, if it would help make me well. Or at least, give us a bit more time.

With that diagnosis, I suddenly had to become one thing and not another. No longer my living daylight self, but a creature held captive to night and shadow and whispers. They said I was in a sleeping trance, a sort of endless swoon, for the first few months of that year. All I recall, though, is a garden.

It lies right outside, but you can get there only through my window. Large and green, almost sunless in the mornings, its plants and bushes elderly, limbs gnarled. Shaded by fruit and pale beech trees, enclosed by a hedge of yews, the borders of its paths are stitched with rows of bloodred dahlias. Camellia bushes bloom in streaks of rosy color. Ferns and violets and lilies of the valley too. But why, I wonder, are they all blooming redly together, at the same time of year? Those last should come up in the spring, and it is still fall. Would I be here still to see that emergence of new life?

Perhaps I am being punished for my sins, by the shortening of my stay here on earth. But what were those sins? I cannot recall, no matter how I try.

The people who visit come at all hours of the day and night—the two Henrys, Clemm and Poe. Granny Poe, even my longlost father. And sometimes a little girl who looks a great deal as I did when a child.

She doesn't speak to tell me who she is when I ask. Sometimes I pretend she's my daughter, the one I was to have with Eddy . . . There was once a queen who dreamed of a daughter as white as snow, as black as ebony, as red as blood. But wasn't it the young daughter in the tale who had to sleep forever? In any case we can go out the window and walk the paths together, the girl and I, and she holds my hand in her tiny one, though I can't feel her grip. It's very odd.

On the sheltered north side of this Night Garden grows a thick, muscular wisteria vine, bare except for a few glossy leaves. It is slowly murdering a poor rickety arbor with its viselike grip. The aged, splintering fence that borders the yard straggles and lists, shedding paint like a leper's skin. Still it strives valiantly to keep wandering beasts from stripping the orchard of its fruit. I don't recognize the hanging orbs that grow there, but Henry teases me when he comes, saying, "It's the Fruit of the Sea, Sissy," and it's strange, but I feel we actually are near the ocean, though I know the seashore is miles away.

It isn't so bad, being entombed for a year. I've a great deal of company. Dear people I haven't seen in years. And I can sing again, in my dreams, unlike the poor Little Mermaid who gave away her voice for love, then did not get that either. I hope my own sacrifice will be worth it—this long yet busy sleep, for the health of youth, the gift of unlabored breath. Though sometimes, even now, I feel a terrible weight on my chest, heavy as iron. Henry says it's the black toad. The heavy cast-iron doorstopper that belonged to Granny Poe, the one that kept our back door from slamming shut.

That frightens me, though I won't tell him so, because he's a big brother and they like to frighten little sisters, who must be brave, or at least pretend lack of fear. The toad was hard and heavy and ugly, so perhaps Henry is right. Its weight feels the way it used to just before I'd begin to cough, when I was awake. Until the blood tide would rise, and the dull knife of pain was finally sheathed for a spell in its sacrificial flow.

It is sheathed now, and so am I—swaddled in sheets and blankets, numbed by the Sleeping Potion, that gentle Poison. Entombed in my soft crypt, roused occasionally by Muddy or Eddy to sip water or eat a little broth or soft mashed egg or potatoes, or to drink beef tea. "No mutton, please," I always whisper, and they must be listening, for I haven't tasted any of that dark, greasy, stringy meat lately.

One day I woke again and discovered the weight on my chest was not the iron-black toad, but the warm furry bulk of Catterina. When I looked around the room, everything was the same. Here was Eddy, and Muddy, and later in the day came Dr. English. Yet while I had slept, apparently the outside world had gone on changing. *The Penn* had failed when Eddy was unable in the end to raise sufficient funds or a large enough list of subscribers. And he would not be working for Mr. Graham ever again.

"Instead, my dear," he told me with great excitement, as he clung to my hand and stroked my damp, tangled hair. "As soon as you are well enough, we'll be packing up everything and moving to New York City."

"New York?" I murmured in confusion. "But—again?"

He nodded vigorously. "The book trade is flourishing there. I must move into writing novels, and I must live in the thick of the literary world. In the meantime I've high hopes of publishing my collected tales, and perhaps a volume of poems."

Muddy met my confused glance over his head, then turned away. As marvelous as they were, these collections never made money. And I lay there recalling the hard cold wind that had tumbled down Bloomingdale Road, New York's broad main way, like an invisible avalanche. The soot and dirt and dust that swirled and blew and grayed the city so that its very air seemed far too busy. How long Eddy had tramped its streets before and found no work, no acceptance from his fellow writers! But then I saw how eager he was, how hopeful. If he believed this was his fate—no, ours—then I would have to believe it too.

He carried me down the stairs as if I were a new bride. I ate my breakfast sitting at table for the first time in a whole year. I finished a slice of bacon and half a biscuit, and drank two cups of coffee, and my previous thoughts seemed silly and melodramatic. After breakfast I went back to bed. Later the same day I was sitting up and receiving company like a duchess. Eating normal food, even walking around a bit. I felt very well indeed.

Dr. English cut back on my medicine, and then for a few days I felt worse. But I hardly ever coughed, and could breathe again without gasping and choking. *Soul, breath, voice,* I told myself. *They are the same.* The doctor came again and smiled proudly, fondly at me. His "sleeping cure" had worked.

I saw things more clearly too. Things I could not have known while I was in the enfolding arms of the Poison. For instance, certain items of furniture were here no longer. Now Muddy went out with a basket full of mending—the kind of drudge work that was a waste of her artistic skill with a needle. Eddy's library of treasured volumes had shrunk even further. And the way they always tried to get me to take my meals upstairs, or in an easy chair in the parlor, while Eddy worked on "The Black Cat" and "The Tell-Tale Heart."

These were good meals indeed, the rich hearty foods Dr. English had prescribed: rare veal and copious eggs, fresh apples and thick cream. While they sat out in the kitchen, furtively bolting meager fare, to afford the means to make me well again.

They claimed I was still not recovered. But I had a plan of my own, prescribed for myself. I began to do something like what Eddy did with the people he made up in his stories: I created myself anew each day. Hoarding strength when no one else was around, resting, holding still as Catterina when she spied a bird in the garden. Not speaking or moving, but waiting like a character in a book whose turn on the page is not yet come round again. Occasionally, when alone in the house, I practiced my scales again, very softly. Then when Muddy and Eddy returned, I became lively, making each gesture, each sentence, each short walk across the room a convincing work of art.

I could sing again, if I did so softly and chose undemanding songs. And if I could artfully create the illusion of health, every day, would it not perhaps come to me in earnest, in time—and even stay?

· 19 ·

Muddy wanted Eddy to go on to New York to prepare the way for us. But when she said so at the breakfast table, a week before the departure date, his hand faltered halfway to his cup. "Go alone?" he mused, biting his lip.

"You must, Eddy. Sissy and I will stay on until you find suitable lodgings. We'll sell the things here we don't need, and close up the house."

He looked down at his plate, as if hoping for some better answer to appear in letters of fire beneath the crackled glaze.

"I'll go," I blurted out.

They both winced and exchanged wordless glances. At last he said, "Well, but . . . are you able?" He looked very hopeful that I would say yes.

Really, I had no idea. But Eddy could not go alone. Imagine what might befall him if he were left unanchored in the city, set adrift! Liable to be invited or even just stumble into any number of temptations. And I could not stay in Philadelphia alone, without Muddy, and do all the work which must be accomplished for yet another move. What if I fell sick here, with no one to care for me?

If he went alone, all the taverns and gin cribs of New York awaited him like unsavory old friends. He would resist, of course,

but in the end be unable to withstand their siren song. Even when
Muddy and I were nearby, Eddy sometimes stumbled off the path
of temperance. Over a hundred miles away, alone in the city, there
would be nothing to stop his unchecked descent into the bottle. I
knew this now as well as I knew the lines on my husband's face,
and all that had put them there: the losses of childhood; the Poe
family's Old Failing; the stubborn refusal of this world to care
much about the things that kept any sensitive soul alive. So it fell
to us—Muddy and me—to be the gatekeepers, almost the gaolers,
of a sane artist, or else the caretakers of a mad, sodden genius.

He loved us, yes, but must also resent us, though I hoped not in
equal measure. Oh yes, I had seen the battle rage behind his eyes
as he sat in the parlor with us and drank Muddy's weak tea and
tried to attend to her mundane talk, and mine—just as clearly,
there behind his gaze, overlaid by a gentle smile and patient mien,
was the *longing*. I'd seen it when we visited the homes of friends,
and he glanced at the rum and whiskey sitting opened on their
sideboards, and then slowly turned his face away. Or when we
passed a tavern or gin shop downtown, and the smell and the sight
of those dazzling displays of amber and crystal called to him, both
at once. So that when he made a great show of looking back at me,
as if nothing were amiss, I could see also—for one clear fleeting
moment—that Imp of the Perverse. The resentment he felt that my
presence, even though requested by him, denied him all those poi-
sonous pleasures as well.

And I in turn would feel, for my own hellish instant, the stirring of my own Imp. An answering prick of what in other circumstances, with any other soul, I might label as Hatred. But this
was Eddy, *my* Eddy, who needed me as no one else on earth did—
and I was certain now, no one else ever would. The feeling fled,
however, as quickly as it came.

At least, for me. But did it flee as quickly for him too? Or did that eldritch worm of resentment burrow into his heart, unseen by us but felt—ah! so keenly—by a heart as sensitive as Edgar Poe's?

But no, I would not in any case allow us to descend into that dark maelstrom again. So I smoothed my damp palms down my skirts and looked at Muddy and Eddy, turning my lips up into a smile. This character was one I'd used before. I thought of her as the Singing Housewife. So I softly trilled a verse:

> *I dreamt I dwelt in marble halls*
> *With vassals and serfs at my side*
> *And of all the company gathered there*
> *'Twas you that pleased me most of all . . .*

"You see?" I looked around with defiance and, I admit, some pride. "Didn't Dr. English say I was well? And truly, I feel fine."

"Yes, but Sissy—" Muddy's broad face creased, working up to a protest.

But I was already rising, heading for the stairs. "Don't worry! I'll see which articles need brushing or mending before we pack to leave," I called lightly over my shoulder.

Once out of sight I slumped against the bannister, aghast at the journey I'd just set in motion. Was I able, *was* I well enough?

"We shall soon find out," I muttered, then gripped the bannister hard so it could help me pull myself up to our room.

We left early on April 6, arriving at the Walnut Street Wharf a little after six on a cloudy, misty morning. Our train was not due until seven-fifteen, so we took seats in the Depot Hotel and Eddy bought us newspapers—the *Ledger, Times,* the *Chronicle.*

"Bah. Nothing of any worth in these yellow rags," he complained. "I'll go buy our tickets." He got up and walked out. I picked up each paper in turn and perused it. He was right: ads for patent cures, for useless knickknacks and beauty treatments, for suspicious moneymaking schemes. Frivolous stories of no-account people celebrated, even idolized, for very little reason.

Still, it passed the time.

The train arrived an hour later and we rode as far as Amboy. There we boarded a steamer for New York. By then the mist had coagulated into a persistent drizzle.

"I want to stay on deck for the view," I proposed. "And it feels less queasy to me that way."

Eddy looked aghast. "Absolutely not. My little wife must retire to the ladies' cabin to keep dry and warm." He took my elbow and guided me like a determined sheepdog all the way to the public compartment for female passengers. This was very elegant, and already occupied by three other ladies. One read a book, one was doing needlework. The other looked up hopefully when we entered, as if bored with her journey before it had well begun.

I sat and began to converse with her. Eddy hovered in the doorway, his gaze as often on me as on the horizon. So I felt triumphant and clever when I did not cough once the whole voyage.

When we docked at the Battery, he left me on board while he went out to find lodgings. He was back in less than an hour, with a hack he'd told to wait at the curb. He rushed up into the ladies' cabin and pushed a long black object into my hands. An umbrella, a very sober black one; a substantial, bankerly appurtenance.

"It cost half a dollar," he said mournfully. I must've looked horrified, for he added, "No arguments. You absolutely must stay dry. We will take no chances, my dear."

"Thank you, Eddy," I said, squeezing his arm. "It's a very good umbrella."

He looked abashed and fidgeted with his tie. "Actually, it cost sixty-two cents."

I laughed, because he looked so much just then like a little boy who'd lost his pocket money. And I was certainly not his mother.

"I've found us a nice room," he went on. "Not too far. Seven dollars for the week, board included." He took the umbrella and with a flourish unfurled it over our heads. Then escorted me as one would a countess, trying to dodge each raindrop, all the way to the curb where the hack driver and horse were both impatiently stamping and blowing.

"One thirty Greenwich Street," he told the driver, who nodded, then swung up into his seat. We lurched off over the cobblestones, teeth chattering as the wheels rumbled and jolted.

"It's on the West Side just before Cedar. You may even recall it. A large old place, a bit ramshackle. Brown stone steps and a porch with brown pillars?"

I shook my head. That could be a description of nearly every other house in our old neighborhood.

"At any rate the landlady is a kind old soul. Very serious. Very . . . sober. Efficient. A bit like Muddy."

I smiled. "Good. Then I will like her."

The place was as Eddy had described it: a very brown house. Even the front door, which held a brass nameplate inscribed MOR-RISON, was painted with brown enamel. The interior did look as if it could be buggy, but then we'd had plenty of insects in Baltimore and Richmond to contend with—large, armored Southern ones, not the small shy Northen variety. Catterina specialized in crickets and cockroach beetles, and was merciless in her final court of dismemberment.

A few houses down I glimpsed the finely painted sign for one place I did recall: the Old Planters' Hotel. So very elegant it would've clearly strained our pocketbook. Still, I wondered what it might be like just once to stay in such a place as if by right, and not think of the cost. Then I feared Eddy would sense my thoughts and feel rebuked.

"Oh, I wish Catterina could see this house! She would faint for joy," I whispered, and squeezed his arm. I meant for its hunting opportunities, but if he thought I meant for its elegance, that was fine too.

He'd taken a back room on the third floor. Our sole window, only lightly coated on the outside with coal dust, overlooked the Hudson River docks. Eddy insisted on carrying me up both flights, though he was fearfully flushed by the time we reached our room. I could've climbed them on my own, if we'd gone up slowly. But I understood: There'd been so little he could do when I'd been ill. I resolved to let him assist me now in whatever way he liked.

When at last we lay in the dark in bed—the mattress high and pleasantly lumpy with something much softer than our own straw ticking at home—he said, "I have a good feeling about this move. It's the right time, and will be the making of my reputation."

He didn't sound cynical or ironic, so I felt cheered. "I think so too. How can they ignore you now? And surely even a New York writer wouldn't hold a grudge this many years."

Then, lulled by the rumble of late-night carriage wheels and faint mournful singing and strumming from a nearby tavern, we both drifted off to sleep.

I did insist on walking down to breakfast the next morning, at least for the last flight of steps. The night before, after Eddy paid for our room and board, we'd gone into the dining room for a respectable supper of strong hot tea, wheat and rye bread, cheese cut from an enormous yellow wheel, and very elegant iced tea cakes. Also there had been large slices of veal on a platter. I'd assumed then this was the standard welcoming feast laid out for new arrivals. But when we got to the breakfast table silver pots of strong black coffee and two large china pitchers of cream were set out on a mahogany sideboard. Then, great dishes of cutlets, smoked fish, fried eggs, and more fresh crusty bread steaming on a cutting board. And a crock of churned butter the color of pure sunlight.

As Eddy pushed my chair in at the table, I burst into tears.

He hovered over me, wringing his hands. "My dear, are you unwell?"

The other lodgers, mostly men, either stared curiously or averted their eyes. "Are you in pain?" Eddy murmured, stroking my shoulder, gripping it lightly as if he could by sheer will drain any hurt away from me, like a galvanic battery in reverse.

I shook my head. How could I make him understand? I'd thought the plentiful food of the night before a temporary thing, meant to welcome and impress. Yet before us again lay a veritable horn of plenty. No one would ever hide in the kitchen here and pretend; here every one of our family would eat well. For the first time I felt as if Eddy was right—coming to New York had been exactly the thing to do.

"I'm fine," I gasped out. "Just so happy to be here. So well, and—with you."

He smiled broadly and sat down next to me, looking carefree and years younger. The creases in his pale forehead, which had settled so deeply the last few months, were smoothed away. When I took his napkin in a wifely gesture, to drape over his lap, I noticed one small flaw. "You have a tear in your good trousers, my dear," I whispered, so the other lodgers would not overhear.

"I know," he whispered back. "Caught them on a nail at the

wharf. But I didn't want to bother about it last night. Do you realize," he said more loudly, "that you haven't coughed once since we
arrived?"

I nodded. "No night sweats either." Then I added, "Buy me
black thread after breakfast and I'll mend your wounded trousers."

He came back later with the thread, plus a skein of lavender silk,
horn buttons, a pair of carpet slippers, and a tin pan to use on the
little stove in our room. It had kept up a good, warming fire all night
long. We were resolved to get a second room as soon as possible, so
Muddy and Catterina and even the bird could join us. Tears burned
my eyelids each time I thought of them so far away—my mother
working hard packing boxes, dear Catterina sitting nearby, super-
vising her efforts, alert for any small unsavory creatures stirred out
of hiding. Eddy had given Muddy leave to sell certain books, to raise
a little cash. And Mr. Graham had asked him to write an article on
James Russell Lowell. As soon as he got paid, he'd send that money
and she'd be on the next steamer.

A week later Eddy did have a great success. "The Balloon-Hoax"
was an imaginary narrative about a three-day transatlantic crossing from Norfolk, England, that landed near Charleston, South
Carolina. It was bought by *The New York Sun,* to be published on
April 13.

When we went to the newsstand that morning looking for a
copy to buy, there were none. Eddy became downcast. "I fear it
hasn't come out after all," he said.

Still, we headed on to the *Sun* offices. There the whole sidewalk
was blocked. The entire square surrounding the building looked
under siege, as if a war had broken out, or a bank had spectacularly
failed. A sea of people kept trying to press forward, toward the
front door.

"What has happened?" Eddy asked a man standing near. No doubt he feared his newest publisher was in some difficulty, perhaps being evicted and shut down.

"Oh, the fools have run out of copies," the man huffed. "The last few just went for a shocking sum, and then a newsboy was knocked down by the angry crowd. Poor lad got a bloody nose."

"You mean," Eddy said slowly, staggering as people coming up behind jostled him, "they are rioting in this way to obtain copies of today's *Sun*?"

"Well, naturally," said the man, looking him up and down. "Haven't you heard? Some fellows have crossed the Atlantic Ocean in just three days! In a balloon! It's history in the making, laddy." He turned away and began trying to elbow his way through again.

Eddy and I stared at each other, wide-eyed, then burst out laughing. "You would not think," I said, when I recovered my breath, "that a headline with the word *balloon-hoax* in it would be considered factual news!"

But it had been, nonetheless. One dirty-faced enterprising newsboy from uptown just then heaved up with a small stack of unsold papers, crying, "Balloon Crossing! Balloon Crossing!" His copies were bought up at once, for any price, people waving their arms as if bidding for some fine medieval scroll. I actually saw an entire half-dollar given for one copy, and heard the dismayed roars of the seekers who'd not managed to get there first.

Eddy's amusement turned to pride and delight. When I saw how broadly he was grinning, a sudden fear struck me. I clutched at his arm and begged, "For heaven's sake, don't tell anyone here who you are. They'll tear your clothing to bits, and dismember your limbs for souvenirs!"

At last we left to try our luck elsewhere, but search as we might the whole day, our quest was in vain. For the actual author of the notorious balloon-hoax story there was not one single copy to be had. Still, annoying as that was, it seemed another good omen: Surely we *were* meant to be here now, in this city of buildings that loomed like sheer rock cliffs. Surely now our luck had changed.

We went out often over the next few days, roaming farther afield as the weather was turning, warming into full spring. Trees in Manhattan were few, but those were lovingly tended, some even surrounded by fancy wrought-iron fences, as if they were not mere wood, bark, and leaf, but preciously wrought objects of art. Here and there sat a fine bit of shrubbery, clipped into a moon-shaped ball or a parcellike square, or even an animal form.

Even more picturesque in a different way were the teeming, abundant shanties of the Irish immigrants and squatters. These tended to be seven or eight feet square, with mud walls and plank roofs, the door usually a barrel set on end—and always with a pigsty tacked on in lieu of a veranda. Eddy was amused by these details, until I reminded him we too were Irish, our paternal great-grandparents having come over from County Cavan less than a hundred years earlier. That sobered him.

"Besides," I pointed out, "they also have a dog or a cat at each hovel. And have you ever seen more contented animals in all your life?"

"No, I have not," he agreed. But then we began to miss Catterina—and of course Muddy—all the more. I even missed the foulmouthed Pym. The closest thing to a talking crow in the shanties was a flock of bedraggled brown hens ranging the confines of one small yard, scratching and pecking at the bare dust and scattered litter.

On the East Side lay a whole village of decrepit clapboard mansions, in not much better repair than the shebangs. They were somehow still magnificent to the eye, with their solemn air of brooding decrepitude.

"Look all you wish now," Eddy admonished darkly. "The Spirit of Improvement has already laid a cold withering finger on them."

As I gazed about the venerable neighborhood I saw he was right, for imaginary streets had been mapped through with raw pine stakes and thick brown string. A flyer tacked to a post in front of one house, edges curling shyly under my gaze, advertised for sale not a suburban residence, but rather a "town lot." The voracious city had already swallowed and partially digested this old neighborhood.

Eddy scowled and tore the poster down. "In thirty years the whole island will be a hive, a swarming cliff face of brown stone. Every *real* cliff will be flattened and turned into a pier! Manahatta will be desecrated by pretentious, towering buildings, cheek by jowl, with granite trimmings and fancy scrolled façades."

"Oh, Eddy, how you exaggerate," I said, giggling. Sometimes it strained one's patience to live with a writer and entertain so many vivid, unlikely imaginings.

For all his complaining he found this hive of strangers full of intense life. The new mayor seemed to have delusions of respectability, for he closed down all the rum palaces and even the rum hovels on Sundays.

"Why not Saturdays too?" Eddy remarked with a sneer. "I am arguing, of course, from a purely constitutional standpoint," he added, after one look at my face.

Certainly on the subject of cleanliness New York still fell far below Philadelphia. No prosperous housewives here fell to their knees to scrub stoops weekly, much less daily. The same paper litter and filth I recalled from our earlier sojourn blew about or lurked underfoot, and you really had to watch where you trod. A haze of coal smoke and wood fires and sometimes eye-watering gin fumes assaulted nostrils and eyes. Eddy was writing away each day in our room, though at times only to pen an irate letter to the editor of one paper or another. The constant din of street cries mixed with the window-shaking rattle of wagon wheels over cobblestones were about to drive him mad.

"I am *not* against progress," he muttered, sealing another letter. "I've only suggested they look into some quieter method of pavement than cobblestones, in order to preserve everyone's sanity."

The Lowell piece was still not finished, but with his payment for the balloon-hoax tale, we could safely send for Muddy and Catterina. "We have three dollars left," he told me the day before they were to arrive, turning out his pockets. "We're paid up for a week in advance, so if I can go out and borrow—"

"Eddy, don't do that. Can't you write something new?"

He frowned. "What would you suggest?"

I thought hard. "Well, there was that bird poem you began, just before we left Philadelphia."

"Oh, good idea. That should be popular." A note of cynicism tinted his voice. Despite the balloon-hoax success, or perhaps because of it, the clannish, snooty New York set had still not taken Eddy much to its bosom.

"Muddy and Catterina arrive this afternoon," I reminded him. "We must go to the Battery to welcome them." That thought cheered him. Having his family together always did. When we greeted Muddy there, she had Catterina in a basket and Pym's cage in hand. "Whew," she said when she spotted us. "Now you can lend a hand. One can only carry so much."

A week later we moved five miles north to the Brennan farm, farther up the Bloomingdale Road. Eddy had found the place through an acquaintance; it had not been advertised. "The country air will be much better for you," he insisted. "And the Brennans are very congenial people."

The family consisted of Patrick Brennan, his black-haired wife, and ten little Brennans ranging from fifteen-year-old Martha all the way down to the latest nursing baby whose name and gender always escaped me. The farm occupied two hundred acres along the Hudson, with a rambling two-story clapboard house.

"This here house," Patrick Brennan proudly told me, "served as a lookout for both Washington and Lafayette during the War for Independence." I didn't see any great advantage to that now, barring another British invasion, but tried to look impressed.

During this glorious summer Eddy took long rambling walks from nearby Mt. Tom to the High Bridge and the other side of Manhattan Island. We had fresh milk from the Brennan cows, and butter and cheese. Eggs aplenty from the hens tended by Martha. Huge squashes and onions and potatoes the size and color of which I had never seen the like, even in the Dutch markets in Philadelphia. And Muddy could cook again for a large company. Mrs. Brennan objected at first to a paying guest working in her kitchen, but gave in when she smelled the hot yeasty perfume of my mother's crusty bread, its browned top shiny with Brennan butter. Pym's wicker cage hung in the kitchen, where both Catterina and the Brennans' orange tabby kept a watchful eye on it.

During these months Eddy seldom went into the city, but he still sent out work. However, as the summer passed he heard nothing encouraging from the New York journals, including *The Knickerbocker,* still the most prestigious magazine in the city. "They'll never forgive an honest review," he muttered, referring to his tomahawking of its editor three years earlier in *Graham's.* Fortunately he still had a reading audience outside Manhattan. He wrote for half a dozen newspapers and magazines in Philadelphia and points south, including *The Columbian, Godey's Ladies' Book, Graham's,* and even his old *Southern Literary Messenger.*

He did receive part-time employment at last, as a subeditor at the *Times.* And then in October, when the cooling fall weather began to strip the trees and force me to spend more time indoors, the poet Nathaniel Willis engaged Eddy as staff on the *Evening Mirror.* "Nate is the most popular writer of the day," he told me.

I had read Mr. Willis's columns. They were well written, yes, but society puff pieces—nothing like what Eddy turned out. But when I ventured this opinion, Eddy nodded. "Yes, indeed. But he has a wife and a young child, and another on the way. What else can the poor fellow do—write poetry?"

I felt this as sharply as a slap. Was that how Eddy thought of us—as a burden that kept him from his true calling? A financial drain, instead of the anchor that kept him sober? When I had extracted that old promise from him, back on our porch in Baltimore, when I was just twelve and he twenty-five, I'd made him swear to take all of us—not just me. But back then I'd thought he wanted a family. That he needed us all to be here when he came home, to keep him from the madness that overtook him when he was cast adrift on his own. And for that reason, I'd come to New York again with him. Had in fact kept myself *alive* for him.

Tears burned my eyes, but he'd already turned back to his desk, scratching away again. As if I'd already left the room—and perhaps I had, as far as he was concerned.

I feared the onset of winter now, with its damp chill fingers that squeezed my lungs from the inside until I was racked with coughs. And coughing so often led to catastrophe. Finally, to ease my mind, I asked Muddy to get me a supply of the old medicine.

Her face paled. "Are you feeling ill?" she whispered, as if an audible mention of sickness might call it down again.

"No, no," I assured her, though I had felt a tightness in my chest the night before, which had been very brisk and cool. "I just want to have a bit on hand, in case—it is a long ride to the city if I should ever truly need it, after all."

She nodded. "Yes, but . . . you aren't hiding anything from me, are you?"

What fictional character should I summon up to fool my parent this time? I finally put on the cool, intelligent Ligeia. "Why no, Mother. Of course not."

She eyed me, but finally turned away to slide a pan of bread into the Brennans' stove. "Very well," she said over one shoulder. "We'll get you some more of the cough medicine. And I think I shall go to buy it myself."

"Yes, why not," I said. "No need to bother Eddy about it." So then I knew we were agreed.

We survived with no calamities into December. I was fine, though the many Brennan children seemed poised to burst with excitement all the way through Christmas Eve. Even the eldest eyed the empty stockings, which hung on the parlor fireplace like a prodigious line of washing, with religious fervor each night. I loved having so many children around, but over the months their presence also tired me. For the first time I thought perhaps it was good we'd never been blessed in this way. Though how Muddy and Eddy would have doted on a smaller version of him, or of me! But I understood now that gift might have also hastened my end.

The new year arrived, and still I did not cough. But the next day a familiar muted pain scraped at the bottom of my lungs, as if someone had taken a dull garden trowel to them in order to plant something there.

"It's pleurisy again," said Eddy. "You must be careful and rest until it passes."

I didn't contradict his diagnosis, merely got up and ate breakfast with everyone. But as soon as he left for the *Mirror* I got back into bed and took enough Potion to ease my breathing—but not so much as would send me into another little temporary death. In this way, I decided, I would heal, and Eddy be none the wiser.

I woke again later to find him sitting by the bed, hat in hand, contemplating me with that old look of despair.

"What—what are you doing?" I mumbled, for the Poison was still working on me.

"There was a heavy snowfall. The roads were impassable. The ice on the Hudson froze all the boats on Stryker's Bay solid. I had to turn back."

"Oh." I tried to sit up, to think clearly so I could explain away my presence in bed at this time of day.

"How long have you been taking this?" he asked, holding up the brown bottle. It was less a medical inquiry than a child's plea: *Tell me a story. Make me believe all is well, and will end happily ever after.*

"Not long. And only as much as you can see is gone now. Really very little, Eddy."

He closed his eyes. "Are you in pain?"

"Only a twinge in my chest. A precaution. It's already much better."

He looked pained. But if I lied and told him I was fit and fine as a Brennan cow he would know I was a liar now, and suspect I'd lied to him before.

He folded his arms like a gaoler. "I won't leave until you're up and well again."

"Eddy, no. You mustn't—I mean, *needn't* do that." I didn't want to risk getting up too soon. But I also did not want him brooding over me like a spying black crow perched on a branch, until he discovered how often I really had to take the Potion. "You have too much work to do. I don't need minding." I laughed lightly, suppressing a wince at the catch in my throat. "How is your bird poem coming along? You must get back to it soon."

He laughed. "Man is only more active, not more happy, than he was six thousand years ago. Don't you agree?"

I could not think how to answer that. He was probably right.

"I'm staying here, right here, to make sure you're well."

He picked up a battered copy of Dickens's *Barnaby Rudge*, opened it at random, and began stubbornly reading to me, with great animation: "'What was that? Him tapping at the door?' 'No,' returned the widow. 'It was in the street . . . 'tis someone knocking softly at the shutter. Who can it be?'"

He went on in his best dramatic tones, doing different voices for the characters. When he got to a passage featuring a droll yet malevolent talking pet, he read the bird's dialogue with much croaking and cawing: "'*Polly put the kettle on. Hurrah! Polly put the kettle on and we'll all have tea. Grip, Grip, Grip—Grip the Clever, Grip the Wicked, Grip the Knowing.*'"

He paused at that point, head tilted, as if he'd just heard something coming to us from far away. Something faint as yet, but very important.

"What is it?" I asked, levering up on one elbow to look out the window. The smooth snow-frosted lane was empty.

He passed a hand over his face as if waking from a trance. "I just—I believe I'll go and work on that bird poem."

Yet he made no move to get up, only sat looking distracted and serious. Though now he perched on the very edge of the hard chair as if forcing himself to stay. After I lay there quietly and talked to him calmly, and did not cough or choke, he seemed to gradually relax. He even smiled.

Suddenly he stood, and dropped the Dickens to the floor. "Excuse me, my dear," he said, and pounded away down the narrow stairwell.

He returned with a few sheets of foolscap, his quill and inkpot, and set up a makeshift desk on a chest of drawers. Then, standing with his back to me, he began to write.

"What are you working on?" I asked, too curious to keep still.

"That blasted bird," he said, voice muffled, as if he were speaking into the cloth of his collar. "Because I know what it is, now."

"Oh good," I said. "Well then, tell me."

"An unreasoning creature," he said. "Yet one quite capable of human speech."

Like Pym, I thought. Or the terrible ape in "The Murders in the Rue Morgue." Or some sort of parrot? The sort of creature that oh so perfectly mimics the speech of another . . .

For a moment my heart seized, as if one of the icicles that hung outside the bedroom window had snapped off and flung itself, with malevolent intent, through the window glass and into my chest. *Rosalie,* I thought. But no, no—he wouldn't.

"What creature is that, precisely?" I asked, trying to keep my tone light.

He didn't answer. Only muttered, as if to himself, without ceasing to write, "It was never a parrot. Never! No, no, of course not. And green? No, it was quite dark. Yes—it could only be black. Certainly a raven all along."

· 20 ·

In a matter of weeks "The Raven" was everywhere. Read by everyone. Praised to the skies. There were two problems, though. First of all, Eddy had sold it to two newspapers at once.

"But how can that be?" I wondered. It seemed a sure way to bring a great deal of trouble down on himself, with the very people he ought to try to please.

"Oh, it was a simple matter," he assured me. "A common publishing tactic."

"What is?" Muddy asked, coming into the parlor as we spoke, bearing a steaming hot toddy for me. I hated the sweet, harsh taste, but she insisted I drink toddies when it was cold out. Like today, with the sky a cast-iron pot lid lowering itself on us.

"I sold the thing first to Colton at the *Review*," Eddy went on, trying to pretend he was not eyeing my toddy. "But I sold my *name* to Willis. To the *Mirror*." He sat back, as if that explanation should satisfy any reasonable person.

Muddy sat down too, looking satisfied—I suppose because he'd made a sale—and also mystified. "Your name, Eddy? But you can't sell a *name*."

I was still trying to grasp what he meant as well. "Then why did Mr. Willis print the poem in the *Mirror* first?"

He sighed. "Well, it's the *Review*'s policy not to publish the author's name on a work."

Under the *Review*'s February version of "The Raven," the attribution "By ———— Quarles" had appeared beneath the last line. While in the *Mirror*'s January version, which had come out on the twenty-ninth, his good friend Nathan Willis had not only appended Eddy's name but also written a glowing preface, calling the poem "unsurpassed in English poetry for subtle conception, masterly ingenuity of versification, and consistent sustaining of imaginary lift and 'pokerishness.'"

I'd laughed at that last word, glancing at the cast-iron poker the Brennans kept at the parlor hearth. Eddy snapped, "No, no, Sissy. He means the game of cards, not a fireplace tool!"

As if I didn't know. "I can't tell who are the more amusing, writers or editors," I'd whispered, kissing his cheek.

"So you see, I sold it anonymously to the *Review*," he went on now. "But then encountered Willis later in the week and he wanted it as well. So he merely published it 'in advance of publication'— that's what he called it—and paid five dollars to print my name with it."

I frowned. The whole thing still seemed wrong.

Muddy cast an annoyed look at me. "Oh, what does it matter. We need the money, and Eddy's worth twice that much. You know it as well as I do, Sissy."

He murmured as if to himself, "It's the most I've ever been paid for one poem." After mulling this thought, his face fell. "But I did lie to Willis. I knew he'd want it badly."

Oh dear, here it comes, I thought. The trouble.

"I told him George Colton at the *Review* had paid me twenty dollars, to make Willis give me at least ten." In the end he'd only gotten five. "And now of course Colton is angry." He sighed and raked his hands through his hair. Which already stood on end, as if the thought of his perfidy and the possible retribution had spectrally raised it.

"Well, but look at all these typographical errors," I said, holding up the *Mirror*. "No, Muddy is right, I think you are even."

"I didn't have time to go over the proofs," he said, groaning. "Dear God, look at this! The word *he* is repeated again in the fifth line. And there's worse." He leaned closer to the page, moaning, flagellating himself with all the little imperfections there.

Nathaniel Willis came that afternoon to visit us, all the way out to the Brennan farm, and he was nothing but flattery. He told Eddy they'd be reprinting the poem in the February 8 issue as well. Muddy and I exchanged a glance over their heads. He had not said they'd *pay* anything for that privilege.

"It is an amazing accomplishment," Willis gushed, accepting a cup and saucer from my mother. "The best fugitive poetry ever published in this country, I tell you."

Muddy frowned sharply, perhaps envisioning dark-caped criminals on the run. How dare this whippersnapper compare her Eddy to thieving riffraff? I raised a corner of my shawl to snort a muffled laugh into it. It was certainly good everyone loved Eddy's poem.

Which brings me to the second problem, which was that *I* did not. In fact, I hated it.

Oh, "The Raven" was all they said, and more. A brooding masterwork. An elegant dirge wrought with staggering genius. But as I first read it—the final fair copy to be proofed after he had pasted the ends together, top to bottom, and rolled that resulting long sheet up into one of his scrolls—I'd hated it more with each line.

Perhaps no one else understood, but I did. *He knows,* I thought. All this time I had worked so hard, and yet he knew, even before, that I was slowly dying. *He's no longer practicing; he's saying good-bye to me now.*

It was not only that. Of course he'd rehearsed my death, the loss of yet another loved woman, many times: Ligeia, Morella, Helen, Berenice, Madeline Usher. A rose by many other names, quite a long roll call of the dead, all women he'd created himself, like a minor god. Stand-ins for his mother, his foster mother, for Jane Stannard. And for me.

The difference was, in "The Raven" he was consigning the dead Lenore—consigning *me*—not just to the grave, but to Hell. In it she was *lost,* gone forever, condemned to eternal separation from him, in some distant so-called Aidenn. Unlike Morella or Ligeia—unlike even poor crazed Madeline, dumped still living into a chilly sepulture—not only would I not return to life, he was resolved he would never even glimpse me again. Anywhere. Ever.

She shall press—Ah, Nevermore!

"How dare you?" I'd whispered, when I read the last line. And then, choking on the words, "How could you?"

But when Eddy had come to collect the pages, to ask if I'd seen anything amiss—"Oh, anything at all!" he'd generously offered—I'd merely bowed my head as I slowly rolled up the scroll, so flimsy in form yet so powerful; the paper dry and dead under my trembling fingers, the words so wretchedly alive.

"No, my dear," I'd said, my tone firm and even. "It appears to be finished. Quite perfectly this time."

In late February Eddy came home flushed, his gaze hard and glittering, but with no smell of spirits about his person. He flung his coat on the settee instead of hanging it carefully from the hook in the

Brennans' front hall. "Sissy, listen to this. I've given my notice at the *Mirror!*"

He grinned, inviting me to rejoice with him.

"Oh no, Eddy," I gasped. I'd never before objected aloud to his leaving a job. But now—surely we had little time left. He knew it, I knew it, yet he would refuse to speak of it even now.

Muddy, who'd been sitting across from me, rose from her chair when he made his announcement. She looked aghast. Then, as always happened when he made such announcements, the emotion playing on her face dimmed and her gaze turned opaque. She seemed to turn inward, closing up like one of the mollusks or anemones from *The Conchologist's First Book*. Whenever this happened I imagined she was either flagellating or soothing herself, or perhaps both, by taking mental inventory: *How many books are on the shelf that might be sold? Which of the pots, pans, spoons, and forks we have left could we do without? What is the name of that last shop owner who'd given more than the usual for the complete works of Plato?*

Eddy chortled. "You both needn't look like such a funeral. I'm not unemployed. I will merely go to work for myself. Standing before you is the new editor of the *Broadway Journal*. Charles Briggs and John Bisco offered me a one-third partnership."

He had published work with the *Journal,* including a review of Elizabeth Barrett Browning's collected poems which he'd read aloud to me while writing it. He'd called her a "wild and magnificent genius," and the whole book "a flame"—fulsome praise which had apparently mortified that shy, gentle lady.

I finally understood. For the first time in his career Eddy would share in the profits of a magazine he helped make successful. Had he been paid a share at *Graham's,* we would've been nearly as wealthy now as the Grahams themselves.

But there was more. "Bisco's the former publisher of *The Knick-erbocker*," he said, with a lopsided, ironic smile. "Do you see what that means?"

Oh, I certainly did. It was as if Eddy had stormed the Bastille all by himself, and now stood on its broken foundation stones in triumph. I clapped my hands. "Wonderful!"

"He offered me the partnership simply for the privilege of printing my name on the bannerhead each month," he exulted. Then pulled me up and danced me—very carefully, as if I were a large porcelain doll—all around the parlor. Three of the youngest Brennans rushed to the doorway from the dining room and looked on with wide eyes, their sweet, grubby fingers plugging astonished mouths.

So the famous black bird had at least brought us more than just praise, more than just the dark, dying knowledge I carried in my breast like a small but indestructible stone.

Eddy's new duties required that he be in town daily. So we regretfully left the farm and took a dingy upstairs back suite at 195 East Broadway. I did not visit his office this time. The heavy dirty air bothered me more, so I stayed indoors and kept the windows closed. Our rooms were like any number of places we'd lived before: small, cramped, dim. Smelling of mold and the cheap cabbage soup the landlady kept boiling night and day.

One evening, a month or so after we'd moved, Eddy came home quite ill. A group of admirers had insistently celebrated him as the author of "The Raven"—yet again—at Sandy Welsh's Cellar down on Ann Street.

"Sporting men," he said ruefully, not meeting my eyes. "I don't know why but they seem to drink even more than literary ones."

Then he staggered off to fall on the bed, rumpled and stinking, still in shirt and trousers.

The next morning, someone knocked at our door just as Eddy finished retching into the chamber pot and collapsed, still in the previous night's wrinkled, malodorous clothes, back onto our bed.

Muddy was out, she'd gone to fetch fresh vegetables for dinner. So I was the one who answered the door, carrying Catterina over one shoulder like a big furry infant.

A well-dressed man swept off his hat. "I'm James Russell Lowell. I humbly beg your pardon if this is an intrusion, ma'am. But I was in New York sitting for my portrait, with Page."

I stared at him, confused and amazed. "Your . . . your portrait? But—"

"Forgive me—you *are* Mrs. Poe? I'm acquainted with your husband. He was so kind as to write an article about me once and—well, I thought I'd take this opportunity to stop and pay my respects to him. And to you, of course."

I was wearing my oldest housedress, actually an old nightgown Muddy had altered. The cat was purring madly, kneading my shoulder and drooling down my neck. I fought a mighty urge to slam the door in his face. It was a nice face, at least. "Well . . . of course. Come in, please, Mr. Lowell." Thinking at the same time: Dear God, is that renewed retching I hear from the back room?

I saw Mr. Lowell in, hoping at least Eddy was through getting sick, and bade him take a seat on an old sprung velvet settee, the best seat in this furnished parlor.

I went to the bedroom door and whispered, "*Eddy*. A Mr. Lowell to see you."

He groaned, but softly, then grabbed two fistfuls of sweaty bedsheet and hauled himself up. He staggered to the washstand and rinsed his mouth, then poured the remaining contents of the pitcher over his head. Good. At least now Mr. Lowell might think his host was soggy with something other than drink.

Eddy turned toward me again, clammy white, pasty faced. Just then I heard Muddy coming in the front door. Heard her soft exclamation of surprise, and Mr. Lowell's gracious self-introduction.

I unhooked Catterina's claws from my bodice. Tipped her like a sack of potatoes onto the bed. Then I brushed at Eddy's suit as he slowly straightened, remaking himself from that sick, shrunken demeanor that always came back to us after such a night, into a mannequin of good humor and welcome—all as he was moving past me, out the door, a hand already extended to greet the esteemed Mr. Lowell.

To most men, I supposed, getting drunk was merely a friendly ritual, a sign of good fellowship, not a fatal weakness of temperament. Not vice, but conviviality. I much preferred the times Eddy was besieged and feted by his female admirers, who were even more numerous, far more decorous, and less prone to tippling. There seemed a good many of them, and their legions only grew after the bird poem appeared. Some were lady poets who desired a word of praise for their amateur verses; some merely admired Eddy's poems and stories and wanted to tell him so, over and over.

And then there was Frances Osgood.

She had requested an introduction from Nathaniel Willis, and he'd obliged, bringing Eddy to the Astor Hotel, where she lived on an upper floor. Later Eddy told me he'd hated it. "The place was decorated in the most excessive style, all quite oppressive. And then Mrs. Osgood! Good Lord, she descended the staircase like some affected Russian czarina."

I could imagine the scene all too well. And him hating, even fearing the lush surroundings, the gilded wood and marble columns and velvet banquettes that must recall the old Richmond life of so long ago. A reminder of all he'd not been able to accomplish—at least, nothing John Allan would've considered a *real* triumph, for that would have to involve some mercantile or industrial endeavor, and certainly include making a large sum of money. I could envision Eddy entering the Astor lobby in his old black suit, which—despite the careful sponging and brushing given it by Muddy each day—had developed worn, threadbare seams and a faint shine which glazed its tired weave. He'd stand there in broken-soled gaiters and dull, secondhand top hat, surrounded by the carefully dressed well-to-do of New York. His friend Willis's so-called One Hundred, the social cream of Manhattan which his columns flattered and mocked in equal measure.

Mrs. Osgood was one of them. A society lady, a poetess, an admirer. I wanted to ask, Was she rosy-cheeked and healthy? Did she look as if she'd live another fifty years? For someday one of these female admirers would surely take my place. After I was lost, to be seen nevermore.

But I did not want to be morbid. So I only asked, as I picked up my mending again, "And was she pleasant?"

"Oh, very," he said begrudgingly. "She writes poems too—not bad ones. Told a funny story about using her poetry money to go shopping. Her husband—well, they're estranged—Nate Willis says he's some sort of painter. She and her two little daughters live on the fifth floor of the hotel. Which means, according to Willis, she hasn't got a cent."

He looked at me with pursed lips and quivering eyebrows and we both burst into laughter, until I feared I'd set off a new, fatal cough. I wiped my eyes, and he said, looking around at our dim room, our cheap things spilling out of crates since we could not afford a chest of drawers, "Hmm. Perhaps we should've moved there, instead."

That sent us off into fresh peals. And if it sounded bitter, well, at least we were enjoying ourselves, and it cost not a cent.

"Oh," he added, as if in afterthought. "She wants to meet you."

I looked up. "Who does?"

"Mrs. Osgood. I am to read 'The Bird' again, this time for the New York Historical Society. Do you feel up to coming?"

I longed to get out. But the thought of going from these near-empty rooms to a brightly gaslit hall packed with a hundred or more people all chattering and staring and expecting witty responses filled me with dread. To have to listen to Eddy's frighteningly sonorous recitation of my own death knell . . .

"No! I—I mean, I really haven't anything to wear to such as that."

As I saw this answer pinch his face, I added, "Really, the truth is, I don't care to be trapped in such a crush, my dear. Could she—could *she* perhaps come here?"

I stopped abruptly, wondering what I'd just done. Invited into our own parlor some simpering society admirer, a poetic black widow spinning a web around my husband? Well, I would find out soon enough, if Mrs. Osgood deigned to accept our humble invitation. Eddy had once told me he felt it his duty to "gently wake up the American poetesses." I just hoped that, once called forth, they would not take up residence in our home, a twittering literary coven.

In July Eddy became sole editor of the *Broadway Journal*. Mr. Briggs had withdrawn. Eddy told us it was for "financial reasons," but later informed me Briggs had been planning to force him out. Since the others on the staff stayed this must have indeed been the case. Thus only Eddy, John Bisco, and Henry Watson were left.

Eddy was to receive his share of the net profits at the commencement of each month. "There can be but one captain at the helm of a
ship," he told me when he came home that evening. "Any two-
headed beast is an abomination."

But the magazine had serious debts. Type compositors, printers,
paper merchants, artists, and writers must all be paid. And he'd
resumed his print attacks on Henry Wadsworth Longfellow. This
drew hostile fire in the form of complaining letters to the editor.
Those from the New England area were quite fiery. I began to wonder if he did it on purpose, to stir up controversy, as Willis had so
often encouraged him to do when he wrote reviews for the *Mirror*.

One night in October, Eddy sat at his desk writing another accusation against Longfellow for the next issue of the *Journal*, lifting
his head from time to time to say, "I'm the *only one* courageous
enough to show him up for the humbug he is," and, "There is room
in American literature for *only one of us,* him or me!"

Muddy and I listened. As I studied the side of his face I saw that
the more he wrote diatribes against the man, the more miserable he
seemed. I began to wonder: Perhaps Eddy really longed to *be* more
like Longfellow, a man who believed in God, and thought His
world made sense. But Eddy couldn't do that. How, when the good
in life was so fleeting, or never arrived? Not when things fell apart,
when he was forever peering into blackness or staring into a disordered wilderness. Always hovering on the verge of something,
yes—but what? Perhaps in his heart Edgar Poe desperately wanted
God to be real. To be the Father—any father, a father to him. And
so he both longed for and was enraged at Him. And in the end,
probably too full of doubts even to notice His presence, should it
ever quietly arrive.

Some good news came on July 19, when Wiley and Putnam
published *Tales* by Edgar Allan Poe. Eddy'd had no say in the

stories chosen, though. "They've omitted 'Ligeia,' 'Eleonora,' 'William Wilson,' and 'Masque of the Red Death,'" he fumed.

"No," I said, shocked, for those were his best. "How could they?"

He shrugged, but looked bleak. "I have no choice but to grit my teeth and accept their decision. For, as usual, we need the money." Then he snatched up his coat and hat, and slammed out. Leaving me to hope he wouldn't encounter any literary admirers or sporting friends who would pay for such surcease from sorrow as the celebrated author himself could not afford.

Eddy was to receive a royalty of eight cents per sold copy of *Tales,* and the book was priced at fifty cents. His anger at its contents was mollified by its critical reception. The *American Review* gushed, "One of the most original and peculiar ever published in the United States, and eminently worthy of an extensive circulation." So George Colton, still the *Review*'s editor, had clearly forgiven Eddy that previous double-dealing sale of "The Raven" after all.

That fall I finally met the celebrated Mrs. Osgood. By then we'd moved to better quarters near Washington Square. The Square was busy each day, and Sundays in particular, with afternoon fashion parades of the local girls and ladies escorted by their gentlemen. When we'd lived in New York years earlier, and I was just sixteen, I would've loved to join their colorful, graceful ranks as they promenaded about. But now I had to save my strength and spend it wisely, to dole it out as the precious commodity it was becoming.

Eddy had conveyed to Mrs. Osgood, perhaps through Willis, my impulsive invitation to visit. By then I'd nearly forgotten it myself. He was at work in the cramped parlor, and my mother was up in her room. I was lying on the lumpy old chaise, reading, with dear, faithful Catterina, my only fashionable accessory, my precious living fur stole. Her bulky warmth always comforted me. So did her excellent hunting skills; no mouse or cockroach or wool-eating cricket, nor even a hapless garden frog, could evade her terrible paws. I took more pleasure in that skill now, for I sometimes dreamed such creatures were crawling over my skin, or trying to find a way into my mouth. Once or twice my screaming had awakened Eddy and Muddy.

What made me dream such nightmares was the toad. It looked, as my brother Henry had insinuated, like the heavy black cast-iron doorstop which had belonged to Granny Poe. She, and then Muddy, had used it to keep the warped back door of the Baltimore house from slamming shut. The toad in my chest was just as hard and heavy and ugly, with a painful, sharp-edged weight completely unlike the comfortable bulk of our dear Catterina.

So I was clad only in a nightdress and Muddy's old shawl when a knock came at the door. "Oh dear," I muttered, sitting up. "Why does this *always* happen?"

The cat mewed, hooking my hem with her front claws, as if she knew what was good for me and it strictly involved lying down.

"Are you expecting someone, my dear?" I asked Eddy.

He shook his head without looking up. He was scribbling furious corrections to a series of papers titled "The Literati of New York," for *Godey's*. "No, no. But I'll get it. You stay put." He didn't get up though.

I rose and went past him on my way to hide in the bedroom. He jabbed his quill like a dart back into the inkpot, and went to the door. I heard the creak of the unoiled hinges, then the murmur of voices. One was a woman's.

Suddenly he stood in my doorway. "It's Mrs. Osgood. Are you well enough for a visit, my dear? She has come expressly to see you."

Thinking of the poems she and Eddy had written back and

forth, which had been printed in the *Broadway Journal* as well—
indeed, that he'd read aloud to me—I doubted that. "Echo-Song"
I knew almost by heart, at least the first stanza:

> *I know a noble heart that beats*
> *For one it loves how "wildly well!"*
> *I only know for whom it beats*
> *But I must never tell!*
> *Never tell!*
> *Hush! hark! how echo soft repeats,—*
> *Ah! never tell!*

"Now you must not be jealous of such nonsense," Muddy had
admonished when I first read it. "He cares nothing for these lady
poets."

I'd laughed, for I wasn't jealous at all. To be celebrated in print
by a poet was not what most people seemed to believe: a pleasant,
painless immortality. It was really a reflection of the poet's ego,
not the subject's life. It spilled forth his mind on the page for all to
see, but it did not define the one celebrated. I assure you, no one
knew this better than I. Poor Frances Osgood. She was only one
of many clever and even a few not-so-clever women who pined
for Eddy's notice. But he loved only me. I had his undying devotion and all his true attention, in life and on the page—*for as long
as I lived*. I think if they had sampled my mixed state of blessing
they would not have scribbled their verses quite so quickly or sent
them off so blithely.

I considered Eddy's entreaty to come out. Looked down at my
disheveled nightgown, then reached for a clean shirtwaist hanging from a peg. I lowered the hand again. Very well—if she indeed
wished to *know me*, let her know me as I was.

"Of course, my dear. Tell her I will be out directly." He smiled and touched my cheek and left. No doubt assuming I'd get dressed, pin up my hair. Instead I dropped Muddy's shawl and pulled on Eddy's old army greatcoat—the nearest thing I had to a dressing gown. I ran the bristle brush once through my tangled hair, then went out to meet her—the new friend, or perhaps the old enemy. It did not matter.

Eddy was seated at his desk chair, a rickety Windsor design of cheap white oak. Mrs. Osgood occupied an upholstered wingback with some still-tied springs. I saw the chaise had been reserved for me—Catterina, my familiar, was sprawled over its length to keep my place warm, her cold slitted gaze impaling the intruder.

Frances Osgood sprang to her feet. As pretty as they said, in gossip and in print. Her lovely eyes, which took in my mode of dress with only a flicker, were large and luminous and gray as moonstones, set under brows arched like swallow's wings. Her gaze was intelligent and attentive, lacking the coquettishness of an idle flirt. Her mouth was such a perfect rosy bow, she must enhance it with rouge. Her tight-waisted yellow day dress, with white lace cuffs and collar, set off a heavy crown of dark, shining hair. She was much shorter than I'd expected though—even next to me. But oh yes, she still fitted the model Eddy had always preferred, to a very T.

She bowed and said, in a low voice that despite its nasal Northern vowels and hard-clipped consonants was surprisingly melodious, "I hope I'm not intruding, Mrs. Poe. I was in the neighborhood. And, having received your kind earlier invitation, thought I might see if you and Mr. Poe were at home."

"We are indeed," I said, settling on the chaise. I picked up Catterina, who made an excellent shield. "I am very glad to meet you at last."

She had the grace to look self-conscious. "Well . . . I've heard so much of you from Ed—from your husband—that I feel we are already acquainted." Two perfect rosy spots bloomed on her cheeks. She leaned forward, then glanced at Eddy obliquely and subsided. As if she wished to tell me a secret, but his presence prevented it.

I was enjoying myself. "Yes, I've heard such a great deal of you too. And please, do call him 'Edgar.' He won't mind. Will you, my dear?"

Eddy cleared his throat. "No, of course not." He looked calm, even pleased. Neither nervous nor guilty.

"Then you must call me 'Fanny,'" she said. When I did not extend the same privilege she inclined her head, as if to acknowledge I had taken the upper hand. I was Mrs. Poe, and still would be. For now.

We then sat for a few moments gazing at each other, as if engaged in a game of chess, and each of us had just called "Check!" To my surprise, we both began to softly laugh, while Eddy blinked with puzzlement. Then Muddy came in with her cure-all—a tray of hot tea, fingers of buttered toast—and the mood became lighter than it had been for a long time.

"Oh," said Eddy suddenly, rattling down his cup. Muddy had given us the chipped ones, I saw, and reserved the undamaged bone china for Fanny Osborne. He walked over to his desk, and picked up several scrolls. "Virginia, could you assist me with a surprise?"

I thought for a moment, then realized what he meant. So I set Catterina aside and went to assist.

"See," he said to Fanny, who was sitting very still with her rose-patterned teacup poised halfway to her lips. "By the difference in lengths, I'm going to show you the varied degrees of estimation in which I hold all you literary people. Inside each, one of you is rolled up and fully discussed."

I nodded. "Yes, that's true."

Then one by one we unrolled them, as Eddy announced just which poet or writer was discussed there. Mr. Griswold's was short and stubby indeed. Other writers had moderately respectable lengths. At last we came to one which seemed interminable; I unrolled and unrolled until finally there was no other option but for me to walk to one corner of the room, while Eddy moved to its opposite.

"And just whose lengthened sweetness, long drawn out, is that, do you suppose?" he asked, grinning at me, then at Muddy and Fanny.

"Surely not—" Fanny began to demur.

"Hear her!" Eddy cried. "As if her vain little heart didn't assure her it is herself!"

"And . . . is it?" she asked warily, biting her lips and lowering the cup as if afraid to spill it.

"Of course," I said, taking pity. Almost loving her, just then, for the longing and uncertainty that showed so plainly. "Of course it is!"

Fanny turned out to be a great mimic. With very little persuasion she acted out two very amusing encounters at a literary club meeting the night before. Soon Eddy and Muddy and I were laughing, in tears. I did not let down my guard, but understood one thing by the time she made her apologies and rose: I liked Frances Osgood very much.

"Oh," she said at the door, where Eddy had escorted her. "I nearly forgot the other reason I came today. To invite you to a party. A get-together at Anne Lynch's home. You will come, won't you, Mrs. Poe?"

Though I normally avoided such things, I wanted to see Fanny again, even to please her. And to discover for myself what it was like to go out to a gathering since Eddy had become so celebrated. Now women of all ages threw themselves at his feet, it seemed. Undoubtedly I would hate it, but I felt the urge to experience his life as it would be later, when I was not present. To bear witness, as one might gaze on a carriage accident with equal measures of pity, revulsion, and awe.

"Oh well, Mrs. Osgood. I'm afraid Virginia—" Eddy began, glancing back at me, turning a palm up.

"Of course we'd love to come," I said, as sweetly as I imagined Fanny herself might.

Anne Lynch lived with her mother in Greenwich Village on Waverly Place. When we entered the tiny foyer, I saw such a crowd in the next room as I would not have believed it possible to cram into the place, judging by its tall but narrow exterior. The good, slightly shabby furniture had been shoved against the walls, which were hung with a jumble of oil paintings, some askew, too high or too low, and of all different styles and subjects: Hudson River landscapes, heaped fruit bowls, clutches of snared rabbits and shot doves spilling out of knapsacks, bleeding onto lace tablecloths. Pale, ethereal women swooning or perhaps expiring on a variety of velvet-upholstered furniture.

The voices I heard raised in argument or debate or laughter or song were like a constant clamor of muffled carriage wheels on cobblestones. A fog of segar smoke and sharp lime cologne masked the musk of damp bodies in satin and wool and pressed broadcloth packed close together. And a faint sweet whiff of sherry, all heated to vapor by a low coal fire in the parlor. Which, in fact, we could not enter, as it was already too crowded.

Still, Miss Lynch endeavored to herd us from room to room like a sheepdog, to introduce us to those she fancied we might take to. And, I suspected, to bask in a hostess's triumph—having snared the author of "The Raven" for her soiree. The tall, thin Anne Lynch I found both kind and intimidatingly efficient. She wore a bead and feather headdress and a green satin gown. She explained how she rose early each day to nurse her ailing mother—they were the reverse of Muddy and me—then caught a ferry to teach literature at a young ladies' academy in Brooklyn. She was only a little older than I—and of course yet another poetess.

"I also sculpt," she added, throwing this last revelation over one shoulder, while parting the crowd before her like Moses at the riverbank.

"Oh my, that too," I said, nearly running to keep up, feeling like a failure.

"It's terrible stuff," she assured me. "But I understand you sing wonderfully well."

I tensed. "Oh. Yes. That is, I *have* sung in public." I recalled again the smoky Philadelphia tavern, the cheering young girls, the men who'd hoisted mugs of beer to my health.

"Then I hope you'll favor us tonight?"

A deep longing to do so rose up in me even before she'd finished the sentence. But I also felt fragile enough to fear the strain on throat and lungs. "Well, perhaps. Or if not this night—"

"Then certainly another," she finished for me, making the obligation formal. "Ah, *here* she is!"

We passed into Anne's small, cluttered study, where Fanny Osgood rose to grasp my gloved hand. "Oh, I'm so glad you came!" She drew me down beside her onto a settee. "You know, your husband never adequately conveyed how young and beautiful you are, Mrs. Poe."

I looked at her narrowly, but she seemed sincere. She wore a low-cut garnet satin frock so well supported with crinolines her skirts engulfed us both like an exotic flesh-eating plant. Whereas my good but old black dress, refurbished with velvet edging by Muddy, had been several times mended. No fashionable petti-coats—we could not afford them. No corset to cinch my waist as waspish as Fanny's, for such constriction would stop my breath and might literally kill me.

"Perhaps he forgot," I said, smiling. "Perhaps he was distracted."

She blinked. "You must think me a frivolous fool. And very un-ladylike."

"No, of course not. You simply . . . like Eddy. You admire him. So many do."

"I want to be his friend. And yours," she went on. "But because he and I both write poetry, and admire each other's work, envious sorts have spread cruel gossip."

I laid my glove atop hers. "It matters little. I know my husband is faithful, that he loves me better than anyone. But—"

"Yes?" she said, her expression eager, or fearful, or merely curious.

"I am not well," I confided in a lower voice. "And haven't been for quite some time." I took a deep breath. How long I'd kept these words even from Eddy, even from my mother. "So I fear he will be left alone one day, perhaps not long from now, and then he'd suffer terribly. Much more so than with any physical pain. Do you under-stand what I mean to convey?"

She pressed her lips together, frowning. "I'm not sure."

I recalled Eddy telling me once that Fanny's estranged husband, Samuel Osgood, the talented portrait painter, was afflicted regu-larly with a terrible black despair. "That's one reason she removed herself and their two little daughters to the Astor," he'd confided, though he did not allude to what the other reasons might be.

"Eddy is a kind and gentle soul," I told her. "He's easily hurt. He *has* been hurt, often. And so he sometimes seeks refuge, or . . . or relief . . . in pursuits which will only injure him more. That is, unless I am there to . . . to call him back to reason. But if someday I am not here, am one day gone away from him, well . . ."

I closed my eyes and looked away, so she would not see the tears that stung and burned there. For Eddy, and for me. "And when I think of all this—"

"You can't . . . can't *rest*," she said to me now, slowly. "For worrying about that day."

Well, that was close enough to the truth. Perhaps she'd had some similar thoughts, in her own marriage. Perhaps she *did* see. How light I felt for a moment, as if my telling another soul at last had driven the Black Toad from my bosom to hop away, its fairy-tale curse briefly lifted.

"So you must be kind to him," I blurted out, holding up a hand for silence, for patience, when her eyes widened and she opened her mouth. I was no fool either. Fanny might be poor, in the New York society way, but she was a veritable heiress compared to me. Used to the sort of life Eddy could never provide, no matter how many poems or stories he scratched out. Whatever her true feelings, she did not wish, or at least could not afford, to ever tie herself to him. Much less marry him. She had no money of her own, and of course no property, and must be dependent on either a husband's income, or her family's.

"He needs a great deal of affection and . . . and *patience*," I went on, feeling traitorous at that last revelation. "He would wish to have a—" I stopped, uncertain of how best to phrase it, fearful of insulting her. "A passion of the intellect. No more. Could you manage that much? For me."

She looked away. So I'd insulted her after all. Now she would rise and leave, then in future cut me dead or cross the street, in the unlikely event we ever met again.

But she turned back, eyes shiny with tears, took both my hands into her small soft gloved ones, and squeezed them. "You are remarkable. I don't believe I've met another woman like you in all of New York, or New England either." And then she let go of my hands to pull a little silk hanky from her velvet reticule—a tiny useless square of fabric which, I could not help but think, had probably cost more than my whole gown. She dabbed delicately at the corners of both eyes.

Oh, I could well imagine what she'd heard of me: *His child wife. His little sickly cousin. An odd marriage. They are so unalike!* Well, perhaps they should give children more credit. Though I was no child now, and all too quickly approaching eternity. My adult life was passing like the pages of a hastily-thumbed volume. Still I would not have done it differently. At least, not the important parts.

"Oh, look!" she cried then, voice still thick with unshed tears as she stuffed the handkerchief back into her bag. She rose from the settee, pulling at my arm. "Dear old Lynchie! She's persuaded your husband to give a recitation of his monstrously popular old bird."

Though I would've preferred to hear anything else, I rose and let her lead me into the crowded parlor. There Eddy stood by the fireplace, somber and self-possessed, a study in black and white. No longer just my husband, or Muddy's son-in-law, or the impoverished orphan left by two dead actors. He'd been transformed into something larger and richer and, of necessity, I suppose, stranger. A thing which I had until then only heard spoken of: the celebrated literary personage called "Edgar Allan Poe."

He drew himself up until he appeared even taller. "'The Raven,'" he announced, in his low, soft Richmond drawl.

"'Once upon a midnight dreary,'" he began. And as he intoned those first lines, I shuddered.

In the early fall I accompanied him to several such events, at least on the nights I felt strong enough. And two significant things happened. The first was that his most celebrated work reappeared, also brought out by Wiley and Putnam, in *The Raven and Other Poems*, in November. The pleasure of that happy event carried us into the winter.

The second thing was less pleasant. I took to my bed again in late November, succumbing earlier than usual to the dreaded winter cough, the Toad's great delight. At first I could conceal this from Eddy by staying in bed all day while he was out.

But it seemed the magazine was in trouble. Alone Eddy could make all the artistic decisions, but he could not turn out work quickly enough to fill its pages and pay everyone as well. By December he was ill too, and writing a valedictory note for that issue. He turned operations over to his new partner, Thomas Lane, then took to our bed, fully as sick as I was. But on January 3, 1846, the *Broadway Journal* finally ceased publication, unable to meet its obligations or the price of production.

So by late spring, burdened with heavy debts and light pockets, we were packing up once again. From time to time, despite fever and hacking cough, Eddy roused himself from bed to go out. "But where are you headed?" I asked. "Stay here with me, you are too ill to traipse about."

"I'm going to find us a house in the country," he said stubbornly, knotting his tie. "It will be cheaper and I can just as easily work away from the city." He came to the side of the bed, leaned over, and kissed me. I felt like pulling him down onto me and keeping him there by whatever means at my disposal. I'd done so before, at least if Muddy wasn't about. But it had been months since I'd felt well enough to even contemplate such things.

"Soon you'll no longer have to breathe this infernal coal smoke," he whispered, and bent to kiss me again.

"That would be pleasant," I whispered back. I felt sure I must be nearing the end of the time which Dr. English, back in Philadelphia, had told me someone in my condition might expect to have left. How nice it would be to spend my final months looking out on a garden and a slice of blue sky, rather than the grimy brick wall a few feet away from our one small window here.

"Your cottage awaits," he said, stopping at the door to look back at me. "I merely have to find it."

21

In March we moved to Turtle Bay. Not to the hoped-for cottage, but a large farmhouse surrounded by acres of gardens and orchards. It sat along the East River just below Blackwell's Island. Eddy and I shared an airy corner room on the second floor. Its bank of windows overlooked an apple orchard on the south end, and the hills of Brooklyn and Blackwell's on the north. I watched the fruit trees blossom as Long Island bloomed into green spring. Yet still I could not rest.

This was not the fault of Mrs. John C. Miller, who owned the farm, for she provided us with such wholesome, homegrown food. Mrs. Miller allowed Muddy to cook our meals. And if I could not come down to table my mother carried up a laden tray. Each time this happened I saw the worry and fear in her eyes. I didn't know how I might comfort her, though.

When the April sun was warm enough I sat out on the upstairs veranda. From my seat, wrapped in a quilt of Mrs. Miller's making, I could watch Eddy row out on the East River as far as Blackwell's Island. I could no longer accompany him, and didn't wish to. It was enough to watch his back curve as he pulled at the oars, till husband and boat grew smaller and smaller. Yet he was never long out of my sight. He always brought me a snail or mussel shell bleached by the sun, or a river stone which gradually lost its subtle rainbow hues as it dried. I lined up these treasures on our windowsills, along with an old jam jar of the flowers—wild and from the Millers' garden—my mother brought up each day. She was fanatical about their life spans now, and grieved all out of measure to see even one wilted blossom. She always whisked these away and quickly brought up new blooms.

I believed life would continue in some ways the same, even after I had to leave the world. From above perhaps I might look down and see Eddy rowing or walking the lanes. See them both as a bird might cock its head to view the world below. Perhaps this will sound odd, that I did not grieve or rage at fate. But by then I could no longer look on death as a terrible leave-taking. I was so very tired, and in some degree of pain almost always. Afterward, I assumed I would not suffer, yet might be with them in some way still. My brother's visit had imparted that knowledge to me.

One day in May, though, Eddy insisted I get dressed and wrap up in the quilt. Then he carried me downstairs and set me up on the seat of John Miller's wagon. We all three drove north, yet though I asked several times, no one would tell me *where* we were going, or why. All Eddy would say was, "We're headed for Fordham." So I supposed he'd arranged some entertainment, or a visit for us there. I felt a bit resentful he would do so without asking if I even cared to go out.

After about fifteen miles of rolling and jolting over dirt roads and farm lanes, we arrived at the busy Kingsbridge Road which, he told me, turned east toward the village of Fordham. By then I was exhausted. My chest felt on fire. The dust from the road scoured my lungs, and I'd twice coughed spots of blood into my stained handkerchief.

"Almost there!" cried Eddy, with maddening cheerfulness.

Angry at being subjected to this torture, I did not even try to answer.

Instead of turning toward the village Mr. Miller pulled the wagon down a side lane and into a yard shaded by gnarled cherry trees. Beyond them lay an acre or two of greensward smooth as a swept velvet carpet. A rock ledge to the east grew a wild profusion of cedars and pines wrapped like ladies in lace shawls of green vine. The whole place was an Eden poised to bloom, with hedges of lilac, and clumps of what might be dahlias and asters and bachelor's button. I felt a little better now that we'd stopped jolting along, but was still confused about why we were here.

"Turn around to look," he said then.

I hadn't noticed the cottage, for it was shaded by cherry trees, and shingled modestly and naturally with unpainted shakes of cypress or cedar. It was small but two-storied, and the long front piazza would be lovely to sit out on in summer. A lean-to shed slumped at one end.

"It's like that poem I might still write someday, myself. Give me a cottage for my home, " I whispered, "and a rich old cypress vine."

The celebrated poet stood next to the wagon, gripping my elbow, watching my face anxiously as a child longing for a parent's praise. "Do you like it?"

"Why, it is my cottage," I said. "But how did you ever find it?"

Eddy's face relaxed. "I'd tell you I was going into the city. Then, when you were no longer at the window, I'd turn and rush up the road the other way. I wore out the soles of my shoes walking, until I came upon this place."

I laughed a little at his rueful expression. We had no money for new shoes, of course.

And then, with no help from anyone I climbed down. I walked a few steps and saw this was in fact the garden from my Sleeping

Poison dream. I knew it right away, and why I was finally here, in daylight, awake. This would be the last place on earth I would live. My waystation from one world to the next. To see its unpainted shingles and green shutters, to understand this was so, made me feel at peace.

"Oh—look, Sissy," cried my mother. "There will be cherries soon. We can put up preserves."

Eddy pointed to stone towers rising on a hill to the southeast. "That's Rose Hill, and St. John's College. It's been taken over by Jesuits. The rector has invited us to use their library."

I nodded absently, already following the black slate-paved path to the porch. I put one foot on the bottom step, but before it could creak under my weight Eddy had a hand under my elbow. I had no need of help yet, but let him support and follow me to the front door.

Downstairs to the right lay a kitchen with a large fireplace on its east wall. To the left spread a good-sized parlor and another smaller room beyond—little more than a cubbyhole, really—which might serve as a bedroom, or a study for Eddy. The walls were freshly whitewashed, the floors pine planks of various widths.

"I want to see upstairs," I said, sounding only a little out of breath.

My mother and Eddy exchanged a look while pretending not to.

"Come with me," I insisted. "Or shall I go alone?"

It was a slow journey up the narrow stairway, Eddy just behind with a hand at the small of my back. But I wanted to see it all on my own. To give my first look at this last place my full attention.

At the top lay a short hallway with a bedroom on either end. There the back roof of the cottage slanted down almost to the floor. Small square windows with clear glass panes, two in each room, were large enough to let in the May sunlight. Large enough to open and feel a summer breeze. Or to allow a spirit to escape. I did not say these things, but hoarded them like a gift I'd been doubtful of, but treasured and put away to take out later and gaze at in private.

It turned out our possessions had already been loaded into the Millers' wagon—Eddy had hidden them under an old canvas sail—so I would not notice and guess. Now one of Mrs. Miller's sons and a neighbor appeared to help unload. As they walked back and forth past me, grunting under the heavy writing desk and the kitchen table, faces growing red and shiny with sweat, I sat in one of the little oak chairs on the front porch, in a patch of sunshine.

"Catterina will love it," I said. "Mice in the fields, birds in the orchard. No back alleys where she must fight to stake her claim. The mistress of all she sees."

"We could hang Pym's cage out here," said Eddy. "I might even acquire a songbird or two."

I slept well that night and didn't cough once. The next morning, after we breakfasted on bread, salt herring, and the last of the coffee, I asked Eddy to read to me from "Israfel."

"Israfel, really?" He raised his eyebrows. "Wouldn't you rather hear something new? I'm finishing up an essay on the literati of New York. Amusing, I think."

"I'm sure it is," I said. It would be both honest and hilarious, and win him no new friends but a few more enemies. "But I'd prefer the other."

"It's so old," he muttered. "But whatever my little wife desires."

He pulled the *Poems* from the shelf and, standing before me, began. I listened with my head back against the settee, eyes closed. I felt transported by his voice, especially at the last lines.

If I did dwell where Israfel
Hath dwelt, and he where I,
He would not sing one half as well—
One half as passionately,
And a stormier note than this would swell
From my lyre within the sky.

The words were so true, his voice so warm and strong and up-
lifting, I forgot myself and murmured, "Yes—yes, it must be so."
And smiled.

The silence that fell then was as profound as if a muffling cloak
had been flung over everything. I opened my eyes to see what was
amiss.

Eddy said harshly, "What do you mean?"

"Only—only that it is beautiful, and—" I tried to think quickly,
for I didn't want to lie outright. "It must be that way. The music.
The peace."

His face darkened to mottled red. "*Never* say that. Don't speak
of death, don't dare. A beautiful young woman must never, should
never—"

But he did not finish, only stared at me in obvious rage, hands
clenched to fists. He'd never spoken in such a tone to me before,
in all the years we'd been married, or before that either.

I stared back in confusion. "But you yourself said it! And still
write of it. You said that—that there was no more fit subject for
poetry than the death of a beautiful young woman!"

He sprang forward, and for a moment I thought he meant to
strike me. Of course Eddy would never do such a thing. He merely
flung the book to the floor, where it bounced, then lay with leaves
splayed and bent, dry and crumpled as a fallen moth.

"That was *before*! A fool might say any number of stupid

things, before he . . . before he saw . . ." He gazed at me with such anguish I was struck speechless. "That is why," he gritted between clenched teeth, "*you must . . . not . . . go.*"

I reached for his hands, but he clapped them over his face, then rushed blindly out, slamming hard into the door jamb, not even hesitating at the impact of that collision. I began to weep without knowing why. For my condition, my fate? For his grief? Because my husband had shouted at me for the first time?

Suddenly he was back. He snatched the book off the floor again and glared at it. "That which I read before was a lie," he growled. "*This* is the truth." And he paged through the poems like a madman, reading at random. "'Al Araaf,'" he spat. "'Thus in discourse the lovers whiled away / The night that waned and waned and brought no day / They fell: for Heaven to them no hope imparts / Who hear not for the beating of their hearts.'"

I wrung my hands in my lap. "But there's more to it, Eddy, I know. I've read—"

But he did not even need a book before him to go on. "'The Raven,'" he barked out like a frenzied dog trying to repel an intruder on the threshold. "'Tell this soul with sorrow laden if, within the distant Aidenn / It shall clasp a sainted maiden whom the angels name Lenore— / Clasp a rare and radiant maiden whom the angels name Lenore. Quoth the raven—'"

I clapped my hands over my ears then and screamed as loud as I could. I would not hear it, I would not suffer that terrible annihilating word to be said aloud. Not in this house.

Muddy stumbled in. "What happened?" she gasped, dropping a dish towel and rushing to my side. "Lord God, are you ill?"

Eddy sagged against the wall and let the book drop again. "I'm a raving madman," he told her, head rolling against the plaster. "Between a few horrible bouts of sanity."

"Eddy! Are you trying to kill her?" It was the only rebuke I ever heard her utter to him.

He gazed at my mother then with an expression so amazed and stricken I moaned and had to turn away. Before anyone could speak again he gave a choked sob and stumbled out. The very angle of his shoulders beaten, exhausted; Prometheus condemned and crushed by distant, vengeful gods.

The front door slammed; he was gone. And who knew how or when or if he would return.

I began to cough. When I held the square of white linen to my mouth it came away heavy and red with clots. Without another word Muddy helped me up the stairs to bed.

I lay there quite still, to placate the vengeful black creature in my chest that would brook no shouting, no infliction of pain except that which it was pleased to dole out. Perhaps the hard and hurtful things we'd said would bring to us both some measure of peace in the end. They were out in the open, at least—our true feelings, our one great divide. I looked forward to a surcease of pain and some continued existence. To a love that did not truly end. But Eddy—what did he look for? Could he not, just once, allow *me* to know better? To let me teach him something for a change? For he could not stop the coming of what would someday be my end. Yet he could not accept it either. We were husband and wife, but he refused to allow me to speak freely.

What would become of him when I was gone?

Thinking of all these things I cried softly, though carefully; for myself and for Eddy. I dared not lift an arm or move a hand to brush the tears away, in case the motion started me coughing again. So they ran from the corners of my eyes and down into my ears, and then I felt both sad and vexed. Finally Muddy came again, to wipe my face and sit with me, humming a childhood song until I closed my eyes and finally slept.

It was harder in confinement, from my small window upstairs, to make out the garden below. Our bed sat just under the sloping back ceiling, but we'd had to saw off the tops of the posts on one side in order to fit it in. I sometimes would lie reversed, my head at the footboard, propped up on the folded threadbare greatcoat, in order to see out. The grounds were large, sunless in the mornings, warm in the afternoons, and all that grew there appeared elderly as time. The yard was shaded by fruit trees, a few beech, and walled by a yew hedge. Among the flowering plants and bushes, I had thought to spy dahlias eventually, but none had put forth their heads.

"Ah well, those we'll plant when you're up again and feeling well," my mother said.

I think she knew that would not happen. I would likely see no more springs, nor have the time or strength to plant summer flowers anywhere.

Camellia bushes bloomed in the late fall, their white petals streaked bloodred. Ferns and violets and lilies of the valley might come up the following spring. But would I still be here to see them?

At times I did feel we were being punished. As if, having found each other, we had somehow erred or sinned in loving. So we were forced to begin to say good-bye almost the moment our fingers had touched for the first time in my mother's parlor, under Granny Poe's beady, bird-sharp gaze.

But why should this be so, when we'd done no wrong to each other or anyone else in the world? I could not comprehend the actions of such a God. Perhaps the brevity of our stay—no, not just ours, but everyone's—was a cruel joke He played repeatedly. Yes, Eddy might say this.

"With a God like that," he'd once impiously quipped, "who needs a Devil at all?" But I didn't want to think it was so.

On the sheltered north side grew the thick, ancient cypress vine of my dream, which was indeed slowly strangling its poor rickety arbor. The splintered fence boards that cordoned the yard had begun to straggle and list, but still strove valiantly to keep wandering cows from stripping the orchard of its few remaining withered apples.

Strange, but on some days I could smell the sea, which lay miles from Fordham. Though anyone with legs and health enough could traipse over to the rocky ledge at the edge of our property and catch a glimpse of Long Island Sound. When I heard the far whistles of the Providence steamers passing by I imagined I again caught that salt-laden breeze, and suddenly would long for Baltimore, the smells and sounds of the wharf. One last look. Wishing for *home,* I suppose, though we never really had the same one for long. So which one was it that I missed?

More often I found myself longing for one unlabored breath. Because that last winter grew cold so quickly, and we had no heavy blankets or quilts left. I huddled under the coat and Catterina perched atop it with tucked paws and slitted green eyes, purring like a coal fire. That became her sole occupation: keeping me warm. She abandoned her campaign against mice and insects, and took the job quite seriously.

Eddy no longer read me poems. He brought newspapers and stories written by others. The wind blew hard, and the chill thrust like frostbitten claws through the chinks in the walls, the cracked panes. One icy morning Muddy came down to the kitchen to find Pym dead, lying frozen and stiff at the bottom of his cage. Though she'd never wanted him to begin with, she mourned the poor creature for days.

She and Eddy joined Catterina in trying to keep me warm. Muddy rubbed my icy feet while Eddy took hold of my hands, which ached and burned in the cold bedroom, and cradled them in his own.

"I am even now working on plans for the magazine, my dear," he would say, clenching his jaw to still his chattering teeth. "I have two or three prospects. An investor who, I think, is quite sympathetic to my goals."

Then Muddy would promise, "I'll make fresh apple pie or a tart, if you'll eat some." Yet we had no butter or sugar, and could afford to buy none.

Still, after a while I'd feel a bit better, and sometimes even get out of bed. Such was the cruel, taunting nature of my disease. I improved so much that one day Eddy let it be known I could receive visitors. And Frances Osgood came up on the train, to see me again.

The first time, she came alone. Muddy had gone off to town to sell books. I only hoped they'd all belonged to Eddy. He had asked her to be sure this time, but she never did pay much attention. To her, the cash in hand was the object, and his friends would not reproach *her*, of course.

When Fanny arrived Eddy had been working, but he threw his pen aside. He always did so, for he loved visitors. He might sit for hours at his desk under the portrait of his mother, tracing in his exquisite chirography and with superhuman swiftness his lightning thoughts. I think, had he not written in this swift way, those fancies would have raced unchecked through his brain, pummeling his skull, to overwhelm and perhaps even kill him. That too, I think, was a reason he sometimes resorted to drink. When the stories were not sufficient, or did not come quickly enough, to slow and soothe the black cyclone that sometimes howled and spun inside him.

So here we sat in the parlor, Fanny Osgood and I, Eddy having returned to his work. By then I'd read some of her poems, including new ones dedicated to Eddy. She'd also written one about me, though it was not among those she showed me herself. He'd brought it home a while back.

> That fair, fond girl who at your side
> Within your soul's dear light, doth live
> Could hardly have the heart to chide
> The ray that Friendship well might give
> But if you deem it right and just
> Blessed as you are in your glad lot
> To greet me with that heartless tone
> So be it! I blame you not!

"Oh my," I'd said to Eddy then. "You've hurt *her* feelings. What did you do?"

"Nothing, nothing." He had looked bemused. "Well, I might've paused too briefly on the street when we . . . or—oh, I don't know." He'd run his fingers through his hair, grabbing at it until it stood on end. "Poetesses are such a prickly lot. Gloomy too, most of them."

Oh, but Fanny was not gloomy. And I was not a girl any longer, nor a fool—though folks often mistake a quiet nature for lack of wits. Mrs. Samuel Osborne was in love with my husband, but she was a lady and would never, ever do anything improper. I liked her still. Rather than skulk about and whisper behind her hand, or smirk and simper in my face as most of his distaff admirers did, she'd set out to befriend me.

Now Fanny said, "If you feel well enough, you must come out with me to hear Miss Fuller speak."

"Oh." I had met Margaret once; she was quite intimidating. "What about?"

"Why, the usual. She will take to the podium and talk on women's God-given rights." Then she did look gloomy. "You know—the ones we are not likely to get hold of in my lifetime, or yours." Then she gasped and blushed, and would not meet my eyes.

I reached out to cover her hands. "Fanny, it's all right to speak of it. I was hoping you would be Eddy's friend, you know. Now and—and afterward."

She looked flustered, but squeezed my fingers back. "I am his friend, and yours too, I hope."

When I told Eddy what she'd said, later that night, he frowned. "Ah. I see. So that is what she wishes?" I might've imagined it, but he looked disappointed. Soon he seemed happy again, though, reading to us by the fire from his newest piece, "Eulalie."

When Fanny came after that first visit it was often in the company of the Misses Fuller and Lynch. This did not vex me; it was amusing to sit and listen to the three of them, to see how they preened and giggled and slapped at each other after a provoking remark. To understand as I watched how each both adored and was wildly jealous of the others. Especially when it came to their work. This was the closest I'd ever come to experiencing this sort of female comradeship, at least since my childhood days back on Wilks Street, playing with Claudine and Juliette.

Elizabeth Ellet came sometimes too. Another friend of Fanny's, but I did not much care for her. When Miss Ellet came to our home, even as she tried to flatter me she never took her eyes off Eddy. Gradually I understood why she would not look at me. The one or two times she could not avoid meeting my gaze, I glimpsed such malignancy, such hate, I drew back. There was something not quite right behind her eyes. If Eddy wasn't at home, or not in the room, her hungry stare never settled. It darted from chair to writing desk to bookshelf, flicking up eagerly at any sound to fasten on the doorway, to see if *he* had finally returned.

One day Fanny did come alone again. I was bored, and glad of the company, though even she seemed a bit low.

First she claimed, "Oh, it's nothing. I'm laced too tight, is all."

But really it was something to do with her estranged husband. She dropped various hints but would not say outright. I wanted to cheer her up. Eddy had left one of Elizabeth Ellet's horrible letters lying out on his desk. He always showed such correspondence from admirers to me, but Miss Ellet's were much more intimate and insinuating in tone, more fawning than the rest; the words of a would-be panderer. Quite nauseating, like the woman herself.

Still, he was always careful with private correspondence. He would not have done what I did next. I got up and brought the letter over to Fanny. Together we read it aloud, giggling and elbowing each other. Fanny used her wicked mimicry to catch Miss Ellet's high, nasal stutter perfectly. "'And *long* for your de-vine inspir-a-tion,'" she intoned, snorting. "'For one so insig-nif-i-cant as *I*.'"

She had her to the very life. We hooted and broke into fresh laughter.

We were so wonderfully entertained, I hadn't realized Muddy was back from her morning errands. At that very moment, while we were still laughing and wiping our streaming eyes, my mother showed Elizabeth Ellet into the room.

"Oh God," whispered Fanny, jerking to attention, crumpling the letter in her thin fingers. "Why Lizzy, my dear," she said aloud.

I felt suddenly overheated and faint. "Miss Ellet," I said. "Won't you come in and sit down?"

She stood rigid between kitchen and sitting room, face lit with two ugly hectic spots, as if I'd slapped both her sallow cheeks. I glanced at my mother, who lurked silently behind Lizzie, wearing her usual black dress, faded yet dignified, even queenly on her tall figure, against that now snow-white hair. Sometimes I wondered how a woman of such heroic proportions had ever birthed someone as small and unimposing as me. Muddy had an odd look, of triumph or satisfaction. For the first time I realized she must hate Fanny Osborne. But why—and did she also hate me? Or perhaps she simply wished me to have no other confidant than her.

Miss Ellet fairly vibrated, but neither moved nor spoke. She was still in her overcoat, holding a leather reticule at one side, cradling a book in the other arm. Suddenly, with a faint cry and a clumsy lurch, she rushed toward us, snatched the letter from Fanny's hand, and stumbled out again. The kitchen door banged loudly.

"Oh my," said Fanny after a moment, voice shaking. "Someone will pay dearly for this!"

I was afraid she was right. I wished I'd never brought the letter out, all just to be clever and entertaining. And yes, cruel. It was wrong, and I wondered why I'd done it. Perhaps my own Imp was at work, for the moment as busy as Eddy's, making me stoop to unworthy actions to secure the admiration and love of a woman who also loved my husband. Was I competing with Eddy for Fanny's love, or vice versa? Whatever the case, I hoped Lizzy Ellet would not be unkind to her, for really the fault was mine.

We tried to talk again, Fanny and I—to restore that light, jolly mood. But by then we could barely look each other in the eye. She left soon after and I went up to my room. Muddy tried to help me up the stairs but I threw off her supporting hand. I climbed alone to my bed and stayed there, feeling certain somehow that my dear friend Fanny would not be back.

22

But Fanny did return once more—in the company of the Misses
Fuller, Lynch, *and* Ellet. She came to ask for the return of all her
own letters to Eddy. I stood in the upper hallway listening to my
friend's voice, which sounded clogged with a cold, or with tears.
Then to Margaret Fuller's reasonable low tones, and Anne Lynch's
apologetic but firm ones. And Eddy's surprised demurrals, the
scraping of the desk drawer as he opened it.

Then came Lizzie Ellet's satisfied whinny. "Is that *all* of the letters you ever wrote him, Fanny? You really *ought* to make certain."

So Lizzie had somehow convinced Fanny—convinced them
all—that her correspondence with Eddy was shameful, scandalous,
and cause for retrieving the evidence. And Fanny had agreed. She
must have, for she was here, and had not asked to see me. It meant
she could never return—certainly not on her own, if at all.

Oh Fanny, I thought. *Not you. Are you really such a coward as
this?*

I did not get dressed and go down.

I did not go downstairs at all after that. Something had seized
and hardened inside, petrified like fossil rock in my chest. I could
not force air down past that obstruction, which at times heated like
a glowing hearthstone and made me writhe and choke in breathless

agony. The Black Toad was back, and *he* would abandon me no more.

I heard Muddy and Eddy sometimes begging me to wake up, to talk to them, to come back. I was able to open my eyes once, to summon enough breath to whisper the truth into my husband's ear: "Lizzy Ellet has killed me."

Eddy and Muddy sit in turn by the bed and read aloud or try to make me eat. Sometimes my mother hands me the remaining sliver of looking glass, from the wall mirror which was broken in the move. I hold it in both hands as she combs my hair out on the pillow. It's strange to look at my own face, which seems still so rosy cheeked and round and full—the picture of health.

You are twenty-four, and you are dying, I say silently to myself as I gaze in the glass. Such deaths are not a marvel. Little children die; adults younger than I. What's odd is that, looking at myself in the triangular silvered shard, I can detect no change. No shadow of the grave, no finger writing upon my pale broad brow. When my mother hits a snarl and tugs to untangle it, I still wince in pain—just as I did when I was a healthy eight-year-old. I'm still hungry. I still need to sleep. I cough at times in long wrenching spasms that feel as if I have swallowed molten lead and must now bring it up again, or perish on the spot. Then the walls of the room shrink around me like a magician's box, only to expand again when I can finally draw a breath.

I am no martyred angel. I still long for the same things: to play my piano, to strum the harp, to feel my husband beside me in bed at night. I still hate Lizzy Ellet. I no longer dream of a daughter, though. I understand now that the little girl who comes to me at night, too young to speak, is my lost sister, Virginia Maria. Not a child of my own. Once or twice I heard my brother sawing and hammering again downstairs, but he did not come up to see me, as before. When he finally does climb those narrow stairs, I suspect it will be for a more serious purpose than the last time he appeared to me.

But yet again I grew a little better, and was able to sit up and talk and feed myself. And then to even have visitors, though I no longer possessed the strength to leave our room.

Mary Gove first stepped into our poor cottage in the company of George Colton, the editor who'd bought "The Raven." I knew of her only what Eddy had written in "The Literati"—that she was a mesmerist, a Swedenborgian, a phrenologist, and a homeopathist. And perhaps most curiously, a disciple of Vincenz Priessnitz, the Bavarian who cured dukes and duchesses by pouring cold water over them, and making them walk barefoot on grass. I wondered what she would think of our shabby little home, with its few rickety chairs, warped kitchen table, and rusting woodstove. The sitting room was furnished only with checked matting, four chairs, a light stand, and a hanging bookshelf holding the few worthless volumes Muddy had not yet sold.

When Mrs. Gove was brought upstairs she clasped my hands and said, "My dear Mrs. Poe. That raven hair, that pearly skin— you are every bit as lovely as I'd heard."

"Thank you," I replied, not knowing what else to say. "I've heard of your work—"

"Psh," she said loudly. "Merely a student of life. I scribble and lecture a bit, is all." She leaned closer and whispered, "Fanny has sent me and her regards."

So my dear friend had not forgotten me. This kind visitor was a gift from her.

We talked a while, and then the others went out for a walk.

When they returned Eddy looked sheepish, chagrined, and very wet. "Mr. Colton and a neighbor man and I were leaping over the brook. It was a competition," he added, not looking at me or Muddy. Then I saw why: His new gaiters—the cheap pair he'd managed to acquire to replace those he'd worn out tramping the roads looking for our little cottage—had split from his exertions.

My mother's face darkened. She took Mrs. Gove by the arm. "You must speak to Mr. Colton about Eddy's latest poem. If he takes it for the magazine, Eddy can have a new pair of shoes."

Mrs. Gove looked flustered. "Oh. Well, I suppose—"

"Muddy," I said. "Please."

She went on as if I hadn't spoken. "He *has* the poem, I took it up to his office last week. Eddy says it is his best work. You *will* speak to him, won't you?"

Mary Gove looked like a trapped rabbit. I could guess why. It must be "Ulalume." Eddy had read it to us the week before, and Heaven forgive us, neither Muddy nor I could make heads or tails of it.

Perhaps Mrs. Gove had played some active role in the destruction of the gaiters, or had at least urged the men on, for she glanced guiltily at Eddy's ruined shoes, then said firmly, "Of course George will publish it. And he'll be damned quick about it too." Muddy looked askance at her profanity. I muffled a laugh in Catterina's furry flank.

That night I endeavored to write a poem, the only one I'd ever attempted. I did not know the rules for making a sonnet, or a villanelle, or any of the classical forms about which Eddy was so knowledgeable. Instead, I decided to take my husband's name and make an acrostic, since he loved poetry and puzzles both. Then I would give it for his thirty-eighth birthday, on January 19. If I could only get the right words down it would show him, and any-one else who read it, what I really felt about our lives, and the peo-ple who tried so hard, so often, to ruin them.

By the time I scrawled the last line, sitting propped against the wall, I was exhausted. The next morning I carefully copied it over. By then I understood it was not actually a birthday greeting, as I'd planned, but an anniversary poem. But surely I would not still be here for that milestone, in May.

When he came up the next evening, bringing supper on a tray, I pulled the page from beneath my pillow and handed it to him.

"Why, what's this?"

"Read it."

I'd meant he should read it to himself. But he misunderstood, for he began to recite aloud.

Ever with thee I wish to roam—
Dearest my life is thine.
Give me a cottage for my home
And a rich old cypress vine,
Removed from the world with its sin and care

And the tattling of many tongues.
Love alone shall guide us when we are there—
Love shall heal my weakened lungs;
And Oh, the tranquil hours we'll spend
Never wishing that others may see!

Perfect ease we'll enjoy, without thinking to lend
Ourselves to the world and its glee—
Ever peaceful and blissful we'll be.

When he finished he hung his head for a moment, silent. I hoped he liked it, even if it wasn't very good. I knew *glee* and *be* was a childish rhyme, though overall no worse than some he'd been forced to read, and even print, by admiring amateur poetesses. And actually a lot better, I thought, than that old lovesick verse he'd once asked me to carry to Mary Starr—which had met its end as fragments in the gutter, back in Baltimore.

Perhaps what was worse was that, in the poem, I'd lied. For I'd certainly had all the love anyone could ever wish for, and it still had not cured my lungs. But I hadn't wanted mine to be a gloomy verse. I did not want to write about the death of a beautiful woman.

"Eddy," I finally ventured. "Is it so very bad?"

He didn't answer, only shook his head. He sank to his knees beside the bed and stretched his arms out over my body, as if to hold me in place there forever. And then, he wept.

By late autumn I was still confined, and had the expected winter cough. But this time it made me much weaker. A glowing flame burned in my chest like an underground coal fire and, just like such subterranean blazes, would not be extinguished. I coughed my way through a gross of linen. These articles began as white as the snow that shrouded my garden outside. But soon I'd stained every pocket handkerchief and flannel and dishcloth we owned with gouts and clots of bright blood. Muddy tended me like an angel, though it was hard on her to climb the steep stairs all the time. Eddy didn't want to leave my side. He sat and read to me, holding one of my hands.

It was very cold in our Fordham cottage. I remember that clearly—how we could see our breath always going before us, as if our spirits were escaping our bodies. Catterina did her best to warm my chest, purring like a steam engine, gazing into my face and pressing her head into my shoulder. Eddy chafed my hands and feet to bring the circulation back. I couldn't even lift an arm by then. I was too tired.

Mary Gove, plainspoken lady of many talents, came again— this time alone. She climbed the stairs and sat beside my bed. I was not embarrassed at this very personal visit, though everything around us shouted of poverty and want. The lack of good bedclothes, for my mattress was covered only with a worn white spread. The tick itself, stuffed with straw. Our only heavy bedcover was Eddy's old army greatcoat. Muddy, who'd had to pawn the last of our quilts, sat at the foot of the bed rubbing my bare feet.

But I found in Mrs. Gove's eyes not contempt nor even pity, but rather that honest and knowing heartache only the poor can feel for the poor. She gazed with clear admiration at Catterina, who lay like a tortoiseshell fur stole—still my one luxury—across my breast.

"Why, I would swear that wonderful cat is conscious of her own great usefulness," Mrs. Gove exclaimed.

Of course she is, I thought. Anyone could see it.

Eddy came in and began to rub my hands. "You still have many friends and admirers, Mr. Poe, who would like to ease your burden," said Mary gently.

"I doubt that," said Eddy, with no malice or anger, but only as one simply states a fact.

"But it's true. And I will show you."

The following week she returned with two men and a wagon. They unloaded a featherbed and an abundance of new bedclothes, and covers for Eddy and Muddy as well. I saw her press a roll of banknotes into Muddy's hands before she left. She visited often after that, bringing a basket of food, or clothing for Eddy or Muddy, or a new nightgown for me.

But then Eddy fell ill of a brain fever. Muddy nearly killed herself nursing us both, until a woman appeared on our doorstep, so
Muddy came up to tell me, with a notice clipped from Nathaniel
Willis's *Home Journal.* "Says she's a doctor's daughter trained in
medicine, and married to a physician. She claims that years ago she
treated Eddy at the Northern Dispensary, the first time we lived in
New York."

Then Muddy handed me the clipping and I skimmed a few
lines:

> *We know that, on Mr. Poe's recovery from former
> illnesses, he has been deeply mortified and distressed by the
> discovery that his friends have been called on for assis-
> tance . . . we hazard this delicate service without his leave,
> of course . . .*

It spoke of bad conduct and worse language charged against
him,

> *. . . the least stimulus—a single glass of wine—would pro-
> duce this effect upon Mr. Poe . . . but public opinion un-
> qualifiedly holds him blameless for what he has said and
> done under such excitements . . .*

This too must be the work of Mary Gove, and other old friends.
Eddy would be furious. He knew—we all knew—of what the article
spoke. But it was an unwritten rule that we did not talk of the Old
Failing aloud, much less publish notices about it to the public. I
crumpled the clipping to my breast, then slid it under the covers
just as Muddy returned with our new visitor in tow. Eddy must not
see it—not now, when he too was ill.

"Hello, Mrs. Poe," she said, bowing as if we were on the street and I fully dressed, rather than clad in a donated nightgown. "I am Marie Louise Shew."

Mrs. Shew was different from the literary women who adored Eddy and plagued us all. She was plain, with a short neck, yellow complexion, long narrow nose, and rather round body. Her best feature was the large luminous eyes which shone out from under heavy lids and finely arched brows. The eyes of an exotic and much more beautiful woman, and through them I saw her kindness clearly manifested.

Mrs. Shew brushed my hair and washed me as a mother would her child, on those occasions when Muddy was tired and could not. She sat and read to me, and sometimes just held my hand. The pain was so intense at times I could not even try to speak. Laudanum no longer helped. I did not sleep, but only dozed and jerked awake.

Each cough began like a thick iron rod striking my lungs. My heart thumped and stuttered, a defective steam engine. The ceiling of my room cracked and split, and a boiling rain of heated stones tumbled down. But I could not move or run away, being a traveler trapped on a sheer cliff, my ledge just a few inches wide. I must traverse this narrow way while clinging to the rock face by fingers and nails, not looking down. Sweat glazed my face and body as the pain boiled my lungs and parched my throat and head. My entire existence narrowed and resolved into stones and blocks and brick walls. Within them, a cage barred with glass shards stood between me and the world and everyone in it. Each cough shook me like the hard pealing of a thousand cast-iron bells. I burned and froze, sweated and parched, and no one could stop it. Only the hot coppery gush of blood brought a moment of respite, as the tide receded.

Then it would begin again.

Finally they gave me so much laudanum it made me docile and numb. I'd sometimes thought of my body as an instrument, like the pianoforte or harp. Now its strings had snapped, its keyboard fallen to pieces. I could no longer bend it to my will and make it sing. When I was awake I thought: Is it really true? Must I fail altogether and turn into a thing with no more feeling than a block of wood or a river stone? I could not envision this part of my journey, not through the dreaming cotton wool of the Sleeping Poison.

Yet it was then, in that floating haze, that I came to the true meaning of that formerly vexing poem, "Al Araaf." The one I'd tried and failed to comprehend so many years ago, while still a child. The one I thought I had understood when Eddy and I argued over it, years later, here in this cottage. It was not just about heavenly music. No, it really said so much more. That when true lovers were both free of the world and of their faulty bodies, they would be reunited, and dwell in a garden again. Not the Heaven of sermons and Bibles—and in some ways that was a shame, for the idea of celestial *harps* had always appealed. But no, this world grew and flourished far away, on a distant star. I could almost see our eternal future together, and it would be on Al Araaf. There was no end, then—only a new beginning. So when the time came to let go and swallow the dark, and be swallowed up by it in turn—to surrender my little spark—I would do so gladly, without looking back. I would not hesitate there on the edge.

I will rush out and fly up like a bird to greet the dawn. Yes, fling myself into space like a fledgling sparrow from the brink of its nest, gripping that twig-laced wall, balanced on the threshold of a world much larger and even wilder than itself.

For the first time since those days when I could still sing and play, something worked within to free me. To make me larger and braver, not smaller and more afraid. Through fevered dreams, beneath the murmur of voices that came and left my room, I heard a hammering night and day. The sound of my dear brother working away downstairs with hammer and saw—though it seemed no one else could see or hear, or certainly they would've mentioned it! Henry's ghost must be taking his time, putting all his skill and love into the crafting of his sister's coffin.

The next morning I called Mrs. Shew to my bedside.

"Yes, my dear, what is it?" she said, smiling down.

I pointed to the table and motioned for her to open the drawer. She did so, and I withdrew a small morocco leather case. She opened it for me. Inside were a picture of Eddy and two creased, faded letters. I pressed them into her hands.

She looked puzzled. "What shall I do with these, Mrs. Poe? Should I read to you?"

I nodded.

They were from Frances Allan, Eddy's beloved foster mother. They told the true story of his disowning by John Allan. Though she would not speak against her husband in life, before she died Mrs. Allan had written Eddy and laid the blame for the break between foster father and son where it belonged—at the feet of that cold, uncaring paterfamilias. This was the second tragedy of Eddy's life, after the death of his lovely young mother. I did not want the world to think, later, he had been the one at fault.

Mrs. Shew carefully folded them again. When she tried to hand the picture and letters back I shook my head. I held out the case again, and she slipped everything inside. "Keep these for me," I whispered quickly, before I could not speak again.

She nodded, looking serious. "Would you like me to bring you anything from the city?"

I smiled and shook my head. The city had nothing left for me.

I woke later that day—or perhaps night, for the light was dim. It darkened further as I opened my eyes. Eddy sat hunched on the edge of the mattress holding both my hands. Muddy was stretched across the foot, holding my feet, trying to rub life back into them. They were both sobbing bitterly. Muddy's hot tears dripped on the arch of my bare foot, and Eddy's fell just as warm on my cold fingers.

Don't cry, I said, or tried to. *We will meet again so very soon. There is no need.*

Footsteps sounded on the stairs, and I thought, *It's Marie.* But just then Catterina growled deep in her throat, then leaped from the mattress and scrambled beneath the bed.

When I looked toward the doorway my brother Henry stood there. He wore one gold earring, like a pirate, and a white sailor's blouse. A scattering of purple and white periwinkle shells were woven into his black, black hair, which was long and tangled and in great need of trimming. I expected him to come take my hand, and pull me up. To say it was time to go out the door and down the stairs with him. But he only stood smiling patiently, and did not speak a word.

Finally I understood, as I gazed again at Muddy and Eddy, both still holding on to me. Holding me down. Or was I somehow still clinging to them? Perhaps it was *I* who must let go. I the one who must decide.

Kiss me good-bye, I said. But no one seemed to hear.

Eddy still grasped both my hands tightly, but I managed to pull one away. With it I reached out to Henry, who stepped forward and took hold. Then my brother pulled and with one good yank I was free. Standing upright again and looking down with compassion, but no real sadness, on the pale wreck of a young woman who had been named Virginia after her dead sister. Looking as well on two sobbing figures stretched out over her silent, unbreathing body, as if to trap the soul there forever with all their force and will.

To my surprise Henry did not turn away then to take me to see the fine coffin. The one I'd assumed he'd spent so long making for my discarded body to rest in at last. Instead he pulled me toward the bedroom window, and climbed up on the sill.

I laughed. It was the sort of thing he would've done when we were small. I followed, and then we were both perched there, and I remember thinking, *How odd*. For we two were large and grown, and my room had a very small window indeed. Yet there we sat on its sill, side by side . . . like two baby birds ready to leave the nest and fly away.

I laughed. "Oh, Henry. How did you know?"

He only pointed out and up, at the tops of the old cherry trees. No—beyond them, at the sky. And then, just as I had decided it would happen, we spread our arms and closed our eyes and let go. Our bare feet pushed us off the edge and out into space.

And then—we flew.

Once around the house, and then we circled the cherry orchard. Sobs and lamentations drifted from the open window we'd just left. For a moment I wondered what was wrong. Who could feel so utterly bereft, and why? Then an orange and black calico cat jumped onto the windowsill, and stood with back arched, watching, mouth wide and mewing as if to call us back. And I remembered—*my mother, my husband*—but when I let the thought make me feel sad, I began to sink toward the treetops. I sank and then fell, the earth rushing up again to claim me, as dark rushes in to envelop the day.

Suddenly Henry had my arm again. He pulled me up, and we were soaring once more.

He headed away on a course that would take us to the river. As we drew closer I saw it there, on the bank, and finally understood: It was no coffin my brother had been tapping and sawing away at for so long, downstairs. No, it was a little boat, curved sweetly as a quarter moon, large enough to carry two souls far away from this world. I should have known. Wasn't Henry a sailor, after all?

And I felt ready to go, to leave the endless bouts of blood and coughing and burning pain behind. Even so, I would never take back any of the time spent on earth in loving. Especially that one love which had given me more of life than I could've ever claimed on my own.

I suppose that was why, despite my brother's hand on my arm and my joy in seeing him again—my joy at all that was to come—I still could not imagine going on ahead, no longer able to see Edgar Poe every day from then on. Or perhaps it was that Eddy, wailing my name from within the sorrowful cottage, bound me by his own great need to the diminishing earth below?

Whatever the case, it was then I made one small yet enormous mistake, still hovering there on the verge: I turned my head. I looked back with longing. And as I did, everything—water, boat, my brother, the stars—rushed away as if sucked into a vortex, a swirling maelstrom made up of the very sky itself. And then, the darkness did descend—but I did not take it in. It took me.

They entombed my body three days later at Fordham Village, on the second of February, 1847. The vault belonged to the Valentines, the kind family who also owned our little house. It was situated in the cemetery of the Dutch Reformed Church, about a half mile from the cottage.

I was drawn there from the dark by the mournful sound of an organ. The day was bitterly cold and windy, yet a number of the New York literati had turned out. I saw Nathaniel Willis, looking pale and grieved, a long black overcoat whipping about him as he laid a consoling hand on Eddy's shoulder. Poor Willis had buried his own wife, dead in childbirth, not so long before.

Six aldermen, strong Dutch farmers and merchants, carried my coffin across the frozen ground of the churchyard. As they approached the tomb, a flock of crows or rooks rose from the bare shivering arms of a great elm and took flight, cawing raucously. Save for one, the largest bird.

Pym, I whispered. But I think, in retrospect, that it was no crow at all.

Eddy stood by the vault weeping, as Muddy held his arm, slack-faced and heavy as a marble monument. As the minister droned out the service they leaned upon each other, clad in funeral black. Though that was nothing unusual, merely their habitual mode of dress. Mourning me would change little of appearances, and perhaps even of feelings. I'd been a long time passing, after all.

Eddy stepped forward and with trembling fingers set a wilted bunch of frost-nipped purple crocus atop my coffin. The aldermen slid the heavy stone lid open, the rough grain of the granite scraping and rasping over the lip of the vault, and then set it back firm and square again to hold me in my place. Afterward they both turned and tottered away—Eddy leaning on Muddy, and she on him in her turn. Of course I saw the grief, the despair in their faces. The grimness of clenched jaws. But I noted as well in their loose, slumped shoulders, a guilty, sorrow-shot relief. They could tend to me no more, and no more would I lie upstairs suffering while they could really do nothing nor bring me any surcease.

For a moment I thought to take one of the flowers and press it for a keepsake—I'd done this before, in life. Those poor blossoms must be shriveling, wilting inside the cold vault. But what need of such things had I now? So I turned away from the scene.

I lay in the dark, still dreaming.

· 23 ·

I don't know how much time passed before I woke again. When I opened my eyes it was to an even, gray dimness. I was lying full length on some hard dusty surface. My nose tickled and itched. I scratched it, then blinked and sat up. Around me stood four walls. One held shelves—of books, or stacks of magazines—perhaps both. Familiar sights for a writer's wife. But I did not recognize this room.

"Hello?" I whispered, feeling tentative, since I did not know where I was or who might answer. Then, louder, "Hello! Is anyone here?"

No answer.

I stood and started toward the shelves, on the way bumping a hip against the hard edge of some furniture—it seemed to be a table or desk. "Ouch," I said reflexively, though it did not hurt.

On the desk sat an oil lamp. Feeling over the tabletop I found a locofoco beside the lamp, lit it, and turned up the wick.

The room sprang into focus, and it was much as I'd thought: four walls, the one across holding shelves, and on those shelves sat books, journals, magazines. A stack of newspapers too. The walls were clean, with the damp, chalky scent of fresh whitewash.

I trailed one hand over their cool, smooth, pleasing surface as I walked around the room's perimeter. Just before I ended my journey back at the wall of shelves, something occurred to me: Such a walk should've put me quite out of breath. Half as many paces used to make me cough and gasp. But I felt well; breathing came easily. My lungs didn't hurt. No pressure, no stony weight— the Black Toad gone. Of course, he'd left before. But this time *I* felt different—fit and strong. I could not say how, but I knew the Toad would not be back.

And what of that cold funeral procession, the open vault? The joyous flight with my brother beside me? "I've been dreaming wild dreams indeed," I murmured.

That made me smile. It might be worth a story, for Eddy. I walked over to the shelves, to see if they held any clue to my location. Perhaps I'd been moved from the cottage to some private hospital, or a sanitarium, and this was its library. I'd been cured, and had no doubt been in here reading, until I had tired myself out and fallen asleep. It would all come back to me shortly.

In the flickering light I leaned in to look at a magazine, which lay open, the preceding pages folded under, as if the reader had been called away for a moment and left it so. I looked at the title of the poem on the page facing up. "To M. L. S———" it read. Below I saw these lines: "For the resurrection of deep buried faith/In Truth, in Virtue, in Humanity."

I frowned, for though I did not recognize them there was a familiarity to the meter and rhythm. I looked down for the author's name at the very end. Imagine my delight and surprise when I saw printed there, "E. A. Poe"!

Then I frowned. *When* had he written this verse? I did not recall it. And who was M.L.S.? Let me see—surely it had to be Marie Louise Shew. So Eddy had written this to thank her for taking care of me. And he'd published it—I squinted at the top of the page—in the *Home Journal.* Then the date of the publication caught my eye: March 13, 1847.

My new, easier breath stopped suddenly.

The last thing I could recall of my life was lying in bed in our Fordham cottage, desperately ill, on the verge of death, and that had been late January. How could nearly two months pass, and I hold no recollection of them? I stepped back from the bland face of the magazine as if from a suddenly-discovered copperhead. I looked about, then turned in a circle, staring at all four walls until I'd made very certain. No, I was not mistaken: This room had no windows. No door. Only those four beautifully finished walls, these tidy shelves—and me.

I am buried, I thought. *They have put me living in the tomb.*

At the horror of this realization a new darkness descended upon me, as quickly as if a thumb and forefinger had suddenly and deftly pinched out the friendly flame of the lamp.

Yet when I opened my eyes again, it was still burning. I was lying down, though not on the floor this time. I was on my back, stretched full length on a settee much like the one in our parlor at Fordham, though its springs felt less weary and it did not sag. The upholstery was not worn, balding velvet, but smooth, thick, silky brocade. I dug my fingers in, pushed myself upright, and looked warily around.

The room seemed otherwise unchanged. I squeezed my eyes shut hard, until I saw stars and red bursts. Then opened them again and looked at the four walls of my tomb, or prison. It was as before. No windows. No door.

Even though my chest felt open and light, unweighted by illness, still when I rose from that couch fear made me move cautiously as a very old woman with fragile, hollow bones and delicate, upsettable organs. I crossed to the bookshelves again and scanned the titles of the volumes. I laid a finger under the embossed words on the first spine. *Tamerlane and Other Poems.* Not a common sight, for few copies had been printed—or so Eddy had told me. I let my finger trail on to the next volume: *Al Aaraf, Tamerlane, and Minor Poems.* Obviously the owner of this place—whatever it might be—was a dedicated admirer of my husband's work.

This idea seemed proved as I looked over the next few titles in line: *Poems by Edgar Allan Poe . . . Second Edition.* Next to it sat *The Narrative of Arthur Gordon Pym.* And next to that, *The Conchologist's First Book.* I moved on to the last four volumes: *Tales of the Grotesque and Arabesque; The Prose Romances of Edgar A. Poe; Tales by Edgar A. Poe;* and finally *The Raven and Other Poems.*

All of them, Eddy's books. I stepped back in surprise, certain there must be more here. That is, other works by other writers. But that was all I found. What sort of library, what manner of obsession was this? I turned to the magazines: *Southern Literary Messenger, The Broadway Journal, Godey's Ladies' Book, The Home Journal . . .* each with reviews or stories or poems by Eddy, and the volumes edited by him as well.

It was a mystery I felt incapable of solving, not without assistance.

"Hello?" I called, less tentatively than before. I waited and listened. No sound of footsteps. No answering cry. And then, even if I had gotten a reply, how would the speaker get inside to me?

Perhaps the bookshelf concealed some secret panel which swung open when you depressed a certain panel or pushed on the right corner. I almost laughed. If so, it would be just like something out of one of Eddy's stories.

I pressed on all the front surfaces of the bookcase, standing on tiptoe to reach the top. But I detected no irregularities. Nothing happened, no matter how delicately I probed or how hard I pushed. I reached in over the books and pressed the smooth back of the shelves. Then shifted all the books aside, one row at a time, and poked and jabbed at the back there too. Nothing. I hiked up my skirt and climbed the shelves like an orangutan, groping wildly around on the very topmost shelf, which was empty. Not even dusty. Panting, I dropped to the floor again. There, crouched on all fours, I had to face the horrible thought skittering like a terrified insect at the back of my mind: *There is no way out.*

I leaped to my feet and screamed, "Help me! Help!"

No answer, no sound from outside the walls.

I screamed again and again. My only reward, finally, was the ragged sobbing of my own breath. I rubbed my face hard, then wandered aimlessly around the room again. Nothing had changed. It seemed I was not to see the world beyond this place. To see Eddy or Muddy or Catterina or the sky or a garden—nevermore.

"Dear Lord God," I said aloud, but did not know whether it was a prayer or a curse.

At last I gave up my frantic pacing and dropped into the straight-backed chair. I propped my elbows on the desk, and lowered my face into my hands.

Some time later a sound woke me. Not a loud noise; more a dry rustle, as of angel wings folding, or the stiff pages of a new book ruffled by an eager hand.

I raised my head. On the tabletop the lamp still burned, though the level of oil in its cut-glass base had not sunk. This no longer seemed remarkable; nothing did. I pushed back from the desk and walked around the room. I stopped beside the bookshelf, and scanned the rows of books. Finally, I saw it.

At the end of the second shelf from the bottom, on top of a stack of magazines, lay a new issue of Nathaniel Willis's *Home Journal*. I picked it up and it fell open as if by design to one particular page. The poem there was cryptically titled, "To ———." But as I looked, the name "Helen" appeared, and the underline vanished. I gasped. What strange magic was this?

I bent my head and read it, all two pages. This was not the old and beautiful "Helen," the poem he'd written so long ago for Jane Stannard, the doomed young mother of his school friend. It was blank verse, far removed from the same class. Not insincere, but overwrought, flowery and adoring—a courtship rhyme. I felt my mouth tighten. This was one of Eddy's Lady Poems. He was wooing someone, as he'd used to do when he needed patronage or a favor. But now he had no wife at home. No excuse not to follow through to the end. But who was she?

Fanny Osgood.

No, no—the tone was all wrong. *The very roses' odors died in the arms of the adoring airs.* Fanny would've collapsed in helpless laughter, reading that.

"Ugh, no," I muttered, then shook my head. Oh, Eddy. Fanny would not take this poem seriously. She would grimace and roll her eyes and giggle—though not to his face. But if the title was truly for a Helen by name? I could not recall any Lady Poets with that name. And in any case, what did it matter, here? I sighed, tossed the magazine back onto the stack, and went to sit down again. To wait.

Over time—that is the best and only way I can describe it, for I had neither night nor day in my sealed chamber—new magazines appeared on the shelves. No more books though. I neither saw nor heard any human being, and I assumed no one saw or heard me. I cannot say how much time passed, for that concept had no meaning now. I did not hunger or thirst, and though I did not seem to need sleep, I often passed into a sleeplike state from which I would rouse suddenly, unaware of how long I'd been unconscious. I thought about my predicament, and wondered, Am I in Hell? Yet this was not a physically painful or horribly distressing detainment, so how could it be a hell?

Juliette and Claudine, my French Catholic playmates in Baltimore, had once told me of a place called Purgatory. In it lingered those souls not damned, but for some reason not free to move on to their heavenly reward. "Even *les bébés*," said Juliette, eyes wide, crossing herself.

Well, I was no Catholic. We'd attended the Presbyterian church in Baltimore, but had not kept up with formal religious services after that. Muddy had gone now and then, and I'd sometimes accompanied her. But Eddy did not like churches—perhaps because he'd spent so much time at funerals. He considered organized religion hypocritical. Still, I had no other explanation, and needed to put a name to my suspended state of existence, or go mad. So I decided I was in Purgatory. But for what sins?

I enumerated the possibilities over and over. I'd stolen sugar from the pantry when I was eight, though Muddy had told me not to. Envied friends who had sisters to play with, and nicer dolls and dresses. I'd torn up Eddy's letter to Mary Starr, but that still did not feel like a sin to me. I'd defied my mother's wishes and crept into my husband's room one night and consummated our marriage. I stopped at that one—could this be it? But he *was* my husband, legally wed. I shook my head, and went on. I'd sometimes been unkind, most notably and recently to the unhappy, awkward Elizabeth Ellet, giggling over her love-sotted letters with Fanny. And hating her for the aftermath. But Lizzy had had her revenge. Still, that did not absolve me, I supposed.

Just then a new magazine plopped onto the stack. By now I did not rush over to peruse these; I knew what they were. But it struck me now, with a sudden clarity of thought I had not felt in a long time, that the answer lay here before me.

I was guilty of a myriad of petty sins, but had never really harmed anyone. I'd never stolen anything—well, save the half loaf of sugar. What if it was not my sins keeping me here in this closeted, dustless limbo, but something else? If I was to blame for my state, why did the blasted magazines keep appearing—as if I had taken out subscriptions? Perhaps those very publications held me captive here. Or rather, their author. For when Eddy wrote his poems and stories, what was he still writing of but me, and for me, and to me? He still would not, could not let go. And I—well, I too had played my part. For instead of freely leaving the world with my brother as guide, as I'd resolved to do, and which Henry had so clearly intended, I had refused. Or rather failed at the critical moment to part with all I had loved on earth.

In the old Greek myth, Orpheus decides that instead of dying to be with his love, he will mock the gods and retrieve her bodily from Hades. To have everything he wants, to make life again just as he wishes. But he loses faith and looks back to reassure himself she is still there, still following, then is punished by losing her all over again.

I could not resist looking back either. And perhaps Eddy still could not let me go.

So together, I thought, *we* have kept me here. Unable to go forward, unable to go back. And he cannot follow. Not yet.

But what could I do about it? If only my mother were here, with her calm and practical advice! Could I appear to her, as my brother had to me, and ask? I did not know how. Then a chilling thought struck me: Henry seemed to come because I was fated to die. If I visited someone out of turn, would it hasten her death? Might I kill my own mother?

"No," I muttered, pounding fists into my temples. "I can't risk that."

Well then, could I simply renounce Eddy—give him up now, once and for all? Be satisfied never to see him again, never to speak with him or to touch his hand? I squeezed my eyes shut. His dark brown hair, large sad eyes, wide brow, and wistful smile. His wild stories, his delighted laugh, his affectionate smile when I said something clever or funny. His handsome nose and dark brows and—

"No," I said to the empty room. "No, I can't."

Well, Sissy, but you must. It was my brother's voice.

"Henry! Where are you?" I rose and looked around wildly, but he was not there. "Help me, please."

He said nothing else, though, and finally I sat down again. If my brother knew this much was true, he himself must have done so—given us both up: me and Muddy. And yet he'd come back for me, to carry me away from pain and suffering. If he could perform that earthly service, after leaving us freely, perhaps I too—

I smiled for the first instance in a long time. Though what *was* time, after all? Here, less than nothing. Very well then, when the hour was right, I would move to free us both. I did not understand yet *how* I'd know that moment had arrived. But I had real faith now, as true and unshakable as the trust I'd felt when, as a child, I'd first looked into the eyes of Edgar Poe.

He had promised me many years ago, on the back steps of my childhood home, that he would always provide and care for us, my mother and I. Now the reverse would be the case—someday it would be my turn to care for and protect and guide him.

· 24 ·

"So now you know why I've come," I say to the distracted man who is still tossing and muttering on the stained and creaking hospital cot. "You must feel as fearful and confused as I once did. But I offer you the solace of the past, and my presence."

He raises his head to blink at me in disbelief. As if I've let him down with this prolonged narrative, or disappointed him by telling the story artlessly, without embroidery. "The Pit," he whispers to himself, as if his worst fears have been confirmed.

"It might at first seem like that," I say. "But really, it's not—"

He flings his head back on the pillow. "Reynolds!" he cries.

That puzzles me. We have no friends or relatives by that first or last name. Then I recall: Eddy once wrote a story about a journey into darkness and distance aboard a phantom ship. He named his hero Arthur Gordon Pym. Our crow's namesake. But Eddy based Arthur Pym's adventures on the real voyages of South Seas explorer Jeremiah Reynolds. In my husband's tortured, dimming brain, he might be hanging on the brink of some great swirling maelstrom, or descending into darkness in a phantom ship like the one in "Manuscript Found in a Bottle." But in that first published story he'd also written of the excitement of embarking on a journey of exploration. A trip to new worlds.

THE RAVEN'S BRIDE   351

"Eddy," I say urgently, leaning to whisper in his ear. To reach him through his own words now. "Don't you see? We are both hurrying toward some exciting new knowledge. Some otherwise never-to-be-imparted secret. I don't believe its attainment must mean our destruction."

"The chasm!" he gasps. "Reynolds! *Reynolds!*"

I smooth the damp hair back from his sweating brow and grip his hand tighter. He lies back, quiet for the moment.

A young man about my age comes in, wearing a doctor's coat. He's followed by a nursing sister. She begins to fuss with the sheet which, in his agitated delirium, Eddy has thrown off.

"No," he mutters, slapping at her hands. "Reynolds!"

"Be easy now, Mr. Poe," says the young man. "I'm Dr. Moran. Do you recall where you are?"

Eddy groans. "Reynolds," he says again, but quietly, fading away.

"Lie back so we may help you," says Dr. Moran. "Soon you'll feel better."

The nurse looks up at this, as if surprised, but the doctor shakes his head at her. "This is Mr. Edgar Poe," he says gravely. "A great writer. A rare, gifted mind."

The nurse gazes down dubiously at the fevered, addled, sweating figure in the cot.

Dr. Moran sighs. "You have heard of 'The Raven'?"

"Oh!" says the nurse, pursing her lips. "*That* Mr. Poe."

"Your cousin, a Mr. Neilson Poe, was here to visit you," says Dr. Moran to Eddy. "And a lady—I believe her name was Mrs. Warner—yes, Dolly Warner. But you were so unwell, I could not let either of them in to see you, as yet."

Eddy merely closes his eyes at this mention of Neilson, the man he always considered to be his greatest enemy—for nearly taking me away from him. Then I know he must be sinking, for any mention of

Neilson never failed to enrage him before. "The little dog," he used
to call him. Quite unfairly.

"I am trying to contact your friends now, Mr. Poe," says Dr.
Moran. "I hope you will soon be enjoying their company."

Eddy looks right at him for a moment with clear, unfevered
eyes. "A true friend would come and blow my brains out with a
pistol," he says. Then his lids sink closed and he falls into a doze.

As soon as the doctor and nurse leave, I take Eddy's hand again,
sit beside him, and wait.

When he wakes some time later, I say, "Can you get up? Please—
come away with me now, my dear."

"Reynolds," he mutters, but with less conviction. "I'm afraid
we—no. *I'm afraid.*" He writhes, rolling his head from side to side
on the sweat-soaked pillow, looking about as if searching for someone, or something. Apparently, it is not me he seeks.

What word or gesture would make him know me? I wonder.
What would make him see it is truly I, and not a demon come to
taunt him?

Then I know the answer. *Voice. Breath. Soul.*

I stand and without speaking or looking at him again, lift my
chin, compose myself, and begin to sing.

> *Ah! Rob me of both riches, rank*
> *If Peace and happiness are mine*
> *With those we love not, life's a blank*
> *With those we love a gift divine*
> *With those we love a gift divine.*

My voice rings out high and pure and sweet, much clearer than
it ever sounded in life. So perfect in pitch it brings tears to my eyes.

I'd never dreamed of reaching such heights. If only Madame Frieda could hear me now! It does not matter that my audience is but one, for who more important to witness my greatest triumph?

Eddy opens his eyes again. This time he looks right at me, as if just noticing my presence. "Why, Sissy," he says, surprised. "I didn't know . . . you've never sung more beautifully!"

"Perhaps you could not hear pure beauty before," I tell him. "Nor could I. But we can now."

I try to pull him upright so he can rise, but the restraints hold him fast to the bed. Just as his and Muddy's hands on me once held me back, as I was on the verge of flying away.

Before I can move to try to free him, his face contorts. He screams, and Dr. Moran rushes back in, attended by two nurses. One begins to sponge my husband's forehead with watered vinegar. He flings her hand away, then convulses as if jolted by lightning. The doctor grips his shoulders and tries to still his thrashing.

Eddy raises his head off the pillow, and says clearly and distinctly into the man's face, "The fever called living is conquered." Then he subsides, even as his grip grows tighter on my hand.

I pull this time as hard as I can, imagining myself as a midwife and he the babe new to the world, about to be born into it.

And Eddy rises then and comes to me. It *is* he who truly stands beside me—even though the doctor and nurses are still bent, working furiously over the limp, ruined husk lying so still.

"Is he gone?" asks the taller nurse, looking over at the doctor.

"Yes, I'm afraid so." Moran sighs, straightening again. "It is too bad. The wages of spirits, and of a hard life. A great loss to us all."

"What was that he said to you at the end?" asks the other nurse, as she pulls the sheet up over the corpse's unblinking gaze.

Dr. Moran frowns, pursing his lips. Then, in a portentous

tone, he says, "He told me—actually, Mr. Poe's final words were, 'God help my poor soul.' Then he breathed his last breath. A moving testament I'll carry to the Temperance Society meeting tonight."

As they turn to go the doctor instructs, "Leave him here for now. I'll make the undertaking arrangements. His wife's cousin in Baltimore is a minister, I believe."

They leave us alone at last, and Eddy looks at me in astonishment. "But that's not what I told him!"

"Never mind. As you said, Eddy, the fever is conquered. It doesn't matter now."

He nods, looking me up and down, taking hold of my other hand. "I suppose not. No doubt others will say much worse of me, in years to come. But you—where have you been, my dear? So many nights, in so many darkened dens, I've cried out for you."

How might I explain it all? Words are such a poor way, but I must try. "For a while I lingered in that hushed, unlighted border between the living and the dead. And I was neither—or perhaps both. And something, well, held me there. Until you needed me here."

"Oh." He looks thoughtful. "But how did you find me?"

"I followed your voice, calling for me." I lean into him then, overcome with joy. He is with me again and feels as alive as he ever has. "I've been waiting such a long time. And you?"

"I've been killing myself for a long time," he says wryly, ruefully. "It seemed—expected, somehow." He squeezes my hand. "Never mind. It doesn't matter now."

I laugh. "Now you quote *me*. But come, we must go."

Still he holds back. "And who—what—am *I* now?" he asks, glancing over his shoulder, frowning at the figure lying white-shrouded on the bed. "And where?"

I lift a hand and turn his face to look at me again. "You're no-where, and everywhere. You are here beside me." Then, in a lower voice, "Above all, Eddy, as we depart, you *mustn't* look back."

He nods as if he understands, though of course he doesn't—at least not yet.

Hand in hand we walk away from the cot and its still, sheeted form. Away from want and disease and terror and human grief. I lead him to the open window, where outside a hundred bats soar and dip like black kites against the silvering light of an approach-ing dawn. They loft up and up, high over buildings and trees, then dive and swoop inches from the cobblestones and walkways be-fore quickly arching skyward again.

"See! Look at them," I say to Eddy, pointing out at the bats. "I'd say it's a bit like that."

He tilts his head as if considering this, one faint line creasing his forehead—which otherwise appears as smooth and young as it did the day I first met him in my mother's parlor. I can see he is almost persuaded.

At last he says, "But I had thought—I'd always assumed death to be the end. And that after dying I should see you, and my mother, and my brother—all the lost ones—never again."

I touch his sleeve and say gently, "It appears, Eddy, you were mistaken."

A light dawns slowly in his eyes and it does not dim. "Ah. So it is truly Al Araaf, then?"

"I don't know." I tighten my grip on his hand as firmly as Henry did on mine. "It may indeed be that heavenly garden. If so, we shall discover it together."

Then we slip through the half-open window, the famous Mr. Poe and I. All around us the bats soar and flit in perfect synchro-nization, diving for moths attracted by the hospital's guttering, flickering gas lamps. Side by side the bats wheel and dip: together, in unison, but never colliding. Signaling to one another steadily with voices as mysterious and unknowable as another creature's soul.

And then, with them—out of space, out of time—we too are lifted. And do not look back.

ACKNOWLEDGMENTS

Many people helped move me and Virginia Clemm Poe along the pages of our briefly shared path. My father, Patrick Hart, was a Poe afficionado. At my birth he named me for the beautiful dead girl in his favorite poem, thus setting in motion my own lifelong association with "The Raven." Kari Stuart, my smart and lovely agent at ICM, was her usual supportive and enthusiastic self during the long writing and editing process. Hilary Rubin Teeman, my editor at St. Martin's Press, read the early drafts and then—as she always does—explained how to bring out the *real* story, which had been lurking just out of sight, off the page. Others at St. Martin's Press I owe great thanks to include Elizabeth Catalano, Amelie Littell, Michael Storrings, Kelly Too, and George Witte, as well as my copy editor, Ragnhild Hagen. David Poyer read each and every draft of the manuscript too, and always found a way to make it a little better. (Or, as he says, "I just marked out every other adjective.") My daughter, Naia Poyer, gave good advice as well, and created some beautiful artwork to help me visualize Virginia. Vocalist Marilyn Kellam and musicians Jerry Gurka and Stefan Dulcie led me back into the nineteenth-century world of popular song and opera. J. Michael Lennon read an early draft and offered invaluable suggestions on the literary Poe. Terry Perrel had some fabulous plot ideas for complicating the characters' lives. Ina Birch, Erin Delaney, and Carol MacAllister offered early advice and enthusiastic support. Lourdes Figueroa kept chaos at bay, at home. The Library of Virginia, the Edgar Allan Poe Museum in Richmond, the Poe House Museum in Baltimore, and the Poe Cottage at Fordham in the Bronx all provided research material, knowledgeable staff, and great period atmosphere. The faculty and staff of the English Department at Elizabethtown College and my E-town landlords, Pam and Jamie Rowley, provided a home away from home in Pennsylvania, where I completed most of the first draft. Director Bonnie Culver, Assistant Director "Mr. Jim" Warner, and the faculty and staff of the MA/MFA Creative Writing Program at Wilkes University offered a receptive audience and a great venue for trying out the work publicly. Suny Monk, Sheila Pleasants, Dana Jones, and the rest of the staff at the Virginia Center for the Creative Arts at Mt. San Angelo once again provided me with the best secret hideout in the world for writers and artists; otherwise how would I ever have gotten it all done? As usual, any flaws, omissions, or errors of fact or in execution are mine and mine alone.

1. Edgar Allan Poe and his cousin Virginia first meet when she's eight and he's twenty-one. They marry before she's fourteen —a bit young, even back in the nineteenth century. Do the circumstances of their courtship and marriage, as portrayed in the novel, work to excuse this great difference, or not? Do you think there can be such a thing as "fate" in love?

2. Virginia's mother, Maria Clemm, is blunt and practical, in personality and financially. Her letter, which swears Poe and Virginia are both 21 years old, lets them obtain a license to wed. Why do you think she agreed to provide this false document?

3. Like many teenage girls, Virginia dreams of fame. But a successful musical career also required money and connections. Another obstacle in Victorian society was gender bias. Women were expected only to be wives and mothers. So Virginia keeps her desire to sing a secret even from her family. How do "secrets" about desires and fears of various kinds affect her personal growth and the novel's action in general?

4. Poe as a raving-mad opium addict was a fiction created by a vengeful biographer, Rupert Griswold. But Poe was an alcoholic—a binge drinker. No AA or effective therapy existed then, so Sissy thinks they've hit on the answer by always being together. The limits of this plan soon become obvious. How does the Poe family dynamic mirror or differ from the ways such relationships play out today?

5. A few biographers have speculated that the Poes never consummated their marriage. Some claimed that since he called her "Sissy," they must've lived as brother and sister—even though it was a family nickname! Poe once told a contemporary that he'd waited until she was sixteen before they "lived as man and wife." In the novel, Maria Clemm forbids Eddy to claim his conjugal rights, then an encounter in a music shop convinces Sissy to initiate sex. Did this seem credible? Why would Poe have agreed to Maria's terms?

A
Reading
Group
Guide

St. Martin's
Griffin

6. To contemporaries, the life of the Poe family must've often looked bleak. Yet the two women don't complain much about their straitened circumstances or lack of comforts. Even Eddy complains mainly about professional slights, rather than a lack of luxury. Why, do you think? How do their attitudes compare with the way we view our work, money, and living environments?

7. When Sissy finally gets the chance to shine on a public stage, it's hardly a refined, classical setting. She's at first shocked, then unsure about actually going onstage. But her dream of singing for a "real" audience wins out. Why did the author choose this earthy setting for a public debut, and how does the experience affect Sissy's character?

8. There is much bird imagery in the novel—not only the famous "Raven" but also other famous literary birds, plus ordinary rooks and crows, even sparrows. When do birds appear in the novel and what discoveries, warnings, or truths do they seem to suggest?

9. If their everyday existence had been easier, do you think Eddy and Sissy would have achieved as much, or more than they did? Or perhaps felt less driven to create and perform?

10. The novel has supernatural elements as well. Sissy in particular is sensitive to the presence of ghosts. Why do you think the author added this supernatural element to the narrative?

11. Sissy dies of consumption (the old term for tuberculosis) at home, slowly, in great pain. In literature, the disease has often been portrayed sentimentally—including by Poe. In the mid-nineteenth century, about 25 percent of the population was infected with TB. Why do you think the disease was so romanticized by artists and writers of the era?

12. At the end of the novel, Poe and Virginia depart the world together. Still, it's not clear that they're guaranteed to find the heavenly paradise imagined by Christians of that era. In fact, by then, Sissy has discovered that life immediately after death is not at all as she'd envisioned. Why do you think the author decided to portray details of the afterlife in this way?